DEATH TRAP!

The tiny hamlet was made up of three buildings—an old service station and bait shop, a small grocery store, and a bar—and about a dozen homes. It was not on any map Ben Raines had looked at.

"What do you think, Father?" Buddy asked.

"They'll attack us tonight," Ben said. "Bet the farm on it."

Dark, savage-looking clouds were gathering in the south and west. The Rebels were tense as the storm approached. Just before dark, the rains began, the sheets of water so intense they limited vision to only a few yards.

"Here they come!" The shout was faint above the roaring storm.

The attack was well-planned, and it was fast.

We're not going to hold them, Ben thought, lifting his M-16. We finally ran out of luck.

"General!" Jersey screamed.

Ben turned and took the butt of a rifle on the chin. The last thing he remembered was falling into a black pit.

ZEBRA'S HEADING WEST!

with GILES, LEGG, PARKINSON, LAKE, KAMMEN, and MANNING

KANSAS TRAIL   (3517, $3.50/$4.50)
by Hascal Giles

After the Civil War ruined his life, Bennett Kell threw in his lot with a gang of thievin' guntoughs who rode the Texas-Kansas border. But there was one thing he couldn't steal—fact was, Ada McKittridge had stolen his heart.

GUNFIGHT IN MESCALITO   (3601, $3.50/$4.50)
by John Legg

Jubal Crockett was a young man with a bright future—until that Mescalito jury found him guilty of murder and sentenced him to hang. Jubal'd been railroaded good and the only writ of habeus corpus was a stolen key to the jailhouse door and a fast horse!

DRIFTER'S LUCK   (3396, $3.95/$4.95)
by Dan Parkinson

Byron Stillwell was a drifter who never went lookin' for trouble, but trouble always had a way of findin' him. Like the time he set that little fire up near Kansas to head off a rogue herd owned by a cattle baron named Dawes. Now Dawes figures Stillwell owes him something . . . at the least, his life.

MOUNTAIN MAN'S VENGEANCE   (3619, $3.50/$4.50)
by Robert Lake

The high, rugged mountain made John Henry Trapp happy. But then a pack of gunsels thundered across his land, burned his hut, and murdered his squaw woman. Trapp hit the vengeance trail and ended up in jail. Now he's back and how that mountain has changed!

BIG HORN HELLRIDERS   (3449, $3.50/$4.50)
by Robert Kammen

Wyoming was a tough land and toughness was required to tame it. Reporter Jim Haskins knew the Wyoming tinderbox was about to explode but he didn't know he was about to be thrown smack-dab in the middle of one of the bloodiest range wars ever.

TEXAS BLOOD KILL   (3577, $3.50/$4.50)
by Jason Manning

Ol' Ma Foley and her band of outlaw sons were cold killers and most folks in Shelby County, Texas knew it. But Federal Marshal Jim Gantry was no local lawman and he had his guns cocked and ready when he rode into town with one of the Foley boys as his prisoner.

Available wherever paperbacks are sold, or order direct from the Publisher. Send cover price plus 50¢ per copy for mailing and handling to Zebra Books, Dept. 4066, 475 Park Avenue South, New York, N.Y. 10016. Residents of New York and Tennessee must include sales tax. DO NOT SEND CASH. For a free Zebra/ Pinnacle catalog please write to the above address.

VENGEANCE IN THE ASHES

WILLIAM W. JOHNSTONE

ZEBRA BOOKS
KENSINGTON PUBLISHING CORP.

ZEBRA BOOKS

are published by

Kensington Publishing Corp.
475 Park Avenue South
New York, NY 10016

First Printing: February, 1993

Printed in the United States of America

One hour of life, crowded to the full with glorious action, and filled with noble risks, is worth whole years of those mean observances of paltry decorum.
                                                            Sir Walter Scott

When neither their property nor their honor is touched, the majority of men live content.
                                                            Niccolò Machiavelli

The Beginning

After years of government waste, government lies, and the almost-total control of its citizens, the United States of America was teetering on the brink of collapse. But it was not alone. All the great nations of the world—the superpowers, as they were called back then—were in trouble. The reasons were many and varied.

War, it seemed, was the only way out. Thin the population. Once the war talk started, it could not be stopped. When the war came, and it erupted simultaneously all over the world, Russia blamed the United States, the United States blamed Russia. China blamed Europe. Israel blamed the Arab nations, England put the blame on Northern Ireland, Germany blamed Japan, and the French blamed everybody.

It didn't make any difference who started the war, a limited nuclear and germ attack, for when it was over, there was not a functioning government left in the entire world.

In the United States, one man was picked to pull the nation out of the ashes of defeat and set it right again. Only problem was . . . he didn't want the job.

7

Ben Raines was an unlikely candidate from the outset. He was a reclusive man, a loner. He had been both soldier and spy. He was a visionary, a philosopher, and a writer of books and articles. He was so controversial in his views that one group or the other had tried a dozen times over the years to kill him. But Ben Raines was a hard man to kill.

Ben Raines was a hard-liner on some issues and liberal to the core on others. Back when such things existed, he was a maverick when it came to voting in any type of election, for he never voted strict party lines.

It took months for a small group of survivors to convince Ben to lead their movement. But when he took the reins of controls, things began to happen. He immediately moved thousands of followers to the northwest and formed a country within a country, calling it the Tri-States. And life was good there. In the Tri-States, there was free medical care for all. There was no crime, for Ben Raines would not tolerate it. The life expectancy of a criminal was very short. Ben built schools and stressed education above all else. All students who were able had at least ten hours of hard physical exercise a week, including paramilitary training, for Ben knew that once the central government of the United States was once more functioning, the politicians would ask the military to move against the Tri-States. Already the struggling central government of the United States was calling those who followed Ben scum and malcontents and traitors. Others called them Rebels. The name stuck. Ben Raines's Rebels.

While the central government of the United States, now located in Richmond, was ruling with typical inefficiency, the Rebels in the Tri-States were living happy and contented lives. The politicians couldn't

8

stand it. It infuriated the bureaucrats to see such a large group of people living with so few rules and regulations, and for heaven's sake, they were actually shooting criminals out there! Everybody who was a permanent citizen of the Tri-States could carry a gun. Criminals had practically no rights at all. And the constitution and the laws of the Tri-States were written so simply that even a child could understand them.

The politicians and lawyers and professional bureaucrats shook their heads at that. That just wouldn't do at all; they couldn't have that. The lawyers especially were unhappy about it. If laws were spelled out so simply and plainly that anyone could understand them, there would not be much need for attorneys. Why, that was practically un-American!

It was pointed out to Ben that only about one in five could live under the laws of the Tri-States. Ben said, "Fine. The other four can keep their asses out or get them shot off."

Actually, it wasn't true that only one in five could live under the laws of the Rebels. The truth was, the other four *wouldn't* live under those laws.

It was a common-sense sort of society. A spokesman for the old Tri-States explained it to a member of the press in this way: "A person who is respectful of another's rights will rake his or her lawn and bag the leaves for proper disposal or turn them into mulch. A person who has no regard for a neighbor's rights will burn the leaves and let the smoke drift into the neighbor's house. Do you understand a common-sense society?"

The press didn't.

But as Ben knew it would, the Tri-States fell under a massive government assault. Only a handful of

Rebels escaped the killing fields. But a handful was enough, especially since Ben Raines was one of them. The Rebels re-grouped and re-formed and began their march against the central government of the United States. Then the rat-borne sickness struck the land and quickly spread worldwide. The Rebels kept their heads down and their wits about them and survived.

The world was plunged backward into medieval thinking. Chaos ruled. Outlaws and warlords took control. Slowly the ranks of the Rebels grew, and ever so slowly they began the job of clearing the United States of crap and crud. It would take them years to accomplish it, but accomplish it they did. The Rebels became the strongest, best-equipped, most highly motivated, disciplined, and most-feared army in all the world. They took back the land from thugs and gangs and returned it to law-abiding citizens.

Then came the day that the nation once known as America was declared a clean zone. It had taken the Rebels, under the leadership of Ben Raines, years to do it, but they did it. The Rebels had established outposts all around the nation. Each state had anywhere from a dozen to several dozen of them. These outposts were towns that had running water that was safe to drink, they had sewerage systems that worked, streetlights and schools and hospitals and churches and libraries. These towns were also places where crime did not exist. Contrary to what lawyers and liberals and sobbing hanky-stompers had maintained over decades of lawlessness, it was very easy to accomplish. Crime was not tolerated. When everyone was of a like mind concerning the criminal-justice system, crime was very easy to control and eliminate. When a citizen could safely shoot a burglar without fear of jail or lawsuits, those so disposed toward crime quickly learned that it was not only unprofitable, it was downright deadly. When every law-abiding citizen had access to a gun, and shooting a criminal was not only legal, it was encouraged, criminals, like rats and other creatures of the night, soon sought a safer clime.

In the Rebel system, everybody that was able worked. There were no free rides in the Rebel system. No police officer had to read anyone his rights, for an individual's rights were taught in school, from kindergarten on up. Public schools taught young people to respect the rights of others and to respect the land and the animals who lived in the woods and forests. Kids were taught both at home and in the schools to respect warnings. They were taught that if they encountered a Keep Out or No Trespassing sign, they stopped and either turned around or found another way to get to where they were going. What few written laws the Rebels had on the books were not there to be broken; they were there to be obeyed.

What the Rebels had done, under the direction of Ben Raines, was to uncomplicate living. Their way of life in the outposts was, by the very nature of the times, harsh, but it didn't have to be complicated. Any Rebel society was based on order and justice. Not law and order. Order and justice. A criminal convicted of any major felony was given a choice, however: a hangman's noose or a firing squad.

As it had been in the old Tri-States, in any Rebel society medical care was free. So was education from kindergarten through college. Kindergarten through high school was mandatory. In the Rebel societies, the teachers were left alone to teach, and the students learned.

The Rebel army was made up of everybody—male and female—who lived in a Rebel society. Everybody

11

became a member automatically at age sixteen. By that time, a person had already completed hundreds of hours of paramilitary training. One either joined the Rebel army or was kicked out from under the umbrella of Rebel protection and put on his own, his ID card destroyed. Without an ID card, no one could receive medical aid or buy supplies from any Rebel outpost.

There were many thousands of people who lived outside the safety zones of Rebel-held territory, many thousands more than who lived in the towns controlled by Rebels. No one was forced to join the Rebels. But anyone with any common sense at all did.

The members of the ten battalions of the regular Rebel army were, to a person, trained to the cutting edge, honed down to hard muscle and gristle and bone. And they liked a good fight. They went out of their way to find one.

Ben Raines commanded One Battalion. General Ike McGowan, an ex-Navy SEAL commanded Two Battalion. Colonel Dan Gray, a former member of Her Majesty's Special Air Service commanded Three Battalion. Colonel West and his mercenaries made up Four Battalion. General Georgi Striganov, a former Russian Spetsnaz commander was in charge of Five Battalion. Colonels Rebet and Danjou commanded Six and Seven Battalions, made up of Russian, French-Canadian, and Canadian troops. Thermopolis, the hippie turned warrior, commanded Eight Battalion. Ben's daughter, Tina, commanded Nine Battalion. And the wild Irishman, Pat O'Shea, commanded Ten Battalion. There was Ben's son, Buddy, and his group of young men and women called the Rat Pack. And there were the ex-outlaw bikers called the Wolf Pack. People of all nationalities and all walks of life and all religious beliefs made up the fighting battalions of Raines's Rebels. And there were the support troops and the doctors. The chief of medicine was a crusty old bastard named Lamar Chase. He was the only person alive who could order Ben Raines out of the field and into a hospital bed, and Ben had to obey. There were the cooks and the truck drivers and the mechanics and the supply people and the pilots and hundreds of others. Raines's Rebels, so far as they knew, made up the largest standing army on the face of the earth. They were also the most feared fighters in all the world. They gave an enemy one chance to surrender. Only one. After that, they rarely took prisoners.

Ben and his Rebels had sailed to Ireland and then England, cleaning it out and handing a reasonably stable government back to the citizens of those nations. Then they set sail for Hawaii, going around the Horn, inspecting each inhabited island along the thousands of miles.

The islands that made up the Hawaiian chain were under the ruthless rule of thousands of pirates and various other assorted thugs.

All that was about to change.

Book One

One

After suffering defeats from the Rebels that came very swift and very hard, the pirates and outlaws and thugs on the islands began beefing up their positions and smartening up. They were, to a person, stunned when they realized that the Rebels now controlled much of the island of Molokai, including the main port and the airport. None of them could understand exactly how the Rebels had managed to land so many troops and go undetected.

"Because we got lax," Jerry James said. Jerry was the leader of one of the largest gangs in the island chain. Jerry James was not his real name, but then, most of the outlaws had long since dropped their real names. "Me and Books here has been talking."

Books Houseman, so called because of his love of reading, stood up. Like Jerry, he ramrodded a large gang and was looked upon for guidance because of his extremely high intelligence. Books was also one of the most vicious gang leaders operating anywhere in the islands. His ruthlessness more than made up for his small size. "What it comes down to is this," Books said. "And you all better realize it. We are in a fight for survival. Unlike our counterparts on the mainland, we have no place to run. We either win, or we die. There is no middle ground. So, we've got to be smarter than Ben Raines. There is no way we can stand and slug it out with the Rebels. While we have many more personnel, they've got us outgunned. They're organized, well-trained, and very highly motivated. We, sadly enough, are no more than rabble. But rabble helped defeat Burgundy in France, and we can do the same here. But we've got to plan carefully, and we've got to have one overall commander of all forces. You leaders think about that for a few minutes; talk it over. Then we'll continue this meeting.''

Rabble was an apt choice of words. But it wasn't quite strong enough. Slick Bowers looked across the large room at Susie Loo, who was sitting next to Vic Keeler. Susie ran a gang that was very nearly as large as his own and about twice as vicious. Vic was a pirate who enjoyed torturing his captives. He was very inventive. Mac Mackenzie sat alone, his back to a wall. Mac was stone crazy and just about as predictable as a Tasmanian devil. But his gang was large and he ran it with an iron fist. Leo Jones sat quietly smoking a hand-rolled cigarette. Leo was just about as smart as Books, but with a lot more common sense. Larry Perkins stood, leaning against a wall. He had a strange expression on his face, and Slick thought he knew what it was all about. Larry was facing reality. They all knew that the Rebels had never been whipped. The gangs had the finest of radio equipment and had spent years monitoring the movement of the Rebels.

John Dodge said, "So let's talk. Hell, we're wasting time." John ran a cattle ranch on Kauai and had about two hundred men working for him, not counting the slaves. Every gang leader and most of those in the various gangs had slaves. They were worked until they could no longer work, then they were given to the Believers, the cannibalistic Night People, those whom the Rebels called Creepies.

Kip Burdette said, "I'm with Books. I think he's our man. Me and my boys will take orders from Books." Kip was a slaver whose ships roamed all over the Pacific, buying and selling human beings.

Rye Billings nodded his shaggy head. A huge bear of a man, the former mainland outlaw biker was known for his brutality. "I'll take orders from Books. I don't much like the bastard, but he's smart, I got to give him that. We're up against the wall, boys and girls. He's right when he says we got no place to run. This is it."

"The plane we sent out never come back," Dean Sherman said glumly. "The last transmission we had was that it was hit and goin' down."

"And that the pilot was looking' at the biggest damn armada he'd ever seen," Polly Polyanna said. No one knew what her real name might have been. Nobody really cared. "My people will back Books. No problem there."

"Same here," a gang leader who called himself Wee Willie said. "We got too good of a thing goin' here. I ain't givin' none of it up just 'cause some overage Boy Scout says to do it."

"Ben Raines ain't no Boy Scout," Tucker said. "Don't none of you ever think that. I fought that bastard from New York City to California. Or rather, I run from him all that way. Now I got no place left to run. If any of you people come out of this alive, and you find my body when Raines's Rebels is done kickin' our asses, bury me up in the mountains if you can. Mighty pretty country up there."

"Aw, man!" a thug called Spit shouted. "Hell, you

act like he's done won this fight. We can whip the Rebels."

"Maybe, just maybe," Tucker said. "But we're gonna have to be awful lucky. You folks don't know Ben Raines. He hates punks and thieves and the likes of us. And in his own way, he's just as mean as we are. Look at who the Rebels has whipped: Hartline, Khamsin, Sister Voleta, the Believers, all the L.A. street gangs, ever army that's ever had the nerve to take them on . . . has lost. Been wiped clean off the map. And I don't know how to fight Ben Raines and his Rebels."

"I do," Books said from the open doorway. "Oh, my, yes. I certainly do."

"Get the general up here," a Rebel sergeant radioed back to Ben's CP. "Fast!"

"What's the problem?" Ben asked, as he was stepping out of the vehicle Cooper had procured for him.

"The enemy is gone, sir. They started disappearing about five minutes ago. There isn't a sign of them down the road."

"Well, it's about time," Ben said, lifting his binoculars.

"I beg your pardon, sir?" the sergeant asked.

"I spoke at length with a local name of Jim Peters. He told me that probably the man who would be chosen to lead the thugs and crud would be a man called Books. Last name of Houseman. Highly intelligent fellow. He was an officer in the American service, a graduate of some military academy; Jim didn't know which branch. Books was court-martialed after he was caught selling secrets to some East European country. Before he could be sentenced, the world blew up. He surfaced over here about five years ago. He's respected if not liked by the other gang leaders. I think that this Books fellow has done something no other group we've ever faced had managed to do." He smiled, noting the puzzled look on the sergeant's face. "He's figured out the only way they might stand a chance of beating us. Bet on it."

A group of Rebels had gathered around, listening.

"If I'm right," Ben said, "and I think I am, we're in for some down-and-dirty guerrilla fighting. This campaign is going to be messy, people. Corrie, bump all batt comms. I want a meeting five minutes ago." He looked at the Rebels gathered around him. "Heads up, people. We're about to engage in a lot of hit-and-run fighting."

"I think you're right, Ben," Georgi Striganov said. "This failure to attack, now that they have hundreds of new troops on this island, is . . . baffling. Or was."

Ben looked at his son. The young man was so ruggedly handsome, half the women in the Rebel army were in love with the muscular young man . . . or thought they were. "I think the crud is breaking up into small teams, son. Take your Rat teams and start head-hunting. Each team take a local with them. Get moving."

His son tossed him a sloppy salute and left the CP, hollering for his team.

Ben looked at the map of the island. "I can't break up the battalions on a hunch. But on the other hand, I can't wait for them to infiltrate us."

Ben turned to stare out the window. "I can't order attack helicopters in to rocket and strafe suspected punk positions on the islands because of the civilian population. I can't order the ships closer in to shell for the same reason. We've got to take the chain island by island. But by doing it that way, it gives the

21

enemy time to beef up and make plans and get set." He turned and thumped the table a couple of good whacks with his fist. "All right, folks. Each of you will pick one full company to be broken up into small groups and start them head-hunting. We've got plenty of local volunteers to act as guides. It's going to be slow and bloody, with the terrain as it is. And if this island is going to be bad, the big island of Hawaii is going to be a bloody son of a bitch!"

Books Houseman, the newly elected supreme commander of all the slime, crap, crud, and those with unhappy childhoods that drove them to a life of crime, read the report and tossed it on the desk. "It didn't take him long to figure it out," he said, with grudging admiration in his tone. "About five minutes. But it's going to take him precious days to clean out Molokai. By that time, we'll be set up all over the place."

"But the citizens will be free," one of his men mentioned.

"It can't be helped. There is no other way to fight Ben and his Rebels. Believe me when I say that all others have been tried. They failed."

"You really think we have a chance, Books?"

"Yes, I do. Albeit a very slim one. This type of warfare is slow and bloody. Both sides are going to take tremendous losses. And that's where we have the advantage. We have thousands more men than the Rebels."

"Books?"

"Yes?"

"Are you a general now?"

Books threw back his head and laughed. "That's a good one, Pete. Me, a general. No, I think not. But for a time I did make a lot of money as a lieutenant . . . by selling secrets to the Russians."

"Did you ever get any of that Russian pussy, Books?"

"Oh, yes. That was part of the arrangement. I slept with several very lovely young Russian ladies. My last contact killed herself rather than be taken alive. Some agents of the CIA wanted her rather badly. They were working in the United States quite illegally, of course. The bastards."

"Ben Raines used to work for the CIA."

"Yes," Books said softly. "I know. That's why I want to take him alive. It would be very interesting to see just how much pain he can tolerate."

Buddy held up a hand and motioned his Rat team to the ground. He smiled and pointed straight ahead of him toward a tangled rise of land. The local who lay beside him grinned and whispered, "There is a ravine that runs to the east of that knoll. It curves and comes in right behind that rise."

Buddy nodded and said, "Lead the way, Pilipo."

The team silently made their way into the rocky ravine and worked around until they were behind the outlaws' position.

"Do we ask for their surrender?" Pilipo asked in a whisper.

Buddy smiled. "We did, last night. We only ask once." Buddy took a fire-frag from his harness and held it up for the others to see. Within seconds, all the team held fire-frags in their hands. "Now," Buddy said, releasing the spoon and chunking the grenade in a deadly arc.

"Grenades!" the shout sprang from the thickness of green.

The vegetation-thick knoll erupted in fire and shrapnel as the mini-Claymores blew. Wild screaming and howls of pain followed. One outlaw, apparently unhurt, ran from the carnage and was cut down, stopped in his tracks and flung backward from the many rounds that tore into him. The Rat team lay silent, waiting to see if the combat would draw others.

No one came to investigate. "Check it out," Buddy said.

The woman slipped to the blood-splattered rise and seconds later called, "Come on."

"Six-man teams," Buddy said, squatting down beside the torn body of an outlaw. A walkie-talkie lay beside the body. It was on, the volume turned down low. Buddy motioned his team to rest and he wiped the blood off the handy-talkie and wrapped a bandanna around the cupped mouthpiece to muffle his voice and waited.

"Jocko," the voice sprang out of the speaker. "What's happenin' over there?"

"Pinned down," Buddy replied, opening and closing the talk switch, deliberately breaking up the transmission. "Come help us."

"You're breakin' up bad. How many?"

"Looks like about ten."

"On the way. Stay loose. We'll come in from the north."

"Drag that dead man up here with the others," Buddy ordered. "Then get set."

Pilipo looked at Buddy and smiled. "You are a tricky one, Buddy."

"You have to be when you're always outnumbered. No noise now."

The outlaws walked into it. When they got within talking distance, the leader called, "Jocko? You okay?"

"I'm hit!" Buddy called. "Come on. They're gone."

Six more outlaws went down hard and kicking. One was only slightly wounded. He was taken prisoner. "Take all the weapons," Buddy ordered. He looked at the badly frightened outlaw. "Let's get this one back to base."

Teams of Rebel head-hunters came back jubilant, carrying dozens of weapons and bringing in a few prisoners. Some of the prisoners were openly defiant, sneering and cursing at the Rebels and expecting the worst. They got it. But most were frightened and willing to cooperate in exchange for their lives.

Even Ben was somewhat shaken when he read the reports after the interrogations.

"Works out to be about nine to one," Beth said, after doing some quick arithmetic.

"And very well armed," Thermopolis said, standing beside Tina Raines. "But the plan of this Books person may very well backfire as we re-arm the citizens."

"Yes," Ben agreed. "That's what I'm thinking. There is this, too: if he's breaking up his forces into teams on all the islands, the men and women who were being held as slaves will have to be freed. Therm, you and Tina take your battalions and move to the island of Lanai. It was sparsely populated before the war; only about two thousand residents. But it was the pineapple capital and I imagine the thugs have slaves working the old plantations. You're going to have to make the crossing in small boats."

Tina said, "I'll get on the transportation end right now."

The hippie-turned-warrior met the eyes of Ben. "You were right, Ben. This is going to be long and slow and bloody."

Ben held out his hand and Thermopolis shook it. "Good luck to you." He smiled. "Take care of Emil."

Therm rolled his eyes and left. Emil Hite had turned into a good soldier, but you just never knew what the little con artist might try to pull next. But like all Rebels, he was one hundred percent loyal to Ben.

Ben returned to his studying of maps of the islands, talking to himself, even though his staff was sitting in the CP listening. Beth, the official keeper of things that Ben had to do. Cooper, the driver. Corrie, the radio operator. Jersey, Ben's bodyguard. "We'll take Maui next," Ben said. "Seven hundred and twenty nine square miles with a prewar population of eighty-five thousand." He looked up as another half-dozen prisoners were marched in, their hands tied behind their backs. So far, the Rebels had suffered only one wounded and no dead. But Ben knew that would soon change.

"General," Jersey called softly.

Ben turned. A Rebel had brought one of the prisoners to him. "Excuse me, General," the Rebel said. "This misbegotten soul says he was second-in-command of the punks on this island."

"I demand that I be untied and treated in accordance with the rules of the Geneva Convention," the thug said.

"There were several Geneva Conventions," Ben replied. "Which one are you referring to?"

"You know damn well which one I'm talking about."

Ben sat down behind the desk and picked up a 9mm pistol. He clicked it off safety. The prisoner was watching him closely. Ben said, "We don't have to abide by those rules. So far as I know, Geneva no longer exists. Besides, you're not in uniform. What's your name?"

"Paul Morris."

"And you were second-in-command of the crud and crap who controlled this island?"

"I resent being called crud and crap!"

"I don't give a flying rat's ass what you resent, you goddamn sorry overage punk. Soldier, take this bastard out and shoot him."

"Now wait a minute!" Paul said, blood draining from his face. "For God's sake, General . . ."

"For God's sake?" Ben shouted, rising to his feet. The prisoner backed up, frightened at the look on Ben's face. The muzzle of the Rebel's M-16 stopped him. "God? You dare to mention God? You're just like every two-bit thug I've ever had the misfortune to come in contact with. Big tough boys until your hand is called and then you're pure shit clear through, calling on the Almighty to help you. Why should He help you? Why shouldn't I shoot you? Have you ever done one decent thing in your entire life? Answer me, you putrid bag of batshit."

"I . . . uh . . . It's my daddy's fault I turned out like I did. My daddy beat me when I was young."

"He didn't beat you enough," Ben told him. "Soldier, get this craphead out of here and over to interrogation before I personally shoot him."

"Oh, let me shoot him, General," Jersey said, winking at Ben and lifting her M-16.

"You people are crazy!" Paul hollered.

"I'll match you for the honor," Cooper said. "I got a coin here in my pocket."

"No, let me shoot him," Beth said, reaching for her M-16. "I haven't shot anyone all day."

"Fine," Ben said. "Go right ahead."

"Good leapin' Jesus Christ!" Paul screamed. "Get

me out of this crazyhouse."

The Rebel winked at Ben and turned the prisoner toward the door.

"Look, man," Paul started babbling. "I'll wash dishes, I'll mop the floors, I'll clean out the toilets. I'll do anything. You can't just shoot me down like I was hog for slaughter, man. Give me a break. I ain't really a bad person. I'm tellin' you, man, I got information in my head. I . . ."

He was still babbling as the Rebel led him off.

"God," Ben snorted. "It's amazing how so many of these slimeballs can turn into a one-man revival when captured."

"Speaking of revivals," Beth said. "Here comes Emil Hite."

"General, my general!" Emil shouted, bouncing into the room. The man had more energy than a generator. "I have found my land of dreams on this beautiful island. Like George Fenimore Cooper and his Paradise Lost . . ."

"That's Milton, Emil," Ben corrected. "John Milton. And it's James not George."

"Whatever," Emil said. "This is where I wish to spend the rest of my days and like Admiral Byrd, let this be my final resting place."

"Byrd is buried on these islands?" Beth asked. "I didn't know that."

"Charles Lindbergh is," Ben said. "Over on Maui, I think."

"General, I heard the most beautiful singing this afternoon. It was so . . . so inspirational, touching a part of me I thought would never be touched again. I thought it had died when my youth faded away. It moved me to tears of joy. It really did. I hadn't experienced anything quite like it since I got drunk one Saturday night and woke up the next morning on the back pew of the Mount Hollyoak MB Colored Church outside Jackson, Mississippi. That was spiritually uplifting too."

"I don't believe you," Cooper said.

"You got drunk and passed out in a church?" Corrie asked.

"I think Jim Nabors lived somewhere around here," Ben said. "Maybe you heard him singing to his macadamia nuts?"

Emil looked confused. "What kind of a nut?"

Ben had started to rise from his chair to physically throw Emil out of the CP when bullets started flying, knocking out windows and putting everybody on the floor.

"Even this is better than having to listen to Emil," Jersey muttered.

Two

Those attacking the CP probably thought Ben had broken up all his battalions into small teams to work search-and-destroy. No one will ever know what they thought because the thousand or so Rebels still in the area chopped the attackers into bloody bits in less than half a minute. The fight was over before Ben could reach his M-14.

"That's it, General," a Rebel said, sticking her head into the CP. "They crawled through a big drainage pipe to get here. Twelve of them. They're all dead."

"Barbarians," Emil muttered darkly, getting to his feet and brushing dust off his clothing. "People must be mad to defile such a lovely place with unwarranted violence."

"Get back to your battalion, Emil," Ben told him. "You're going to Lanai."

"What's over there, General?"

"Pineapples. Move!" Ben walked out of his CP to watch as the bodies of the attackers were stripped of weapons and ammo and dragged off to be buried in a mass and unmarked grave.

Those who elected to take up arms against the

Rebels were accorded very little respect when it came time to be buried.

Using the toe of his boot, Ben rolled one dead attacker over on his back. The young man, probably in his early to mid twenties, had taken a dozen M-16 rounds in the chest. His eyes were frozen open in death. Ben knelt down and went through his pockets and found a clear plastic bag containing a white powder.

"Cocaine," Buddy said, walking up. "Almost every one of the enemy we've killed had cocaine on him. Those we've interrogated say it's a big business on the islands."

Ben tossed the bag on the man's bloody chest and stood up. "I never understood why people use drugs. I'm from a different era, I suppose." He looked over at Thermopolis. "Of course, I never understood why people wanted to wear their hair down to their shoulders, either. Seems like a lot of fuss and bother to me."

Therm smiled. "We're making a statement."

"Horseshit," Ben said, and walked off.

Thermopolis laughed and yelled, "You'd look cute in a ponytail, Ben."

"Not as cute as you'd look in a crew cut, Therm," Ben said over his shoulder. Ben smiled as he returned to his CP. He had never given a damn how people wore their hair. He always felt it wasn't any of his business. "Gather up the crew, Jersey," he said to his little bodyguard. "We're moving to the airport."

By midmorning of the next day, once Ben was sure the airport and the area around were clear of punks, attack helicopters began hammering in from the ships still at sea, and from the port where they were off-loaded from the ships by crane. There were many airplanes parked around the tarmac—all of them with flat tires—and Rebel mechanics got busy getting as many of them as possible airworthy again.

Tina and Therm had left for Lanai during the night, making the short run in small powerboats. They had reported only light resistance so far, but they were not advancing very far until the bulk of the two battalions were ashore and geared up. Tina had reported that the civilians living on the island—those they had encountered thus far—were in appalling physical condition, many of them near death due to repeated beatings at the hands of their captors. They were forced to work long hours in the fields, under all sorts of adverse conditions, and were poorly fed.

"Send them over here on the returning boats," Ben told her. "Chase has his MASH units up and will receive."

"Ten-four, Eagle. Civilians on the way."

Striganov joined Ben on the tarmac, a clipboard in one big hand. "Intelligence reports that the military on the islands destroyed most of their equipment when the end was certain," the Russian told him. "There is no evidence that the enemy possesses any type of surface-to-air missile delivery systems. They are well armed with various types of automatic weapons and have rocket launchers and probably thousands of hand grenades. But all military planes, tanks, and other large offensive weaponry were rendered useless at the end."

"Another plus for our side," Ben said.

"Yes. Quite. Also, intelligence confirms what the prisoners have told us. We're outnumbered about ten to one." The Russian shrugged his shoulders. "So what else is new?"

Ben smiled at that. Although he spoke perfect English, Georgi had picked up a lot of American expressions over the years.

"Armed with the captured weapons, we've got about a battalion of locals working with our people in the search-and-destroy teams. The batt coms told me that their teams are letting the locals handle more and more of the missions. They do deal rather harshly with the enemy."

"I just bet they do."

"Also, night patrols state that a lot of small craft left this island during the darkness. I think the pirates and thugs have fled."

"I agree. At least, as many as possible have fled. But I want this island sterile before we move on."

"I think that can be accomplished within seventy-two hours."

"Good. Then we take Maui."

Books listened as the leaders of those who had fled Molokai babbled on, each one trying to talk over the other. Exasperated, he had to hammer on the desk with the butt of a pistol to quiet them.

"Calm down. I get the point," he told the group. "But Raines no longer has the element of surprise working for him. We certainly know he's here and we can prepare for him. We've got time. He'll save Oahu for last. Bet on that. Right now I want you people to get a grip on yourselves and calm your men. You're in a panic."

"That's easy for you to say, Books," he was told. "You wasn't there. Raines's people are like ghosts. They can be on you before you can blink. They can cut the throat of the man not five feet from you and you'll never know it until you try to talk to the guy and he don't answer. And I ain't lyin' neither."

"I know you're not," Books replied. "I believe you.

33

What can I say? What do you want to do, surrender? You know what would happen to us then. The citizens would hang us. We don't have a choice, people. We have to fight."

"The people on the other islands?"

Books shrugged. "I'm open for suggestions."

"What you're sayin' is, they've had it."

"I'm afraid so. But there is a bright spot. They'll kill a lot of Rebels before they pack it in. So they'll be less for us to fight."

One gang member recently from Molokai wanted to tell Books that as far as he knew, no Rebel had even been wounded, much less killed. But he kept his mouth closed. He knew Books was right. They had to fight. They just didn't have a choice in the matter.

Books picked up a sheet of paper. "The Rebels have landed on Lanai. Then I think they'll hit Maui, then the big island, then they'll strike at Kauai and us simultaneously. We've got a lot of work to do and not much time to do it. Let's get at it, people."

"Eight to Nine," Therm radioed.

"Go, Eight," Tina replied.

"What is your situation?"

"Bogged down for the moment. These people are putting up a stiffer fight than those on Molokai."

"Same here. And it'll get tougher with each island. Hold what you've got, Therm. Let's set up mortars and start softening them up."

"That's affirmative. At your signal."

Mortar crews quickly set up and at Tina's signal, the two battalions started dropping in a mixed bag of 60mm mortars. They pounded enemy positions for thirty relentless minutes, then dropped in smoke and the Rebels surged out of cover and moved forward.

But the thugs and punks had lost their taste for battle under the barrage and had fled, many of them losing their weapons in their haste to get the hell gone. Those weapons were picked up, cleaned off, and given to the former slaves who had joined in the fight. Those that still had the strength to stand. The bodies of the enemy were left where they were sprawled. They would be buried or burned later.

The two battalions linked and headed for Lanai City. Therm and Tina both ordered the locals who had joined their battalions to head for the brush and take care of their former captors. They smiled and said they would be delighted to do so.

"No doubt," Therm muttered.

The Rebels pressed on, meeting a large group of men, women, and children streaming up the highway.

"They are waiting for you in the town," an old man with snow-white hair told the Rebels. "They are in a panic. When we saw them rushing into the town, we slipped out. They paid us no attention at all. They are all very frightened now. But I think they will fight to the death."

"Stay here," Tina told the man. "We'll set up a medical tent and see to your needs."

"We have sick with us," the old man said. "But if you will arm us, we will leave the road and seek out those who fled. You will not have to worry about them."

"Don't ever let anyone take your guns again," Tina told the group, as they were being armed with what the Rebels had picked up along the way and taken from the dead.

"You do not have to worry about that," the elderly man assured her. He straightened up, tall and proud. "We are now part of General Raines's Rebels."

"Amazing," Therm muttered. "Just the mention of his name puts steel in the backbone."

"You've never understood that, have you, Therm?" Emil said, wiping the sweat from his face.

"Oh, I understand it. It's just astonishes me that so many people are so eager to fight and possibly die for a man they have never seen. And before you say it, Emil, I know it is the man, and not the cause."

"It's both," the little con artist replied. "You and the general, Therm, you're a lot alike. Whether you'll admit it or not."

"Is that supposed to be a compliment?"

"Nope. Just a fact."

Therm smiled. "Perhaps you're right, Emil. Perhaps you're right."

At the small town of Lanai City, located almost directly in the center of the island, the two battalions of Rebels threw a loose circle around the town and began the wait. The hours dragged on and the outlaw defenders of the town began to sweat. There were few shots fired, for no one on either side offered a target, especially the Rebels. The only casualties were among the defenders and they were self-inflicted, a half-dozen outlaws choosing suicide rather than being handed over to the citizens to face a sure hanging.

Tina and Thermopolis held their battalions and waited.

"We can take all the time we need," Ben said, after reading Tina's short dispatch. "Starve the bastards out." He turned to West, seating in front of his desk. "What's the word on the creepies? I was under the impression the place was crawling with them."

"Intelligence says they are concentrated on the big island. Some sort of deal was struck with the outlaws and pirates. Peaceful coexistence and all that crap.

that he actually stopped at the proper place. He also thought he heard sirens, so he stopped in adherence of the emergency vehicle.

But he was certain there were police lights behind his car a few seconds after he stopped. He looked into his rearview mirror and said, "Damn."

"Pull your vehicle out of the intersection," the officer said through his loudspeaker.

Paul did as instructed, but he knew a bottle of wine—not to mention what he consumed at the hotel—probably took him over the legal limit for alcohol consumption while driving. He did not want a DUI. Worse, he did not want to go to jail.

So, before the officer reached the car, Paul closed his eyes to gather his balance. "You can do this," he said.

The officer approached and tapped on the driver's side window.

"Sir, are you all right?" the officer said, looking as much into the car as he was at Paul.

It was dark out now, around eight o'clock and the cop shined his flashlight into Paul's face.

"I'll be doing better if you didn't have that light in my face," he said.

"Why did you stop in the center of the intersection?" the officer said, the light still in Paul's face.

"I got confused, officer," Paul said. He got the words out, but did not enunciate as clearly as normal. "I'm visiting here for a few days and I was looking around at the town and looked up and it seemed like the light turned red and I lost where I was. I thought for that second I was behind the crosswalk."

"I see," he said. "Can I see your rental car contract and license?"

Paul looked in the car's glove compartment, but the contract was not there. He feared Ginger took it with her, as she was holding it some of the ride to Napa from the airport. Then he checked the center console, found it and handed it over to the officer.

"Sir, have you been drinking?" the police officer asked.

"Yes, I just left the wine lounge, 1313, a few blocks away," Paul said. He figured lying was not going to work, so he surmised that giving him something would be the better strategy. "I had the best glass of wine in my life. A 2008 Caymer: amazing wine, especially considering it was so young."

"Where are you staying?" the policeman said.

"Not too far away, at the Marriott," Paul said.

"Can you turn off the engine and step out of the car?" he told Paul.

"Is this really necessary? I got confused about the light and where the crosswalk was," Paul said.

"Yes, it's necessary," the officer said, his tone much more aggressive. "The fact that you couldn't determine where to stop is a problem. You admitted you were drinking and you smell like more than one glass of expensive wine. And your eyes are glassy."

"I'm just sleepy," Paul said as he exited the car. "I've

traveled all the way from Atlanta. Still trying to adjust my body to the three-hour time change. If I were at home, it'd be going on eleven-thirty and I would already be in bed."

The officer was not having it. He directed Paul to the side of the street away from traffic. People walking around and driving by in the quaint town could not help but notice Paul going through a field sobriety test.

He was not happy. He was embarrassed. And he felt the pressure of proving that he was not inebriated. But he didn't. He couldn't. Too much drinking impaired his center, so he could hardly walk a straight line in the awkward fashion cops demand: one foot literally in front—heel-to-toe—then turn around and do it again. Stand on one leg with arms stretched out, extend right hand away from body but touch the tip of the nose. Then do it with the left hand.

"This test is not a fair test," Paul told the policeman. "How can you test me on something I have never done before?"

"Sir, that is the law and nothing I can do about it," he answered. "Furthermore, turn around please and place your hands behind your back."

The officer placed the handcuffs on Paul and walked him to the police car when he did what people see on television all the time when someone gets arrested: He put his hand over Paul's head and held it down as he folded into the back seat. He even said, "Watch your head."

Paul sat in the scrunched-up seat totally uncomfortable and completely humiliated. His high was gone. He was going to jail, and that fact ripped away all the feel-good of the wine he experienced a few minutes before.

Worse, he started to feel nauseous and lightheaded. It was warm in the car and he began to sweat. The officer stood outside the car speaking on a wireless device about having the rental car towed. Paul began breathing out of his mouth to get more air, trying to prevent a panic attack. For someone who had a fear of flying, being confined in cuffs in a cramped space was tantamount to torture.

He felt caged, trapped…like a prisoner. The officer finally came back to the car.

"I don't feel good; it's hot," Paul said. "Can I get some air, please?"

The cop turned around and looked at Paul and saw the distress on his face, the sweat on his brow. He nodded his head and blasted the air.

"We have to wait here another ten minutes or so for the tow service to get here," he said. "Meanwhile, I'm going to do some paperwork to make this whole process quicker."

"Can I get a phone call? I'm not trying to spend the night in jail," he said.

"Well, you're likely going to do that," he said. "By the time you get a bail bondsman and he gets it over to the jail, it'll be several hours. Unfortunately, it's not a quick process."

"What's the charge?" Paul said.

"Suspicion of driving under the influence of alcohol," he said.

"Ah, man, come on now because of that sobriety field test?" Paul said. "That's pretty unfair."

The officer did not respond at first. Finally, after an extended pause, he said: "You'll be able to make a phone call when I get you to the station. You have someone here who can post bail for you?"

He said, "Yes," but it was not a call he wanted to make. He was fortunate that he even remembered Ginger's number. Hers, his mom's and Helena's were the only phone numbers he committed to memory.

His instinct was to call Ginger, but the pettiness in him moved him to call his mother. This would be a slap in Ginger's face. Not on the same level as her getting an abortion without consulting him, but a slap in the face nonetheless.

But that would have to wait. It was another fifteen minutes before the tow truck arrived. The officer filled out paperwork in silence and Paul listened to the calls from the dispatcher come in on the radio.

There was an arrest at Lincoln and California of a man who ran a red light—on his bicycle. The bigger problem for the guy was that he was in possession of a meth pipe with meth in it. He was headed to the Napa County Department of Corrections/County Jail.

Then there were officers and medical personnel called to the 700 block of Lincoln Avenue. A two-year-old male was suspected of taking medicine a two-year-old child was not supposed to take. He was transported to Queen of the Valley Medical Center for evaluation.

And then there was a fifty-nine-year-old man who was caught walking out of the local Target on Soscol with a jacket and sweater he did not purchase. An employee made a citizen's arrest, holding him until police arrived.

Focusing on those crimes helped Paul to calm down and take his mind off the discomfort he felt. Finally, the officer began the short drive to the jail on First Street. Paul looked at the people on the streets going about their lives without the specter of being placed in a prison cell. It made him feel worse.

They arrived and immediately Paul was struck by how the correction officers had either disdain for him or looked at him as if he were invisible, not even a person. He was lumped into the lot of criminals because he drank too much and got behind the wheel. He felt less than whom he was.

The cuffs were finally taken off and he rubbed his wrists that were pained by them. He wiped the remaining sweat from his face and composed himself. The police turned him over to the correctional officers, who would "process" him.

The place did not look horrible—it wasn't Alcatraz. But there was an air of oppression about it, a feeling of troubled souls resonating the place.

Shit got real for Paul when he was told to stand on

the blue line and look at the camera, turn to his left and to his right—his mug shot. That didn't feel good at all. Then he was taken to the fingerprint area where a woman did the honors, one by one placing his fingers on a machine that resembled a copier that captured his prints.

He was amazed at how routine the processing in process was. It sobered him up. He was as coherent and observant as he could be. He understood completely that he was an inmate.

"Excuse me," he said as an officer led him to a cell that was narrow and smelly, with aluminum benches on either side. Best of all, it was empty. The last thing he wanted was to have to deal with others. "Can I make a phone call?"

The correctional officer led him to a phone that sat on the desk at the command center. On a pillar next to the phone was a list of local bail bondsmen. Under it was a sign that read: "5 Minute Limit on Phone Calls… No Exceptions."

Paul dialed his mother's number. He was worried that she would not answer; she did not take calls from numbers she did not know. But Brenda was concerned about Paul after Ginger told her that he left in a huff and without his cell phone. She was hoping it was her son.

"Vino?" she said into the phone with a sense of desperation, bypassing the traditional, "Hello."

"Ma. Hey," Paul said. "I'm in—"

"I know," she interrupted. "Don't even say it."

"Jail, Ma," Paul said.

"DUI?" she asked.

"He said 'suspicion of DUI,' which makes it, to me, hard to prove," Paul answered. "I didn't take the breathalyzer. So he's going by what he believed."

"It's his judgment as an officer to determine if you're a threat behind the wheel," she said. "Why the hell did you leave us here at the hotel anyway? Ginger wouldn't say."

"We can talk about it when I get out of here," Paul said, "which is the reason I'm calling."

He gave her three options of bail bondsmen from the list by the phone. He could hear Ginger's voice in the background, and she was not singing.

"Here's your wife," Brenda said.

"Paul, you're in jail?" she said.

"Yeah."

"So why didn't you call me? You called your mother?" she asked.

"Doesn't feel good, does it," Paul responded, "when something important happens and you turn to someone other than your spouse?"

"This is why I had an abortion; you can be so mean," she said.

Paul heard Brenda's response in the background. "Abortion? You had an abortion? Madeline, you knew about this?"

Then he heard all three of the women's angry voices talking all over each other. It was audio confusion.

"Hey, hey, hey," Paul said so loudly into the phone that a correctional officer came over and warned him about his volume. Ginger finally got them to stop bickering. "Can y'all do that later—*after* you get me out of here?"

"Well, I'll let your mother handle that since that's who you called," Ginger said with attitude.

She passed the phone back to Brenda. "You OK, Vino?" she said as if she were talking to a kid.

"Ma, I'm fine," he said. "I'm at the Napa Correction Center/County Jail. It's not that far from the hotel. They just told me my fine is five thousand dollars, but I can bond out for five hundred. Can you work on this now so I can get out of here? Please?"

"OK, I will," Brenda said. "But we've got a lot to talk about—you driving and drinking and your wife having an abortion? Really?"

"OK, I gotta go, Ma. I won't be able to call you again, so please get me out of here now."

And with that, he hung up and was led back to the cell, which, in those few minutes had welcomed three guests: a twenty-something young man who reeked of alcohol and the streets; an elderly man who seemed to be either drunk or mentally challenged; and a man close to fifty who laid on his back on one of the benches.

It was close to ten o'clock at night the day after Thanksgiving and Paul Wall was in the Napa jail, a place he never even considered when he planned the trip to his dream destination.

CHAPTER 14
YOU HAVE THE RIGHT TO REMAIN SILENT

"You can forget about getting out of here tonight," the elderly man said. He was disheveled, with long, dirty-blond hair and thick facial hair, a sort of filthy Santa Claus. Paul studied his face and determined there was a younger man than he first thought beneath all that hair and behind those wrinkles.

Paul was not interested in having conversation with his fellow inmates, but had to respond to the man.

"How do you know?" he said.

"How do I know?" the man responded. "You ever seen *The Andy Griffith Show*?"

"Andy Griffith? Yes," Paul said.

"Well, I'm Otis from *The Andy Griffith Show*," he said.

"Who's Andy Griffith?" the younger man asked. He had tattoos of snakes and a skull and bones and other random images on his arms and shoulders and around his neck.

The man looked at Paul, who explained: "He's an old-school actor who had a TV show before you were born. He was the sheriff in a small town called Mayberry. Otis was…he was…"

"He was the town drunk," the older man said, "who spent a lot of his weekends in jail, so he knew how the system worked."

"So you saying that about yourself?" the young man asked, smiling. "You're the Napa town drunk?"

"Pretty much," he said. "But you can call me Otis. Funny thing is, that's actually my name."

"You," he went on, looking at Paul, "you don't live here."

"How you know that?"

"Because you have a Southeastern accent, probably from Georgia," he said. "The way you almost sing certain words. Your accent is not as bad as could be. You're educated. Went to college, but probably in the Northeast, didn't you? In Virginia or Washington, D.C., or Philadelphia. That region."

Paul looked on in astonishment. The man was right about everything.

"How could you know that?" Paul said. "I haven't even said ten words. Haven't been sitting here but three minutes."

"Wait," the young man said, "he's right? All the stuff he said is right?"

"He's right," Paul answered.

"How could you know that, old man?" the kid said. "You just said you're the town drunk. But you're psychic, too?"

"Not psychic," the man said. "To be psychic is to be outside human knowledge. What I do is not that."

"How do you know these things?" Paul inquired. "I'm amazed."

"I wasn't always the town drunk," he said. "I once, not that long ago, worked for a government agency that shall remain nameless. I was a profiler. My job was to study human behavior.

"For instance, I can tell by how you are sitting that you've never been in jail before, that you're…put off by this whole experience."

"I wouldn't call this an experience," Paul said.

"Are you kidding me? Everything is an experience," Otis said.

"So what happened to you?" the kid said. "I mean, you're obviously smart and had a good job. What happened? How you end up being the town drunk—no disrespect."

"Neither of you would be here long enough for me to explain it in full," he said. "Let's just say that some things happened in my personal life that I didn't—and still haven't—handled so well."

For Paul, that meant death. What else could eat at a man so much that he let his life disappear into dust. Having experienced losing his job and the depression it brought him, Paul could imagine how something more serious—death—could overtake a man's psyche.

Before the conversation could continue, the man lying on the bench sprung up. "Damn, ya'll ain't got no respect for a man trying to get his beauty sleep," he said. He was smiling. "I'm fucking with you. I had to get a power nap to get my head right. Been a long night and it's still early."

The young man laughed. "I was thinking the same thing," he said. "What you in here for?"

The man stretched and yawned and said, "Quota. These cops gotta get their quota of arrests," he said. "It's the end of the month. More people end up in here the last eight, ten days of the month than any time in the month. I'm telling you some good shit."

"That may be true," Otis said, "but they arrested you for something."

"Oh, yeah, they got me on some bullshit," he said. "Said I had an open alcohol container in my car. It was a beer can from earlier in the day that I had drank."

"But why did they stop you?" the young guy said.

"Oh, 'cause I was doing sixty-seven in a forty-five," he answered and then laughed.

"What you want from me?" he added. "I had a lot of things working against me: I was late to this girl's house for a little, you know; I had to piss like nobody's business; and I don't like driving the speed limit."

Then he turned to Otis. "I heard you say you can tell about people based on their body language. What's my body saying about me? I want to hear this."

"You're a liar," the old man said immediately. "You lie to distract you from the truth that pains you. You lie to hide the pain."

"What are you talking about, old man?" he said to Otis. "You don't know what the hell you're talking about."

"You asked me to tell me what I noticed about you," he said.

"What have I lied about?" the guy responded.

"You lied about why you're in here," Otis said. "I watched you. Not one word about your arrest was true."

"Did you lie?" the young guy asked.

The man did not respond at first. Finally, he said, "How can you know this shit?"

"I just do," Otis said. "It's instinctive but it's also a learned skill."

"But, if you don't mind me asking, what happened to you?" Paul asked.

Otis ran his hand through his thick beard and briefly looked away. He was not sure if he should share his story because he was not sure they would get something out of it. But then he looked at Paul again, and he knew he could take away something that might influence his life. He thought of asking Paul what bothered him. Instead, he told his story.

"When I was young and dumb, I didn't even give the idea of marriage a thought," he began. "I didn't trust women, didn't need them for more than sex and felt like most young men do: the goal in life is to get as much sex as possible."

"That's right. What's wrong with that?" the young man interjected.

No one bothered to answer him. Otis went on: "Then I met Darlene Wilkinson on a blind date. My friend introduced me to her. He gave me the buzzwords that meant she was just OK: 'nice,' 'sweet,' 'smart.' A young man wants to hear 'sexy,' 'hot,' 'cute.' He didn't give me any of that because he knew, while it mattered, in the end I was gonna need substance and heart and a good mind.

"Well, I was mesmerized by Darlene and less than two years later we were married. I had never envisioned what true love could feel like. But we had it. There probably is no such thing as a perfect person or a perfect relationship. But she was perfect for me and our relationship was perfect for us.

"Two years ago, she got pregnant. When she told me, I cried. I was overwhelmed with knowing she and I would produce something so great together: a child."

Otis' voice got lower and the words did not come out of his mouth so freely.

"She carried our child, a daughter, for almost nine months. I was away for work and she experienced pain and then hemorrhaging. Our neighbor rushed her to the hospital. Doctors could not figure out what was wrong for a while. I will spare you the technical details, but she had a rare condition that flared up.

"I cut my trip short to get back and be there with her. But by the time I arrived, my daughter had died."

None of the men knew what to say, so they didn't say anything. A pall fell over the cell.

"It was beyond devastating. My wife, who was a strong woman, could not get out of bed for a month. She literally stayed in bed all day. She didn't eat. She hardly slept. She just cried and cried.

"You see, we had tried for years to get pregnant, but couldn't. Doctors told us she just would not. Well, maybe eight months after they told us that—after we had considered artificial insemination and adoption—she was pregnant. It was the happiest time of our lives.

"She was a beautiful pregnant woman. And happy. No aches. No morning sickness. It was a beautiful experience for her and for me. But to lose our baby killed her spirit. She died when the baby died, except hers was a slow decline in health to where she passed from a broken heart. One night, as I held her and wiped away her tears, she fell asleep and never woke up. She died in my arms.

"So, in six months, I lost the person I was closest to in the world and the baby we talked about bringing us even closer together. So, what happened to me, you ask? A big part of me has died, too. The person I was, the life I had and thought I was going to have…it's all gone.

"There's no other way to put it. Others have experienced similar tragedies and they moved on, eventually. I think their 'eventually' just came sooner than mine. Mine will come. One day. Maybe. Hopefully. But until it does, I have to function the best way for me to function—through drinking to escape this hell that's living in my heart."

Otis amazed Paul again, but in a different way this time. How could he share such an emotional story in a jail cell to three strangers? And how ironic that his story had to do with his pregnant wife?

"Damn," the youngest man said.

"Otis, man, I am really sorry to hear this," Paul said. "I cannot even imagine."

No one else said anything for several minutes. Paul thought about how he would react to losing Ginger and Helena and it saddened him. It scared him. Maybe he would be just as floored as Otis.

It made him realize that having Ginger and Helena was the world to him. Another child from his bloodline would have been great. But he had his wife and daughter. That was a lot to embrace, far more than Otis.

He absolutely was angry and disappointed about Ginger having an abortion. But hearing of Otis' losses made him appreciate his family more than he ever had.

It came down to the whole "life is short" thing. Whenever there is a tragedy, people are reminded to appreciate life, that it has an expiration date, that not living it to the fullest is wasting time, that it could be worse than it is, that someone is worse off than you. Paul felt all that, and he was so moved that he wanted to hug Ginger and not strangle her.

Once he let go of his feelings of anger and disregard, he was able to feel for Ginger. Otis' wife also was told she could not conceive, but defied the medical expectation and got pregnant. Losing her child killed her. Paul thought about how Ginger lost their baby through abortion, and how, as a mother, that had to be a gut-wrenching decision.

And this was important: The fact that she did and Paul did not even sense something was wrong spoke to how disconnected he was from her. And he started to feel bad and ashamed. He understood better how hopeless Ginger felt and how, if he were not wallowing in self-pity, he might have been able to sense something with her and thereby spark a conversation that led to a different outcome.

Back at the hotel in Ginger's room, she, Brenda and Madeline were in the throes of drama.

"I can't believe what I just heard," Brenda said to Ginger. "You had an abortion?"

"Now just wait a minute, Brenda," Madeline jumped in. "You're not going to attack my daughter, especially when it was your son who basically pushed her to this."

"How in the hell did Paul push her to do something like that?" Brenda asked.

"By the way he treated her—or didn't treat her," Madeline said. They stood practically nose-to-nose, close enough for any loose spit to hit the other's face. "He said he wanted a divorce. Why would she want to have a child with a man who wants out?"

"Why would a woman who was told she couldn't get pregnant, actually get pregnant and then get rid of it?" Brenda said. "That was a blessing from God. He told those doctors who's in charge and performed what the doctors considered a miracle, I'm sure. So to just get rid of it…that, I do *not* understand."

"You don't have to understand," Madeline said. "This isn't about you."

"And it's not about you, either, Mother," Ginger said from across the room. She sat in the single chair by the window with her feet up on the ottoman. There was a calm about her that was surprising.

"You all are talking about me and my life as if I'm not here. Well, I am here and I have heard enough. I love you both. I do. And I am glad and appreciate that you all care so much about Paul and me. But this is our business, our life and we have to work it out—or not work it out. Not you.

"So, you two can talk about me all you want after I'm gone. I am going to bail my husband out of jail. And I want to do this by myself. I will catch a cab and will call you later to let you know what's going on."

With that she rose from the chair and walked past the ladies and out of the room.

Brenda and Madeline sat on the double beds across from each other and didn't say a word. They shook their heads and sat there for a minute. Then Madeline said, "I'll be honest: I didn't agree with Ginger's decision, either. If she had told me what she was thinking before she went to the clinic, I would have talked her out of it. And I would have called Paul. I understand why she did it. I just don't understand how she could do it."

"I don't, either," Brenda said. "Kids today are so emotional. I wasn't really ready for a baby when I got pregnant with Paul. But I didn't think about an abortion, either. I guess it's a different time."

"You know what?" Madeline said. "I guess we should go to the bar and have some wine until they come back."

"Good idea," Brenda said.

CHAPTER 15
SAY WHAT?

Before stepping out of the room, Ginger politely took the sheet of paper from Brenda listing the bail bondsmen in the area. She did not bother to look back at her mother and mother-in-law. She just kept it moving.

When she got out in the hallway, though, she breathed a sigh of relief that was so big that she got lightheaded. She gathered herself and went to the front desk, where the manager called a taxi for her.

While en route, she called Awesome Bail and gave the infor-mation about Paul's situation. She figured that would expedite the process. But hardly is anything easy in times of trouble.

The company wanted all kinds of documents that she did not have—pay stubs, social security card, passport.

"We live in Atlanta; we're here on vacation," she said. "He left his wallet in the room; I have that. There are all kinds of documentation about where we live, credit cards, whatever. We're not criminals. We are not trying to jump bail. I'm just trying to get him out."

"Miss, there is a mandatory forty-eight hours of jail time with your first DUI charge in California," he said.

"So, even if he were to post bail, he would still have to serve two days."

"What?" Ginger said.

"The only thing that could change that is if the judge rules the time could be converted into work service," the man added. "But because you all live in Georgia, I don't know if that's a possibility."

"Do they hold court on Saturday here?" she asked.

"You're lucky; not all of California does, but here we do," he said. "So, he will see a judge in the morning and will determine what happens."

Ginger had the cab driver drop her off at the jail. There, she found a worker who gave her the deal: Paul would have to spend the night. He would have an eight o'clock appearance in front of Judge Davis. His bail was set but the judge would determine in the morning if he would have to serve another night behind bars and his court date.

Ginger was upset. She wanted to get Paul out; she felt somewhat responsible for him being there. Having to stay another day would totally ruin their trip; they were scheduled to leave on the red-eye Sunday night.

She did not have much cash on her, so she sought to piece together the money. She was not sure how much Paul had in his account, but she had a duplicate card to his account and she knew the PIN number. He'd had her use it in the past and the PIN was the address to their first apartment: 2406.

So, she walked to the nearest ATM and was astonished when the balance read: $48,106. She wondered if the bank got it wrong. There was a time, years back, when her account balance read five hundred dollars more than she actually had in the bank. When she tried to get out more than she knew she had, she was refused. That had to be case here, she surmised.

If that was the case, it did not allow her an accurate balance, so she was not sure if there really was eighteen hundred available. That made her nervous because the last thing she wanted to do was have to go to her mother for the money to help bail out her husband.

Before she could contemplate that much more, Ginger got woozy. She had been feeling strange off and on, but this time she felt really disoriented—and scared. It was not like what she considered a panic attack in the garage several months before. It was more of a light-headed, dizzy feeling and an uneasiness in her stomach.

Her family had a history of bleeding ulcers, and she was always fearful she would get one, too. This time, she was more fearful than ever. Ulcers can be brought on by worry, and she certainly had been worrying and was worrying quite a bit about Paul—and her marriage.

Instead of trying to dismiss it, Ginger found a bench on the street, took a seat and used her phone to call a taxi—and locate the nearest hospital.

Before she could do either, however, Madeline called her.

"Ginger, what's going on? Is Paul out?" she inquired.

Ginger explained the dynamics to her and told her she would be back at the hotel later and that she was working on the bail money—anything to get her off the phone.

She succeeded in that and contacted Black Tie Taxi to pick her up near the detention center. She waited on a bench with her mind racing to many places: a potential ulcer, Paul, the abortion, Helena, her mother, her marriage. None of the thoughts gave her comfort.

"Queen of the Valley Medical Center on Trancas Street," she said when she hopped into the back seat of the cab.

It was a short ride from where she was, maybe ten minutes. During that time she texted Helena, although it was around two in the morning on the East Coast. She missed her and always found a base of comfort in communicating with her child.

Unlike many mothers and daughters that go through antagonistic crises during the child's teenage years, Helena and Ginger had no such issues. They got along more like sisters who actually liked each other.

"We are having an adventure here in Napa. Lots to share when we get back. Hope you're having fun. Sure you're at a party. Be safe," was her text message to her daughter.

A return message came back in less than a minute. "Surprised to hear from you. Is everything OK?"

Ginger sent her back a smiley face because she did not

want to lie. Then Paul's phone chimed. She took it with her from the room. It was a text message from Helena.

"Daddy, is all OK? Mommy just texted me. I am at a party, but I wanted to check on you all b/c Mommy texted me when you all should be having fun."

Ginger texted her back from Paul's phone. "Hi, sweetheart. All is good. We just miss you. We love you."

At least she had that to feel good about as she exited the cab and walked into the hospital's emergency room. She actually felt better than she had, but decided to go anyway. An ulcer gets progressively worse, and so she was intent on dealing with it at that moment.

The receptionist greeted her with a smile, had her fill out paperwork and she took a seat in the waiting area. She looked at the others waiting for service and wondered what their ailments were. It was a calm waiting room, much unlike when they had to rush Helena to Piedmont Hospital in Atlanta when she tripped on a street curb and cut her hand, requiring seven stitches. There was blood in that waiting area, and it was not all Helena's.

One teenager had a bruised shoulder and neck from apparently falling off a skateboard. *Probably was riding on the railing of some steps,* Ginger thought. *If that's the case, then he probably deserves this. Maybe he'll cut out that nonsense.*

The other few people looked to be not sick at all or battling something internal, like she was.

Within minutes, she was called to the back to see a

nurse, which shocked her. *That would never happen at home*, she thought. She explained her symptoms to the doctor, who examined her family history, took some blood and a urine sample and gave her some ginger ale to help settle her stomach.

All her vital signs were fine. "Is this your first time in California?" Dr. Margolis asked.

"It is," Ginger said. "Beautiful place. The feeling I'm having is getting in the way a little bit. It's nothing dramatic, but the dizzy spells concern me."

"And they should," the doctor said. "Dizziness should never be taken lightly. It could be some kind of brain issue. I'm not saying that at all. There's no reason to think that at all. I'm just saying that in general, the brain is so complicated and sometimes it gives us clues that something isn't quite right. So it's important when we get those clues that we explore them."

"I have so much going on in my head right now, I wouldn't be surprised if my brain exploded," Ginger said.

"Well, let's not have that happen," the doctor said, and they laughed.

He told Ginger she could rest on the examination table until he returned with the blood work results that might give him some clue as to why she felt as she had.

She lay there thinking about her cousin, Rita, who was sick for months and went to many doctors who could not figure out her health concerns. The not knowing drove

Rita batty. Ginger fretted the doctor coming back and telling her there was nothing they could find out of order.

Finally, she dozed off on the table and dreamed the doctor came back to tell her she had an ulcer, appendicitis and a stomach virus. When she looked at him with concern, the doctor said, "Well, at least you know. That's what you wanted, right? To know?"

Before she could get too scared, the door opening awakened her. It was Dr. Margolis.

"Doctor," she said as she got her bearings. "Did you find anything?"

"Let me ask you something," he said. "Have you been drinking a lot of our wonderful wine we harvest up here?"

"Yes."

"Well, that's it," he said.

"What do you mean?" Ginger asked.

He said: "As good as our wine is, it does not go down so well when you're pregnant."

Dr. Margolis walked toward the door, turned and added, "Congratulations."

Ginger did not respond. She sat on the table, dumbfounded.

CHAPTER 16
A NIGHT TO NOT REMEMBER

I f Ginger's head was spinning before Dr. Margolis' discovery, it was *really* going with the news that she was pregnant. Again.

"Doctor, how can this be?" she asked. "I mean, I was told in no uncertain terms that I could not get pregnant. Now you're telling me I am?"

"I'm going to tell you a secret that I don't want you to repeat," Dr. Margolis said. "This is covered under doctor-patient confidentiality, OK?"

Ginger nodded her head. She anticipated the knowledge he was about to share.

"Sometimes," Dr. Margolis said, "doctors are wrong."

And then he laughed. And she did, too. "That's the only real, honest answer there is," he said. "This is not an exact science, as you know. Sometimes, no matter all the research and knowledge, we don't get it right. I'm kind of glad the doctors missed on this one. And I bet you are, too."

"I am, doctor," she said. "You have no idea."

Dr. Margolis left the room and Ginger looked down at her stomach as she placed both hands over it. Then she looked toward the ceiling, and with tears flowing down her face, said, "Thank you, God. Thank you."

She spent a few minutes in the room, rejoicing at the blessing bestowed upon her, the miracle she never even considered. *And they say lightning doesn't strike twice in the same spot?* Ginger thought.

When she left the hospital, with pamphlets on healthy eating as a pregnant woman, breast-feeding and exercise, she didn't even bother to call a taxi. She began walking.

Her cell phone rang and she expected it to be her mother, who was looking for her to return to the hotel by then. She was not ready to speak to her. But when she looked at the phone, she saw an unfamiliar number. Immediately, she thought it was Paul, so she answered.

"What's going on?" Paul said. "My mom said you were working on the bail."

"I did," she said, "but there's nothing that can happen tonight. I was told you'll have to see the judge in the morning and he'll determine if you have to stay another day."

"What? Another day? Are you serious?" he asked. "Where did you get that from?"

"Paul, we have a lot to talk about," Ginger said. "Are you OK?"

"I'll be OK when I get out of here," he said. "They let me use the phone again, so I only have a few minutes. Who told you about staying here two days?"

"That's the law out here," she said. "Only the judge can

make an exception. I'll be back at court in the morning at eight. I can use a debit or credit card, so I'll have the bail money—it's hard to get a bond because we don't live here—and let's hope the judge lets you go."

"This is so messed up," Paul said. "This guy didn't even give me the breath test. He went on his instincts. How can I get a DUI based on his beliefs?"

"That's what you should tell the judge," Ginger said. "I hope he lets you go."

"Yeah, me too," he said. "Well, I gotta go."

"I'm sorry this has happened, Paul. I really am."

"Thanks. Me, too. But it'll be all right. See you in the morning."

Paul got off the phone and was confused when a correctional officer directed him and the others to another area of the building. It was then that his little arrest experience turned totally humiliating and dehumanizing.

They were ordered to strip, and Paul watched in amazement as the men got naked, turned their backs to the officer and bent over so he could determine if they had stuffed "contraband" up the cracks of their anuses. When it was his turn to do so, Paul felt numb, like he was in a horrific dream.

He felt like cattle, like he was less than the man he was before entering that building. The officer ordered him to place his clothes in a paper bag and to grab a towel, a set of jail-issued clothes, plastic flip-flops and to take a shower in the stall that reeked of filth.

Paul did so in a daze. He could not believe all this was happening to him. But it was. He was no longer someone arrested on a DUI charge. He was an inmate and treated as such.

Once clothed, they were directed to a pod where there were two levels of cells and an open sort of recreation area. It was after midnight, so the televisions were off and the other inmates were already in bed.

Please put me in an empty cell, Paul prayed to himself.

It did not work out that way. He was walked to a cell on the upper level, in the center. He walked in and when the officer shut that heavy metal door behind him, Paul's heart dropped. He truly was in jail.

Adding to his misery was someone on the lower bunk that Paul thought was sleeping. *What if this guy is crazy and I have to fight him?* he thought.

He placed the toothbrush kit he was given on a small table and climbed on the top bunk, banging his knee in the process.

He had never seen and even heard of a mattress as thin as the one he stretched out on. It was about four inches thick. Paul was totally uncomfortable, but not because of the bed. He was an inmate.

He didn't like breathing the air, and the idea of actually going to sleep was far-fetched. He tossed to try to find a manageable position to rest, which apparently irritated his cellmate.

"Hey, if you gonna flip and flop all night," he said, "we gonna have a problem."

Paul was not sure how to respond. He didn't want to punk out, although he hardly was some roughneck. But he had his share of fights in his day and had gotten himself in shape in recent months. He thought he'd better let dude know he was not to be played with.

"Man, go to sleep," Paul said. He was not sure where that came from, but he blurted it out. "Don't worry about me."

He held his breath, hoping the man would not respond or would not take it as a declaration of war. Paul's response seemed to disarm the man. "That's what I'm trying to do," he said.

Paul did not respond. He felt lucky he got away with those reckless comments. He didn't want to push it. So he found a relatively comfortable position on his back and looked up at the cold ceiling. Paul counted the minutes, and they went by molasses-slow.

"Hey, why you in here?" the guy in the lower bunker asked.

"I thought you were trying to sleep," Paul answered.

"*Trying* to, but can't," he said. "First time in jail. I ain't too comfortable, you know?"

Paul was relieved. Maybe he didn't have a serial killer as a cellmate.

"Same here," he said. "I came out here from Atlanta to enjoy the wine. I guess I had a little too much last night."

"Wow, same here," the man below said. "I live in L.A. Having some drama on the job and at home and said, 'Let me get away.' This is my refuge. Been coming up here for years. Love it up here. Right now, though, not loving it so much."

"Tell me about it," Paul said. "I got my wife, mother and mother-in-law here with me. So imagine what I'm gonna face when I get out of here."

"Damn. I'll pray for you," the man said, and they both laughed.

"So you're into wines?" the guy asked Paul.

"Love wines," he answered. "Trying to get more into them. So this is an important trip for me. Had some great wines already, though. Had the best wine I ever had tonight."

"The crazy thing about this place is that if you went out every night out here, you could probably say that every night," the cell-mate said. "That's why I come up here. I watch the movie *Sideways* and I get on the road."

"Ah, man—what's your name?" Paul asked.

"Roger."

"I'm Paul, Roger. I can't believe you mentioned *Sideways*. I watched it before I left, too. There are so many scenes I like. But there's this scene where Virginia Madsen's character tells Paul Giamatti's character why she loves wine… What she says and how she says it, it makes you want to drink wine."

"Paul—Paul, right?"

"Yeah."

"I know the scene you're talking about," Roger said. "I know it by heart."

"Come on, man. No way," Paul said.

"OK, check it out. She says, 'The more I drink, the more I liked what it made me think about…like to think about the life of wine. How it's a living thing…like to think about what was going on the year the grapes were growing, how the sun was shining, if it rained? I like to think about all the people who tended and picked the grapes, and if it's an old wine how many of them must be dead by now. I like how wine continues to evolve. Like, if I opened a bottle of wine today it would taste different from if I opened it any other day, because a bottle of wine is actually alive and it's constantly evolving and gaining complexity. That is, until it peaks…and then it begins its steady, inevitable decline… And it tastes so fucking good.'"

"Oh, shit," Paul said. "That's amazing. How could you— wait. You said you live in L.A… You're an actor."

"Yes," he said. "Typical struggling L.A. actor. But I loved what she said and I used that as one of my monologues for auditions. It's easy to do because I agree with what she says, so it's almost an emotional thing, like it's really coming from me."

"That's crazy you would recall *that* particular scene," Paul said.

"I know," Roger said. "I wish I could write like that. Just thoughtful writing."

"And the person had to be a wine-lover," Paul said. "How else could he be so emotional about wine?"

Paul's experience took a turn for the better. He was paired in a jail cell with a wine lover and actor who loved to talk about wine. In Atlanta, Paul had a few friends that appreciated wine, but none of them could really discuss wine the way they would sports or the stock market—with passion and knowledge.

"I'm like you—someone who likes wine and wants to get better at understanding them," Roger said. "I was up here one time and happened to meet someone who took me to a sommelier event where there were about thirty of the best wine experts in the world in one room.

"So there is this contest—whatever sommelier that can identify this one red wine would win ten thousand dollars. I was standing there, saying to myself, 'This is going to be fun.'

"Well, it wasn't fun, really."

"What?" Paul said.

"It was amazing," Roger said.

"These guys…let me tell you what happened. So, the wine is in this decanter. They pour each sommelier some of it. They're sitting around this huge table. So, you realize there are millions of wines in the world. Millions. But they have to identify the year, the region of the world and the actual name of the wine.

"I'm thinking, 'How can this be? No one can do that.'

"So, they get the wine and everyone looks at it on the table for about, I don't know, seven, eight minutes. They just stare at it. Then they pick it up and hold it above their heads and look at it again, trying to determine the age. The next thing was to smell it. So they stick their noses damn near in the wine. It was crazy. They got a clear, deep smell of the wine.

"They do that a couple of times and then they begin swirling it in its glass—two fingers between the stem and circulate it while it's sitting on the table. They're helping it to breathe. This goes on for about five minutes. And I'm like, 'I don't care what you do. No way someone gonna be able to figure out one out of a million wines. No way.'"

Paul listened as a child would a bedtime story. He was totally engrossed.

"So, it's literally about forty-five minutes later," Roger continued, "and no one has said a word. They are all studying this wine, swirling, it, smelling it, staring at it. Finally, after all the foreplay, they finally start tasting the wine. Still, no one has said a word because the one thing they can't afford to be is wrong. It would be horrible for their reputation.

"So finally, almost an hour into this thing, one guy raises his hand. He says it's a 1976 Chateau so-and-so from Southern Italy or some place. I can't remember exactly what it was. But he was *right*. Can you believe that? This guy figured out this wine was forty-something year-old wine from Italy from just studying it and tasting it. The other guys clapped politely for him. I wanted to give my man a hug and a high-five. It was amazing."

"Damn," Paul said. "That's what you call being an expert in your field."

Both men were quiet for a moment as they took in the story. For those few minutes, they were not in jail. They were in that room with some of the best wine experts in the world.

"What was the wine that made you fall in love with wine?" Roger asked.

"It was a Fairview Pinotage 2002, I believe," Paul answered.

"A South African wine?" Roger said.

"Yes. My boy, D.J.'s wife, Wanda, went there for a visit and brought me back a bottle," Paul explained. "I had never had a Pinotage before. It's grown only in a few places in the world but especially in South Africa. Something about the soil. Well, I loved it. It made me feel like wine could be a meal. It was hearty and fruity and robust. It was different from any wine I had ever had. It was the wine that brought me all the way in."

"I understand how you feel," Roger said. "What did it for me was a 2008 Tobin James Fatboy Zinfandel. I always liked wine, but this one goes down smooth, like an expensive cognac. All the dark berries are evident. And it's 16.2 alcohol content, so it gets you there. I heard a guy call it 'sex in a bottle.' And you know what? You drink a bottle of that with your woman and you'll get lucky for sure."

They talked of wine—viogniers, pinots, chardonnays, merlots—until the sun came up, starting a day they hoped would not end like the day before. They talked because they couldn't sleep and because discussing wine kept them from thinking about where they were.

So into the discussion was Paul that he hardly thought about Ginger and the abortion. And he was glad about that because he still had not figured out how to process it. But Ginger said they needed to talk and he hoped something would come out of it to make him feel better. But that would be later.

Paul and Roger were corralled along with about twenty other inmates and shepherded to the courtroom in the detention center. Paul felt the weight of his trip as he stood for before Judge Jenson, who looked fresh and alert. He had an upbeat spirit.

Paul looked around the courtroom and spotted Ginger, who offered a reassuring smile. He was glad to see her; he smiled back. Paul watched how the judge interacted with the inmates before him. He was expeditious, thorough and seemingly fair, giving Paul a sense of hope. When it was Paul's turn, Judge Jenson said, "OK, you look like an upstanding citizen. What's your deal?"

It was a rhetorical question and Paul realized it, so he did not say anything as the judge examined the paperwork. "OK, Mr. Wall, I don't see any results of a breathalyzer. Did you take one?"

"No, your honor."

"I see," he said. "Looks like you took the field sobriety test. Didn't do so well, huh? What were you drinking?"

"Sir, I had the best wine of my life at 1313 Main—a bottle of Caymus 2008 Cabernet Sauvignon."

"That place is great," the judge said. "I go there on occasion… OK, let's see here. So you stopped in the middle of the intersection, didn't fail the sobriety test but didn't pass it, either. The officer used his judgment, which he is entitled to. But he did not administer a breathalyzer. Can you pay the bail?"

Paul turned to Ginger, who nodded her head.

"Yes, I can, sir," he said.

"OK, Mr. Wall. They don't have much of a case against you without the breathalyzer, but because it is a DUI case, I'm going to set a court date. See the clerk on your way out and then pay the bond, which is ten per cent of five thousand dollars. And, if I were you, I'd hire a lawyer to negotiate this thing so you don't have to come back out here just for this."

"Thank you, judge."

And just like that, Paul was again a free man. He looked at Roger, who was a few feet away. "Good luck, man. Call me," he said, and Roger nodded his head.

Paul saw the clerk, got some paperwork and went through a side door to claim and change his clothes. Ginger, after paying the bail, waited in the lobby for her husband, unsure of how he would receive her. It was her news that she aborted their child that led him to leaving her at the hotel and the ensuing drinking binge. *Would he blame me?* she worried.

At the same time, she remained flummoxed by learning she again was pregnant. *How could I go from not being able to get pregnant to pregnant twice in about five months? When do I tell Paul? My mother? Helena? Are we ready to have a child?*

She was overwrought with concerns and not confident on what to do. She was sure she would tell Paul, though. *This pregnancy was a blessing from God, a chance for me to redeem myself to Him and regain whatever I lost from my husband.*

Then she thought: *What if he's so angry with me that he wants out? What if he believes he can't trust me?*

She was going to play more games with her mind, but Paul emerged from the locked doors. Their eyes met… and there was no animosity between them. There was only relief.

Otis' story about losing his daughter and wife resonated with Paul. He wasn't sure if he would not deteriorate as Otis had without his girls. And now that he had financial means, it was the time for them to come together, not pull apart. He faced the fact that while Ginger's decision on abortion was extreme, she never would have taken that path if he hadn't lost all confidence in who he was and said he wanted a divorce.

Ginger was remorseful that she acted out of spite and anger instead of calm and responsibility. Despite Paul's claims, she came to the belief that it was her responsibility to share her pregnancy news with her husband and let them decide together what route to take. She told him what she did as a way of overcoming her guilt, but it only heightened animosity in the relationship.

So now they were face-to-face after so many personal revelations, and they were unabashed in their remorse and shared responsibility for their plight.

"Thank you for being here," Paul said, hugging Ginger. "I'm sorry about all this."

"I'm sorry, too, Paul," she said, holding her man tightly. "I am so sorry."

They hugged for an extended period. When they finally let go, Ginger used the back of her hand to wipe away tears.

"It's OK," Paul said. "I'm OK, and we're OK. Let's get back to our vacation. We have one more day in California. I have some plans for us."

Ginger pulled out her vibrating phone. It was Brenda, Paul's mother.

"He's right here," Ginger said, handing over the phone.

"I'm good, Ma. No problem. Everything's fine. We're headed back to the hotel. Ah, huh. Yes… It was bad, but… Ma, we'll be there in twenty minutes. No, maybe longer. We've got to go get the car. They impounded it. So we'll get the car and be there in the next hour… OK. Ma, I'm fine. OK. Love you, too."

He ended the call and looked at Ginger. "It's not like I was in Sing Sing or Alcatraz," he said.

"A parent will be a parent until the end," she said.

He nodded his head, grabbed her hand and they headed out to retrieve the rental car.

When they got back to the hotel, Madeline and Brenda were in the lobby, waiting.

"Let me look at you," Madeline said to Ginger.

"Why are you worried about her? I was the one in jail," Paul said.

"You don't know?" Brenda said.

"Know what?" Paul asked

"I wasn't feeling well last night," Ginger said, "so after I left the jail I went to the emergency room."

"You OK? What did they say?" Paul asked.

"I'm fine," she said. "Better than ever. Just had some stomach issues."

"What did they say, though?" Paul asked.

"That I'm fine," Ginger answered. She did not want to tell him standing right there in the lobby. She was not sure the best scenario to tell him, but she knew that was not it. "I had some ginger ale and I felt better."

She was convincing enough that no one questioned her.

"Well, what's the plan for the day?" Paul said. "I've got to get a nap. I did not sleep at all last night."

"I bet you didn't; I wouldn't," Brenda said. "How bad was it?"

"Terrible. Humiliating," he said. "But I met some interesting people. But I can't talk about it now. I need a good, long shower and at least a two-hour nap. Let's have lunch by the pool around twelve-thirty."

They agreed to do so, and Ginger walked with Paul back to their room. The in-laws went for coffee and fruit.

In the room, Paul hardly delayed in getting into the shower. "I have to wash away that experience," he said. Under the hot water, he felt himself come back to life, the smell and grime and aura of the jail flowed down the drain. He spent an extra ten minutes in the shower, letting the flow douse his hair, the water serving as therapy.

"This has been a crazy trip," Ginger said when Paul exited the shower. "You feel better?"

"I feel like I washed the Napa Valley Correction Center/ County Jail off me," he said. "I don't get why a jail has to be so disgusting."

"I'm just glad you're out," Ginger said. "But it's not made to be a resort, you know?"

Paul, with his silk robe wrapped around him, nodded his head knowingly, and rested on the bed. He let out a sigh of relief. Not too long before then he was on a super-thin "mattress," staring at the ceiling and wondering how his life degenerated to that situation. Being in the confines of his hotel room was so welcomed.

Ginger had the television on ESPN, but the sound was down, and Paul rested on his back as if he were in a coffin: hands clasped together across his chest.

She went to the bathroom and returned after several minutes. "Paul, we really need to talk. There's something important I need to tell you," she said. Ginger had gathered the courage and the words to give Paul the news that would turn his mindset.

Paul's response? He snored.

"That was fast," Ginger said. She sat on the adjacent bed and stared at Paul as he slept. She looked down at her stomach and put her hand over it. And she started to cry—tears of joy and regret. Then she figured out why she cried so much. Her hormones were screwy.

Life is growing inside of me, she thought to herself. And

when she thought of the abortion, she cried more. *God, please forgive me.*

To have a second chance when much of her life she was told she had no chance to get pregnant, well, it made the miracle of child bearing that much more miraculous. She was anxious for Paul to wake up. She wanted to apologize to him again and to share news with him that she was sure he would embrace.

But he slept and slept—and Ginger alternated between staring at him and reading the literature on how to eat for two. She knew right away she would be obsessed with making sure she gave her child the best chance to be born healthy.

She also thought about how to tell Paul; what to say, where to say it, how to say it. Her mom and Brenda were not going to join them for dinner later that night, so Ginger thought it would be better to tell Paul first, over dinner, before sharing it with anyone.

Make it a special announcement in a special place, she thought. Paul had identified French Blue in St. Helena as their dinner destination. There was something special about that place because it was in a town named after their daughter.

Yes, that's the place to tell him, Ginger thought.

CHAPTER 17
DAWN OF A NEW DAY

For the first time in their lives together, Paul's snoring did not bother Ginger. There were times when she slept in the guest bedroom or demanded he sleep elsewhere because the noise was so distracting. But on this day, with the news she had to share and all that they had been through, she wanted to be close to her husband.

She was in a remarkable place in her life. All the pain and hurt and disappointment of a few months before were gone. Ginger lay cuddled up with her snoring husband feeling as alive and womanly as ever.

As much as she felt like a mother in raising Helena, she was shocked that knowing she would birth a child changed how she felt about herself. She was so broken and disenchanted when she was pregnant several months before that she never gave herself the opportunity to embrace the magnitude of the responsibility.

This time, she did, and even though she was in the very early stages of the pregnancy, she intuitively placed a hand on her belly often, as if she was protecting the fetus from impending danger.

Mostly, she felt extra womanly. She knew it was a silly notion; she was a full-fledged woman all along, a mother, a wife. But having life growing inside her injected Ginger with a sense of pride and self-esteem that she had not felt. Ever.

I have a life growing inside of me, she said to herself while resting in the bed. *Oh, my God.*

Before she fell asleep, she thought about names for the baby and how the child would look and how her mom would spoil it and how she wished her dad were alive to see the baby, to see her pregnant. She also thought about Helena. She was such a delightful young lady, a teenager without the teenage attitude or sense of entitlement. She prayed her child would have the same temperament.

But mostly she prayed that Helena would forgive her and Paul for not telling her that she was adopted. Theirs was parents-raising-a-child, genuine love that was strong and everlasting. But Ginger could not help but wonder how Helena would feel about not being told the truth about her parents all these years.

For a second, she thought that maybe Paul was right. *What good would it do to tell her? We're her parents.* But that thought passed swiftly. *As her parents we are obligated to tell her*, Ginger told herself.

Still, the effects it would have on her concerned Ginger. Would Helena accept hearing the truth and not judge her parents? Would she want to meet her birth parents? And with Ginger pregnant, how would Helena receive that news? Would she resent the forthcoming child?

All those scenarios scared Ginger. Helena was her world, and she could not fathom their relationship not being the same as it always had been. Telling an eighteen-year-old she was adopted at virtually the same time as revealing her mother was pregnant would be a lot to take in at once.

It was a lot for Ginger to take in, and so she finally closed her eyes and drifted off to sleep. She rested peacefully, with dreams of Helena posing for photos with the new baby, proud that she was a big sister.

Paul, meanwhile, dreamed of being in jail and having to fight his way out of closed-in places to prevent being raped. There were two guys, one bigger than him, one smaller. They approached with caution and bad intentions. "Been waiting for this since you got here," the little one said. "You gonna be mines."

"And mines," the bigger guy added.

Paul grabbed a bottle of wine, a 2011 Alouette Pinot Noir and blasted the smaller man across the head with it, knocking him out and breaking the bottle at the same time. In his hand was the neck of the broken bottle with its sharp edges. Confidently, he approached the big guy and stabbed him in the gut with it, and he fell to the floor.

Paul let out a primal scream, and raised his hands in victory. He had conquered them. But in his salutations, he realized he had become one of them, and it scared him so much that he shook himself out of his dream and woke up.

His movements in his sleep startled Ginger, who moved away so she wouldn't get struck by a flailing arm.

"Paul, you OK?" she said. "You must have had a bad dream."

"Oh, man. I did," Paul said. "I dreamed I killed two men—or at least hurt them badly while I was in jail. Hit and stabbed them with a wine bottle."

Ginger laughed. "A wine bottle? You had a wine bottle in jail?"

"I did," Paul said, wiping his face. "And a good bottle of wine, too."

They laughed. Paul turned his body and embraced Ginger. It was just before 1 p.m. "I tell you, Gin," he said, "I hate we have gone through some of this drama. But I really believe it can—it will—make us stronger and closer.

"Jail was not a good experience, but I'm almost glad I went through it. I ain't that religious, but I can say with confidence that I believe God puts us in positions that are uncomfortable so we can learn from them. I felt like I was sub-human part of my time last night. It's humiliating to be in handcuffs and to be locked into a space. But I met people with *real* problems. It makes you understand that as bad as something may seem to you, it's not even as bad as it could be.

"You would think we would know that. But we take it all for granted. I mean, I met this man who looked so haggard—he was in the holding cell with me when I first got there. But I could see that he really wasn't as old as he looked. He was just unkempt. Anyway, the man could look at you and tell you about certain things about you because of your body language.

"He worked for probably the CIA or FBI—he wouldn't say. But he lost everything when his newborn baby died as his wife was delivering. And then his wife eventually died because she never got over losing the child. And those two deaths broke him down. He lost his job and is basically a bum. Said his name was Otis, like Otis from *The Andy Griffith Show*, the town drunk, frequently locked up. It was really sad.

"But it was also an eye-opener for me. I thank God that I didn't totally lose my mind with losing my job. But I did let it change me."

He rubbed Ginger's arm. "And I am so sorry for that," he said. "When you look back on things, you see things better. At the time, I felt less than a man; I couldn't provide for my family. But I should have been thinking how great it was that I had a family. That's the positive over negative thing. If I had done that, I probably would have handled that situation a lot differently and you'd be pregnant with our baby...I'm sorry, Gin."

It was then that she was going to tell Paul. Over dinner would have been more romantic or dramatic, but him saying that at that time let her know how much he wanted a child with her.

Before she could utter a word, however, Paul kissed

her deeply; so deeply that she got dizzy. She was not sure if it was the kiss or more effects of being pregnant, but she lost her equilibrium for a moment.

She looked at her husband and she saw the kind of love in his eyes that she saw at the height of their marriage. She kissed him, and they caressed each other like lovers do.

As Paul lay on his back, Ginger tugged the belt on his robe and pulled it open, and his rocket-hard penis sprung up like a telescope. She immediately stroked it gently, causing him to moan.

At the same time, Paul meticulously handled her ample breasts, squeezing them at first before centering his attention on her thimble-sized nipples. They were Ginger's sensitive spots, her hot spots, and in response she stroked his manhood with more fervor. He leaned over and began licking and then sucking her nipples, and the pleasure rifled through her body.

She held his head as he sucked her titties, and she breathed heavily and spread her legs. He knew his wife, even if their love life had become far less frequent. And so he placed his hand between her legs, and he could feel the heat rising from her like steam.

She shifted her weight to her upper back and raised her hips off the bed, and Paul pulled down the draw-string pajama pants she wore. One side first, then the other...until they were at her ankles.

Ginger kicked them off using her feet, and bent her

legs again so Paul could insert his middle finger into her. And he did, with great care and attention to her desires. The moisture from her insides doused his finger and she slid her body up and down on it to manage how deep she wanted it to go.

Her eyes were closed but her heart was open. She needed passion in her life, and the closeness that came with it. She missed the physical pleasure it brought her. After several minutes, Paul slowly dislodged his finger, and Ginger rolled on her side, her back to her husband.

Paul did not hesitate to angle himself so he could enter her from behind, and the initial insertion made Ginger flinch. Inside her, he adjusted his body so he could grab and smack her ass as he stroked her slowly and deeply. She moaned and he kissed her on her back, and the feeling that only intense passion can bring covered them.

"I love you, Gin," he said, still inside her, still pushing himself deeper.

She tried to answer, but the force of his movements stifled her breath. She could hardly get a word out that made any sense. She grunted and moaned as Paul pounded harder and faster and penetrated her until he could go no deeper.

Ginger needed a good fucking like that. They both did. So many pent up emotions, so many frustrations, so many desires. It all came out in this lovemaking session that traveled from one bed to the next, from one position to another.

"Damn, baby. You're getting it," Ginger said to Paul, her legs on his shoulders.

He extended her legs out and held her by her ankles as he pounded in rapid-fire succession, like a jackhammer. "Yes, baby," he managed to get out. The rest of what he said was profanity: "Shit." "Damn." "Goddamn." "Fuck." No sentences. Just single words that, in this context, meant pleasure.

"Get it, Paul. Get it," Ginger implored, and those words charged Paul to stroke harder and deeper and come in from different angles to touch all her walls. She was in pain and pleasure at the same time. Only during sex could this happen.

Someone's cell phone rang, but neither of them entertained answering it. They were in the throes not only of making love, but truly reconnecting after a period of discomfort, distrust and uncertainty.

Paul finally felt the sensation of an orgasm rise at once from his feet and descend from his brain to converge and explode at his penis, swelling it up even bigger as it unleashed a load of semen into Ginger, who felt the tingly feeling of being suspended that climaxing brought.

"Oh, God," she yelled. "Oh, God."

She held him tightly as they reached an orgasm in unison, an event that was rare but significant because it epitomized their connection. Paul thrust on until his almost limp body collapsed on top of hers. They breathed heavily into each other's ear.

"Damn, Paul," Ginger said. "Damn. That was so good that I think I'm pregnant."

Paul laughed and Ginger kissed him on his chest. They lay together in silence, exhausted and fulfilled, and before long he dozed back off to sleep.

Ginger cried.

CHAPTER 18
ANTICIPATION

Madeline was giddy. She received a phone call from Mitch, who seduced her with his words. There were not Don Juan type of sentiments, but they seemed sincere and honest, and that's what she needed.

Getting over the death of her husband was a daily chore. First of all, she did not know how to move on. More importantly, she did not know *when* to move on. What was the perceived "proper" time to pick herself off the floor and date again.

She aged gracefully and, when she wanted to, had a younger woman's spirit about her. Mitch was not the first man who expressed interest in the widow. But he was the first to be chivalrous and humorous and who did not pressure her. The words that sold her on him were these, uttered about six months after her husband's sudden death:

"The last thing I want to do is come into your life as some whirlwind. At the same time, I do not reject when I have a chance to add good people into my life. I could be wrong—I was once—but I see you as a good person.

So, just know I am here to build on what we started when you are ready."

It was an approach that made so much sense, which explains why so many men didn't get it. Madeline had a few men her age approach her as if she was some horny, lonely woman, dying to have someone warm her bed. "Everybody needs a little loving, you know?" one man said to her on their second phone conversation. That was their last talk.

Other men figured she must have had some life insurance money, so she was financially secure and could take care of them. One man told her: "So, I think we'll get along. You seem like a woman of today. You understand the value of being the bread-winner. I'll do my part—keep you feeling good and take out the trash."

She told him: "Leave. When you do that, you'll be taking out the trash."

Mitch was strong on his own merits, but clowns like those magnified his stature in Madeline's mind. She figured she would always, in some way, grieve for her deceased husband. But she knew the only way to have a fulfilling rest of her life was to live it. That did not mean with another man. It meant being open to another man who was worthy.

"So," she said to Brenda in the lobby as Paul and Ginger made love, "Mitch said they will be here at seven-thirty to pick us up. He said he had an Italian restaurant in mind."

"Girl, it could be Waffle House at this point," Brenda

said. "I just look forward to having fun, good conversation with good men. If we get that, then I will be fine."

"I can't speak for Mitch's friend, but Mitch always has a lot to say about a lot of things. So, we'll be fine."

They noticed it was time for their kids to be downstairs and they were not. So Brenda called. No answer.

"The car is right there, so they have to be in the room," Madeline said. "They might be asleep. Paul had a long night. Come on, let's go knock on their door and wake them up."

So they took the walk to the room, chatting the whole way. But just before Brenda could knock on the door, she heard something and pressed her ear against the door.

"Madeline. Listen," she said.

And they blushed as they took in the lovemaking sounds of their children.

"Come on, Brenda," Madeline whisper. "This isn't right."

"OK," Brenda said, and they tiptoed off.

When they got to the elevator, Brenda said, "That was weird."

"Kinda creepy," Madeline said. "I remember Ginger walking in on me and her father one time. She was young, around five, and she heard all this noise and I guess she was concerned. Girl, it was embarrassing. I was bent over, holding on to the rear of the bed and her father was behind me doing his business."

Brenda laughed loudly. "Oh, no. How did you get out of that?"

"Shoot, we didn't," Madeline said. "I just said, 'Ginger,

go back to bed' and she turned around and left. And we kept doing what we were doing. Thinking about it now, she might have just stood there and listened to us.

"When I saw her in the morning, there was this awkward feeling I had."

"It probably was just you feeling that way," Brenda said. "Kids have a way of moving on."

"I hope so," Madeline said. "I'd hate for her to have that image of me burned in her memory."

"I know what you mean," Brenda said. "Paul never caught us doing it. But we caught *him*. One night my husband went in his room to get a basketball—he was still playing at the time—and I went to check on Vino. Well, he was so into masturbating that he didn't even realize we were standing in the doorway. When he did, he just stopped and pulled the covers over his head."

"Wow," Madeline said. "Did you ever address it?"

"I didn't; his father did," Brenda said. "I don't know what he said, but he told me he had a talk with him—man-to-man—and we never talked about it again. But Paul did seem a little strange or embarrassed when I saw him the next day. He was about twelve."

"I think we're going to be waiting down here for a while," Madeline said. "So, let's have some wine."

"How about a white? Paul loves reds, but I like some whites, too," Brenda said. "A chardonnay?"

"You pick it, I'll drink it," Madeline said.

"So how do we handle this date thing?" Brenda said.

"I'm a little out of practice. Haven't really dated in a few decades."

"I know what you mean," Madeline said. "You know why it's sad? Because even though we were married, we still should have been dating our husbands. That's where marriages go wrong. We get stuck in the rut and let it slip away.

"Having a so-called 'date night' wasn't enough. You do that once a month or so. What about the other twenty-nine days?"

"I know," Brenda said. "It's amazing how people don't get it with relationships. Older people who have been through stuff should be the relationship experts. What do these youngsters know?"

They kept sipping the wine and before long, they were feeling especially good.

"I'll tell you what the real problem is with relationships," Brenda said. She was on her third glass. "Not enough of what our kids are doing right now is going on."

They gave each other a high-five and fell all over each other laughing.

"Seriously, though, the problem," Brenda continued, "is that we make wrong decisions when we choose life partners. Sounds like you got it right—your husband was your soul mate. But most of us choose a husband or a wife for all the wrong reasons or not enough of the right reasons."

"As an example…," Madeline said.

"As an example, I'll use myself," Brenda said. "James was a good man, overall. But he did not have that energy and real zest for life that I wanted in a man. Still, I ignored it, even though it bothered me. I felt like I could change him or that he would grow into the man I wanted him to be.

"Having fun and laughing and being joyous are important to me. We had fun, to a degree, but he was more conservative and laid back than I needed. I needed a take-charge man. He wasn't that. And I knew it and yet I went along with it anyway because I figured he was a good man who was going to be good to me.

"As it turned out, that wasn't enough. I knew it wasn't enough a long time ago—*years* ago—but I literally suffered in silence. And when your kid moves on, that's when it really hits, you know? Then it's just you and him and it all comes out in a rush. Even at that I took it, stayed until I couldn't take it anymore."

"One thing you said," Madeline chipped in. "You said you thought you could change him. That's one of the big mistakes people make in relationships. You can't change anyone. Now, you can *inspire* someone to change by how you act. Maybe. But people's natural defenses come up when you are clearly trying to change them.

"They're like, 'What's wrong with me? Why do I need to change?' And instead of getting what you want, you get more of what you don't want. But I agree with you on decision-making. You know how many friends and family members I know who married someone that I knew wasn't right for them? A *lot*. If I knew it, they *had* to know it, too. But some people just want to say, 'This is my husband' or 'I'm married.' And that's the mistake."

"Yes," Brenda chimed in. "They say the divorce rate is fifty percent. I say of those who stay married, more than half of them wish they weren't married. They stay because they feel trapped or that it's cheaper to keep her or easier to stay—even though they are unhappy.

"I tell you, it took everything in me not to cheat on James. I was bored to death. Nice man. But he wasn't for me. And at the end, when I realized I had to leave, is when simply looking at him irritated me. I was in a bad place."

"Well, I give you credit for doing what was the strong thing to do," Madeline said. "My sister right now has been married eleven years and unhappy with nine of them. Just not happy about how she's living, where she's living and who she's living with. But she won't do anything. She said she's stuck. It's sad."

"I tell you, I was concerned about Paul and Ginger," Brenda admitted. "I never saw my son as he was. He never said it was Ginger, but what was I to think? Finally, he told me he lost his job and how that really knocked him off his feet."

"And it knocked Ginger off hers, too," Madeline said. "There was a time when she was miserable, very upset. There was no communication, that's what I gathered."

"Well, they are communicating now—in the language of love," Brenda said, and they laughed again. And when they looked up, there were Ginger and Paul, smiling.

"So," Paul said, "how many drinks are we behind?"

"A bottle and a half," Madeline said, "and you're not gonna catch up because we ain't stopping."

"Oh, boy," Ginger said. "That doesn't sound good."

"What have y'all been doing?" Brenda asked. "We've been waiting on y'all."

They were not about to say what they *really* were doing. But Paul didn't want to lie, either. So he told the vague truth. "We were in the bed," he said.

"Yeah, I bet you were in bed," Madeline said.

"Mother? What does that mean?" Ginger asked.

"Nothing, child. Let's go eat. You've got to be hungry," Madeline said.

"We're going to a place in Yountville called Bistro Jeanty. Supposed to be good," Paul said. "Then we have a four o'clock at Sterling Winery."

"Oh, I read about Sterling," Ginger said. "Up on a mountain with a great view of the valley." And then she thought: *That's the best place to tell Paul he will be a father again.*

Which would have been great if it wasn't where Paul had planned to tell Ginger he hit the lottery for $8 million.

CHAPTER 19
MOUNTAIN HIGH

They drove to Yountville for lunch, which was on the way to Calistoga, where the Sterling Winery was. The sun was brilliant; it was another day that highlighted the magnificent of God.

The conversation was light, but everyone wanted to hear details about Paul's night in jail. He wasn't so keen on talking about it. Not because he did not want to share, but because he was not sure if they would get why it was an experience he was glad he endured.

"I can sum it up this way," he said. "It was embarrassing, dehumanizing, funny, enlightening and interesting. Overall, I'm glad I went through it. It's a crazy system, the prison system. Even in a little town like this people are troubled by guns and drugs and violence.

"I told Ginger about the man in the first cell I was in as they processed me. He had a great career in the government but his daughter and his wife died within months of each other and he was just broken down. He lost it and now he's an alcoholic who can't let go of his grief.

"Thank God I didn't lose my family, but I understood how important family is to me because I put myself in his place. It made the things that bothered me seem inconsequential.

"And then there was a guy there who said he was arrested for speeding. But the other guy, Otis, told him he was lying. He could tell you about yourself through your body language. Like, he said I was from the southeast, that I was educated up north. This wasn't like some fortuneteller. This was a man who studied my speech patterns and body language and could tell me about myself. I was blown away.

"So this other guy has all this mouth. He's saying how he was in for speeding. Otis told him he was lying. Told him he could see in his eyes and how he shifted his body. The guy got mad and eventually admitted that he had shot someone, someone he thought had been seeing his girlfriend. Turned out it wasn't the even the right guy."

"I have a question," Brenda said. "When someone catches his or her mate cheating, why is it they want to beat up or shoot the other person? You shouldn't go after anyone; you should walk away. But if you just *had* to shoot someone, shoot your mate. That's the person who really did you wrong."

"Or just shoot yourself," Madeline said.

"I liked it better when you said don't shoot anyone," Ginger said.

"Anyway," Paul concluded, "it was an interesting experience. Met a guy in my cell who was in for the same reason I was—and he loved wine. An actor from L.A. I got lucky: We talked about wine all night. It helped us forget where we were."

They drove along mostly in silence for the next several minutes, taking in the sights and admiring the beauty and quaintness of the place. Then Ginger spotted an ideal picture-taking spot: A roadside sign in Yountville with glorious mountains in the background, that read: "Welcome To This Famous Wine Growing Region: Napa Valley…and the wine is bottled poetry."

So Paul pulled over and they took turns taking photos of each other in front of the sign and in different groups. And they got another tourist to take a few group photos of all of them.

Brenda and Madeline were a little tipsy, so their excitement was magnified. They wanted several photos of themselves—alone and together. And they kept checking the photos after they were taken and not approving before finally Paul took control of the moment.

"The car is leaving in thirty seconds. I'd like you all to be in it when I pull off," he said. "But if not, I know where to find you after I eat."

"I guess it's time we get in the car then," Brenda said.

Everyone piled in, and Ginger turned and looked at her mother-in-law. "You think you're slick, don't you?" she said. "You never told your embarrassing story."

And everyone reiterated Ginger's point. "OK, OK," Brenda said. "I wasn't trying to get out of telling it. I just forgot."

"Well, remember now," Madeline cracked.

"OK, so, as cute as I am now, I was even more cute when I was younger," Brenda began. "I was in my early twenties and my hair was pretty long. But it wasn't long enough for me, so I got this long, flowing wig that went almost down to my butt, girl."

Madeline laughed.

"And there was this guy I really liked. His name was Peter Richardson. All the girls liked him but I heard he liked me, too. We were going to meet at this club, this beautiful place with really high ceilings, candles burning on candelabras, velvet drapes, dancers in cages, the works. We were in New York.

"I have on this chiffon dress that's falling off my shoulders—really sexy and cute but not too revealing. And so Peter is there, looking handsome and in charge. And my friends tell his friends I'm there looking good and his friends tell my friends we should meet up near the bar area.

"So we do, and it's like a movie, like he's moving in slow motion toward me and I'm moving in slow motion toward him. The crowd parts and it looks like everyone in the club, hundreds of people, has their eyes on us and excited about us finally coming together.

"Now, I'm a little nervous but not that nervous because I had a few drinks—top-shelf Long Island Iced Teas. Yeah, I was drinking big girl drinks back then. So, anyway, I get closer to Peter, about five feet away, and all of a sudden, he has this strange look on his face. Then he starts backing up and pointing at me and the whole place gets loud and I'm looking around like, 'What the hell is going on?'

"Then I started to smell something; smelled like something was burning. I looked around and didn't see anything, but my friends were pointing at me and screaming. Finally, I felt this heat—my wig was on fire."

Ginger spit out the ginger ale she was drinking and Paul and Madeline were in stitches.

"And I'm not talking about a little flicker; my wig was an inferno. I pulled it off and threw it and it landed on one of the drapes and set the drape on fire."

"Get outta here," Madeline screamed.

"Someone threw something on the drapes before the whole building burned down. But I was standing there with the stocking cap on my head looking crazy. Peter tried not to laugh, but he couldn't hold it back.

"One of my friends came over and grabbed me and rushed me to the bathroom…I was never so humiliated. But I was lucky that fire didn't catch my chiffon dress. I could been a crispy critter."

They all laughed a good long time. "That was a good one, Ma," Paul said. "And it didn't involve someone's bodily function, either."

"I'll be sure to look out for candles tonight," Madeline said.

"Huh?" Ginger said.

"We have dates tonight, remember?"

"I'm not sure about this," Paul said.

"You don't have to be sure about it," Brenda responded. "We're more grown than you are. We're not some rookies trying to find our way. How do you all say it? We got this."

"Well, we need to know where you're going—and I want to meet them before you go."

"I want you both to meet Mitch and Lionel—that's his friend," Madeline said. "He's a nice man."

"Yeah, well, we'll see," Paul said.

They arrived at Bistro Jeanty and were attracted by its charm outside with beautiful flowerbeds on either side of the entrance, under red and white striped awning. Inside, it had the feel of a French bistro, cozy with wicker-backed chairs, food specials written on a blackboard, French art and waiters clad in long white aprons.

The menu was expansive and pricey, but no one fretted over it, especially after indulging in the delicious treats and wine. Ginger had water with lemon, green bean salad with warm goat cheese over roasted tomatoes and honey vinaigrette.

Brenda had the short rib, roasted carrots, pearl onions and buttered egg noodles. Madeline had the chicken, mushrooms, black and red wine sauce and Paul had the grilled rib eye with fries and a side of Brussels sprouts.

There was not a lot of talking during lunch. Every so often someone would throw out a random comment, which usually was about how outstanding the food was.

"Ginger, I can't believe you're passing on the great wine," Paul said. "It wasn't as great as the Caymus I had last night—that was the best wine I ever had—but this Syrah, Novy Family, it's good."

"My stomach still isn't right," she offered. "The doctor said I probably should lay off the wine for a few days."

"Damn, baby, that's too bad," he said. "We're in Napa, for Christ's sake."

"You haven't called me 'baby' in so long I can't remember," Ginger said.

"Well, it's a new me and we have a new marriage, as far as I'm concerned…baby."

"I read on Facebook on a post that said what your man should do," Ginger said. "I can't remember everything, but it said a few things like: 'A man should make a woman laugh and he should call his woman 'baby.' I do remember that."

The bill came and the women started digging in their purses for their wallets.

"Let me get this, baby," Paul said, smiling. "We're celebrating my freedom, our last full day in Napa and family love."

They agreed with Paul. But when Madeline and Brenda went to the bathroom, Ginger said to her husband: "You know, when I went to the ATM with your card to get some bail money, the balance said forty-something thousand dollars."

"What?" Paul said, trying to act surprised. "Is that all?"

"I'm serious," she said. "It was crazy."

"That's happened to me before," Paul said. "Not that much of a difference in the balance, but a few hundred dollars. I even tried to take out the money I knew wasn't really there. It didn't work."

"Same thing happened to me once," she said. "Anyway, you should check it when you get a chance."

"I will," Paul said. He felt he quickly needed to change the subject, so he said, "I'm kinda glad our moms are going to dinner. We can have one night out by ourselves at a nice restaurant. It will be nice."

Almost immediately they both thought the same thing: To share their big news over dinner instead of at the winery. It would be more private, more personal.

And then we can tell our parents the great news together, Ginger thought.

And then we can share the news with our parents together, Paul thought.

"I can't wait," Ginger said.

"Me, either," Paul said.

"When was the last time we looked forward to spending time together?" she asked.

"That's part of the proverbial marriage trap," Paul said. "You're married long enough, you start taking some things for granted. Some things, not people. It's not intentional. It just happens."

"Well, I don't want that to happen with us anymore," Ginger said. "I want something different."

"And that's what you will get because that's what I want, too, baby," Paul said. "I mean that."

Ginger smiled at him.

"Now let's go taste some wine," Paul said.

And so, they did. They cruised to Sterling Vineyard, where the line to get tickets for the tour was long. But Paul had paid for theirs online in advance, so he went to the Will Call window where their passes awaited them. He chose Sterling as one of their stops because of its reputation of having the best view in Napa Valley.

Problem was, getting to the top of the mountain required a two-minute ride in a small tram that swung back and forth in the wind. For someone who was afraid to fly, it was not comforting to step into that little carriage-like contraption suspended in the air by a cable.

It only sat four, so they went in as a group. Each of the three women paid Paul special attention. "It's going to be fine; it's a short ride up. Enjoy the view," Brenda said. "Right, Vino?"

Paul took a deep breath. He said, "I'm all right," but he didn't feel all right. He felt uneasy, like he was confined.

"Should we really be on this thing?" Madeline said. "I mean, there are a hundred wineries here. Why are we at the one that he has to go up in the air to get to it?"

"It was my choice, Miss Price," Paul said. "I'm OK. It'll be all right. It's not like we're flying."

"Look at that little boy," Brenda said, pointing to a kid around eight years old who was in the tram behind them. "Look at him. He's perfectly fine. So why aren't you?"

Mother knew best. She knew how competitive Paul was, so to be compared to a kid, well, that ate at his pride.

"Trust me, I am good," he said. "Let's go."

And up they went, ascending above the earth at a methodical pace. The view got more and more beautiful the higher they rose. "Oh, my, look at that," Madeline said, pointing down at the fountain that spouted out water into a pond.

"And look over there," Ginger said, pointing. The sun illuminated the full, green trees, the vineyard below and the prodigious mountains that virtually surrounded them. "Just beautiful."

Paul looked out briefly, but quickly turned back to the kid, who was posing for photos and having a good time.

"Where's the camera?" he asked. "Let's capture all this beauty."

And so, Ginger, who had the camera around her wrist, began firing away, documenting the beautiful nature all around them. Paul relaxed some and while he was not as carefree as everyone else, he did not have any overblown anxieties, either.

"That wasn't bad," he said as he stepped out of the tram. "But do we have to take it back down, too?"

He was joking, but figured he'd worry about that an hour or so later, when they would be ready to leave. It was on to the tasting.

Sterling Winery was ideal for the gorgeous, sixty-five degree, clear afternoon on the expansive deck that overlooked the valley. They made they way there after tasting three different wines that they all seemed to enjoy but were not particularly excited. The chardonnay poured on the deck, though, was light and fresh and went with the day's weather.

And although they were only tastings, the sum total of the wines provided a nice buzz—not that Madeline and Brenda didn't already have one since before lunch.

They walked back into the building to read some of the history of the winery and to get another look at the huge barrels where the wine was fermented.

Paul and Ginger stayed outside. They found a corner overlooking the valley and beautiful landscape, an image a painter would put on canvas. "Maybe we should take you back to the doctor. You love wine, and yet you're feeling so bad that you can't even taste some?" Paul said. "That's not a good thing, especially where we are. This is the purpose for coming here."

"I thought the purpose was for us to find our marriage, Paul," she said.

"That's the main reason we came here," Paul said. "But we could have gone anywhere to try to reconnect. We picked Napa because we love wine so much."

Ginger, with her right hand over her stomach, nodded her head. "Gin, what's wrong?" Paul asked.

She could not wait any longer. Holding it in another few hours would have been torture. She looked around at the wonderful setting and looked up at the man she loved—the man she crushed when he learned she had aborted his child. It was time to share her wonderful news.

"God is so good," she said, shaking her head. "God is so good."

Paul just looked at her, concerned. Confused.

"Honey," she said, "when I went to the doctor last night, he told me the news. I was in shock."

Paul was clueless. It was not registering for him. "What?"

"I'm pregnant."

It was as if Paul was frozen stiff by a genie. He didn't move. He stared at her, as if he was waiting for her to say something else. But she had said enough.

"What do you mean?" Paul asked.

"What do I mean? I'm pregnant," she said, smiling.

He looked down at her stomach. "But you said you had an abortion."

"Paul, that was four months ago," she said.

"You mean, you're pregnant *again*?" he asked, still not quite getting it.

Ginger smiled and nodded her head.

"Are you serious?"

"*Yes*, Paul."

"Oh, my God," he said as he hugged her. Then he pushed away from her. "Oh, I'm sorry. I don't want to hurt the baby."

"It's OK. It's not a baby yet," she said. "I'm in the first trimester."

"I can't believe this," he said. And then he did something Ginger had never seen: He cried.

"Baby, this is crazy…crazy in a good way," Paul said. "I can't believe it. I mean, I believe it, but…I guess I'm shocked. Oh, my God. God knew we wanted a baby. He knew we *needed* a baby."

Ginger started crying again, profusely.

"Through all this, you're carrying our baby. This is God's will. This is God's will."

They hugged and cried and would not let go of each other. In the distance, Madeline and Brenda, returning to the deck, could see them embracing.

"Oh, Lord, what's going on with them now?" Brenda said.

"Come on, let's go find out. But let me get another shot of this wine here before we do," Madeline said. "I might need more of a buzz."

"Yeah, good idea," Brenda said, and she had some chardonnay, too. Then they walked over to the elated couple.

"Hey, what's going on?" Madeline asked.

They separated and turned to their curious parents. Brenda saw the tears of her son and got nervous. "Paul," she said with anxiety in her voice.

"We have something to tell you," he said. He looked over at Ginger.

"You're going to be a grandmother again," she said. "I'm pregnant."

And all three of the ladies started screaming, drawing the attention of everyone on the massive deck.

"My wife is pregnant," Paul announced to the onlookers.

People clapped and came over and congratulated them. One couple stopped and told them: "You picked a good place to tell him this," the man said. "This is where I proposed to my wife—right over there, in that corner. That was twenty-nine years ago and a day a lot like today. Just a beautiful day."

"Beautiful because I said yes," his wife said. "It was overcast that day. It had rained."

"No, it hadn't," the man said. "It was sunny and seventy degrees."

"Listen, you were so happy that I said yes it seemed the sun came out," the wife said. "But it was a cloudy day. I remember it like it was yesterday."

"You can't even remember where we parked the car twenty minutes ago."

Paul and Ginger laughed at the hilarious, lovable couple.

"You all go ahead and enjoy your day. Congratulations," the man said. Then he turned to his wife. "Now see if you can remember to walk away when you should. Come on."

Everyone laughed as they left and playfully bickered as they did. Madeline, Ginger, Paul and Brenda found a table and sat down.

"How can this be?" Madeline asked.

"Paul and I already talked about it," Ginger said. "This is God's work."

"Amen," Brenda said. "That's what I was going to say. To get pregnant twice in the last whatever the time-frame is? This is a gift from the Man above."

Paul threw his head back so that he was looking skyward and closed his eyes. "Thank you, God," he said. "Thank you, God."

CHAPTER 20
GOOD NEWS,
AWKWARD NEWS

The rest of the Sterling Winery tasting was wonderful but overshadowed by the news that Ginger was pregnant. She had not seen Paul so buoyant since they brought home Helena eighteen years earlier.

"Look at him," Brenda said. "He's beaming."

"I know," Ginger said. "I was trying to wait until the right time to tell him."

Paul returned from a bathroom run. He had purchased them the Gold Experience, meaning they had a private tasting of three more Sterling wines: a 2008 Reserve Chardonnay; a 2010 Malvasia Blanca; and a 2011 Viognier. The staff wine steward serving them enjoyed their celebratory spirit so much that she also poured them a 2007 Sangiovese and a 2007 Reserve Cabernet Sauvignon.

Ginger had water.

"Baby, I am so sorry you cannot taste these wines," Paul said. "They are so good. Then again, I'm not sorry."

"Me, either," Ginger said. "I was telling your mom that I was waiting for the right moment to tell you. I was in shock myself for much of last night. I hardly slept. I almost told you in the room before we left. But we were talking about a romantic dinner and I thought that was the best time.

"But being out there in the sun, looking at all that God created, it felt like the right time and place."

"It was perfect," Paul said. "Perfect."

"We've got to tell Helena," Ginger said. "And we also have that other news to tell her. Thinking about that last night gave me a headache. What do you all think? How should we handle this? I don't want to burden Helena with the news that she was adopted and pile on that there's a new baby coming."

"Sometimes kids have problems with a new child because the focus won't be on them anymore," Madeline said.

"But Helena is eighteen; she should be beyond that stage," Brenda said.

"She should be but she's been spoiled all her life and gotten all the attention," Madeline said. "When she comes home next year for a visit from college, will she be OK with seeing everyone give so much attention to the baby?"

"Well, she's gonna have to be OK with it. And she will be," Paul said. "When a new kid comes the older kid has to adjust. That's how it is. We have to make sure Helena doesn't feel left out. Plus, she's so sweet. She'll be a great big sister."

"But I'm worried about the dynamic of her learning she's adopted and learning about a new baby coming all at the same time," Ginger said. "Should we tell her both things now? Should we wait on telling her about the adoption?"

"You've got to tell her everything," Madeline said. "Now. That's my opinion. She's a good young lady, mature. She'll handle it all. It might be a lot in the beginning, but she won't go off in hiding or anything. She's pretty expressive."

"Ginger, I get your concern," Paul said. "She learns that we are not her birth parents in one breath and then learns that we have a baby on the way in the next breath. Does she feel like she means less to us because of the baby?"

"She knows how much she means to you both," Brenda said. "I do. I was against telling her at all that she was adopted. But I have changed on that. She deserves to know. But the reason I changed is because I thought about the person Helena is. She's a great kid. She calls me every week—from college. And I am sure she calls you, too, Madeline. What teenager calls her grandparents consistently while they are away in college?

"So I'm sure she's calling you both all the time. My point is, family is important to her. You all mean the world to her. She's going to be strong about it. She's not going to feel you all will love her any less."

The discussion went back and forth for several minutes, all the way in the tram down the mountain to the car. It was so involved that Paul didn't even bother to be bothered with his fear of heights and enclosed places. He simply rode with it.

They headed back to the hotel feeling great physically from the wine and great mentally from the news. But they could not come to a consensus on Helena. "So, if we tell her both at the same time, which do we tell her first?" Paul asked.

The car fell silent. "Well, if we tell her the baby is coming first," Ginger said, "she'll be happy. She'll be excited. Maybe with that joy in her she will not be so impacted by learning she's adopted."

"See," Madeline said, "I think differently. If you tell her the hard news first—that she's adopted—then telling her the good news lifts her spirits. It's like, 'What do you want to hear first? The good news or the bad news?' Most people say, 'Gimme the bad news first, so the good news can make them feel better.'"

"Not necessarily," Brenda said. "I would want the good news first so it could cushion the bad news. And then there's the chance that she could receive the adoption news so strongly that it cancels out the good news."

"It has to be in how we position it," Paul said. "We can't position it as bad news or as something that's so disconcerting. We have to present it to her as news that she's old enough and mature enough to accept. We should say we probably waited too long to share this with her—put the burden on us, where it should be. Tell her that we will find her parents for her and take her to visit her parents if she'd like.

"I have a friend who learned she was adopted when she was twenty. She learned it because her natural parents' family found her. She wasn't upset with her parents; she knew they loved her and that they were trying to protect her; that they were not trying to deny the child anything, despite how it looked. I will tell her that story."

"And you also tell her that you and her mother and her grandparents love her more than life itself, which is true," Brenda said. "And tell her that her little brother or sister will need her to help raise him, to teach him, to guide him, to set the example for him. Give her some responsibility in her sibling's life."

"Yes," Ginger said. "You're both right. We have to let her know that she's even more important to us now. Let her know we want her to be a strong influence on the baby's life, which we really do."

"That's true," Paul said. "I kinda hope it's a boy because I don't think I can take another girl having me wrapped around her finger. I need a boy to wrap his mom around his finger."

"Oh, I cannot wait," Brenda said. "We haven't had a baby to play with in eighteen years. That's too long. I have missed being a grandmother to a little one, watching her grow up, learning to walk and talk and get into things."

"Yeah, that Helena was a mess," Madeline recalled. "She'd come to my house and right away run to her grandpa. She loved her granddaddy. I never saw him so proud as when she sat on his lap and would fall asleep there."

"I thought about that, too, Mother, last night," Ginger said. "I wish Daddy would be here to see the new baby. He'd be so happy."

Her voice trailed off and she got a little teary-eyed. Much of the focus after her father's death was on her mother and how she would handle losing her mate of more than forty years. But even as he was dealing with his loss of job around that same time, Paul monitored his wife. She was a daddy's girl who took his death hard.

Most people did not see her pain. Paul pulled her through, although she would never get past not having her daddy.

"Losing your father probably has something to do with why you're so emotional about this, Gin," Paul said.

She nodded her head. "I still miss my daddy," she said. "There's no other way to put it. The pain I feel won't go away. I can put it off from time-to-time. But it's there. And that's what kind of scares me about this thing with Helena: What if she feels she's losing you, losing us?"

"We have to make her understand she'll never lose us," Paul said. "I believe she already knows that, but we'll make sure she does."

They arrived at the hotel after stopping at a grocery store and picking up some sparkling cider. They wanted to toast with Ginger.

Paul stopped at the hotel restaurant and picked up four champagne glasses. In their parents' room, he made a toast.

"To my wife, who I love so much; to our unborn child, who we will love with all of our hearts; to Helena, our daughter and granddaughter that I could not love anymore than we do; and to God, thank you for blessing us with this incredible gift of growing our family."

They tapped glasses and drank up.

"I cannot wait to see you with your little baby bump in a few months," Madeline said.

"I'm gonna keep it sexy," Ginger said. "I refuse to be some oversized human blimp in frumpy clothes with swollen feet, sliding across the room."

"Yes, we can't have that," Paul said.

"Look who's talking now," Brenda said. "He's gotten himself together and lost a bunch of weight and now he can talk?"

"That's right," he said. "I earned it."

"Well, I can tell you right now that I'm breastfeeding— they say you lose weight quicker that way," Ginger said.

"How do you know this?" Madeline asked.

"I got some information from the hospital last night, some pamphlets," she said. "I couldn't sleep. Between thinking about Paul in jail and Helena and being pregnant, it was too much for me to sleep. So…"

"I would have done the same thing," Madeline said. "I'm so happy you are pregnant. Isn't it something to realize you have life growing in your stomach? How big of a miracle is that?"

"That's why I keep touching it. There's nothing to feel

yet," Ginger said, "but it's in there growing, little by little. An embryo, to a fetus to a baby to a real live person. It's amazing."

"It is amazing, but we're going to have to set up very regular doctor appointments," Paul said. "You're not a spring chicken anymore—although you still look young; don't look at me like that. I don't want anything to go wrong."

"He's thinking about this man he was in jail with last night," Ginger said.

"Hold on—that sounds too casual, like I'm always in jail or something," Paul said, laughing.

"Never know," Brenda said. "This could be the start of some-thing."

"Not here," Paul said.

"Anyway, before the pregnant woman was so rudely interrupted, I was going to say that we have to be positive. Nothing negative; not even thoughts. I'm going to eat right, drink right, rest, exercise, take vitamins. These nine months are going to be the most disciplined of my life. And it's going to be easy. As much as I love wine, I didn't look at you all drink it and feel like I had any urge for it. I am so into this."

"That's the right attitude," Brenda said.

They chatted for another ten minutes or so, but never came to an agreement on how to share the important news with Helena.

"We don't have to figure it out today," Paul said.

"Agreed—until *he* is born," Paul cracked.

Ginger participated in the little game, but she did not care if it was a boy or a girl. If anything, she leaned toward a boy because she had the experience of raising a girl—and she knew Paul was serious about wanting a boy.

They debated the issue from the room to the lobby, where they were to ask their parents of their preference. But then they got to the lobby, Madeline and Brenda were not there. Ginger went to check the bathroom and they were not there. Before they could call the room, Paul's cell phone rang. It was his mother.

"Paul, we're in a taxi," she said. "Mitch and Madeline got things mixed up. He thought we were meeting there. She thought he was coming to pick us up. The restaurant does not seat unless all parties are present—and we couldn't move the reservation back. So we jumped in a taxi so you and Ginger can go on with your night."

"Ma, we could have taken you to the restaurant," Paul said. "Which one is it? Maybe we can meet you there for drinks after dinner."

"OK, good. It's called Tra Vigne," Brenda said.

"That's close to where we're going. We passed it twice today," Paul said. "OK, keep your phone on. I will call you after our meal. Or you call me before you all leave the place."

Tra Vigne was an Italian restaurant just beyond a railroad track, with vines covering the building and a green and white awning. It looked like something carved out of Italy.

Mitch and Lionel waited at the bar for Madeline and Brenda, who were looking elegant and younger than their sixty-plus years. Both wore dresses and heels, but not too high. "You'll never catch me falling on my butt," Brenda said.

Mitch, tall and distinguished with gray hair and a mustache, noticed Madeline immediately, and he and Lionel met them at the reception area. He and Madeline hugged while Lionel—who was not as tall as Mitch but was handsome with a wide, engaging smile—introduced himself to Brenda.

Madeline and Lionel and Brenda and Mitch exchanged hand-shakes and pleasantries and they were escorted to their table. The restaurant was alive and noisy, full of people. It was an ideal setting for a double/blind date: nice, but not overly romantic.

Mitch said, "To eat good food is to be close to God. It's an Italian saying. And I agree with that. Eating is one of my true pleasures."

"Mine, too, Madeline said. "This place is supposed to have good food."

Madeline sat at the square table to Mitch's left, with Brenda next to her and across from Mitch and Lionel to Brenda's left. Madeline and Brenda strategized on this arrangement. They wanted it so that if Mitch desired to engage in private conversation with Madeline, he would be able to do so without talking across the table. And the same with Lionel, who was an interesting man.

He spent the latter part of his life running a foundation for underprivileged boys, after retiring from the military. He played the saxophone. He seemed genuine. And he had an edge about him.

"Our foundation was legit; I can see how you're looking at me," Lionel said. "You're thinking about that Jerry Sandusky fool from Penn State who molested all those boys. Don't get any ideas."

The ladies laughed.

The evening flowed nicely. The food was delicious and hearty. The wine was nice and flowed like water. The conversations ranged from raising kids to travel to the Presidential election to the awkwardness of blind dates.

"Funny, but I never felt uncomfortable tonight," Lionel said. "This has been great. My man Mitch took care of me, introduced me to a couple of nice women."

Something in those words forced Brenda to focus more on Mitch. She found herself looking across the able at him, as if drawn to him. She could not understand it— until then. She was not just looking at him anymore; she was staring.

Her heartbeat increased and she excused herself to go to the bathroom. "Want me to go with you?" Madeline asked.

Brenda sipped some water. "No, it's fine. I'll be right back," she said.

She collected herself and made it to the restroom. She was glad it was empty. She looked at herself in the mirror.

She was shocked. But she was sure: Madeline's friend, Mitch, was the young love of her life, Mitchell English.

Brenda had not seen him in more than forty years. When last she did, he walked away with tears in his eyes after she refused to marry him. She was pregnant by her eventual husband, James, but he still wanted her to be his wife.

Now there he was, sitting across the table from her. How could it be? How small is the world? More importantly, what would she do? Should she tell Madeline first? Should she pull Mitchell to the side? Should she do it at the table? And did he realize who she was?

The more she thought about it, the more she realized that every time she looked at him, he was looking at her. He did know, she thought. *At the very least he was studying me, trying to figure out how I'd look more than forty years later,* she thought.

Brenda did not know what to do, how to handle it, but she washed her hands, took a deep breath and went back to the table. Both of the men stood up to greet her. Lionel held her chair for her.

"Gentlemen," Brenda said. "Thought they went out with bell bottoms. Thank you."

She got settled in her seat and refused to look up at Mitch. She immediately started talking about a bad blind date experience.

"My friend, Celeste, set me up with this man about three months ago," Brenda began. "And, look at me, I'm five-foot-five. This man she introduced me to was the same height as me. Now, I don't have anything against short men. Just keep them away from me."

Everyone laughed. She glanced at Mitchell and her heart fluttered. That smile was the one that owned her heart when she was twenty. She knew for sure then. And she was panicked.

She also knew then that he knew because he stared at her as if he was sending a message.

"Mitchell," she said to him. Just hearing her say his name made him sit up in his seat.

"Mitch," Madeline corrected Brenda. "Not Mitchell."

"Actually," he said, "Mitchell is my given name. Only a few people in the world still call me that."

He stared at Brenda as he spoke. "But most people call me 'Mitch,'" he added. Then he said, "You were going to ask me a question."

"I was," Brenda said. "I was going to ask how did you pick Lionel to bring with you for me to meet?"

"Good question," Madeline said.

Mitchell smiled and looked away. Then he said, "From the way Madeline described you, I figured you deserved to meet a man who is a good man, committed, smart... someone you'd be comfortable with. Did I do you justice?"

Brenda glanced at Lionel and looked back at Mitchell. "Let me put it to you this way: I am really glad I am sitting here right now," she said.

Everyone smiled as Brenda reached for her wine. Then

she remembered that Madeline called Mitchell from Brenda's phone because Madeline's battery was weak. She had his cell number and thought of texting him to meet her near the bathrooms. Her mind was consumed with how to broach the subject and how to get a few minutes alone with him.

She did her best to learn more about him while not seeming as if she was prying.

"So how is it that two fine men like you are single?" Brenda asked, while grinning with Madeline.

"Yes, I'd like to know the same thing," Madeline said.

"Unfortunately," Lionel said, "I am a widower. My wife passed a few years ago now. Kidney failure... And I have not found that one woman since. Didn't even know how to begin to start my life again, really. So..."

"Sorry to hear that, Lionel," Madeline said. "I can relate to losing a spouse. My husband died about a year ago, suddenly."

"I understand what you're going through," Lionel said. "Be patient. Somehow, you'll find your way."

"And you, Mitchell?" Brenda asked. She was not in a mood to hear Madeline's story.

"Well, I have been divorced for a while now," he answered. "I think there could be just one person really meant for you. And she was not it."

She knew Mitchell was speaking to her in code. She was so excited and amazed and scared that she did not know what to do.

"Lionel, so where did you meet Mitchell?" she asked.

"We actually met in the Army many years ago in North Carolina and stayed in touch. Then we ran into each other years later in Korea. I'm from out here, Oakland. Always felt I'd come back this way when I retired. So I have been back on the West Coast for a long time now. When he told me he was moving to San Diego, it was great because we could get together regularly."

"And you and Madeline met in Atlanta, right, Mitchell?" Brenda asked.

"We did," Mitch said. "I was visiting a few months ago."

"That's it?" Madeline asked. "There's more to it than that. Lionel gave a better answer about meeting you than you gave about meeting me."

She smiled as she said it, but Madeline was a little perturbed by his answer. "Oh, I wasn't trying to bore folks with the details," he said. "I was just getting to the point."

"Why would anyone be bored by how we met?" Madeline asked.

"Excuse me; wrong use of words," he said. "Brenda, I was visiting your fair city to play golf before the weather broke and visiting with my sister, who I hadn't seen in a long time. She and Madeline here happen to go to the same church. And at the end of service we were introduced by a friend of my sister's and have been sort of pals since then."

"Now that story was sounding good until the 'pals' part," Madeline said.

"Everything is a process," he said. "Gotta be pals to get anywhere else."

"Pals sounds a little too buddy-buddy for me," Madeline said.

"It's really just semantics," Mitchell said. "I came all the way up here from San Diego and then drove ninety minutes because I wanted to see you. And I'm glad I did."

He looked at Brenda as he said that last sentence. And she knew he was trying to say to her that Madeline meant nothing to him. But to draw his attention back to her, Madeline leaned into Mitchell's ear and whispered into it. It was if she sensed his interest in Brenda or Brenda's in him—or just felt that she was not getting enough attention.

The last thing Brenda wanted to do was upset Madeline. They had spent the better part of three days together and had overcome some hang-ups in order to, for the first time, feel like friends, like family. Their kids were elated about it, and so she did not want to upset that which was just built.

At the same time, she had told the group on Thanksgiving that she remained in love or "the idea of love" with Mitchell after more than four decades. Now, miraculously, he was sitting across from her. How could she simply let him drive off, even if she did have his phone number? She was headed back across country the next evening.

Then a small miracle happened: Lionel excused himself

to take a call from his son and Madeline spilled a little Shiraz on her dress and excused herself to tend to it. This happened at the same time.

Brenda took a deep breath as Madeline rose from the table. Mitch helped her out of her chair and he did not sit back down. Rather, he stood across from Brenda, staring down on her. So, she rose from her chair, all the while looking into his eyes, the same eyes that were so hurt many years before.

He moved Madeline's chair out of the way and approached Brenda, who was defenseless. Mitchell delicately placed his hands on her shoulders.

"Brenda," he said.

"Mitchell," she said. "I can't believe this. It's really you."

He shook his head. "This is amazing," he said. "I have thought about you so often over all these years."

"I have never stopped thinking about you," Brenda said. "I even got on my daughter's Facebook page and put your name in there to see if I could find you."

"That's funny," Mitchell said. "I remember the last time I saw you."

"I remember it, too," Brenda said. "I remember it well."

"You look fantastic," Mitchell said, smiling. "When I saw you, I felt something. Just through seeing you, I felt something."

"You felt familiar to me," Brenda explained. "And then suddenly, I knew it. And my heart started beating so fast."

They stood there for a few seconds, looking into each

other's eyes just as Lionel was returning from his phone call and as Madeline emerged from the bathroom. They stopped side-by-side in their tracks, stunned by what they witnessed.

"How could this happen?" Mitchell said.

"I don't know," Brenda said. "I guess it was meant to happen. What else could it be? I mean—"

Mitchell leaned in and kissed her in midsentence. She kissed him back and Lionel and Madeline looked at each other. "What is going on?" she asked.

"Hell if I know," Lionel said. "But let's go find out."

He let her pass and they headed to the table, where Brenda and Mitchell stood in loving embrace.

"Ahem," Madeline said as she returned. "Y'all been busy since we left."

"Oh, please, sit down," Brenda said. "You won't believe this."

"I already don't believe it," Madeline said.

Everyone got seated and Brenda said, "Madeline, do you remember on Thanksgiving I told you about the love of my life when I was twenty?"

"No way," Madeline said.

"Yes, it's him, Mitchell," Brenda said. "I'm so shocked I don't know what to think."

"Wait. The man you said went off to the Army when you were a kid? This is the guy?" Madeline said.

"You told her about me?" Mitchell asked.

"Just a few days ago I told her about you and about us," Brenda said.

"Wow," Lionel said. "So, I guess it's safe to say this is the woman you spoke of on our drive up here."

"Huh?" Brenda said. "What did he say?"

"He said his heart has only been broken once in his life—about forty years ago," Lionel recalled. "Said he never told anyone that he was practically in tears over this woman. Turns out *you're* the woman."

"I feel like I'm dreaming," Brenda said.

"Me, too," Madeline said with sarcasm. Then she gathered herself. She stood up and hugged Brenda. "I'm so happy for you. This is incredible, really. Of all the people in the world…Anyway, Lionel, would you like to join me at the bar for a drink?"

"I'd love to," he said, leaving the table to Brenda and Mitchell.

CHAPTER 21
JACKPOT

Ginger and Paul arrived at French Blue and were floating. The realization that they would have a child set in with each passing minute, and it injected their lives with a joy they simply had not had since Helena was declared theirs.

The restaurant was located on quaint Main Street, across from a chic boutique hotel, lined with specialty shops and restaurants. There was a coolness in the night air, a freshness, which was perfect for the occasion.

A white brick, lit fireplace greeted them outside the entrance of the destination, where people sat outside in light jackets and sweaters enjoying the climate. Inside was open and airy, with beautiful light hues and sparkling lighting. The huge windows stretched the entire width of the front of the place, and fresh flowers and tasteful art adorned the walls.

There was a wonderful vibe to the dining room, a wonderful smell. It felt like a celebration.

They were seated at a table near the front windows. Paul insisted Ginger take the seat with her back to the window so she could take in the entire restaurant.

This type of thoughtfulness had abandoned Paul many years before, and it had become so routine that Ginger forgot how special it felt to be treated like a priority. She could not pass on the opportunity to let him know that.

"It's very nice to be treated like you love me," she said.

"I do love you and I'm sorry it took all that we have gone through to get back to showing you that I do," Paul said. "But now that I'm here, I'm here for good."

"I believe you. I do," she said. "But we're going to have a baby pretty soon and definitely be wrapped up in her. I don't mean to spoil this great feeling we have, but we've got to figure out the financial part of this. A kid, as much as you love him, is costly."

Paul smiled. "What are you smiling about?" Ginger said.

"You're extra pretty when you're pregnant," he said.

Ginger smiled, but she was not thrown off course. "This is serious, Paul," she said. "We've got to get on a budget. You know how much stuff we have to get? Clothes, crib, bassinet, stroller—"

"Wait," he said, "I thought that's what the baby shower was for."

"I see you're in a silly mood so we can talk about it another time," Ginger said. "But keep in mind I have to get maternity clothes, too, as I get bigger and bigger."

"Hold that thought," Paul said as he addressed the server.

He ordered a glass of sparkling water for Ginger and

a glass of champagne for himself. They perused the menu; everything read divinely, as menus do when you are especially hungry.

"I'm thinking fish," Ginger said.

"Good; fish has the Omega3s that everyone is saying we need in our diets now," Paul said.

"Yes, but not all fish, though," Ginger added. "It's wild salmon, tuna, trout, sardines and maybe one other that have the most benefits… And I see trout on the menu. That's what I'm having."

"I am so hungry," Paul said. "I'm going to start with a salad, the Living Butter Lettuce with rosemary-butter-milk dressing and candied pecans. Then I want the Head-On Wild Gulf Shrimp with harissa butter, roasted garlic and something called levain. And for my entrée I'm going to have the Fisherman's Stew with sea scallops, red snapper, squid, tomato-fennel broth and pine nuts. And whatever they have for dessert."

"You act like you're the one pregnant," Ginger said.

"I *am* pregnant," he said. "I might not be carrying the baby, but I am so connected to you and this pregnancy."

Ginger smiled. She could not believe how her life had evolved in a matter of months. The same person who was distant and docile and eventually asked for a divorce was now caring and thoughtful and doing a nice job toward rebuilding their marriage.

She turned away to retrieve hand sanitizer from her purse and when she turned back toward Paul, there was a small jewelry box in front of her. Paul's sleight-of-hand was impressive; Ginger did not see him move at all.

"What's this?" Ginger asked.

"Looks like a box to me," Paul answered.

The surprise on her face was priceless as she slowly opened the small box, revealing a stunning diamond in platinum setting.

"Paul…"

"I hope you like it," he said.

"It's beautiful," she said. "But why? And how—"

Paul cut her off. "Why? Because I love you and because you're here with me, still here with me after all of my craziness," he said. "You deserve nice things and so much more."

"All I really want is for us to have a great family; that's it," she said.

"Well, let's do that," he said. "But there's one thing I have to tell you."

Ginger's face went from joyous to concerned. She did not want to hear anything that would take away from their jovial spirit. And she told him so.

"Maybe I should hear this at another time," she said. "We're in such a good place right now. Let's let it last a little longer."

Paul smiled. "You sure?" he said. "I can wait. But I think it's time you know this."

His smile helped Ginger; he wouldn't smile if it were bad news. *He got a job*, she thought. She wanted to say it, but didn't want to take away from his moment.

"Okay, go ahead," she said.

"Now, don't be mad I didn't tell you this before now," he started.

"See, you're making me nervous," she said.

"Don't be," Paul said. "All this time and I never really thought about how I would tell you this."

"Just say it," Ginger blurted out.

"We're rich," Paul said.

She was stumped. "What?"

"Baby, two months ago, I hit the lottery—eight million dollars!"

He pulled out and handed to her a copy of the check and a bank statement with their names on it that had two million dollars deposited in it and another that had another two-million plus in it.

"I...I... I'm...I'm....Ginger could not get out a sentence.

Paul sat back in his chair with his arms folded, smiling.

"Paul, what is this?" she finally said.

"Breathe," he told her. "Take it easy. I hit the lottery, baby. I couldn't believe it. I read those numbers over and over again at least ten times. I literally pinched myself to make sure I wasn't dreaming. It was real. Gin, it was a little more than four million after taxes. Pinch yourself so you know you're not dreaming."

Ginger closed her eyes for a few seconds, and then tears seeped from them and down the sides of her face. And then she let out a scream.

"Oh, my God," she said.

The people in the restaurant thought Paul had proposed to her because they saw the ring on the table. Those in adjacent tables clapped.

"Baby, can you believe this?" he said.

Ginger did not answer. She held her hand over her mouth. Paul went around the table and hugged her. "Our life is set up to be anything we want it to be now, Gin," he said. "Anything."

She still did not say a word. He helped her wipe away tears before going back to his seat.

"This is so crazy," Ginger finally said. "Paul…"

"I know," he interjected. "I still can't believe it."

"I can't believe you didn't tell me," Ginger said. "How could you not tell me? Why didn't you tell me?"

Paul's salad came before he could answer. "Congratulations," the server said. They said in unison: "Thank you."

He reached across the table for Ginger's hands and he blessed the food. "Dear Lord, we thank You for this food we are about to receive for the nourishment of our bodies. And we thank You for the amazing blessing You have delivered to us. Only You could be this gracious. Thank You, God. Amen."

Paul grabbed a small plate and shared his salad with Ginger. He bit into his third piece of bread with rosemary butter, which was so delicious that he asked the server if they sold the butter.

"Baby, I didn't tell you at first because I wasn't sure you still loved me," he said.

"What?"

"When I won, we were in hell. I was in hell," he explained. "I had said I wanted a divorce. I didn't mean it but I said it because you deserved better than what I was at that time. That's what I thought then in the state of mind I was in. So now here comes this miracle and it's like, 'I have a chance to fix all this.' But I needed to know that you would come back to me because of me and not because of money."

He braced himself for Ginger to snap. He knew it was insulting to her to think she would be motivated by money in a matter of the heart. And subconsciously it is a reason he did not tell her sooner. He was afraid of what she might think of him. But the longer he waited, the deeper his fear became.

"So, you think I'm a gold digger?" she asked calmly. She took a sip of the sparkling water. "You think I would stay with you because of money? That's what you think of me."

"What I thought was I love you and I want you to love me," Paul answered. "That's it. I didn't want any outside influences playing a role. So, I said, 'Let's go on a trip and see if we can find the magic.' But I knew we would because I was a different person from the last eleven months. I was out of my funk and, even though we had fallen into a rut, at the core of everything was that we had a true love for each other—and for family."

"Still, you put me through a test," Ginger said. She wasn't mad; almost nothing could make her mad at that point. There was too much to be joyous about in her life.

"I don't think it was the right thing to do, looking back on it," Paul said. "So I'm sorry. But for a man, it's important to know that his woman loves him for who he is, not money. I needed to know that for my psyche."

"The fact that I even agreed to go should have told you where my heart was," she said.

"That's true," Paul responded. "And the fact that I bought that ring should tell you what I believed would happen."

They smiled at each other.

"Don't be mad, Gin. Please," Paul said. "We have too much to be thankful for, too much to look forward to. Plus, being mad ain't good for the baby."

Ginger smiled a big smile then, just as the food arrived. Her grilled rainbow trout with Yukon golds, bacon, Gravenstein apples and grain mustard was delicious. And Paul devoured his seafood stew.

She let go of her concern and wanted to scream again, but suppressed it. "What are we going to do with all this money?" she asked.

"Save it, a lot of it, for Helena and our new baby," he said. "Donate some of it. Get a reputable financial adviser. Don't you think?"

"No doubt about it," Ginger said. "There are so many people we can help—women who have been in abusive relationships, cancer research, homeless shelters, foster kids, disadvantaged youths. I am so glad you said that.

"See, this is the Paul I fell in love with. You could have answered that question by saying what you were going to buy for yourself and where we would travel and so on. But your first thoughts were to provide for our children and to help other people. Those are the qualities I fell in love with a long time ago."

"Thank you, Ginger," he said. "And you're the same way, which makes us a good match. I can look back on it now and be honest: A man tying his success or who he is to a job is too much. I put my whole stock in a job, in what I did for work. I'm not saying it's not important. I know it is. But to lose my job—and lose it the unjust way I did—messed me up. And it almost messed up my life.

"Big Al was helping me come around, telling me to 'man up' and do what I needed to be a good husband. Crazy as he can be, he knew how much you meant to me."

"Wait until you tell him you won the lottery; he's going to go off," Ginger said.

"Well, actually, he already knows," Paul revealed.

"What? You told Al, but you didn't tell me?" Ginger said, disgusted.

"I wasn't trying to stay married to Big Al," he said. "And I had to tell *somebody*. My head would have exploded if I hadn't."

"You didn't tell your mother? Does she know, Paul?" Ginger asked.

"No. But I did tell my father," he said.

Ginger shook her head. "So we have a *third* important thing to tell Helena," she said.

"Yes," Paul said. "Maybe we should tell her about the money first. That'll keep her little butt under control."

They laughed. The more they ate, the farther away they got from Paul not telling Ginger about the money. They were a couple in love, pulled together by love, not money.

CHAPTER 21
NEW FRIENDS, OLD FRIENDS

Paul called his mom after their meal to see where they were. He still wanted to meet Mitchell and Lionel—and he wanted to tell her about the lottery.

She answered on the first ring. "What are y'all doing?" she said into the phone. "OK. We're here."

"That was my son, Paul," she said to Mitchell. "He and his wife will be here in about ten, fifteen minutes."

Brenda and Mitchell caught up on each other's lives and essentially fell in love all over again.

When Madeline and Lionel left them alone at the table, they reverted to their youth almost instantly.

"You broke my heart," Mitchell said. "I'm not ashamed to say it."

"It's a little late, but please let me fix it," Brenda said. "I can honestly say that I never forgot you. I never forgot how I felt about you. I never forgot how you felt about me, offering to marry me although I was carrying another man's child."

"I look back on that time of my life as something that was special, but it also scarred me," Mitchell said. "It scarred me in the sense that I spent the rest of my relationship life trying to feel like I did with you, about you, and I couldn't. I actually had two marriages. I hardly even count the first one because it was less than a year after I last saw you. Classic rebound. And it only lasted fourteen months."

"I married Paul's father when he was two, almost three, and stayed married to him until about a year ago," Ginger said. "Nice man... But he wasn't...you."

They were working on their second bottle of Pinot Noir.

"What are we going to do, Mitchell?" Brenda asked. "You live in California. I live in Atlanta. But I really don't want to let you walk away from me again. This wine has made me super aggressive, but it's the truth."

"And the truth is, I don't want to walk away from you,' Mitchell said. "Twice in one lifetime? No. That can't happen. I'm not such a spiritual person, but I believe this was fate. It *had* to be."

"It *had* to be," Brenda agreed. "When we met at the front, I said to myself that you looked familiar. But it was more than that. I felt something...I never envisioned you at sixty-three years old. But then, I never envisioned seeing you ever again, either."

"I will come to Atlanta as often as I can and I would love for you to come to San Diego," Mitchell said. "It's beautiful. Laid-back. The perfect weather."

"Can't wait to experience it," she said.

"So, what do we do about Madeline and Lionel?" Mitchell said.

"Forty-something years ago, I was concerned about other people's feelings and thoughts about me," Brenda said. "I'm too old and too smart to worry about them now. I don't mean to sound cold, but it's the truth."

"I don't think they are that concerned," Mitchell said. "I met with Madeline two times. Nothing was happening there. She's a nice woman. But you…I have held you in my heart all my life."

Brenda looked up and Paul and Ginger were approaching. "Oh, here's Paul, my son. They got here fast."

Paul hugged his mom and turned to Mitchell. "So, you must be Lionel. Nice to meet you," he said, extending his hand.

"Actually, I'm Mitch," he said. "Nice to meet you. Lionel is over there at the bar with Madeline."

"Huh?" Ginger said, puzzled. "Madeline is my mother."

"Nice to meet you," Mitch said.

"Nice to meet you, too. But I thought my mom met you at church in Atlanta."

"She did," he said. "It's a long story."

"Actually, it's a short story," Brenda said. "Remember when I told you about the love of my life when I was twenty years old? The man I really wanted to be with but I was pregnant by your father?"

"Yeah," Paul and Ginger said.

"Well, incredibly, this is the man. Madeline met

Mitchell in Atlanta," she said. "And when we saw each other, it all came together."

"*What?*" Paul said.

"How's my mom?" Ginger asked.

"I need a glass of wine," Paul said. "What's this? Pinot?"

"How could you tell that by looking at it?" Mitchell asked.

"I just know," Paul said. "The color. The density. But wait. Ma."

"I know, Paul, it's crazy," Brenda said. "It's a miracle."

Ginger bolted over to her mother and Lionel. "I guess you heard?" Madeline said. "Small world. God is working on this family.

"This is my daughter, Ginger. This is Lionel."

"How did this happen?" Ginger asked. "I want to know all the details because this is something else."

Madeline and Lionel shared the details as they saw it.

"Looking back, I did notice that they were making a lot of eye contact," Madeline said. "But I didn't think anything of it. I thought they were just being good communicators, looking those in the eye you're speaking to."

"I noticed that, but I also noticed that Mitch was a little more quiet than normal. Somewhere at the table he figured it out and when he did, his mind was churning on how to say something instead of talking to us," Lionel said.

"But guess what, honey?" Madeline said. "It has worked out great. Lionel and I have a lot in common. And we're going to keep in touch."

"That's nice," Ginger said.

It was so surprising that Paul and Ginger forgot to share the news of the lottery money—until Paul told Brenda at the table. She had told Paul that she would have to save money to travel back and forth to California to see Mitchell. That's when it registered to Paul that he had not shared the news.

When he did, she screamed. That's how Ginger, standing at the bar, knew Paul had told her.

"Wow," Madeline said. "Did you hear that scream? What was that about?"

"Well, mother, it was probably because Paul told her that he hit the lottery for eight million dollars," Ginger said.

And then Madeline screamed—and Paul knew his wife had told her mother.

The three of them left the bar and went over to the table. Hugs were shared. Lionel said to Paul: "I guess I'm meeting you at the right time," and they laughed.

Paul called over the server and they ordered another bottle of Pinot—and a glass of sparkling apple cider.

Lionel pulled up two more chairs and the six of them talked and laughed and marveled at the stunning developments until long after the last diner left.

When the bill came, Paul picked it up.

"This one is on me," he said.

No one argued with him.

CHAPTER 23

MUDDY WATERS

They had an evening flight back to Atlanta the next day, and Paul had one more surprise for Ginger.

"A mud bath?" she asked.

"Yes. We cannot come all the way out here and not experience a mud bath. Calistoga is the mud bath capital," he explained. "We have a noon appointment. It's like a spa treatment. But there are these crazy minerals in the water and the mud that reinvigorates your body. And my back hasn't been right since that long flight.

"And you said you feel a little achy, too, right?"

"I do, but you sure about this?" she said.

"I already told our moms what we were doing. They're having lunch with Lionel and Mitchell," he said. "When we get back, we can head straight to the airport."

And so they took the drive to Golden Haven Hot Springs spa in Calistoga. Along the way, Paul talked to Big Al and Ginger called Serena, who were ecstatic about all the developments.

Paul called Helena right before they got to the destination. "Been an amazing trip, honey," he said.

"So you and mom are doing better?" Helena asked.

"Better?" Paul said. "Who said we weren't doing well?"

"Daddy, I'm not a kid," she said. "I lived in the house with you. You hardly talked to each other."

He was surprised. He thought she was so caught up in her own life that she did not notice theirs.

Paul repeated what Helena said so Ginger could hear it. "You noticed we weren't talking to each other?"

Ginger told her girlfriend, "I'll call you back."

Paul then put Helena on the speakerphone. "Honey, Mom can hear you. I have you on speaker."

"Hi, Mom. Dad still thinks I'm a kid. He didn't know I knew you and he were having issues."

"Well, to be truthful, I didn't know you knew, either."

"You don't remember what I said to you right before you left me in my room at college? I said, 'Mommy, take care of Daddy. He loves you.' That was my way of saying I understood what was going on. You didn't get it?"

"I didn't but you're even smarter than we thought," Ginger said.

They pulled up to the spa, which looked like a motel. "Helena, we're about to take a mud bath before we head back to Atlanta. But we're going to call you later. There's a lot we have to talk about."

"A mud bath?" she said. "You old people... Anyway, okay. Call me. Have fun. Love you!"

They checked in at the desk and were taken to the room for their couples' mud bath. Immediately, the smell of the mud was jarring. "Stinks in here," Ginger said under her breath.

The young man gave them instructions on how to enter the tub that was virtually spilling over in hot mud. There was a hot tub to the right that did not look inviting. And there were showers to the left.

"OK, enjoy," the man said. "I will check on you later."

Paul and Ginger got undressed and approached their side-by-side tubs of mud. Paul was eager to get in. His back bothered him and his neck was a little stiff, too, from sleeping awkwardly and lying on that thin jail mattress. He went in butt-first, as instructed, and was almost immediately soothed by the mud and the heat.

"Oh, baby, it feels weird the more you submerge yourself, but it's hot and it's like you're floating," he said.

Ginger took her time but finally eased her way into the tub. Her facial expression didn't convey that she was happy. But as she got more comfortable, she relaxed.

"It's hot," she said. "And sand is in the crack of my butt."

They laughed and in a minute or so she was in and covered and totally relaxed. The guy came in to check on them, put a smoother version of the mud on their faces and a cold towel across their foreheads.

"You should stay in about twenty-five minutes and then you can shower and get in the hot tub or get a warm body wrap," he said. "Enjoy."

They settled into the mud and found a comfort zone. Paul was so relaxed that he almost fell asleep. Ginger was not as comfortable, but she enjoyed the experience.

They talked for a short time, but then drifted into a totally relaxed place. Paul actually fell asleep for a few minutes. Ginger lay in it, but her mind was so filled with emotions and thoughts that she could not doze off. Plus, the heat bothered her.

She did feel better about it when she got out and the aches in her lower back she felt were gone. Just like that. Paul said, "I feel like playing basketball. I cannot believe how fresh I feel. Amazing."

They showered and took their time cleaning themselves off—they passed on the hot tub and warm body wrap—before heading back to Napa to pick up the luggage and their parents.

"That probably was a little messy and stinky to you, Gin," Paul said on the drive back. "But I'm glad we went for two reasons: One, I wanted us to experience something together neither of us had. That's one way to keep things fresh in a marriage. Do different stuff."

"I like that way of thinking," she said. "What's the other reason?

"I didn't know it at the time I planned it, but that mud was symbolic of what our marriage had been like," he said. "We were stuck in the mud. Just lying there, floating. If we didn't do something, we were going to sink deeper and deeper until we drowned.

"But on this trip, we pulled ourselves out of the mud. And just like our bodies feel now, coming out of that mud bath, our relationship has been reinvigorated."

Madeline reached over and held Paul's hand. They listened to music and enjoyed the beautiful countryside the rest of the ride back to the hotel, where their parents were in the lobby.

Mitchell and Lionel had said their goodbyes. The ladies were ready to head home. Paul loaded up the car and they were on their way. They decided they would eat at the airport.

"The mud bath was great," Ginger said. "I feel totally refreshed."

"Really? I probably could have used one after all that wine last night. My goodness," Brenda said.

"Brenda, I am so happy for you—Mitch, I mean, Mitchell, is a nice man," Madeline said.

"Thank you. He is," Brenda said. "And it seemed like Lionel was really into you."

"I like him. We got along great. Who would have guessed this?" Madeline said. "But I'm trying to figure out why we aren't in a limousine, Mr. Millionaire."

Paul laughed. "Next time," he said.

His phone rang. It was Helena. "Hi, honey. I'm gonna put you on speaker so you can say hi to your grandparents, too."

Everyone greeted her.

"So, Dad, what is it you want to talk to me about?" Helena asked.

"Well, there are three things, but the one I want to speak with you about first is very sensitive and we should talk about it in person," he said. He looked around the car and the ladies nodded their heads in agreement.

"Dad, it can't be that serious? Is anyone dying?"

"No, no one's dying, Helena."

"Then tell me now. I don't want to wait."

Paul looked around the car for a consensus and everyone shook their heads "no."

"Baby, come home this weekend so we can sit down as a family."

"Dad, what is it? That I'm adopted?"

Paul nearly veered off the road. "What?"

"Dad, come on. I'm eighteen. You told me this two years ago."

"What? What are you talking about?"

He looked around the car and was greeted by puzzled faces.

"Daddy, you and I stayed home one weekend when Mommy went on that bus trip with Grandma Madeline to Savannah," Helena said. "You and I cooked dinner and then I went to the movies with my friends. You said you were going to stay home and drink some wine that you ordered. Malbec, I think it was.

"When I got home that night, you were watching TV and I asked you how the wine was. You said it was so good you were into the second bottle. I didn't think that was a lot at the time, so I sat down with you and you just told me."

"I…I can't believe this. What did I say?"

"You said you and Mommy love me very much and that you had to tell me something very important and that I had to listen really carefully. You said, 'You are your mom's and my daughter. We raised you from the first days you were born. But you did not come out of your mother's stomach. We adopted you.'

"I didn't say anything. Then you said, 'Listen, you are our child.'

"I asked you whose stomach I came out of and you said, 'Her name is Rita.' You said if I wanted to meet her and the man who got her pregnant—you were so cute; you wouldn't call him my 'dad' or 'father'—that you and Mommy would make it happen. I said, 'No. You are my parents.'

"I was trying to let it go but that wine had taken over. You said, 'They are probably good people but they did some bad things, so they are in prison.' You told me their story. Then you started crying, Dad. You said you were sorry that you made Mommy not tell me before then. I said it was 'OK because we are a family and I love you both, no matter what a birth certificate says.'"

Ginger wept, again. "Did I say anything else? I can't believe this," Paul said.

"You said, 'Your mother and I love you with everything we have.' And we hugged and you passed out. And I just laid there in your arms and fell asleep, too."

"Oh, my God," Paul said. "Why didn't you say anything after that?"

"Because it didn't matter," she said. "You are my parents. And that's it."

"I'm so sorry we didn't tell you the right way," Ginger said.

"Mom, it's OK, it's fine," Helena said. "I love you."

"Still," Ginger said, "we want you to come home so we can talk about it together."

"OK," Helena said. "What are the other two things?"

Paul was so emotional he couldn't talk. Ginger wiped her face and said, "Well, your daddy told me something last night that was shocking."

"That he hit the lottery?" Helena said.

"*What?* How could you know that?" Ginger said. "Did you tell her, Paul?'

"No," he said.

"Daddy didn't tell me," Helena said. "Grandpa did."

"That damn James," Brenda said. "He knew?"

"Yeah, I told Dad about a month ago," Paul said.

"You told him but not me?" Brenda asked.

Paul said, "I told him because I knew—or I thought—he could keep a secret. I know you can't, Ma."

"Well, I'll be damned. What secret haven't I told?" Brenda inquired.

"Do I really need to list them, Ma?" Paul said.

Brenda thought about it and said, "Never mind."

"So you know about the money? Why did he tell you?" Ginger said.

"Well, I call Grandpa probably every two weeks," Helena said. "We had our 'pop' call—that's what he calls it. And I asked him: 'So, Grandpa, what's really going on with the family?' And he said, 'You're my little angel and I cannot lie to you.' And he told me. He said you would tell me when the time was right and to not say anything until he said it was OK. Last night he said it was OK."

"So how do you feel about it?" Madeline asked.

"I feel good because now I can finish college without my parents having to spend all their money," she said. "I felt kinda guilty about that."

"What a sweetheart you are, Helena," Brenda said.

"My goodness," Paul said. "OK, so we have that to talk about to and how we're going to manage it and not let it manage us."

"OK," Helena said. "So I guess that means the third thing to talk about is the baby."

"*Huh?*" Paul shrieked. "This is crazy. Who told you about the baby?"

"Grandma Madeline and Grandma Brenda called me this morning," Helena said.

Paul and Ginger turned around to look at their parents.

"See what I mean, Ma?" Paul said.

"I'm sorry," they said in unison. "We were too excited. The girl needed to know she's going to be a big sister. That's a big thing. She has to get prepared for that," Madeline said.

"I totally agree," Brenda said, smiling.

"But we talked about this last night," Ginger said. "She should not have gotten the news from you."

"It's OK, Mommy," Helena said.

"Soooo, how you feel about that, Helena?" Paul asked his daughter.

"I'm so happy," she said. "I can't wait. I hope it's a girl. Then I can dress her and show her the ropes. But then again, if it's a boy I can teach him about girls and when he gets old enough he can beat up boys that get on my nerves."

"I can do that for you," Paul said. "Gladly… Anyway, I guess that's it. You're all caught up."

"Nobody gonna mention that Grandma Brenda is in love?" Helena said.

"Ah, what did you say?" Brenda said.

"Mommy told me that you met your childhood sweetheart last night and you're still in love with him," she answered.

Everyone looked at Ginger in astonishment.

"Helena, we're going to call you later, when we get home," Ginger said.

"OK, have a safe trip," Helena said, laughing. "I love you all. And have a drink for me."

ABOUT THE AUTHOR

Curtis Bunn is a national award-winning sports journalist and author of six critically acclaimed novels that explore compelling relationship dynamics. His debut book, *Baggage Check*, ascended to No. 1 on the *Essence* magazine bestsellers list.

His most recent books, *A Cold Piece of Work*, *Homecoming Weekend* and *The Old Man in the Club*, have been lauded for their authenticity and gripping storylines.

Bunn spent twenty-five years writing sports at *The Washington Times*, *New York Newsday*, *New York Daily News* and *The Atlanta Journal-Constitution*. Over that time he wrote about every major sporting event, including the NBA Finals, Olympic Games in Seoul, Korea and Sydney, Australia, Super Bowls, NCAA Final Fours, World Series, boxing championships and so much more. He now serves as Deputy Editor of www.AtlantaBlackStar. com, a leading online news organization.

In 2003, Bunn, who also taught journalism for four years at Morehouse College, created the National Book Club Conference, an annual event that brings together some of the top African-American authors and readers from across the country.

You can find him at www.curtisbunn.com. He also has a presence on Facebook and Twitter @curtisbunn.

READER DISCUSSION GUIDE

Questions to help facilitate a book club or group discussion *(Don't cheat and read these questions before reading the book. :-)) :*

1. Have you experienced getting a loose tongue under the power of alcohol? What was the occasion(s)? What secret or truth did you reveal?

2. Was it acceptable for Paul to keep his incredibly good news a secret from his wife until he learned that she wanted to make the marriage work?

3. Considering Ginger's emotional state at the time, do you understand her drastic decision she revealed in California that really upset Paul?

4. What is your position on telling a child he/she is adopted? Should you reveal it or keep it concealed? Why?

5. How would you accept learning your father had killed or contributed to someone's death in protecting you?

6. Would you, as Ginger did, have tried to make the marriage work after your husband (or wife) told you he/she wanted a divorce?

7. What did you think of Paul's jail experience?

8. What did you think of the main characters telling funny stories that they had not shared with anyone?

9. Were you surprised by the twist with Mitchell and Brenda? What did you think of it?

10. How would a trip with you, your mother, mother-in-law and spouse turn out?

THE CRAFT
WRITING
THE TRUTH IS
IN THE WINE

I typed the final words of this book at exactly 1:59 p.m. on Friday, February 1, 2013. I let out a sigh of relief, closed my laptop and placed it on the hotel bed. I then retrieved a bottle of Fairview Mourvèdre, a red wine that traveled with me from Atlanta to Chesapeake, Virginia, where a book party was to be held for me that evening for my previous release, *Homecoming Weekend*.

I saved the wine, purchased six months before in Cape Town, South Africa, just for this occasion. And it was *good*.

In the past, I celebrated completing books by cooking, which is one of my favorite pastimes, along with golf and more golf and movies and making cocktails. In this case, considering the title of the work and the relief that came with finishing it, wine was the appropriate way to mark the occasion.

It was appropriate the way you might need a libation at the end of a long day, to, at once, steady the nerves and to reward yourself for surviving the challenge. That's how I felt: accomplished and like I had endured in the face of significant odds.

The truth is, staring at an empty computer screen with the idea of filling it with eighty thousand words is quite a daunting thing. Even after having written five other novels, it remains intimidating. But it is an amazing thing when the characters you create grow and live inside you. You take their journey together, making it kind of strange when you are done and it is time to discard these "people" that have resided in you and become a part of you for so long.

The good news is that Paul, Ginger, Madeline and Brenda will never leave me; they will hover in the recesses of my mind, and probably emerge again and demand that I write a sequel.

They were fun characters because they were honest. They said things they wanted to say, things that were on their heart. Many times it was the influence of the wine that released those reservations, but at least they cleared their conscience. Some of us cannot say that.

To get to their place, I had go to Napa and indulge in the wine, take in the country, breathe the spirit of the place. And it was a wonderful experience. For someone who has gained a strong interest in wines, it was great research.

Strange, but I find myself still "researching," even though the book is done! That's how much I enjoyed learning about wines and ingesting them. Now, wine is very much a part of my life.

I sipped wine as I read back on this book, and I was

reminded of the deadline pressure I put on myself. In the last forty-five days I had to write about fifty-five thousand words. I was doing more research (if you know what I mean) than writing.

But in that last month and a half, the book took life, as I crafted storylines that challenged love and piqued curiosities. The characters became more clear to me—and more complex. The themes of the dilemmas strengthen as characters' inhibitions weakened.

For an author, it is a beautiful place to be—in command of your imagination and story, knowing where you are going and how you're going to get there. I found myself writing wherever I was—the couch, bed, coffee shop, airplane, airport, dining room table. When you feel like you must write to feel good about yourself, well, that's where you want to be.

"Truth" was no more difficult or easy to write than any other book. But it is always a challenge to create interesting characters with interesting stories. It is in the complexities of each that make a book thought provoking. I had fun doing that.

So I partook of the wine when I was done, and I have not failed to think of this book each time I have poured a glass since then. It's like each sip represents a celebration of the work.

CURTIS BUNN'S
FAVORITE WINES

I am hardly a wine connoisseur, but I have grown to really appreciate it, how it is made and cultivated. And I enjoy it. I make sure some wine is consumed on most days, especially reds because of the health benefits. *(Wink, wink.)* Here are my ten favorite wines. If you try any of them, I hope you enjoy.

—CURTIS

REDS

TOBIN JAMES FAT BOY ZINFANDEL 2008

"Sex in a bottle," it was described to me by Frank Ski of Frank Ski Restaurant in Atlanta. And I get his point. 16.2 percent alcohol. Need I say more?

THE PRISONER ZINFANDEL

"Subtle hints of berries and spice. The more you consume, the more you want."

FAIRVIEW PINOTAGE 2010 (SOUTH AFRICA)

"Distinct flavor and taste. Perhaps my favorite wine of all. Good for celebrating."

PHEBUS (MENDOZA) MALBEC
"*Spicy and flavorful. Good to drink while in bed watching a good movie.*"

STERLING 2007 RESERVE CABERNET SAUVIGNON
"*Elegant wine that makes you want to close your eyes with every sip.*"

WHITES
OYA RIESLING
"*Flavorful and delicate. Delicious. My favorite white wine of all. Order it at www.oyawines.com.*"

ST. SUPERY CHARDONNAY 2009
"*There's a sexiness to this wine, first consumed at The Lamb's Club in New York—or maybe it was just the woman drinking it...*"

STERLING VIOGNIER 2011
"*First of all, it looks great in the glass— light and bright and ready to take in. It's refreshing and fruity, but not too sweet.*"

ZOLO SAUVIGNON-BLANC
"*Crisp and light, ideal for a summer day while wearing sunglasses, sitting out on a patio. Cool and refreshing.*"

VEUVE CLIQUOT PONSARDIN (CHAMPAGNE)

"The ultimate celebratory drink. I'll take this over any other champagne. It is refreshing with fruit flavors bursting in every sip. Just look for the orange label. Want to impress? This is the one for every toast."

The Believers have massive breeding farms on the big island."

"How many are we facing, West?"

"Thousands," the mercenary said. "Prisoners confirm that. This is their last bastion."

Corrie walked in—none of Ben's personal team ever knocked—and laid a dispatch on his desk. Ben noticed the worried look on her face.

"From General Jefferys at Base Camp One," she said, pointing to the paper. "And it's bad."

Ben picked up the paper and read aloud. "Extremely large force, estimated size several divisions, on the march from central South America. Expected to reach the southern borders of Mexico in four to five months. General Payon is moving his entire army to the borders. General Payon says there is no way that he can hold for very long."

"Shit!" Ben said. "Corrie, get Cecil on the horn and ask him to define division size. Is he talking about prewar size? My God, even if he's talking about light divisions, that would mean a corps size of approximately fifty thousand troops. Where did they come from? Who is in charge? How well equipped are they? I need more than this, Corrie."

"I'll get right on it, sir."

Ben cut his eyes to West. The mercenary arched one eyebrow. "All that chatter we heard rounding South America. We listened to them and they listened to us. They deliberately fed us nonsense, all the while carefully plotting our course."

"Probably," Ben agreed. "But fifty thousand troops? Get the batt comms in here, West. By the time you round them up, Corrie will have Cec on the horn and we'll know more about this situation."

Ike helicoptered in from the convoy at Ben's orders. The battalion commanders sat in Ben's office, waiting for Corrie to receive and decode and Beth to type up Cecil's message. It was anything but good.

"Read it, Beth," Ben said.

"Preliminary reports place the army in excess of fifty thousand men. At least three and possibly four full-sized divisions. Resistance fighters in central South America report them to be Nazis."

"Nazis!" Ike almost shouted the word. "Hell, the last of those people died years ago."

"But their dream didn't," Ben said. "We've known for years that in certain sections of South America Hitler's ideology was flourishing. Before the Great War a very large Hitler Youth movement was growing. Go on, Beth."

"Four or five months to reach the borders of Mexico is not realistic, General Jefferys states. More like eight months to a year. The divisions include much heavy armor, and they're having fuel problems since the tanks are diesel and roads down there have deteriorated badly. The troops are supported by many helicopter gunships, make and model unknown, but resembling the old Russian Mi-24 Hind."

"Damn!" Striganov said.

"How many gunships?" Ben asked.

"A very large number. Intelligence reports just in state that factories in South America are producing about fifteen a month."

"For how many years?" Ike asked.

"Doesn't say, sir."

"Go on, Beth."

Before she could continue, Corrie ran in. "More, sir."

"Let's have it."

"Confirm that troops are wearing the lightning bolt or the death's-head insignia on their uniforms.

38

They are Nazis, sir."

"Son of a bitch!" Rebet said.

"Stay with the radios," Ben said, holding out his hand for the reports. He read them and leaned back in his chair, hand-rolling one of his rare cigarettes. "Well," he finally said, "we've fought everything else over the years. No reason to doubt the reemergence of the Nazi party. Hell, it never really died. I'll have Cec send Spanish-speaking Rebels down into Mexico, with General Payon's permission, of course, to assess the situation. We need first-hand, eyes-on information. At least we have some time on this one. Cec can radio all the outposts and have them send people in. That will give us another couple of thousand Rebels. Approximately two and a half more battalions."

"Against fifty thousand," Danjou said. "And you can bet they are highly trained."

"Oh, yes," Ben agreed. "No doubt about that. They've had years to do it. Let's get it wrapped up here, people, with minimum losses. We've got the biggest battle we've ever faced looking right over our shoulders." He paused, then added very dryly, "With the deaths of millions of innocent people waving on the banners they so proudly march under."

Three

The news of the impending invasion against what had been known as the United States swept through the Rebel ranks. With that news, knowing they had to wrap this up and do it quickly, the battalions of Tina and Thermopolis hit the small town of Lanai City with a fury that scared the defenders so badly many of them threw down their weapons and refused to fight. They sat on the ground, their hands in the air, dread in their hearts, and crap in their pants. Those who resisted died very quickly, the Rebels showing them no mercy. Those thugs, pirates, and other assorted crap who had chosen to run to the brush were never heard or seen again. The citizens of the islands, now freed, disposed of them, stacked their bodies in piles, and burned them. The islands of Lanai and Molokai were clear.

All prisoners were taken to Molokai and placed under the guard of citizens. A few decided to test their captors. They were shot dead without hesitation. The crap and crud of the islands were learning very quickly that Ben Raines and his Rebels, and the citizens who had joined the movement, had very little compassion for those who turned to a life of crime. Trials were held almost immediately, and those accused of the most heinous of crimes were hanged in full view of the prisoners. To say that watching their fellow cohorts in crime dangling from the end of a rope and kicking their life away had an extremely traumatic effect on them would be a gross understatement.

Ben and his batt comms began planning the invasion of Maui. Special-ops teams had already been sent in and had linked up with citizen resistance groups. It was very disheartening for the thugs and pirates and slavers to wake up in the morning and see the heads of friends stuck up on poles outside their houses, eyes bulging and faces frozen in horror in that last moment of life. Those who had chosen a life of crime were learning very quickly that the Rebels played by no rulebook and that they did not give a damn for a criminal's so-called rights. If they had been expecting lawyers and appeals and fine points of law, they soon learned they had no rights, there were no lawyers, and to fight the Rebels meant death. It was the most demoralizing situation the criminals had ever found themselves facing.

On the island of Oahu, the gang leaders went over plans, checked their heavily fortified installations, and waited. Many had tossed away their plans to split up into small groups to combat the Rebels. Quite a few of those who had split up and disappeared into the rural areas had never been heard from again. They had fallen victim to the many citizen resistance groups that had been formed and now roamed the countryside outside the cities and towns, looking for their former captors.

All in all, summed up a gang leader named Wee Willie, it was a really lousy situation.

*   *   *

Ben made a final inspection of Molokai and Lanai and was satisfied that the islands were clean of crud. He knew that a few had escaped back into the brush, but they posed very little threat and would eventually be flushed out by the citizens and killed. The finer points of law were being ignored. One either was with the Rebels or was against them. For the moment, to choose the latter meant death.

A link had been established between Base Camp One on the mainland and General Payon's command post in Mexico. Teams of Spanish-speaking Rebels had been sent down to the front lines along the border of Guatemala and Belize. So far, the Nazi divisions had not yet reached Central America, but they would. There was nothing to stop them.

The Nazi divisions would be the largest, the most highly trained and best-equipped army the Rebels had ever faced, and Ben wasn't all that sure his people could contain them. They had the heart, but not the numbers. So in his spare time he was busy drawing up contingency plans for an all-out guerrilla war should it come to that.

On the mainland, Cecil had his people working feverishly caching supplies all over the country. Factories were being relocated, pulled back into the country's heartland, and Base Camp One was being turned into a death trap for anyone foolish enough to blunder into it.

Ben knew one thing for a dead bang certainty: he had to wrap up the Hawaiian campaign in plenty of time to sail back to the mainland and get his people in place for a major confrontation. The thugs and crud and crap on the islands were an annoyance, a boil that had to be lanced, but the Nazi divisions were a cancer; stop them soon, or the patient would die. And the patient was liberty.

Tina and Therm's battalions would launch against Maui from the island of Lanai. Ben's battalion and three others would strike from Molokai, the other battalions remaining in reserve. He told the Rebels to gear up; they were moving out that night and would strike in the predawn hours.

Special-ops people started moving out just after dusk. When they got about five miles from the island, they would start fanning out and go ashore in small teams, all of them heavy with explosives and ammo, and light on food. Buddy was leading the first team in.

"Ashore," he bumped his father's CP back on Molokai.

"Affirmative," he received the one-word acknowledgment.

Buddy stowed the radio, and he and his Rat team slipped past the beach and into the tangled overgrowth of brush and palms and kiawe trees. The other teams would not make contact with him unless they ran into trouble they could not handle. All special-ops teams carried silenced weapons and each carried spare sound suppressors for pistol and assault weapon. They were also very proficient with wire and knife, and they could kill with their bare hands. Dan Gray had seen to that.

They had gone into an area that once had been crowded with tourists. Now the fine hotels loomed in front of them like giant, many-eyed monsters, staring blankly at them in the gloom. Buddy's team was made up of four men and three women, not counting himself. Diane, Judy, and Anita. Pete, Harold, Roy, and Carson. They had worked together for a long time, and each knew what the others would do in any given circumstance. They all froze at the sound of talking off to their right. Without having to be told,

Pete and Diane slipped into the darkness, their specially made soft-soled boots making no sound.

Several very faint chugging sounds drifted back to the remainder of the team. Seconds later, Pete and Diane slipped back and squatted down.

"Machine-gun emplacement," Pete whispered. "We pulled the bodies back into the brush."

"Good," Buddy whispered. "Let's go place some charges and make some noise."

From Lahaina to Honokohau, dark shapes with cameo-painted faces were flitting through the night. They left behind them sudden death. They planted their charges and then slipped back into cover, waiting for the main assault force to arrive.

The Hawaiian leaders had told Ben, "We will not know tourist trade again in our lifetime. Probably not in our children's lifetimes. The cities are useless to us, as are the fine hotels. Bring them down if you want to. We must return to the land for our survival."

Just before dawn, moments before the main body of Rebels struck, those outlaws who had decided to dig in and fight were going to be in for a large surprise.

The other gang leaders on the other islands had voted down Books Houseman's suggestion to break up into small groups to fight the Rebels. They had decided to fight them in a conventional manner.

"Fools!" Books had said.

One of the few gang leaders who had managed to escape the wrath of the Rebels in Los Angeles and had just now agreed to throw in with Books looked at him. "I tell you what we better do."

Books looked at him and waited.

"We better just stick the muzzle of a gun in our mouths and pull the trigger. 'Cause we ain't gonna beat Ben Raines. I was in northern California, and I

44

was in L.A. You don't know how this man operates."

"Then why did you pitch in with us?" Vic Keeler asked.

The L.A. punk shrugged his shoulders. 'If I gotta die, I might as well die among friends . . . or at least them that live like I do."

But Books was paying little attention to Keeler or the street punk. He had read and reread the message from communications. He didn't know whether to believe it or not. An extremely large force was moving up toward the United States from South America. And communications had concluded that they were Nazis. Nazis! Books's father hadn't even been born when all that mess was going on. Nazis!

He drummed his fingertips on the desk. If they were Nazis, Books Houseman sure as hell didn't want to get tied up with them. His mother had been a Jew. He remembered his grandfather—just barely—but enough to recall the old man telling horror stories about the Nazis.

Books looked out the window at the darkness. He had to smile, but it was a rueful smile.

"You think all this shit is funny?" Keeler asked him, an edge to his tone.

"Oh, in a manner of speaking," Books replied. "Here we sit by lantern light."

"So?"

"First thing the Rebels would have done would be to fix the power plants."

"What the hell are you driving at, Books?" Keeler asked.

"If you can't see it, Keeler, then there is no point in my discussing it with you."

"Well, go to hell then," the pirate said, but without any real rancor. He stood up and stalked out of the room.

"What are you driving at, Books?" the L.A. punk called Spit asked.

"That we aren't very progressive or far-sighted," Books said. "We live like pigs, satisfied with the minimum of amenities. As long as we have enough mud to wallow about in, and enough slop to eat, we're content."

"What are we supposed to do?"

Books waved that off, knowing he was dealing with a near-cretin, and unhappy that he was forced to associate with the likes of Keeler and Spit.

For a moment, he toyed with the idea of trying to make a deal with Ben Raines. Some kind of arrangement whereby he and his followers could join the Rebels in exchange for a vow to help the Rebels fight the Nazi hordes. Raines had done that with gangs in the midwest, so he'd heard. He wondered how many of his followers would go along with something like that, and concluded there would be damn few of them. He knew—or at least had heard, and had no reason to doubt it—that the Rebels had an elaborate screening system. Fail it, and you were in serious trouble.

No, Books summed it up, there was nothing for those on the islands to do except fight and hope to win. It was root-hog-or-die time. And Books Houseman had an uncomfortable feeling it was going to be the latter.

Ben's battalion was the first to hit the beaches in the darkness of predawn, followed by the battalions commanded by West, Rebet, and Striganov. Seconds after the planted charges blew, the Rebels stormed ashore and put the defenders along the beach into a panic. The charges planted by the special-ops personnel had been a mixture of heavy HE and incendiary, and all along the beaches, stretching for miles, the raging fires laid an eerie backdrop for combat as the Rebels ripped through the thin lines of outlaws and thugs and pirates and secured a beachhead.

Ben and his team ran onto the brush-covered grounds of an old resort hotel and hit the dirt as machine-gun fire sprang from the lobby. From behind the scant cover of a palm tree, Cooper checked behind him to make sure no Rebel would get scorched by the backblast and leveled a rocket launcher. He sighted in and let the rocket fly. The lobby exploded in flames and ripped and torn body parts.

"Burn it out," Ben ordered.

Rockets tore into the hotel and soon the structure was burning out of control. Thugs and outlaws began screaming from the windows of floors above the flaming lobby. When they saw that the Rebels were not going to lift a finger to help them, they began cursing the Rebels, then many of them jumped, choosing to smash the life from their bodies on the grounds below rather than be burned to death in the rapidly raging inferno.

The Rebels moved further inland, leaving the once-magnificent hotels and resorts blazing behind them, the grounds around the buildings littered with dead and dying.

The outlaws and assorted crud and crap on the islands fled in fear and panic. None of them had ever expected anything like the cold and callous warfare that the Rebels were dishing out. After the first few abortive attempts, they had given up trying to surrender. They had been given a chance to surrender and had chosen to ignore it. Now it was too late for most of them.

The Rebels did take a few prisoners. They would not shoot those who simply sat down in the streets or sidewalks and lifted their hands into the air, many of them bawling like a hurt child. Those were jerked to their feet, their hands tied behind their backs, and handed over to the growing crowds of civilians.

"No torture," Ben and the other batt comms told the leaders who had stepped forward. "We won't tolerate that. Try them and punish them. Hang them or shoot them, if that is your judgment. But no torture."

The Rebels moved inland. By noon, they had advanced and driven the outlaws into the West Maui Forest Reserve. There, Ben halted the momentum of his people.

"Start distributing the weapons we've collected," he ordered. "Let the locals hunt them down; they know this reserve. West, you and Rebet take Highway 340 and start clearing the towns along that route. Georgi and I will be on the other side of the island on Route 30." He turned to Corrie. "Have Tina and Thermopolis stay in reserve and order Danjou and Colonel Gray's battalions into Makena and start clearing that area."

Books Houseman sat by the radio in his command post on Oahu and listened to the frantic signals. The island of Maui was rapidly falling into Rebel hands. The Rebels were putting the defenders into a panicked rout. The lawless were not even making much of a fight of it.

"Jesus God!" came the scream out of the speaker. "Help us! Books! Send help, for the love of God."

"For the love of God," Books muttered. "Do they actually think God gives a big rat's ass what happens to them?"

"I was raised in the church," an aide said softly.

Books looked at him and smiled. "You want to pray, Bobby? You want to pray for forgiveness of your multitude of sins? Go right ahead. I'll just sit here and laugh while you do."

"God will hear me," the young man said. "He hears everybody's prayers. He forgave the thief on the cross."

"Right, Bobby. And everyone lived happily ever after, floating around on clouds plucking on harps and fucking angels. Why don't you go outside and give yourself up to the slaves now wandering about the island? See if they forgive you. After they hack you to death with machetes, that is."

"You're serious?"

"Sure, Bobby. If you want to surrender to them, you go right ahead. I won't stop you. That will probably beat the hell out of hanging."

Bobby stared at him for a moment, then shook his head. "You've resigned yourself to death, haven't you, Books?"

"We don't have a choice, my boy. Ben Raines or the Nazis or the former slaves. Take your pick. Or maybe you'd like to go over to the big island and join the Believers?"

Bobby looked at him in horror.

Books laughed. "Sure. They'd probably welcome you with open arms. And then eat you!" He threw back his head and laughed.

Bobby shook his head. "You're sick, Books. You really need help."

Books wiped his eyes. "Help? You damn right we need help, Bobby. With Ben Raines and his Rebels breathing down our necks, we need all the help we can get. Do you have any suggestions . . . besides prayer, that is?"

Bobby shook his head. "You need me anymore today, Books?"

"No. Take off, Bobby. Go to church. Pray for your lost soul. Just get out of here until you get over all this religious crap."

At the door, Bobby turned around. "I'd like to get out, Books. But that's the problem with an island. There just isn't anyplace to run."

Four

The outlaws on Maui just quit.

Communications intercepted no radio call and no flares went up; the outlaws, bandits, pirates, and trash just threw down their weapons, put their hands in the air, and quit. It was the most astonishing sight Ben and the others had ever seen.

Ben walked up to one group and stared at the men and women. None of them would meet his sharp and piercing eyes. "Look at me!" he said. To a person, they jumped at his voice. They lifted their eyes and Ben could see they were scared half to death. "Why?" he asked them. "Why just give up?"

The group exchanged glances and a woman said simply, "We can't win. Not here. Books and them others with him won't give up, and neither will them stinkin' Believers, but we can't win. So why fight on? Besides, we really didn't want to fight anyway."

Ben blinked at that, then looked at a young man; no more than a boy. "How old are you?"

"I . . . don't rightly know, sir. I think I'm fifteen."

"I'm Jenny," another woman said. "The boy has never killed, raped, nor tortured," she said. "He's basically a good kid. He was the only survivor on a

51

pleasure boat that drifted up here a couple of years ago. A big yacht. Me and Marge here kind of took him in."

"The pleasure boat?" Ben asked. "It belonged to your parents?"

"No, sir. Slavers. They grabbed me and my sis and mom off Midway. We were shipwrecked there. No one else alive. Some sort of disease hit us about four days out of here. I got sick, but I got well. I was the only one left alive. It was . . . kind of bad. I buried my mom and sis at sea, along with the others as they passed."

"You think you can look after Jenny and Marge, boy?"

"What? Oh. Yes, sir. I guess so. They sure took care of me."

"Then the three of you take off and find you a piece of ground to farm and get to doing it."

Jenny and Marge exchanged glances. Jenny said, "But we were—"

"I don't care what you were. General Georgi Striganov was once my bitter enemy. Colonel West was a mercenary who fought against me in the south of the United States. I've got two thousand or more men and women in the ranks who used to be outlaws. But I saw a spark of decency in them, just like I'm seeing in you."

"How about us joining up with you?" Jenny asked. "There is a lot of crap and crud on this island, for sure. But there are a number of pretty decent sorts who never took a part in torture or rape or murder. They stole, yes. They had slaves, yes. But they didn't mistreat them. You see these locals standing around here. They aren't making any threatening moves toward us. That should tell you something."

Ben looked at a local, standing with a shotgun in

his hands. The man nodded his head. "She's telling the truth, General Raines. Of all the islands, the people on this one were the most easygoing. It's on Oahu, Kauai, and the big island that you're going to run into trouble."

Ben smiled and shrugged his shoulders. "All right. But you people better get ready for the roughest time of your lives. Joining this outfit is anything but fun."

Buddy and some of his Rat team rode up on motorcycles, accompanied by Beerbelly and Lead-foot and Wanda and some of her Sisters of Lesbos. The prisoners blinked at the sight.

"Like I said," Ben told them. "We have a strange mixture in the Rebel ranks." He turned to his son. "Take your . . . contingent, son, and go with these people. We have a lot of new recruits to train and not a whole hell of a lot of time in which to do it."

Not all the outlaws on the island were so willing to give up the fight. Plenty remained that were brutal hard-core criminals. But within a week's time, those who chose to fight on were either dead or prisoners.

By the time the Rebel doctors, under the command of Lamar Chase, had checked out the new recruits, Ben found that he had over three thousand people to train. He knew that approximately twenty percent of them would not make it through the training. But if six hundred fell out, that would still leave him enough to form three new battalions. He pulled Major Greenwalt from Dan's command to head up Eleven Battalion, Lieutenant Jackie Malone from his own command platoon to head up Twelve Battalion, and Captain Raul Gomez to take over Thirteen Battalion. He split up the volunteers into three groups and told the new batt comms to each take a group and get to it.

Immediately, several men decided they didn't want to take orders from a female. Jackie washed them out on the spot and central records recorded the reasons why. Those three would never be a part of any Rebel organization.

There were those who were blatantly racist. They were kicked out quickly. Still others could not or would not respond to the discipline needed to be a part of the Rebel army. They were soon gone. Some could not meet the physical requirements and others just dragged their butts.

While the weeding out and the training of the new members intensified, the war went on.

"The creepies live in underground bunkers," a special-ops spokesman told the batt comms, after he and his team had returned from a dangerous visit on the big island. "One of their main breeding farms is located at the old Kulani Prison site. It's going to be a real bastard to get into. Establishing a beachhead will be easy. Most of the towns along the coast have been long deserted. But digging the creeps out of the interior is going to be time-consuming."

"We destroy as many as we can," Ben told the commanders. "We don't have to kill all of them, just knock them down enough so the locals can come in after us and manage it. Has Jim Peters really put together a fighting battalion?"

"I'll say he has," Tina told her father. "And he's itching for designation."

"Call it Fourteen Battalion," Ben told Beth. "We're going to need everybody just to hold our own against those people coming up from South America. G-2 has informed me that the advancing divisions do not have nuclear capabilities. That surprises me, but it's welcome news. Our new battalions are shaping up, and by the time we're finished here, they should be fully operational. Now then, I have gone against my own policy and offered surrender terms to those on Oahu and Kauai. Their commander, someone called Books Houseman, refused. The only way they would consider surrender is if we offered them full amnesty. That is unacceptable to me. I warned them that once we start, it's going to be harsh. Books personally told me by radio to, in his words, 'Get fucked.' I told him he wasn't my type."

After the laughter had subsided, Ben walked to a wall map and picked up a pointer. "All right, people, here it is: I'm taking my battalion straight into Hilo. I'll secure the town and the airport. Dan, you take the airport here at Upolu Point. Georgi, you go in here at Paauhau. West, you're going in down here at Ka Lae. Rebet, take your battalion in here, at Hookena, drive straight in and take and hold the airport just outside of Waimea. Danjou, go in here at Kalapana. Therm, you seize the airport at Kaupulehu, then split your battalion, move south, and take the airport at Keahole Point. Everyone else stays in reserve. Once our objectives are secure, we'll start using gunships to punish the creepies. Map packets are in front of you."

"Bastards!" Books said, sitting at his desk and looking out the window. "I should have guessed those wimps over on Maui would roll over."

John Dodge had come over by boat from Kauai and said, "The Rebels are beginning to shift their armada around. They're layin' just outside the channel now. This will probably be the last time I'll be able to come over. They're runnin' PT boats all over the damn place. I'll go back tonight and that'll be it for me. The run is gettin' too risky."

Books nodded his head. "No vacillation on the part of any of the gangs on your island?"

"No." John was adamant. "Don't none of us want no part of Rebel law."

Books looked at him. "Start killing your slaves. We can't have them at our backs once it starts. I ordered the extermination on this island this morning."

John nodded his agreement. "I noticed. Bodies are beginnin' to pile up and stink. You better start burnin' them 'fore you have a disease problem."

"Communications says that Raines is going to hit the big island soon. Two, three weeks over there, and then it'll be our turn."

John Dodge stood up and shook hands with Books. "I got to say hello and good-bye to some buddies over here. I'll see you in hell, Books."

Bobby sat in a corner of the room, listening and watching the two gang leaders. He was scared and doing his best to hide that fear. He had never thought it would really come to this. Actually, none of them had. He didn't want to even think about dying. He had gone to a church and tried to pray. But he felt so guilty about being there, after all the hideous things he'd done over the long years, he'd left the old sanctuary. He didn't know what to do. Now the slaves were being killed . . . those that had not fled into the brush. Bloated bodies were littering the streets, rats eating on them. It was terrible. For the first time in his life Bobby was seriously considering suicide. He knew one thing for a fact: he wasn't going to allow himself to fall into civilian or Rebel hands. He'd been Books's aide for too many years. They'd hang him for sure.

"Did you find a church to pray in?" Books asked him with a smile, breaking into Bobby's thoughts.

"A church?" John said with a sneer. "You really went to a fuckin' church?"

"Yes," Bobby said. "I went to church. But I didn't stay very long."

"What's the matter, Bobby?" Books asked, that same sneering smile on his lips. "Was your conscience bothering you?"

Bobby did not choose to reply. He walked out, leaving the derisive laughter behind him.

"What's wrong with him, is he queer?" John Dodge asked, the words reaching Bobby.

Whatever was Books's reply, the words did not reach Bobby. The gunfire of outlaws killing slaves blotted them out. Bobby looked at the body-littered and bloody streets and shook his head in disbelief. Bobby was anything but a prude. He'd done his share of killing and raping. But this was so . . . senseless. Needless. The gang leaders were acting like a bunch of spoiled children: if they couldn't have it, then destroy it.

Suddenly Bobby wanted out. Just to get away. He could get on his motorcycle and ride up into the mountains and hide. Grow a beard and stay hidden for a long time. He could . . .

Do nothing, and he knew it. He was too well known. Sooner or later, those former slaves who had escaped into the interior when the wholesale executions started would find him and kill him.

He walked around the corner and started to step over a woman who was lying in a gathering puddle of blood. She moaned and rolled over, looking up at him through anguish-filled eyes. Somebody had shot her twice in the stomach and left her to die a painful death.

"Big brave man," the woman sneered at him, blood leaking from her mouth. "It'll take me hours to die like this. Finish it, for the love of God, finish me. Stop the pain."

An outlaw called Big Jess stepped out of the alley. "No, Bobby, you don't do nothin' of the kind. I want her to holler. This is the one that no matter how I beat her, she never would suck me off. So I want her to holler."

Bobby looked at the outlaw, disgust in the gaze. He stepped over the woman. She grabbed at his jeans and he kicked her hand away.

Big Jess chuckled. "You a good boy, Bobby. Faithful to his woman, too," he said to the gut-shot woman. "Yes, sir. He's been with the same wahine for some years now."

Bobby turned his back to the outlaw and walked to his motorcycle. Whole goddamn island was going crazy.

"Beg, you bitch!" Big Jess said.

"Go to hell!" the woman told him.

Bobby cranked his motorcycle and headed for his house, up in the hills around the city.

Not wanting to be left out of all the action, Ike was now in command of a reworked and refitted modern-day PT boat. Ben knew about it and kept silent. If Ike wanted to roar around the ocean looking for trouble, that was fine with Ben, just as long as the ex-Navy SEAL returned to the armada every now and then to check things out. Actually, Ben had been about to let Ike come ashore with his battalion when Ike decided to shift the armada around. But now that Ike was having so much fun roaring about the ocean in a seventy-foot rocket, Ben decided to leave him alone.

Ben walked to the wall map and checked out the new positions of the ships. When Ike was finished shifting vessels around, he would have effectively closed off all island travel for the outlaws and pirates. Any ship or boat found in the channels was subject to being blown out of the water. Several already had been and the pirates had gotten the message.

With a sigh, Ben returned to his desk and looked at the mounds of reports on it. With the addition of the four new battalions, the paperwork had drastically increased. Ben picked it all up and threw it on the floor, in piles. Hell with it.

Jersey watched him from the door. "You need some aides, General," she told him. "You're either gonna be out in the field, or tied to a desk. You're gonna have to start delegating authority. Now, which one is it gonna be? 'Cause everybody is tired of hearing you bitch."

Ben looked at her and started laughing. General of the Army he might be, but Jersey pulled no punches with him. She told it like she saw it.

"Enlarge my staff, is that it, Jersey?"

"Has to be, General. The army's gettin' too large for one man to do it all. When we had nine battalions, it was too much. Now it's really gotten out of hand."

Beth and Corrie and Cooper came in. Ben stared at them and they stared back. "Speak your minds," he said.

"We been talkin' to Doctor Chase," Corrie said. "He's worried about the work load on your shoulders. So are the rest of the batt comms. Tina and Jersey have been meeting with them from time to time. General, you're a soldier's soldier. You hate the office and love the field. You enjoy planning and tactics, but you're happiest in the field. We now have

59

more than twelve thousand people in infantry units alone. I don't even know how many others are in armor and artillery and engineers and truck drivers and cooks and medics and all the other stuff."

Ben smiled. "Tell you the truth, Coop . . . I don't either. But I do have the figures around here someplace."

"That's the point, General," Beth said. "You've talked for months about setting up a real Headquarters Company with a real XO to take all this crap off of you. Let's do it and take some strain off of all of us."

"Who do you have in mind?"

"Thermopolis."

That startled Ben. But the more he thought about it, the more logical it became. Thermopolis was a detail man; he loved that kind of work. And while Thermopolis was a good battalion commander, he did not like the killing involved with being in the field and had often said so. Therm was a gentle man by nature, and so were the people who had come with him several years back.

"Therm might not go for it," Ben said.

"Oh, I think he will," Beth replied with a grin.

"Suckered again," Ben grumbled, but with a smile.

Five

"Why in the hell is he waiting to strike?" Books bitched to the roomful of gang leaders. "He's up to something." He stood with his back to the men and women, staring out the window at the street below. The bodies of the slaves had been removed and burned and the scene looked almost tranquil.

"Do we have anybody left on the islands the Rebels control?" Vic Keeler asked.

"No. Well, if we do, they're not sending out any radio signals. I just can't understand why Raines is waiting so long to strike at the Believers on the big island. I don't know what he's planning and it's frustrating."

"I hope he waits ten years," Polly Polyanna said. "I'm not that anxious to die."

Susie Loo glanced at the gang leader. "I still say we got a chance to come out of this."

"A damn slim one," Polly muttered.

Bobby entered the room, carrying a dispatch from communications. "Books, the big ships laying offshore have shifted. They've come in closer and gone broadside toward us."

"Now what the hell does that mean?" Slick Bowers asked.

He, along with the others, got their reply in the form of a dozen 155mm rounds impacting against buildings and earth. When Ben had learned of the wholesale killing of slaves, he had ordered the ships to commence their bombardment of the major cities on Oahu and Kauai.

"Son of a bitch!" Big Jess shouted, as a round came dangerously close to the building being used as Books's command post.

"Grab anything of importance!" Books yelled over the din of incoming rounds. "Clear the city. Raines is going to bring it down."

120mm mortars located on board ships joined the 155s and the 105s and began pounding at the city of Honolulu. The outlaws and assorted crud and crap went into a panic as willie-peter and HE rounds started dropping in full force, blowing away the tops of buildings and starting fires. Those caught in the streets were showered with bricks and other killing and maiming debris.

Freshly resupplied, the Rebels would keep up the bombardment until the cities were burning out of control and useless to the outlaws. Books's plan to kill the slaves had backfired and blown up in his face.

Thermopolis accepted his new assignment and did not make any effort to hide his pleasure at the reshuffling. He now was in complete charge of Headquarters Company with two hundred and fifty men and women under him. And for the first time in years, Ben's desk was clear and he could take to the field without having a guilty conscience.

Buddy Raines was given command of Eight

Battalion and the young man was understandably nervous about it.

"Nothing changes, son," Ben told him in his office. "Your battalion goes into Kaupulehu, take the airport, then split your forces and move down to Keahole Point and seize the airport there. You'll do just fine. If I didn't think you could handle it, I wouldn't have put you in charge."

"What are you grooming me for, Father?"

"Someday, you've got to assume command of all the Rebel forces, son. I won't live forever. Tina doesn't want it. She and West will be married before too much longer and she wants to settle down and have babies. Colonel West is not much younger than I am, and he's going to want to retire when he marries. I think as soon as this Nazi threat is over, there will be some major reshuffling of command. If this Nazi threat is ever over, and that is one hell of a big if. Who did you put in charge of your Rat team?"

"Diane."

"Good choice. She's tough as a keg of nails. Did you get any flak from the men?"

"Oh, no. They all like and respect her."

"Get to your command and meet with your officers and sergeants. We hit the big island in seventy-two hours."

Ben walked over to Headquarters Company and was pleased to see the place humming. Thermopolis had taken hold and jerked things together almost immediately. There were huge boards showing placement of troops and ships. Maps with colored pins showing areas of combat, possible combat, and landing sites. Therm could put his finger on every scrap of material belonging to Rebels anywhere in the world. The place buzzed with efficiency. Made Ben nervous.

"What'd you do with Emil?" Ben asked.

"Put him in charge of all portable toilets," Thermopolis said with a grin. "Believe it or not, that is one hell of a large responsibility."

"I believe it. Especially when you're trying to find one of the damn things."

"Look here," Therm said, taking Ben's arm and leading him to a huge wall map that covered much of one wall. "The red pins denote trouble spots all around the world. The black pins are the Nazi columns moving up through South America. The orange pins are General Payon's troops. I'm in contact with Base Camp One and with General Payon's liaison several times a day. The blue areas are Rebel outposts in America. Over on this map are highways. You can see where bridges are blown and sections of highway that are impassable. This map denotes Rebel storage areas and fuel dumps. I'll be fully operational in here in a couple more days."

"How long would it take you to pull this down and pack and move?"

"Less than an hour."

"You've taken a hell of a lot of trouble off of my shoulders, Therm. And I appreciate it."

"Not nearly as much as I do, Ben," the hippie-turned-warrior said with a smile. "Now I get to sleep in a real bed every night . . . with my wife!"

On the big island of Hawaii, the creepies waited for the assault against them. They were under no illusions. They knew the Rebels did not take prisoners of Believers. Even if they tried to surrender, the cannibals would be shot on sight.

The Night People, Believers, creepies, whatever one chose to call them, were the most hated of all the enemies the Rebels had ever faced. Ungodly and inhuman, Doctor Lamar Chase called them.

Ben usually added a few other words to that.

On the evening before the jump-off to the big island, Ben walked over to Headquarters Company and had coffee with Thermopolis.

"Now you're going to see just how big a responsibility I've handed you, Therm," he told the men. "Once we're on the island and moving, this room becomes the hub of all operations. Don't expect to get much sleep for the first twenty-four to thirty-six hours. This isn't exactly what a Headquarters Company is supposed to do, but here in this army, we tend to do things differently. I'll be in contact with you quite often once we hit the big island." He held out his hand and Therm shook it.

"Luck to you, Ben."

"Keep it running for me, Therm."

"Will do."

Ben walked back out into the night, a smile on his lips. It was about to get real busy around the HQ.

Back at his office, he went over his equipment. His personal team was doing the same. "We board the boats in one hour," he called to his people. "Double-check everything. Once we enter Hilo, we don't get resupplied for some time."

Ben slipped into his body armor and then slung his battle harness on and hooked it in place. He slipped his pack on and picked up his M-14. He did not realize it, but he was smiling. Ben was a warrior, not a desk soldier. He would die fighting in some battle, somewhere, not keel over with a heart attack laboring over paperwork in some damned office.

Corrie and Cooper and Jersey and Beth stole glances at Ben, then looked at one another and smiled. This was going to be an interesting campaign, for they could see that Ben was all fired up and hot to go.

Ben walked out of his office and into the anteroom. He winked at Jersey. "What'd you say, Jersey?"

She smiled. "Let's go kick some ass, General!"

Boats of all description were being loaded when Ben and his team arrived. Ike had rumbled in, leading his fleet of PT boats, and Ben and his people climbed on board. "Straight to the docks at Hilo, Admiral," Ben told the ex-SEAL.

Ike looked hard at him. In the distance, the big guns on board ship were still pounding away at Honolulu, the barrage never letting up. If there was anyone left alive in the city, they either had nerves of steel or were totally insane after days of shelling.

"Hilo hasn't been softened up, Ben," Ike reminded him.

"Resistance will be light in the towns," Ben replied. "We're going to have to dig the bastards out of the caves and tunnels. Crank it up, Ike. Let's go."

Ike slowly grinned. "I heard that you had changed into a real fire-eater after having all that paperwork lifted off you."

"Not me, Ike. I'm still the same old peace-loving person I always was."

Ike said a very ugly word and shoved off.

"Mountains, deserts, and rain forests," Beth said, when they were out of the harbor and on their way. "Four thousand square miles. That's the big island."

"It isn't going to be a picnic," Ben said, his words just audible over the rumbling of the power plant.

Ben, Danjou, and West were the first to leave, followed by Georgi, Rebet, Dan, and Buddy. Ben studied maps and rested below decks as the armada made its way toward the big island. Hours later, Corrie stepped down the ladder.

"Danjou laying offshore, General. Hilo coming up fast now."

Ben went up the ladder into the predawn darkness and Ike handed him binoculars. Ben could see no sign of life in the town of Hilo. No fires, no smoke, no movement, nothing.

"It had a population of about thirty thousand before the Great War," he said.

"Maybe the creepies had a big banquet," Cooper suggested.

"Gross-out, Coop!" Jersey said.

"I hate these goddamn people," Ben muttered, handing the night lenses back to Ike. "Corrie, order the attack to begin. Let's go, Ike."

Hilo was a ghost town, the buildings long abandoned and thick with dirt and mold.

"Well, where the hell are they?" Ben questioned the dawning day. "They could have inflicted heavy casualties on us during the landing. Something is all out of whack here."

"Buddy, Rebet, and Dan reporting heavy fighting," Corrie said. "West is just hanging on at Ka Lae. General Striganov and Danjou reporting only very light resistance."

"Gunships into West's position," Ben ordered. "Advise West and have him radio coordinates."

"Scouts report the airport is heavy with creepies," Corrie said, after getting the gunships up.

"I might have guessed," Ben said. "What is their fascination with airports? I have never understood that." Ben looked around him. "Where is Coop?"

"Rounding up some transportation," Jersey told him. "He'll probably come back in a damn hearse."

Coop came panting up. "Not a usable vehicle to be

found, General," he reported. "But I found a whole bunch of bicycles."

"Well, shit!" Jersey said.

Ben laughed. "How many bikes, Coop?"

"Whole warehouse full, General."

"Come on, gang," Ben said. "Let's go pedal our way into battle."

Six

Once the bike riders reached the airport, the scene was anything but funny. The buildings were filled with creepies and they were putting up a fierce battle. Since the Rebels were armed with only light weapons, with no tanks to spearhead, the fight was building-to-building and hand-to-hand and the forces were very nearly evenly matched up.

Ben and his team fought their way into the main terminal and were immediately confronted by a screaming, stinking horde of creepies. Grenades thrown by Rebels turned a part of the terminal into a blood-splattered mess. One howling creepie jumped onto Jersey's back, riding her down to the floor. Ben stuck the muzzle of his M-14 to the creature's head and brains splattered the wall. Jersey struggled out from under the man, cussing as she crawled to her knees.

"Stinkin' son of a bitch!" she panted. "God, I hate these people."

Then they were all belly-down on the dirty floor as automatic weapons fire ripped over their heads, the lead howling and screaming off the walls behind them. Creepies came leaping over chairs and benches in a last-ditch suicide charge, shrieking their hatred for the Rebels, and Ben and his team poured the lead to them, stopping them cold on the blood-slick floor.

The terminal building fell silent as the nearest creepie lay dying, still cursing the name of Ben Raines. Cooper walked over to him and shot the cannibalistic creature in the head. Ben and his team walked through the building, shooting the wounded where they lay. It was a callous act, but a necessary one. For the Rebels had found out the hard way that no Believer could be rehabilitated. The Rebels had lost personnel attempting that. Not even the young could be brought back to any type of civilized behavior. It was not something the Rebels relished, but all knew it had to be.

Outside the terminal building, the battle was waning as the Rebels finished the grisly job at the airport.

"Corrie," Ben said. "Get our mechanics in here to get some vehicles running. We can't pedal all over the damn island. We've got to have trucks."

Corrie listened to her headset for a moment. "General Ike says we sure looked cute pedaling our way out here," she said with a smile.

"You tell Ike," Ben looked at her, "I said to kiss my . . ."

Corrie quickly tucked both ears under the pads, blotting out Ben's words. She smiled sweetly at him.

"Get me a report from the other battalions," Ben said, then lifted one of her earphones and repeated it when he realized she could not hear him. "I'm through cursing now, Corrie," he added.

"West is now secure and moving inland," she said, after checking with communications. "General

Striganov is moving inland along the Mamaloha Highway toward the inland airport. He reports no resistance but is expecting heavy fighting once at the airport. Buddy, Colonel Gray, and Rebet are secure. Danjou is reporting no resistance of any kind."

"We're going to have to dig them out," Ben said, disgust in his voice. "Corrie, bump Therm and tell him I want every flamethrower we have over here ASAP. Plenty of fuel. Also start flying C-4 over here today. Lots of it. I'm not going to lose people by using them as tunnel rats. We'll find the creepie hidey-holes and exits and blow them closed. Has anybody found any survivors on this island?"

"No one is reporting any, General," Corrie said. "I think the creepies wiped them out."

Jersey looked startled. "You mean they ate a hundred thousand people?"

"I doubt it," Ben said. "But they probably worked their way through a lot of them."

"Blakk!" Jersey said, a grimace on her face.

"All right, people," Ben said. "Let's get this airport cleaned up and get ready to receive some planes. Start dragging out the creepies and burning them. Anyone with an open wound is not to touch any creepie." Doctor Chase and his lab people had found that the Night People were highly infectious.

The runways were clear by noon and the planes started bringing in supplies. Food, fresh water, ammo, flamethrowers and fuel, and lots of explosives. Ben split his command and sent two companies south on Highway 130. They were to reconnoiter the small village of Keaau and then cut southwest to the village of Kurtistown, on Highway 11, and hold their positions.

Before they left, Ben told them, "You know the

71

creepies just as well as I do. They'll probably be coming at you tonight. Heads up, people." He ordered two platoons into town with these words, "Check every basement, everything that leads underground. I don't believe for a minute they all went into the brush. They've left some behind, bet on it. If something is suspicious-looking, blow it."

Ike intercepted the transmissions and got on the horn. "You're too light, Ben. If they hit you now, you'll be in deep shit. I'm sending some of my people in to beef you up and no arguments."

"None from me, Ike," Ben told him. "I was going to request backup from you." He smiled. "But I figured you'd be snooping like an old gossip on a party line anyway."

He broke the connection as Ike was sputtering and cussing. Within thirty minutes, some of Ike's SEAL teams were helicoptered in and set up around the airport. Ike used the same training methods as he had gone through as a young man, and as a result, the SEALs in Ben's command were ranked as extremely dangerous fighters, and all were at the peak of physical conditioning. Ike never let up on his people. That was the way he was trained, and he saw no reason to change it. One either cut it or got out. There was no middle ground with Ike. His people got all the shit jobs anyway, just like it had been back when the nation was whole, so nothing had changed.

"First and second platoons under heavy attack in town!" Corrie yelled from the makeshift radio room. "Creepies coming out of the woodwork."

"Goddammit!" Ben said. "I knew those bastards were close. "Ask if they need assistance."

"That's negative for right now, sir. They're in good defensive positions and holding their own."

72

Ben started to ask the SEALs to go into town, but checked his tongue. That would put them in a bad spot, for he knew that Ike had ordered them to stay close to him. "Pull back those two companies I sent down Highway 130, Corrie. Let's settle this here and now." He checked a map. "I want the Rebels' exact position in town. Once that is established, tell them *do not move,* I'm sending in gunships."

"Gunships diverted and on the way," Corrie told him.

"Hit the town and rearm here."

"Yes, sir."

From the airport, the Rebels heard the gunships as they began their vicious attack. Smoke began spiraling from the town as rockets set buildings blazing. Creepies began scurrying like rats from the inferno and Rebels chopped them down. Helicopters began setting down for rearming and the pilots reported to Ben.

"We got them cold, General. Our people are tucked in tight and secure. It won't be long now. We're leaving an avenue clean for our guys and gals to get out, if they choose. But the creeps are running this way."

"We'll be ready for them. Encourage them to head this way."

The chopper pilot smiled. "Will do, General."

But the creepies never made the airport. Somewhere between the town and the airport, they veered off to the west and disappeared.

"Heading into the Hilo Reserve," Ben said, consulting his map. "Let's go into town and look it over."

Corrie had found transportation—a Ford station wagon—and the team piled in, falling in behind two trucks filled with Rebels—a few SEALs had gone ahead of the trucks—and more Rebels fell in behind the station wagon. Ben pulled out just as the two companies he'd sent scouting returned and took up positions around the airport.

The small city of Hilo was burning and the Rebels made no attempts to put out the fires. Ben ordered backfires lighted to contain the flames and then ordered his people out of the city and let it burn itself out.

"West's people have secured the towns of Wai-ohinu and Naalehu," Corrie informed Ben. "Creeps have retreated back into the Kau Reserve. He is not pursuing at this time."

"Tell him to hold what he has and wait for orders. The other battalions?"

"Firmly in control of their areas. I'm waiting on a report from Five Battalion now."

"Tell them to dig in for the night and do it right. They're sure to be attacked."

"General Striganov has reached the airport on 190," Corrie reported. "Heavy fighting there. He's calling in gunships while he still has light."

Ben nodded his head. "The flybys of the breeding farm at the old prison camp?"

"Thermopolis says that initial reports have been confirmed, sir. The camp has been destroyed. Bodies all over the place."

"God help those poor people," Ben muttered. In a way, he was relieved that it had happened, for the Rebels had found that liberated people from creepie breeding farms had a very poor chance of ever attaining any degree of normalcy. Being slowly fattened for food drove most of them over the edge.

"Order our people back to the airport and dig in for the night. It's over here."

The Rebels put the fires behind them and headed back to the security of the airport.

Only a few attacks occurred that night, and they were minor ones. The creepies had retreated into the interior of the big island, into caves and pre-dug tunnels. But in doing so they had sealed their own fates. So much of the big island was covered with old lava flows that the search areas were restricted and predictable. However, it was still a huge undertaking, and it would be time-consuming.

The Rebels spent the next several days going from one village and town to the next. And they took their time doing it, carefully inspecting each house, every building for hidden cellars and tunnels. When they found one, they sealed it with high explosives. The Rebels could tell if the holes and tunnels were occupied—the smell was a dead giveaway. After the holes were sealed shut, the house was burned to the ground.

Mechanics and engineers got enough of the old cars and trucks and motorcycles left on the island running so the Rebels did not have to ride bikes . . . unless they wanted to, and some did. The Rebels found no survivors on the island.

"Almost a hundred and twenty thousand souls lived on this island," Ben said, closing a map case. "Now they are gone. Vanished." He was standing in the center of the old prison camp/breeding farm. The bodies had been removed and buried in a mass grave. There was no way of knowing the names of those the creepies had killed, for the Believers had kept no records. A single cement cross was all that marked the site.

He picked up his M-14 and slung it. "Now it gets down and dirty," he said aloud. "Corrie, all battalions into the interior. Search and destroy."

Planes and helicopters using heat-seeking equipment had pinpointed many of the creepie strongholds, but getting to them was dangerous and slow work, for the creepies had booby-trapped the paths and they had to be cleared. The Rebels worked slowly and carefully and lost no one in the clearing of the mines and other booby traps.

The tunnels they found had been skillfully camouflaged, and the Rebels knew they would probably miss some of them. Those they would leave for the locals to deal with.

"Jesus!" Ben said, recoiling from the foul odor that sprang from the mouth of the cave.

"Really smells wonderful, doesn't it, Ben?" Georgi asked, his face a twisted grimace from the odor.

They were in the Mauna Kea Forest Reserve. They had blown closed a dozen holes that day, and the Rebels were tired and disgusted at the sickening odors that emanated from the creepie hideouts.

"We will control the world someday!" the shout ripped out of the odious darkness of the cave. "You will all eventually die at our hands!"

"Eat shit!" Jersey said, and leveled her M-16, giving those in the cave a full thirty-round clip. The other members of Ben's team followed suit, and lead began howling and bouncing around the stone walls of the cave.

"You people feel better?" Ben asked them.

"Lots," Beth told him, shoving in a fresh clip.

Ben and Georgi looked at each other and smiled.

"Why not?" the Russian asked. He and Ben leveled their weapons and sent more rounds into the yawning, stinking darkness.

A demolitions team came forward and told Ben, Georgi, and the others to clear out. Being careful to stay clear of the mouth of the cave, the Rebels drilled holes in the stone, planted their charges, then backed off and blew it. When the dust had cleared, tons of rocks covered the cave entrance.

"I hope it takes you a long time to die, you creeps!" Jersey said, then turned her back to the cave.

The Rebels did not know it at that time, but they were about to confront a force that they would come to hate even more than the Believers. Although none of them would have thought that possible at the moment.

Back in the mid-1980s, years before the Great War ravaged the earth, many terrorist groups from nearly every country in the world learned of the impending war and sought refuge in several South American countries. They not only brought their blood-drenched ideas with them, but they also brought hundreds of followers. Only a handful of the terrorists actually were of German origin. They were Palestinian, Japanese, Irish, Italian, South American, South African. They came from France, Spain, Mexico, Bulgaria, England, Holland, and from countries all around the globe. Their organizations bore such names as the Military Sports Group (Wehrsportgruppe), Baader-Meinhof, Al Fatah, Black September, the NAP, Armata Rossa, Red Help Group, June 2nd Movement, Holger Heins Commando (which originally recruited its members from a nuthouse at Heidelberg), People's Socialist Army. Other groups were the Red Army (Sekigun), known as the JRA, the Popular Front for the Liberation of Palestine (PFLP), As-sa'Iqa (the Thunderbolt), the DFLP, the PFLP-GC, the NAYLP (a Palestinian youth group whose members were now grown men and women), Black June. In South America, these dangerous but nutty fruitcakes and yoyo brains were embraced by the Ejercito Revolucionario Del Pueblo, the Montoneros, the Junta de Coordination Revolucionaria (JCR)—other members of the JCR were Bolivia's National Liberation Army (ELN), Chile's Movement of the Revolutionary Left (MIR), Paraguay's National Liberation Front (Frepalina), and Uruguay's Tupamaros (MLN). Others included the French Front De Liberation De La Bretagne—Armee Revolutionnaire Bretonne (FLB-ARB). From Holland, the Republik Malaku Selatan. From Spain, the Group De Resistencia Antifascista Primo De Octubre (GRAPO). From Puerto Rico, the Fuerzas Armadas De La Liberaction Nacional—(FALN). From Italy, the Muclei Armati Rivoluzionari—Armed Revolutionary Nuclei (NAR). Brigate Rosse—Red Brigades. From Turkey, the Turkish Peoples Liberation Army (TPLA). And hundreds of other small terrorist groups from all over the world that came together and combined into thousands, and then more thousands after they finished their recruiting drives, promising everything under the sun and more to a people who never had anything to begin with. They were anarchist, antibourgeois (so they claimed), revolutionary, and especially anti-American and most especially anti-Ben Raines and the Rebels.

Their leader was a South American self-styled

general with the strange name of Jesus Dieguez Mendoza Hoffman. His grandfather had come to South America just after the end of the Second World War and stayed.

Jesus Hoffman was about to cause Ben more trouble than Ben had ever before experienced in all his years of warfare.

And that was saying a mouthful.

Seven

Ben and his battalion walked slowly down the mountain toward the lushness that lay below them. They were, to a person, tired, stinking of sweat and the clinging odor of creepies, and disgusted with the day's events. To a person they wanted a bath and fresh clothing, and after a time, a hot meal. They had found yet another of the Believers' breeding farms, the force-fed human food source all dead, lying in bloated mounds in the camp. They had been lined up and shot, men, women, and children.

The Rebels had found the caves where the creepies had taken refuge and were particularly vicious in dealing with them, forcing them out of the tunnels with tear gas and shooting them as they exited the cave. The Rebels talked among themselves about leaving many badly wounded creepies behind that day, considering leaving them behind to die slowly. In the end they did not. They put them out of their misery and dumped them back into the caves, forever sealing them in the dank darkness.

The Rebels—to a person—were beginning to hate this lovely island. They hated the creepies, hated what they were forced to do, and longed for the day they could leave and put it all behind them.

But they had many more long and brutal days ahead of them before that could happen. The Rebels had cleared all the towns and villages. They had secured all the roads and cleaned up many of the historical sites. The major airports were secure and receiving traffic. And daily the Rebels pulled on their boots and slogged out to kill creepies.

"They're getting harder and harder to find," Ben said, wearily pulling off his boots and looking at his big toe sticking out through a hole in his sock. "They're deeper now than they've ever been."

Dan Gray was with him in his CP, on the northwest side of the Mauna Kea Forest Reserve. The two battalions had searched all that day and had not found one cave.

"Analysis says that of the original number, less than ten percent of the creepies are still alive on this island," Dan said.

"Analysis is sitting on their asses over on Maui, eating hot food daily and sleeping between clean sheets every night," Ben replied. "They do a valuable and much-needed job, but sometimes I think they're out of touch with reality."

A guard stuck her head inside the small building. "Buddy and Rebet coming up, sir."

The two batt comms entered, shook hands, and poured coffee. Dan was having tea. "Our sectors are clean," Rebet said, sitting down wearily. "West reports nothing in the past three days."

"I spoke with Danjou this afternoon," Buddy said. "He is convinced his sector is sterile."

Ben nodded his head in agreement. "So is Georgi. Personally, I am not so sure. But if we haven't killed them all, we've knocked them down to the point where they pose no real threat. Tomorrow we'll start going over this island to make damn sure there are no survivors we've missed. Since the creeps eat only human flesh, if we leave them nothing to munch on, it's a good bet they'll start on each other. If the leaders will agree to keep this island unpopulated for a couple of years, the creepie problem will, or should, solve itself." Ben stood up and poured fresh coffee. "I want daily head counts of all personnel. Make damn sure no Rebel falls into hungry hands. I don't want to see anyone walking alone. It's too dangerous. If we do this right, we can be out of here in a week; no more than ten days."

"I would like to return here someday," Dan said softly. "Once the memories have faded. It is a beautiful place."

The Rebels began their slow search of the island, on foot and from the air. They found one more cave during that ten-day time and sealed it. No survivors were found on the island. It was void of human life.

Ben ordered the big island evacuated. No one was sorry to put it behind.

Back on Maui, Ben began preparations for the invasion of the two remaining islands, Oahu and Kauai. The only other island, Niihau, the 'Forbidden Island,' as some called it, was surely occupied by outlaws and thugs, but because of its size, it could be easily taken and would be the last one the Rebels struck.

And Therm had compiled a great deal of additional data on the divisions coming up from South America. All of it spelled out very bad news.

"The commanding general of the army is a man called Jesus Dieguez Mendoza Hoffman. Approximately thirty-five years old. The grandson of a very famous, or infamous, Nazi of World War Two fame. Since the army is made up of people of all nationalities, no one is quite sure what their ideologies might be. We do know this: They hate America and they despise you and the Rebels, Ben. They are goose-stepping, heil-Hitler types, made up of terrorist groups from all over the world. They are well-trained, well-armed, and they are fanatical in their desire to destroy what is left of the United States."

Ben shook his head. "How far up are they?"

Therm smiled. "They're bogged down in Paraguay, having a hell of a time moving all that equipment. Word we're receiving is that the Indians and the resistance groups down there are really giving them a hard time."

"I hope every one of those goose-stepping bastards comes down with malaria and dies!"

Therm was still laughing as he left the CP. Ben returned to his maps.

"We're next," Books told the roomful of gang leaders. No one from Kauai was in attendance, for crossing the channel was just too dangerous with Ike and his PT boats prowling around. "The Rebels wiped out the Night People on the big island. I don't think the Rebels lost a person."

Crazy Mac MacKenzie was muttering to himself. If anything, he had gotten crazier since Ben and his Rebels started knocking on the door.

Big Jess looked at him. "Mac, if you don't shut that stupid mouth of yours, I'm gonna slap it off."

Mac stopped mumbling and stared at Jess. "You'll

die when you try," he warned.

"Knock it off!" Books said. "What we don't need is for us to start fighting among ourselves. Believe me, there'll be plenty of fighting to go around when the Rebels get here."

"Are we going to just let them land on the islands, Books?" Polly Polyanna asked.

"I don't see that we have a choice in the matter. Now here is the plan: Just as soon as we know the ships are on the way, we break up into small groups and take to the brush and the villages. Slick, are the booby traps ready to go?"

"They're in place." He grinned. "And they're nasty ones, too."

"Everybody know where they're to go and you've all your radios, food, ammo, and other gear set to grab and run?"

"All set, Books," Jerry James rumbled out of his beard. "We'll give them damn Rebels something to think about, for a ironclad fact."

"I guess all we can do now is wait."

"To die," Susie Loo said softly.

"I'd rather go down with a gun in my hand killin' them damn law-and-order bastards than dangle from the end of a rope with a broke neck. Or slow-strangle like I've seen others do," Big Jess said.

"For a fact," a punk called Spit said. "I wanna fuck me one of them Rebel bitches 'fore this is all over. Pass her around to the boys for a real fun gang bang. Listen to her squall when we turn her over. Just like we used to do back in L.A." His face darkened with anger. "Before that goddamn Ben Raines destroyed it."

Bobby was looking out the window at the still-smoking remains of Honolulu. The bombardment from the ships had really done a number on the city. From Kamehameha Highway all the way over to Diamond Head, the Rebels had blown it all to shit. There were a lot of buildings still standing, but one hell of a lot more were gone to rubble.

"Have you talked to John Dodge, Books?" Polly asked.

"Yeah. John and his boys are going to try to block the landing. But they're making a bad mistake by doing so. I don't think it will take them long to see that. But if they wait too long, it'll be all over for them."

"They didn't touch Pearl Harbor," Bobby said, more to himself than to the others. But all heads turned toward him. "That's where they're going to off-load their tanks and other heavy stuff. Bet on it."

"I think you're right, Bobby," Books said. "Do you have a plan to thwart that?"

"No," Bobby said. "None at all."

"You sure haven't been yourself here of late, Bobby," Susie said. "What's the matter with you, your old lady cut you off or something?"

Bobby smiled. "No. Actually, we're getting along better than ever before. Our situation sort of reminds me of an old, old movie I saw one time. It was called . . . *On the Beach.*"

"Yes," Books said. "You're right, Bobby. It was taken from the Nevil Shute book by the same name. Yes. 'In this last of meeting places/We grope together/And avoid speech/Gathered on this beach of the tumid river . . . /This is the way the world ends/This is the way the world ends/This is the way the world ends/Not with a bang but a whimper.'"

"That's beautiful, Books," Polly said. "Brings

85

tears to my eyes. Did you write that?"

"No," Books said with a smile. "That was penned by T. S. Eliot."

"I ain't goin' out with no fuckin' whimper," Mac snarled. "I aim to kill me a whole bunch of Rebels 'fore I go down."

"That's the spirit, boys and girls!" Books said. "Semper Fi and all that Marine Corps bullshit. We shall not flag or fail. We shall go on to the end. We shall defend our island, whatever the cost may be. We shall fight on the beaches, we shall fight on the landing grounds. We shall fight in the hills; we shall never surrender."

"You sure have a way with words, Books," Susie said. "Did you just make that up?"

"Actually, no. Winston Churchill said that."

"Who the hell is he?" Vic asked.

Ben walked the long lines of Rebels standing in loose formation. The Rebels did not stress skills in standing at attention, saluting, marching, or any of that other b.s. that armies have been known to emphasize over the long and boring years. Ben was fond of quoting Jean Larte 'Guy's comments concerning armies: 'I'd like to have two armies: one for display with lovely guns, tanks, little soldiers, staffs, distinguished and doddering generals, and dear little regimental officers who would be deeply concerned over their general's bowel movements or their colonel's piles: an army that would be shown for a modest fee on every fairground in the country. 'The other would be the real one, composed entirely of young enthusiasts in camouflage uniforms, who would not be put on display but from whom impossible efforts would be demanded and to whom all sorts of tricks would be taught. That's the army in which I should like to fight.'

That's the army that Ben Raines had put together and called the Rebels. That's the army that he stood in front of on this morning before the invasion.

The four new battalions were there, but of the four, only Jim Peters's Fourteen Battalion would take part in the invasion. Eleven, Twelve, and Thirteen were still in training, but getting close to receiving the coveted black beret of the Rebels and with far fewer dropouts that any training officer originally anticipated.

Ben stood in front of over ten thousand Rebels, a microphone in his hand. "We've got big trouble brewing back on the mainland, people. An army five to ten times our size is on the move up from South America, and their objective is to destroy what is left of the United States, and to wipe from the face of the earth every trace of the Rebel army.

"We're going to take the remaining islands, and we're going to do it quickly but carefully. Then we're going to head back to the mainland and get set for the biggest battle we've ever experienced."

As he spoke, although the majority of the gathered Rebels did not know it, Ike's SEALs and other special-ops personnel were already on the islands of Oahu and Kauai, clearing paths through the maze of booby traps and getting ready to raise a little hell of their own come the night.

"We've taken damn few losses thus far," Ben said. "So let's keep it that way. You're too valuable to fall under the guns of worthless street punks and assorted dickheads. And on that subject, the first person I see without helmet and body armor is going to get an ass-chewing they'll not soon forget.

"Spend the rest of this day going over your equipment and relaxing. We start moving out just after midnight. Good luck and God bless you all. You're the bravest men and women I have ever had the pleasure of serving with. That's all."

Eight

Ships and boats of all sizes began moving out, all heavily loaded with troops and equipment. Ben was taking his One Battalion and Three, Four, Five, and Six Battalions onto the island of Oahu. Ike was taking his Two Battalion, and Seven, Eight, Nine, Ten, and Fourteen Battalions against the island of Kauai. SEALs and other special-ops people were waiting at ports on both islands. As soon as the first few Rebels and equipment were ashore, the special-ops people would move inland and start their own private little wars against the defenders. For the first few days, they would be the forward eyes and ears of the Rebel army.

Ben knew that this assault would be a mean and nasty little war, but nothing like what faced them in the months ahead once they reached the shores of America.

He had no doubts about the Rebels' ability to win the conflicts that faced them, but he also knew that their losses against the divisions of Hoffman would be enormous. Every Rebel man, woman, and child would have to do his or her part if the advancing hordes were to be stopped.

"Thinking about the mainland, General?" Jersey broke into Ben's thoughts.

"Yes, Jersey. I am."

"Going to be a real bastard, isn't it?"

"Yes. And there is no way in hell we're going to be able to stop them at the borders. Not with the size of that army. We just don't have the personnel to plug up all the holes."

"What do they have against us and the way of life in America? Or the way it used to be?"

"The United States was the most giving country in the world, Jersey. For years we gave and gave and gave, of time and effort and billions of dollars, and the majority of the world's countries hated us for it."

"That doesn't make any sense, General."

"It does when you consider that outside of the big and powerful industrial countries, the rest of the world was largely ignorant and poverty-stricken and the citizens very easily manipulated. No matter what we did, those people wanted more from us. It reached the point where we just couldn't give any more.

We gave money to other countries when we should have been using that money to help our own citizens. It reached the point where the politicians were not paying any attention at all to the people who put them in office. Ah, it's a long and complicated story, Jersey. We had many problems at home that should have been addressed but were not. The United States became the object of hatred from a lot of countries we had poured money into. But it's all moot, now, Jersey."

His other team members had gathered around,

listening. They were all young and never tired of hearing about the old days, as they called the prewar time, a peaceful time that they had too few memories of.

Cooper said, "I recall a saying, maybe from some member of my family, I don't know, something about you could be too good to people. That if you went over a line, the more you gave, the more they expected you to give."

"That's right, Coop," Ben said. "And America gave until she busted herself. If ever a war came at a right time, the Great War did. Our great nannies in Washington had spent us into bankruptcy, trying to be all things to all people, all the time. That's impossible. It can't be done."

"General," Corrie said, pointing at a great land-mass visible under the clear and starry skies. "That's Oahu, right?"

"That's it."

"The first thing Rebels do, when they move into an area, is get the lights back on, the plumbing working, and the sewer system and water-management facilities operational. These punk dipshits can't even get the electricity working, for Christ sake!"

Ben laughed and laughed at her, and the others joined in. Finally Corrie got caught up in it and the laughter felt good. "You're right, Corrie," Ben said, wiping his eyes with a handkerchief. "That's why they're punks and dipshits. But back when the United States was functioning, more or less, the liberals, who seemed to run the news departments of every TV network and every newspaper and maga-zine in the nation, would have said something like this about those thugs on that island in front of us: 'Because all those poor criminals were socially, economically, and physically and mentally abused as children, they can't be expected to maintain the same high standards as those of us who were more fortunate.' Or some such crap from the mouth as that."

"You're putting us on, right, General?" a young Rebel from Dan's battalion who had joined the group asked.

"Oh, no, son. Not at all. You see, back in the 1960s and '70s and part of the '80s, the thinking of liberals was this: If you parked your car in your own driveway and left the keys in it, and it got stolen, it was your fault. Not the fault of the thief."

"Well . . . that's the dumbest damn thing I ever heard of!" the young Three Battalion Rebel said. "Who would believe something that stupid?"

"Not anybody with their head on straight," Ben replied. "But the country was run by liberals, and their ideology was just what their name implied. Liberal. Very soft toward all crime and all criminals, and very generous with the taxpayer's money toward any social program—whether it worked or not. But all the problems of the United States cannot be laid at the liberals' doorsteps. The conservatives in Congress did their best to throw away the taxpayer's money, too. Expensive military boondoggles that didn't work, pork-barrel projects that weren't needed and only benefited those who lived in whatever district or state got the fat. The blame cannot be equally shared between the old liberals and conservatives of the past, but it damn sure can be shared." He looked at Jersey. "For instance, Jersey, if you got pregnant and wanted an abortion, there were those who were trying with all their might to stop a woman from doing that."

"What damn business is that of anybody except the woman?" Jersey flared.

"It isn't anybody else's business. But so-called religious zealots and a lot of conservatives were working very hard to stop all abortions."

"It seems to me," Corrie said, "that if back in the old days, children were going hungry and being neglected and being birthed by women who, for whatever reason, didn't want them and, from past experience by health workers, couldn't or wouldn't care for them, then abortion would be the humane thing, right?"

Ben chuckled as the ship began to slow. They would start a slow circling and the troops would begin to disembark an hour before dawn. "That's the logical way to look at it, Corrie. That's the way we, as Rebels, look at the issue. But back in the 1960s, '70s, and '80s, there was very little logic being applied to a whole lot of topics in America. Shoot a man who was trying to burgle your home, and odds were very good that the homeowner would be booked, jailed, tried, and put in prison, or at best, if he was lucky, he'd be sued by the burglar, or the burglar's family . . . and the homeowner would lose. That's logic applied by liberals."

"That system sucks!" Jersey said.

"You're right," Ben agreed. "And a great many taxpayers—probably the majority—agreed with your assessment, but the courts and the Congress just turned their asses to them and ignored their pleas."

The young Rebel from Three Battalion said, "You mean, sir, that if I had lived back in the old days, and I came home and found a bunch of punks looting my house and shot some of them, I might be put in prison?"

"That's right. Wonderful system we had back then."

"Will it ever return to that?"

"Not if we're careful," Ben said. He looked at the island of Oahu, a huge darkened blob in the night. "Very careful," he added.

Ike stood by the railing as the ship turned broadside to the island of Kauai. His thoughts were on the upcoming conflict with the thugs and slavers on the island, but a part of his mind was on the battle that faced the Rebels back on the mainland. The middle-aged warrior felt that the forces of Jesus Hoffman could be beaten, but at what cost to the Rebels? And what if there was yet another force waiting in the wings, ready to launch an attack against America while the Rebels were battered and bloody after doing battle with Hoffman? That was something that he and Ben and the other batt comms had discussed. Afterward, Ben had asked that Cecil, back at Base Camp One, increase the size of his communications staff and more closely monitor the airwaves for any sign of hostile traffic.

For the moment, that was all any of them could do.

Ike shook his head, clearing it of all thoughts except the battle at hand. He turned to an aide. "What's the latest from my SEALs and the other special-op people on shore?"

"General Raines is not going to have any trouble when he lands. The punks on Oahu have pulled back and appear to have broken up into small groups. We're going to have a fight of it on Kauai."

"We'll bust through without a lot of problems. Ben's going to have a real fight on Oahu . . . right from the git-go. The commander over there is smarter than this bunch we're facing. He's going to make Ben split his people up into small teams and come after him. Once we establish firm beachheads along the highway, the punks will begin to fall back into the interior and then they'll probably pull the same thing on us that Ben is facing." He checked the luminous hands of his diver's watch. "Get the people ready to board landing craft. We're close to jump-off time."

Ike took the phone set from his operator's backpack and cued Ben. "Eagle, this is Shark. We are in position."

"That is affirmative, Shark," Ben replied. "You ready to go make bang-bang with the bad guys?"

Ike smiled in the night. "You watch your butt, Eagle. That's a smart one you're facing on Oahu."

"He's not too smart, Shark. He's facing us, isn't he?"

Ike laughed. "Launching boats, Eagle."

"Talk to you in a few hours. Eagle out." Ben turned to Corrie. "All troops into landing craft. Let's go, gang."

When John Dodge saw what was coming at him out of the night, all along the southern coast of Kauai, he quickly revised his plans and ordered his people back. If he'd been half as smart as he thought he was, he would have ordered bridges to be blown and would have slowed Ike's advance to a crawl and severely hampered Ike's tanks. But John didn't think about that. He took a long look at the landing craft filled with Rebels, all heading his way, and panicked.

At Pearl, SEALs and special-ops personnel secured the old harbor without having to fire a shot. Moments after they radioed the all-clear signal, hundreds of Rebels stormed ashore, with Ben and his team leading the way.

"Any problems?" Ben asked a burly SEAL.

"Nary a shot fired, General. You're going to hit some booby traps further on, but the harbor is all clear."

"You boys take off and do your thing," Ben told.

The SEAL grinned in the darkness of predawn. "We'll go have some fun now, General. It's been boring so far."

"Get out of here," Ben said with a laugh.

All the military bases around Pearl had been looted and picked over so many times that nothing of value had been left. And the Rebels met no resistance as they worked their way around Pearl Harbor. They secured Hickam AFB and Honolulu International Airport without firing a shot. They saw no sign of the enemy. By seven o'clock in the morning, ships were off-loading equipment and not one shot had been fired.

"Ike's meeting stiff resistance, sir," Corrie reported. "But he's got a toehold and gradually pushing the punks back."

"What about our forward people?"

"SEALs reporting Honolulu is one dead damn place, sir. They're rounding up what few survivors are left in the city and bringing them here. Doctor Chase is setting up at Hickam and is ready to receive."

"Has my wagon been off-loaded?"

"That's ten-four."

"Let's go visit Honolulu."

With two Dusters ahead of him, and a company of Rebels behind him, Ben set off to see what was left of Honolulu, staying south of H1.

The days of bombardment from the guns offshore had devastated the city. The fires which had gone unchecked had finished it. Everything south of the interstate was tangled rubble and burned-out buildings. Ben rode over as far as the Honolulu Zoo, and that sight made him so mad his team thought he was having a heart attack. Even after all these years, it was obvious that the poor animals had been left without water or food and had died horribly. A citizen confirmed it.

It was very fortunate for the gang leaders and their followers that Ben did not run up on any of them the day he visited the zoo. Had he done so, judgment would have been very swift and very final.

"You got to see this, General," one of Gray's scouts radioed. "We're just south of the interstate on Kapiolani. Where some old construction work was started and never finished."

The Scout pointed to a mass grave, the earth so shallowly scooped out, already hands and arms and legs were sticking out of the ground due to the recent rains.

A local the scouts had found explained. "The outlaws didn't want us running around after they split up into small groups. So they rounded up all the slaves they could find and killed them."

"Jesus!" Cooper said.

"They didn't bury them for several days. It was . . . not a pretty sight."

"Get some earthmoving equipment in here and cover these people," Ben said. He turned to the local. "Where are the gangs of outlaws?"

"They scattered all over the island, General. In groups of five and six. They're in the pineapple fields and the brush and the mountains. They'll be hard to dig out."

"We'll dig them out," Ben assured the old man. "How many of you escaped the carnage?"

The man smiled. "More than you might think. The outlaws killed maybe . . . oh, two or three thousand. But most of us had long since taken to the hills and the brush. This morning, when we saw the thugs leaving, many of us came back, to fight alongside you and your Rebels. I have a weapon that I hid when the outlaws came." He held up an old double-barreled shotgun with a broken stock. It had been recently taped back together. "I know many of the faces of the outlaws, and I intend to kill every one I see." He said that defiantly, and Ben knew there were probably many others just like the man.

"You certainly have my permission to do just that," Ben told him. "But for now, why don't you gather up all the survivors you can find and come with us to the hospital for a checkup and some hot food?"

The old man had whip marks all over his bare arms. Scars on top of scars. Ben had a idea that Doctor Chase was going to go right through the ceiling when he took a look at the old man's back.

"That's very kind of you, General. Thank you."

"My pleasure to be able to do so, sir." Ben waved at a Rebel and the old man was led away.

"It is mostly the old people who are left around here," the old man told the young cammie-clad Rebel. "It was mostly the young ones the thugs killed. I guess they thought we were too old to present any danger to them."

Ben was grim-faced as he checked his M-14 and said, "Seeing how this scum mistreated old people just makes the job a lot easier."

"And the animals," Beth said, her voice menacingly low. Beth was an animal-lover who had murder in her heart for anyone who mistreated an animal.

Jersey smiled. "Kick-ass time!"

Nine

Ben made no moves until all his equipment was off-loaded and ready to roll. On the island of Kauai, Ike had established a firm toehold on several docking areas and was doing the same as Ben. As Ike had predicted, once John Dodge actually saw what he was facing, he broke his people up into small groups and they headed for the countryside.

During the lull, Ben and Ike had shifted people around, putting them back on ships and landing them all over the island, off-loading tanks and heavy artillery whenever possible. The second phase of the invasion was about to begin and it was going to be done very efficiently, accomplished as quickly as possible, and conducted ruthlessly.

The outlaws huddled in small groups and waited to die.

Those outlaws who did not leave the immediate area of the city soon found out how deeply—although not for very long—the hatred for them ran among those they had enslaved.

As the Rebels began their push out of the ruined city, scouts began discovering the mutilated bodies of outlaws. Some had been shot, but most had been hacked to death with machetes and axes. The Rebels viewed the carnage impassively and moved on. Their feeling was that the outlaws got exactly what had been coming to them. The Rebels also noted that all of the weapons and ammo had been removed from the bodies. Never again would the people of these islands be enslaved. They were rearmed, and this time they would remain armed, and the blithering and blathering of politicians be damned.

The Rebels were quietly amused at how quickly the islanders were adopting the Rebel philosophy. Any future politician who suggested any type of gun control would more than likely be shot before the words left his or her mouth.

The slow flushing out of the outlaws and thugs and self-proclaimed pirates began, and it was classic textbook search-and-destroy on the part of the Rebels. The cat-and-mouse game played out to the death in some of the most beautiful country in all the world.

Only a few miles outside the city proper, Ben and his team found themselves cut off and coming under hard fire.

"They're all around us," Cooper said, after crawling to Ben's side. "Nearest friendlies are half a klick away and pinned down just like us."

"We're in a good position," Ben replied. "The bogeys will have to cross that little clearing to get to us and I don't think they want to try that. Just sit tight. What's all that traffic about, Corrie?"

"B company. They were a little concerned about us. I anticipated your reply and told them that we

101

could handle it."

Ben smiled and looked around at his team and the half-dozen other Rebels who were trapped with them in the gully. "Hang tight, people. They'll lose patience before long and do something stupid. They always do."

"Come on out and get us!" The shouted challenge was hurled at the Rebels from out of thick brush only a scant fifty yards away. "Come on, you bastards!"

"And bitches," Jersey muttered. "Don't forget us, you worthless pricks."

Ben chuckled. Jersey was a mean, vicious little fighter who had about as much back-up in her as an angered wolverine. Jersey and the other women in the Rebel army had long put to rest the question of whether women could hold their own alongside men in combat. Not every woman was cut out for combat, but then, neither was every man.

The outlaws began firing wildly, the slugs hitting only air and the brush behind the Rebels' position.

"Idiots," Jersey muttered.

"Hold your fire," Ben said to Cooper, over the rattle of automatic weapons fire. "Pass the word, Coop. Hold your fire. They're getting nervous."

The word passed, Corrie said, "B company wants to know if you want them to drop in some mortars, General?"

"No. Save them. That pack of crud over there will flush themselves in a few minutes. They're getting antsy."

"Big brave boys and girls," the sneering words came across the clearing. "You're like every pig I ever met. All mouth and no guts."

Ben looked around and caught Jersey's eyes. She smiled at him and winked. Like many of the Rebels,

102

Jersey had played this game so many times she had lost count. If the outlaws really felt they could anger a Rebel into doing something foolish, they were dumber than Ben originally thought.

"Why don't you surrender?" Jersey raised her voice, taunting the crud. "We'll give you a hot meal and a cup of coffee before we shoot you."

"You bitch!" a man shouted. "I get my hands on you, I'll show you the only thing you're good for."

Jersey laughed at him. "Wrong. Pus-brains and needle-dicks have never appealed to me."

The outlaw cursed her.

Jersey didn't let up. Raising her voice, she said, "Hey, Alice," she yelled to another Rebel. "Can you imagine bedding down with that crud? Christ, I can smell them from here. I bet they haven't taken a bath in weeks."

The outlaw's cussing became wilder.

"Yeah," Alice said, loud enough for the outlaws to hear. "They probably use their fingers to wipe their butts."

"And then eat with the same fingers," Corrie shouted.

"Yeah," Beth added her opinion. "Those types are the reason you see signs in bathrooms urging people to wash their hands after using the toilet."

Ben lay on the sloping ground of the gully and smiled, letting the women have their fun with the crud. And then Jersey and the others really started letting the outlaws have it. It got downright crude when the Rebel women began loudly referring to them as a pack of pus-gutted, unwashed, ignorant, needle-dicked bug fuckers.

Corrie, lying beside Ben, looked at him and shook

103

his head. "They won't take much more of that," he said.

"You damn whores!" the same outlaw screamed. "Stand up and I'll fight you like a man."

The women laughed and jeered at that.

"Does that idiot realize what he just said?" Cooper questioned.

"I doubt it," Ben said. "He's probably too scared to think straight." Ben raised his voice just a bit. "Let's get this over with, Jersey. They're not going to rush us and time's a-wasting."

"I've done everything I know to do to make them mad," Jersey said.

"I ought to put you ladies over my knee and give you a good spanking for all that bad language," Ben told them.

"Promises, promises," Alice called with a laugh.

"Take your team and work around," Ben told a squad leader. "Flush them out with grenades and we'll take it from there. Corrie, advise B company we'll have people working between positions. Let's don't shoot our own people."

It was an easy shoot after that. What the grenades didn't do, Ben and the others did. They chopped the outlaws up like so much liver. Ben stood for a moment with his team, looking over the slaughter site. Ten dead, two badly wounded.

One of the wounded looked up at Jersey. "You that bad-talkin' bitch?" he gasped.

"One of them," she told him coldly.

"You one hell of a fighter, for sure," he managed to push the words out of his mouth. Then his head lolled to one side and he closed his eyes.

Another team of Rebels joined Ben. Because they had left the city behind them, and had moved into rough country, this team was armed with shotguns, the barrels sawed down to twenty inches. The shotguns were loaded with three-inch magnum #00 buckshot and usually made a terrible mess out of a human body.

"We've still got daylight," Ben said. "Let's go."

They hadn't advanced a quarter of a mile before being forced into and around an old house by intense fire coming from across the road.

"Get used to it," Ben said, worming his way to a shattered window. "This is the way it's going to be until we clear these islands. How badly spread out are we, Corrie?"

"We sure aren't bunched up," she replied.

"Put some rifle grenades into that building directly across from us. Let's see what happens."

The roof collapsed, pinning those outlaws inside.

"Finish it," Ben ordered.

It was unconventional and many would say inhumane. But the Rebels had learned over the long bloody years that hard-core criminals either could not or would not be rehabilitated. They poured lead and fired grenades into the ruined structure and moved on. If there were wounded under all the mess, they could damn well stay there. On these remaining islands, Ben had sent out the word: fight us, and you die.

The Rebel battalions on the island of Oahu were working clockwise around the island. Striganov was on Highway 930, and after securing and clearing Dillingham AFB he moved on toward Haleiwa on Highway 83. Dan was on the north part of the island, and after securing Kawela was working south on 83. West had put ashore just north of Kaneohe and was working south, while Rebet and his battalion had landed on the extreme eastern tip of the island and were working toward the ruins of Honolulu. As the major highways looping the island, and the villages and towns on them were cleared, the Rebels would then begin slowly tightening the noose, working inland toward the Koolau Range.

On Kauai, Ike and those battalions under his command were following suit, first clearing the coastline highways, and then moving inland.

For all the Rebels, it was slow and dangerous work. The outlaws had booby traps all over the place and had laid out antipersonnel mines that had to be cleared before any advance. Each day, a thousand acts of courage above and beyond the call of duty were performed by Rebels. No medals were given out, no bands played, and there were no parades held in their honor. It was just something they all knew had to be done, and they did it.

On both islands, locals were resurfacing and being armed and used as scouts and trackers by the Rebels, and no outlaw wanted to fall into the hands of a local. Those that did were not treated well at all.

Many of the outlaws, now seeing the writing on the wall, and knowing there was no way they were going to stop the advance of the Rebel army, wanted to surrender and let due process take its course. They assumed that since civilized behavior appeared certain to replace anarchy and lawlessness, they could surrender and they would be given lengthy trials, with long-winded lawyers and appeals and all that.

Wrong.

A group of men approached Ben at breakfast one clear and glorious morning and requested a meeting with him.

"We are attorneys, sir," one said.

106

"So?" Ben asked, spreading jam on a piece of toast.

"I was with the local ACLU chapter," another said.

"Don't spoil my breakfast," Ben warned him.

"We were wondering," another said. "When—"

"It won't," Ben said, sugaring his coffee.

"You did not allow me to finish, General."

"That is certainly my plan," Ben replied without looking up.

Dan walked in, carrying a plate of food in one hand and a cup of tea in the other. "What's all this?" the Englishman asked, sitting down.

"Lawyers," Ben told him.

"Before breakfast?" Dan questioned. "How ghastly."

"I don't like you," one attorney said to him.

"I cannot possibly begin to tell you how deeply affected I am at that remark. Since I am basically a very sensitive fellow, my psyche has been bruised sorely."

"You're English?"

"How astute you are. What could have possibly given that away?"

"Get out of here," Ben told the lawyers.

"These islands have been in the grips of lawlessness for a decade, sir," another attorney said.

"The man is so sagacious it boggles the mind," Dan said, winking at Ben. "Don't you agree?"

"Oh, quite." Ben lifted his eyes and stared at the group of men. "There may come a time when people like you are needed. I hope not, but it's a possibility. Albeit not one I'm looking forward to. But for now you are not needed. We ordered the outlaws on these islands to surrender. They chose to ignore that order. Now, we might take a few prisoners. But if we do, they will not be represented in any way familiar to you people. We don't care what their childhood was like. We don't care whether the devil made them do it, or if their parents beat them, or if they weren't allowed to play first team or if their neighbors complained because they played music too loud or they were deprived of a certain brand of tennis shoes. Do I make myself clear?"

"Now, see here, General," the sixth and last lawyer spoke up. "We, all of us, have been subjected to a myriad of indignities since the hoodlums took over the islands. But for all that they have done, and many of them have done terrible things, they still have the right to a trial. I . . ."

Ben stood up at that. Ben was not a physically overpowering man. For his age he was in marvelous shape, but it was his eyes that made a wise man shut up. The lawyer showed uncommon good sense and closed his mouth.

"We took the best of the outlaws and are training them on another island right now," Ben told the group of barristers. "They will become part of the Rebel force. As for the scum left on Oahu and Kauai, the only trials they'll receive is from the muzzle of a gun. Now, before you go, let me warn you of this: After we have cleaned these islands of trash, and have returned to the mainland to meet the largest known army on the face of the earth, don't try to force a return back to your old type of law and order. The people that we have freed and will leave behind won't tolerate it. The days of legal mumbo-jumbo are gone forever. No back-room deals. No plea-bargaining. No jailing or suing a citizen for using lethal force to protect what is his or hers. You all know how we operate. I don't have to explain it to you. Or I

108

shouldn't have to. Now get the hell out of here and let me finish my breakfast in peace."

Whatever reception the attorneys were expecting from Ben, this certainly wasn't it. They left in a huff.

"Twits," Dan said, spreading fresh-put-up jam on a piece of bread.

Ben sat down and began eating his breakfast. "They must be brainwashed in law school. That's all I can figure out. Either that, or they are actually much more decent and fair-minded men than I."

Dan was coughing and choking on his toast, his eyes bugging out in astonishment at Ben's remark, when Jersey, Beth, Corrie, and Cooper came running in to see what all the commotion was about.

Ten

Ben stood with his team on the side of the highway, looking up at a long row of homes perched on a mountainside. "Two- or three-million-dollar-plus houses," he said. "Back when the world was whole, the people who lived in those mansions had servants, security, the very best of everything . . . or so they thought."

"What do you mean by that last bit, General?" he was asked by a young woman.

"They were prisoners, trapped by their own wealth. They lived in fear of extortionists, kidnappers, terrorists, and burglars. They couldn't move without security. And you can bet on this, too: when the end came, their money couldn't save their lives or make their lives any safer . . . because it was worthless. Let's go check out those mansions."

"I can't believe the crud would be so stupid to hide out in something so obvious," a young Rebel recently assigned to Ben's A Company remarked.

"Wanna bet me a week at KP the homes are empty?" Ben asked with a smile.

"No, sir!" the young man was quick to reply. He was walking beside Ben; Cooper had parked the

110

wagon off the paved and curving drive of the first mansion.

Ahead of them, a scout suddenly raised his hand and made the *hit the dirt* movement. The Rebels scattered, jumping off the drive and into the bushes.

A dog barked, then another joined in. They came running down the drive, two dogs of so mixed a breed they were mutts. But they were happy, playing and jumping and barking and rolling and yelping as they came. Ben stood up and watched the dogs at play until they were out of sight. He looked at the embarrassed scout.

"Don't be embarrassed," Ben called. "They could have just as easily been bandits."

A rifle round slammed into the helmet of the scout and knocked him to the ground. The round was not of sufficient caliber to penetrate the much-improved-upon Kevlar helmet, but the scout would have one hell of a headache when he woke up.

"I'm glad I didn't take that bet," the young Rebel lying beside Ben muttered.

With precision movements, one squad of Rebels opened fire, covering medics who dashed into the drive and hauled the downed Rebel to the safety of the brush.

"He's okay," a medic called. "But he's gonna have a whopper of a headache."

"First squad come with me," Ben said. "Corrie, advise the company commander we are going around to the back of the first house. Do it and let's go."

Corrie bumped the CO and the team was off, first squad running behind them. Most of them were used to the general's antics and thought nothing of it, but some had just come in and were not yet accustomed to seeing the commanding general of the army taking such chances.

111

Flinging themselves down behind some huge flowering bushes at the rear of the house, one young Rebel said, "Jesus, the old man must be fifty at least and he's ahead of us!"

"Don't count the Eagle out of it yet," a sergeant told him. "A lot of folks have tangled hand-to-hand with him. I helped bury some of them."

"Been with him long?"

"Five, six years. I was a young punk outlaw when the Eagle jerked me up by the nape of the neck and saw something worth saving in me. I'd die for that man," the sergeant said, fierce loyalty behind his words.

From his position near the rear of the house, Ben leveled his M-14 and waited for a shot. It was not long in coming. One outlaw exposed a forearm and Ben sighted it in, gently squeezing the trigger. The big slug tore into the outlaw's elbow, shattering the bone and knocking the thug to the littered tile of the kitchen. He howled and thrashed on the floor, cussing the Rebels through his pain.

"Rifle grenades," Ben ordered those equipped with launchers.

All but one of the grenades bounced off the stone of the house and exploded on the patio. One 40mm grenade sailed right through a shattered window and made a mess of those in the kitchen.

Two Rebels ran through the brush behind the house, carrying a Big Thumper, a third Rebel just behind them, carrying the mount. The team quickly set up and began pumping 40mm grenades through the back windows of the mansion. Explosions rocked the earth as the grenades blew, the concussion inside the rear rooms of the house blowing out what remained of windows and doors and bringing with the debris various body parts of thugs and outlaws.

The Rebels on both sides of the mansion and those behind cover on the gently sloping front lawn waited for the thugs to exit the now-burning house.

The outlaws made no move to surrender, for they had seen what happened to others who did surrender . . . when the Rebels were in a charitable mood. The locals promptly took them out and hanged them.

The Rebels waited with the patience of the trained man-stalker for their prey to show themselves. They would. They always did.

The outlaws in the house made a screaming suicide charge out the front of the house. The luckiest got about twenty feet from the door before relentless Rebel fire from three sides cut them down.

"Secure the house and put out the fire in the back," Ben ordered, rolling to one side and pulling out his canteen, taking a long swig of the now-tepid water.

Gunfire came from the house near the end of the secluded row of fine homes overlooking the Pacific.

"Locals," Corrie said. "They're working this way. I'm in contact with them. One of the lawyers who talked to you this morning, General?"

Ben snapped his canteen cover closed and cut his eyes to her. "What about him?"

"He got in their way."

Ben didn't have to ask what happened to the man. He knew. He didn't particularly like mobs or vigilante movements, but in cases where the lawless have held sway over decent people for years, he sure as hell didn't blame the newly freed locals for their actions . . . or overreactions.

"We'll rest here," Ben said. "Let the locals handle the remainder of the homes along this strip. Set up a line running west to east in case any of the crud try to escape in our direction."

Corrie gave the orders and the Rebels repositioned and waited. Corrie listened to her headset for a moment and said, "Hang on." She looked at Ben. "The locals are asking if we have any rope to spare."

Ben's eyes were bleak. "Give it to them," he said. "It's their show."

Moments later, a half-dozen husky young men of Hawaiian descent yelled for permission to approach the Rebel position. They were armed with weapons of various calibers and makes and some of them were vintage. "Rearm them with the outlaws' weapons," Ben ordered. "And give them all the rope they need."

After they were rearmed and briefly instructed on the nomenclature of the weapons, one of the young men said, "We'll take care of the thugs along this stretch, General, if you have someplace else you'd like to go."

Ben smiled at him. "I hear you had some trouble with some of your own citizens today."

"The one who was shot always did think he was God's gift to humanity," the young man replied. "He was also a collaborator. For him, it was just a matter of time."

"We're not hanging them indiscriminately, General," another young man said. "We're sparing nearly as many as we hang. But they'll serve many years on forced construction and cleanup crews, working to put this island back in shape."

"That's as it should be," Ben replied. "Good luck to you all."

Ben and his people pulled out, leaving this battle to the locals. They glanced once at the swaying bodies hanging from limbs and lamp posts and moved on up the highway.

Ben and his battalion rolled into Makakilo City to find that the small town had been turned into a battleground between locals and small groups of thugs. Scouts halted the column a few hundred yards from the city limits and Ben walked forward to the checkpoint, his personal team strolling along with him.

"The locals control this end," the scout told him. "The assholes are in the downtown area and everywhere else. A bunch of small groups came together, I guess."

One of the locals came running up to the blocked road. He was carrying an old World War Two vintage .45 caliber spitter that the troops nicknamed a grease gun. "We've taken prisoners, General." Although Ben wore no insignia of any kind, he had a command bearing about him that only an idiot could miss. "Over twenty of them. We have no way to house them. First thing the thugs did when they invaded us was to burn down most of the jailhouses."

"We'll take them off your hands," Ben told the man. "You need some of my people in there with you?"

The man grinned. "You betcha, sir!"

"We're going to tear up your town when I send tanks in," Ben cautioned the man. "And I will send tanks in to spearhead."

"Hell with the town. It can be rebuilt."

Ben smiled at the man's exuberance. "Corrie, order third and fourth platoons in and send four Dusters in with them. First and second platoons stay here. Bring your prisoners to us, sir."

"Yes, sir!" The local ran off down the road, hollering that the Rebels were here.

"I guess after years of being shoved around and beaten and enslaved, I'd be jumping for joy myself," Beth remarked.

"If the damned United States Congress hadn't

115

taken the guns away from people," a older Rebel said, "I don't think much of this would have happened. Do you, General?"

"It would have happened in certain areas of the country," Ben said, taking time to hand roll a cigarette after looking around to see where the medics were. Lamar Chase had them spy on Ben, reporting back to the crusty old bastard how many cigarettes Ben smoked a day. There were times when Ben felt as though he were back in grade school, sneaking off behind the gym to take a few puffs. "It would not have happened in the rural areas of the nation. But the punks would have taken over the cities. And also the towns located in heavily industrialized states. The northeast and California especially. For in those areas were where the strictest gun-control laws were enacted. There is this, too: for years Americans were literally beaten over the head with public-service ads—written by nitwits—that one should never shoot simply to protect personal property. And a lot of people just can't pull the trigger on a human being." He watched as the prisoners were led up, being prodded along by rifles in the hands of Rebels. "Even worthless pieces of shit like that."

"What do you want done with these dickheads, General?" a woman asked.

"Who you callin' a dickhead, you goddamn whore?" the outlaw standing nearest to her asked.

She turned and put the toe of one jumpboot into his crotch—hard. The outlaw hit the pavement, puking and howling.

A burly Rebel leaned over, jerked him to his feet with one hand, and shook him like a naughty child. "You will learn to watch your mouth, punk."

"Take them to the medics. They'll draw blood and

run tests checking for communicable diseases. These bastards probably have everything, running the gamut from TB to AIDS."

"Son of a bitch!" one outlaw cussed Ben.

Ben waved it off. There was nothing they could call him that he had not been called a thousand times before, and by better men than these trash.

"Get them out of here. The first couple who check out clean, bring them to my CP. It'll be around here somewhere. We might as well bed down here. It'll be dark in a few hours."

"I ain't tellin' you a goddamn thing, Mister Hot Shit General!" an outlaw blustered.

Ben smiled and then chuckled. "That's what they all say, partner. That's what they all say."

Eleven

"Sit," Ben told the outlaw. He had been checked out and bathed and then fumigated for fleas and other bugs that sometimes inhabited the unbathed human body's exterior.

The outlaw had lost all of his bluster. The Rebels had learned what prison guards had known for centuries: order a man to strip naked—if he refuses, you take his clothing by force, and do it with no more effort than handling a little child—and that man loses much of his resistance. Then after an anal probe is done, and not done gently, he is tossed into a shower and scrubbed pink, all his hair is shaved from his head, and he is forced to stand holding his britches up with one hand—for he has no belt—you usually have a very passive person on your hands. Not always, but usually.

The outlaw sat.

"Were you fed?"

"Yes, sir. Good grub, too. I was hungry. I appreciate it. I reckon that's my last meal, ain't it?"

"I doubt it. I don't know what you've done, so we won't try you. The locals will."

"That's even worser."

"Now what do we do? Do you start telling me about your poor, miserable childhood and how your father beat you and all that happy crap?"

The outlaw chuckled. "I would if I thought it would do any good. But with you, I'd be wastin' your time and mine."

"Thank you. Sad stories always make me maudlin. I wouldn't want to weep at all your recollections of past misfortunes. What can you tell me that might help us in this campaign?"

"Probably nothin', to be honest about it. You know who runs the show?"

"Books Houseman."

"Right. We busted up into small groups at his orders. Most is still in small groups, probably. Don't make no difference no way. We're still gonna lose. They's somethin' about you people that just scares the shit outta lots of us, includin' me. They's somethin' about you people that none of us ain't never seen 'fore. I can't name it."

Ben knew. Total dedication. Discipline. The hardest training in the world. Experience. And the knowledge that what they were doing was right. "Go on."

"There ain't nothin' left to say that you don't already know. We ain't got no fancy weapons like you people. No tanks, no artillery, no bazookas, no helicopters, nothin' like you people. It's just a matter of chasin' us down and killin' us."

"Then why don't you people just give it up? Odds are, many of the locals are wearying of the hangings by now. So you would be imprisoned or work on a chain gang. You'd be alive."

The man smiled. "You don't understand the criminal mind, do you, General?"

"I am forced to say that I don't."

"Oh, you'd get a few who would change. I mean, really change. But not the majority. You'd get a lot who would say they would change. But they'd be lyin'. Once you people pulled out, most would be right back stealin' and killin' and rapin' and doin' everythin' they did 'fore you showed up."

"And you?" Ben asked, giving the man an opening, a way out.

"I don't know, General. I been on the wrong side of the law all my life. Years before the Great War come. My daddy was a farmer and my mamma a schoolteacher. They brought me up right—or tried to. It just didn't take. Some people are born bad. I really believe that."

"So do I." Ben studied the man for a moment. "I'm going to take a chance with you . . . what is your name?"

"John Morris."

"All right, John. I think you've been honest with me, so I'll reward that. You asked if I understood the criminal mind. Who does? So I'm going to send you back to let the shrinks pick your brain. But with a word of caution: you won't find Rebel shrinks to be anything like the ones you probably came in contact with before the Great War. Don't try to bullshit these people. They don't play those kinds of games. You can go."

John stood up, holding his deliberately ill-fitting pants up with one hand. "And if I'm honest with these people, General?"

"You might get another shot at making a new life."

"Or I just might get shot, period."

"That is always an option, John."

*　　*　　*

Ben stepped out of his CP long before dawn the next morning. Not a man who required a lot of sleep, Ben had slept his usual few hours and felt refreshed. He got a cup of coffee from the mess tent and walked back to his CP.

"Must have been real quiet last night," he said to the sentry.

"It was, sir. It didn't take the locals long to deal with the crud once they had the Dusters and the Rebels along."

Ben sat down in an old chair on the front porch and rolled a cigarette, then drank his huge mug of coffee—actually it was a beer stein—and smoked in the predawn hours. At 0430 his team was up and dressed and having coffee with him on the porch.

"This has been a picnic so far, General," Jersey finally spoke, after a refill of coffee. She was self-admittedly a real bitch in the mornings until she had at least one cup of coffee. Cooper gave her a wide berth until she had her coffee. "I talked with a guy from Tina's battalion last night. Our people are kicking the crap out of them over on Kauai."

"Say what's on your mind, Jersey," Ben told her.

"General Ike could handle this operation and we could get the hell back to the mainland and start setting up for all that crap that's coming up from the south."

"These people aren't professionals, General," Beth said. "It's nothing but target practice for us. It's boring."

"A lot of strain on General Jefferys back home," Corrie said. "And he's not in the best of health."

Ben had been giving that a lot of thought. Cecil was not in good health and with this new threat from South America, Cec had a lot of pressure on him. But to leave in the middle of a campaign . . . ?

Corrie's radio started squawking and she went inside. She came out a few moments later, her face grim-looking in the dim light. "This Hoffman person is on the move, General. That was Therm from HQ. Base Camp one had just bumped him. General Jefferys wants you to holler at him as soon as possible."

Ben walked over to the communications truck and got Cec on the horn. "What's up, Cec?"

"It's bad, Ben," came the voice from thousands of miles away. "Hoffman's sent infiltrators into the States. Intelligence thinks they were sent in months, maybe years ago, and kept their heads down . . . in a manner of speaking. What they've been doing is recruiting while you've been gone. Obviously this move was planned years back. The infiltrators have been in contact with extreme-right-wing, hate-filled survivalist groups for a long time. You know the type. I've got to have some people over here as fast as possible. We've got to nip this in the bud right now."

"All right, Cec. I'll get back to you by 0900 my time. Hang in there. Eagle out." He put a hand on the operator's shoulder. "Get all batt comms over here right now, son."

"We going home, General?" the young Rebel said.
"Some of us are."

"Ben, we're falling all over each other on these islands," Ike said. "Hell, we've collected enough weapons from the outlaws to outfit every man, woman, and child left."

"We're just backing up the locals on Kauai," Buddy said, and the other batt comms nodded their heads in agreement.

122

"Yes," Danjou said. "Two battalions on Kauai and two battalions here would be more than sufficient to do the job. And it would not take us long. There are so many of us here now, we run the risk of shooting at each other."

"Cecil would not call for help if he didn't need it," Georgi Striganov pointed out.

"Take Therm's Headquarters Company," Tina said. "He's got to get set up and running Stateside. Hell, Dad, the outlaws here are falling apart."

"They might pull themselves back together if the majority of us pull out," Ben said.

"I hope they do," Pat O'Shea said. The wild Irishman grinned. "That way we could say we've been in a real fight."

"The ships are ready, Ben," Ike said. "You could be sailing in three days."

Ben toyed with a pencil for a moment. "All right. Ike, you're in command here. I'll leave your battalion and three others. Buddy, your Eight Battalion will remain, along with Ten and Fourteen Battalions. Everything else, including Therm's Headquarters Company, will move back to the mainland and start setting up to meet Hoffman's divisions. I'm going to take all the special-ops people."

Ben looked at Thermopolis. "You and your people are the first out of here, Therm. Start taking your operation apart and packing it up."

Corrie intercepted the runner and took the message. "General, about three hundred punks just surrendered to B Company of Two Battalion. They said there are about five hundred more ready to pack it in."

"Well, shit!" Pat O'Shea said. "What the hell is the matter with these people? I haven't seen a decent fight since we got here!"

123

Ben sat in the bleachers of an old football stadium and looked at the mass of punks being held on the playing field. He was glad he was leaving so he would not have to listen to all the sob stories that were surely going to come out of the mouths of the captured outlaws. It had reached the point where it seemed like everytime a Rebel looked up, a group of outlaws was walking down the center of a road, their hands in the air. But several thousand hard-core still remained full of defiance and ready to fight to the death.

With Ike in command of the battalions remaining behind, those outlaws would surely get their wish. Ike was not known for his gentle, humanitarian leanings.

One of the outlaws on the playing field looked up at Ben and waved. Others saw him and began waving and cheering . . . probably due to the fact that they had surrendered to Rebels and were still alive.

"Wonderful," Ben said, halfheartedly returning the wave. "Now I have a cheering section."

Corrie, Beth, Jersey, and Cooper did their best to hide their grins.

Ben looked over at them. "Oh, go on and laugh!"

They did.

Ben spent his time watching the loading of equipment and troops. There was nothing left to do. The outlaws were surrendering in droves, and the four remaining battalions still in active service were hard-pressed just to find places for them and to help with the guarding. What had started out to be a major operation was ending with all the sparkle of a glass of flat champagne.

The Rebels on Kauai had found the bodies of half a dozen gang leaders. They had committed suicide rather than face the hangman's noose. They were identified as Larry Perkins, Kip Burdette, Wee Willie, Rye Billings, Dean Sherman, and a woman that was known as Sarah.

"There is no way the good people on these islands can house and feed and guard all these slimeballs," Ben said at a final meeting of batt comms before he was to shove off for the mainland. "So I have a plan. I've talked with a dozen ex-captains of ships and they like the plan and will go along with it. They've already started working on those cargo ships in the harbors of these islands. They're to transport these thugs and creeps all over the Pacific Ocean, dropping them off in small numbers on every island . . . inhabited or not. Oh, it'll be checked out for water and food sources; I'm not leaving them to die some horrible death. And if the island is inhabited, the people will be told what they're getting and asked if they want them. The hard-core will be taken to the west coast of South America and kicked out there. To hell with them."

Georgi Striganov grinned, nudged Ike in the ribs, and held out his hand. "Pay me," the Russian said. "I told you that was what he'd do."

Ike handed him a fistful of worthless old American money and Georgi used a one-hundred-dollar bill to light a cigar.

Therm and his Headquarters Company had already pulled out, on a ship loaded with excess supplies. They would be met by Rebels in America and escorted to a location near the border with Mexico and set up there.

The battalions sailing back to the mainland were

packed up and ready to board the ships.

"We've got nearly twenty thousand locals armed to the teeth, Ike broke into Ben's thoughts. "Hell, they outnumber us!"

"General," Pat O'Shea said. "I thought Hitler's dream was a pure Aryan nation?"

"It was, more or less. Why do you ask, Pat?"

"Well, in this latest dispatch from General Jefferys, it says that the divisions coming up to do battle with us are made up of people from all over the world. All colors and all nationalities. I don't get it. That isn't what Hitler envisioned."

"These people aren't really followers of Hitler, Pat. Very few of them are even German. These people are terrorists, for the most part. But dangerous. In that last dispatch, Cecil talks about the Hitler Youth Corps. But now it's called the Hoffman Youth League. That tells me that he's had years to train these people. And that means that we'll be up against the largest, best-trained, best-equipped, and most highly disciplined and motivated army we have ever faced."

"You're really worried, aren't you, Ben?" West asked.

"Damn worried, my friend. We've never met a force we couldn't beat. But this time, I'm afraid our losses are going to be staggering."

Book Two

One

Ben paced the decks during the cruise back to the mainland. He was not given to much conversation and his team left him alone with his thoughts. When he wasn't pacing the decks, he was in his stateroom, studying maps of the United States' long border with Mexico. It was impossible to defend with the troops under Ben's command. Even if General Payon pulled his army back from southern Mexico and joined forces with Ben, the border was just impossible to defend.

Ike was reporting by radio that the campaign in the islands was fizzling out as the thousands of now heavily armed locals were overwhelming the outlaws by sheer numbers, flushing them out of their holes and usually killing them on the spot. Ike had pulled the Rebels back and was letting the locals handle it.

He reported that Books Houseman was dead. The appointed leader of the outlaws had been killed by an aide. Someone named Bobby, who had apparently gone insane and slaughtered everyone in the room, then turned the gun on himself. After the death of Books, the outlaw resistance seemed to fall apart. Ike said that if the fight—or the lack of it—continued as it was going, he and the remainder of the Rebel battalions would be leaving Hawaii just about the time Ben docked.

Thermopolis and his Headquarters Company had been met in California and flown to a newly built base just outside what was left of Laredo, in Texas. They were fully operational.

Whoever was doing the planning for General Hoffman knew what he was doing. The Rebels Cecil had sent down to the Mexico-Guatemala border just got out alive. Hoffman had landed paratroopers behind Payon's lines, and about half of the Mexican Army was trapped in extreme southern Mexico and fighting on two fronts. Payon had pulled what remained of his army back and stretched it out along major points from Poza Rica on the Gulf of Mexico down to Acapulco on the Pacific.

"Blow all the bridges," Ben had radioed to the Mexican general from on board ship. "Slow him down just as much as is humanly possible. Give me time to get my people into position. When you feel it is impossible to hold any longer, get the hell out of there and join me on the border."

Ben had ordered planeloads of explosives down to Mexico, and teams of Spanish-speaking Rebels to assist in the blowing of bridges and the blocking of major highways leading north. As many bridges as possible on Mexico's 200, 190, 150, and 180 were being destroyed in a desperate race to buy Ben and the Rebels some time.

Had Mexico and the United States worked this closely together before the Great War, every problem that had faced the two nations back then could have been resolved, and Canada, the United States, and Mexico could have emerged as the greatest combined superpower in all the world, rich in resources, workforce, and culture. But that didn't happen—due in no small part to a great many very stupid, greedy, and bigoted people on both sides of the border—and because that did not occur, the lack of cooperation contributed to the world going to hell in a bucket of shit.

When Ben's ship docked, planes were waiting to take Ben, his team, and First Platoon, A Company, to the site of Therm and his Headquarters Company in Texas.

Ben stood for a long silent moment looking at the huge map that covered half of one wall of the operations room. He experienced a feeling of despair unlike anything that he had ever felt before. "The black-flapped pins are Hoffman's troops?" he asked softly.

"Yes," Therm said. "The blue-flagged pins are General Payon's forces."

"Therm, the goddamn black-flagged pins run all the way to San Salvador!"

"Yes. Obviously Hoffman was much more powerful than any of us first thought. We believe his movement was going on long before the Great War. We have revised our estimates of his strength. We now believe that he has five fighting divisions."

Ben was stunned and his face clearly mirrored that astonishment. He put out a hand and gripped the edge of a table. His personal team stood in shock facing the wall map. "Therm, if he's running light divisions of infantry, that's approximately eighty-five thousand men."

"Our estimates place Hoffman's numbers at one hundred and five thousand. And at full strength, we can field just over twenty-one thousand people. And Ben, that's using everyone who can tote a gun."

131

"Our people who got out of the pocket down here," Ben said, pointing at the map. "What are their reports about Hoffman's troops? Discipline, fighting ability, equipment."

"Top notch, Ben. Everything is top of the line. Our teams report the enemy is awesome. Absolutely first rate. They captured one and he went to his death without uttering anything more than his name, rank, and serial number."

"Who killed him and why?"

"He killed himself, Ben."

"An army of fanatics," Ben muttered. "A big army of fanatics. Do we have anything additional on this Hoffman person?"

"Very little. He is supposed to be a great leader of men. Brilliant. Cunning. A great tactician. But we don't know that. We don't know that he's ever faced an army of any size."

"Hell, Therm, we can't butt heads with this army. We've got to make him split his forces and come at us that way. But even at that, it's going to be his full division against a brigade of our people. And four of our battalions have never been tested in battle." Ben sighed. "Well, we've got a month, maybe two months, to make plans and get set. I want Ike here, Corrie. Tell him to leave Hawaii to the locals and get here as quickly as possible. Get those battalions and equipment on board ship ASAP and fly Ike back. Like today."

"Yes, sir."

"I'm getting ready to make some personnel changes, Therm. I'l brief you just as soon as I've spoken with Ike. If he gets his fat ass in gear, he'll be here late tomorrow." Ben smiled to lighten the tense mood. "And tell him I said he's a fat ass, Corrie."

"Right, sir."

* * *

"Fat ass!" Ike said, after reading the short communiqué. "Why, that long, lanky . . ."

The runner handed him the second communiqué.

"Jesus Jumpin' Christ!" Ike said. "Five divisions? Five! Get me a plane ready to go."

"Theoretically, sir," a young lieutenant said, "I believe the Apache AH-64A, fitted with four auxiliary fuel tanks, will hold enough fuel to fly you back to the mainland."

Ike fixed the young man with a very cool and steady gaze. The lieutenant got awfully nervous. "Young man," Ike said, "I didn't like helicopters when I was either hurling my body out of one or rappelling down a rope years back. I have absolutely no intention of rattling across the Pacific Ocean in a goddamn whirlybird."

"Yes, sir."

"Have you ever tried peeing in a damn Apache?"

"No, sir."

"Neither have I, and I don't care to. Besides, I believe you said theoretically?"

"Yes, sir. I read it in a training manual."

"Who wrote it? Had to have been a chopper pilot. Hell, they're all nuts. Besides, I . . . What are you smiling about, Lieutenant?"

"I believe the general was a Navy SEAL, was he not?"

Ike tried his best to stare the young man down. He could not. Finally Ike smiled. "Well, yeah, you're right. But SEALs are only half-nuts."

"All the serviceable planes have left, General," an aide told him. "Ferrying medical and special-ops people. Crazy Zeke Andrews says he'll fly you across."

"Crazy goddamn Zeke is going to fly me across the goddamn ocean in his goddamn helicopter," Ike muttered. "At about a hundred and seventy-five miles an hour. What happens if I gotta take a goddamn dump up there?" he yelled.

"What took you so long?" Ben asked Ike. "Did you come across by helicopter?"

"I don't want to talk about it," Ike mumbled, sitting down gingerly in a chair.

"What's the matter with you?" Ben asked. "Your hemorrhoids bothering you again?"

"I don't want to talk about it!" Ike yelled.

"Touchy, touchy," Ben said.

"More than you know," Ike muttered.

"All right, all right, Ike. You give our situation here any thought?"

"Oh, my, yes. I had plenty of time to think about it, believe me. That and worrying about cotter pins working loose," he said under his breath.

"Beg pardon?"

"Nothing, Ben. Nothing. Yeah. I thought about it, and I think we're in one hell of a pickle. That's what I think."

"Yeah. I agree with you. Come over here to this table. I've got a map all marked out."

Ike grunted as he got to his feet.

"Would you like for me to order you a wheel-chair?" Ben asked.

"No, I don't need a wheelchair. I'm just a little . . . stiff, that's all."

"I think you're falling apart," Ben said, bending over the table.

"Put your lanky ass in a chopper seat for twenty-five hours and see what happens," Ike muttered.

"Ummm?"

"Nothing, Ben. Nothing."

"When did you start talking to yourself, Ike?"

"Get on with the business at hand, Ben. Never mind me."

"Until Hoffman and his bunch cross over onto North American soil, Ike, I want you in charge of all special-ops people. That mean you and your teams will be taking a lot of helicopter rides."

"Oh, wonderful," Ike muttered.

Ben gave him an odd look and said, "We'll leave three exit holes for General Payon and his army. At here, here, and here. El Paso, Laredo, and Brownville. All the other crossings are to be destroyed. I've spoken directly with General Payon and he agrees with it. They'll be blown on my orders only. Wire them and move on. We'll be receiving a lot of people from Mexico during the next few weeks. I've got people setting up emergency receiving centers now, from Tucson all the way over to Brownsville, and trucks moving with food and water and blankets. I'm going to put Tina and Raul Gomez in charge of training all the new recruits from Mexico. They both speak the language and we're going to need all the help we can get, old friend. Believe me."

Ike straightened up with an audible creak and said, "Oh, I do believe you. Five full divisions, Ben?"

"At least. Probably more than that. But Payon's got lots of artillery and he's going to give Hoffman's boys a damn rough row to hoe. He'll buy us as much time as he possibly can. Now then, we're got Hoffman's infiltrators working all over the nation. This nation. Cecil's got about two thousand Hummers ready to go for us at Base Camp One. His mechanics have gone over them and they're tough as mountain goats and ready to roll. About five

135

hundred are on the way here now. Fuel trucks are being placed all over the southern borders; they should all be in place in a few days. We're going to fan out and hit the known trouble spots in America. We'll be moving fast and light and we're going to hit these goose-stepping bastards so hard they'll never recover from it. We've got to do it; we can't have them at our backs."

"Have you given any thought to driving deep into Mexico and beefing up Payon's army, Ben?"

"I thought about it, then rejected it. General Payon says the roads are in terrible shape down there. Our supply lines would be stretched to the max. We don't know the country and accurate maps are not available. Besides, we've got to contain those infil-trators in this country. That's a must-do priority."

Ike nodded his head. "I'll start putting my teams together today and laying out gear. I want first on the list for those Hummers, Ben."

"You got it. Check with Therm on the locations of the fuel trucks."

The eyes of the two warriors touched and held for a moment. Ike said, "You know we're not going to stop these bastards at the border, Ben."

"I know. To butt heads with them, force against force, would be suicide for us."

"First time in a while," Ike drawled, "that we'll be on the hard defensive."

Ben shrugged. "I think we'd better get used to it, old friend."

Ike sighed. "Well, Hawaii was nothing more than a realistic training exercise. But at least it got some of the new people blooded. Now comes the real test."

"Yes. But if we fail this exam, we don't get to repeat the course."

"A real final exam."

"With hard emphasis on the final."

"Yeah. Well, I got to get busy. See you around, Ben."

Ben stood alone for a moment, staring out the window. Beth quietly entered the room, a slip of paper in her hand.

"General?"

Ben turned, noting the expression on her face. He mentally braced for the worst.

"Those troops of General Payon's who were trapped in southern Mexico? . . . They've been wiped out. Only a handful escaped. Hoffman's troops are not taking any prisoners. General Payon is now blowing all bridges on highways leading north and is extensively mining Highways 190, 185, 180, and 150. He is in the process of destroying all major airports."

"Damn!" Ben said softly.

"Makes Hawaii seem like sweet dreams, doesn't it?" Doctor Chase said, entering the room.

The two old friends shook hands. "How are you doing, Lamar?"

"I'm well. What's the matter with Ike? I saw him limping out of the building and asked about his health. He almost bit my head off."

"I don't know. Maybe he's due for a checkup."

"I suggested that. He told me where to put my checkup. Sideways. And stick a helicopter up there with it."

"General," Cooper said, sticking his head into the room. "All the batt comms are here. And General Jefferys's plane just touched down."

"Thanks, Coop. You want to sit in on this, Lamar?"

The chief of medicine shook his head. "No, thanks. I'll say hello to Cecil and be on my way. Ben,

137

my people are going to be stretched pretty thin."

"I know, Lamar. We all are. General Payon is flying in medical teams from Mexico to take some of the strain off your people."

"They'll damn sure be welcomed and put to work. See you, Ben."

Cooper walked to Ben's side. "General, are we gonna win this one?"

"I don't know, Coop," Ben said softly. "I just don't know. But for humanity's sake, we'd better."

Two

Cecil looked bad. Ben was shocked at his old friend's appearance. Cecil's hair was almost totally gray now, and his face was haggard. We're all getting old, Ben thought. We've been fighting this damn war for more than a decade and it's telling on us.

When all the men were seated, Ben said, "Ike won't be here. He's out of this until the full-scale fighting starts. He's in charge of all special ops. Might as well give you the bad news first. Southern Mexico has fallen to Hoffman's troops." He picked up a pointer and walked to the wall map. "From 185, here, up to Mexico City is a no-man's-land. We don't have much time, people. We've got to do a year's work in approximately two months. General Payon has promised me two months, and I think he'll hold for that long. Then he's got to get across the border and beef us up."

"How many troops does he have, Ben?" Striganov asked.

"The question is, Georgi, how many will we have left?" The Russian smiled grimly and nodded his head in agreement. Ben said, "If he gets up here with five full battalions, I'll be both shocked and pleased."

"Dad, are his battalions about the same as ours?" Tina asked.

"Exactly the same. He patterned his army after ours. Tina, I want you and Raul to act as training officers for the new recruits we'll be receiving from across the border. We've got about a hundred young men and women now over at McAllen. I'll have them brought over here ASAP."

"How many are you expecting?" Tina asked.

"Hundreds."

"How intense do we make the training, General?" Raul asked.

"Just as tough as you think they can stand. All right, people. Here is how it lays out." He went to the map again and pointed to a dozen different locations, marked with tiny black flags. "These are trouble spots. Hoffman's troops are known to be there, working with hard-right-wing groups that have had the good sense over the years to keep their heads down and out of our sight. We're going to pick teams right now—at this meeting—to go in and kick the shit out of them. We're not going to have much in the way of heavy stuff. We'll be traveling fast and light, in Hummers. They'll be here within a day or two. We'll be supported, whenever possible, by Apaches and other attack choppers. The old PUFFs are out. Hoffman's people have too much in the way of high-tech weapons; they'd blow them out of the sky. Let's start picking teams and drawing equipment. We shove off within hours after the Hummers arrive."

General Payon's expression was bleak as he listened to his scouts report. He had lost a lot of good men and women when they had gotten trapped in that pocket down south. Good men and women.

140

Highly trained and loyal to the core. It was a blow that still had the general reeling.

He dismissed his scouts and sat for a time behind his desk in the old ranch house he was using as a CP. Like Ben Raines, General Payon was a middle-aged man who was battle-hardened by years of fighting. And like Ben, Payon was a true professional soldier. A soldier's soldier. He had not always been so, but like General Raines, when his people turned to him, he reluctantly agreed to lead the fight. And like Ben, he suffered silently and stoically when he lost personnel. But he knew, like his counterpart north of the border, those were the fortunes and fates of war and warriors.

He called to an aide. "We must have a more personal liaison between us and General Raines. Send Captain Tomas to me."

The captain standing in front of his desk, Payon said, "You will pick a small team and travel to the border, to General Raines's command post. You will be my eyes and ears and voice with General Raines. We will be in daily communication. You stay with General Raines. No matter where he goes, you stay with him." He handed the captain a sealed envelope. "This is to be hand-delivered to General Raines, and only to General Raines. God speed, Tomas." He rose and extended his hand.

After the young officer had left, General Payon sat down and rolled a cigarette. He felt better now. Now, if anything was to happen to him, his carefully chosen and trained army would remain intact. He smiled. Although Ben Raines might not be happy with the contents of the letter he was about to receive.

"Do you know what this letter says?" Ben asked the

captain, after carefully reading the letter.

"No, sir," Tomas replied stiffly.

"Relax, son," Ben told him. "We're not all that big on spit and polish and protocol in this army. Sit down and have some coffee. Real coffee."

Ben had a knack of being able to put people at ease, and Tomas sat down and slowly relaxed. He tensed as Ben poured him coffee. Commanding generals did not do things like that in his army.

"Sugar and milk, Tomas?" Ben asked from the small table in a corner of the room.

"Please, sir."

"How many personnel did you bring with you?"

"Eight, sir."

"All experienced combat veterans?"

"Oh, yes, sir. Veterans of dozens of campaigns. Dependable and steady people. Six men and two women." Ben handed him a mug of coffee. "The women are ferocious fighters, General. I will admit that at first I was dubious. No more. They pull their own weight and then some."

"Same in this army. So you are to stay with me, is that right?"

"Yes, sir. Those are my orders."

Ben handed him the letter and watched Tomas's face as he read it. The letter stated unequivocally that should anything happen to General Payon, General Ben Raines was to assume command of the Mexican Army and the officers and personnel of that army would obey Ben Raines's orders without hesitation or question.

Tomas carefully folded the letter and placed it on Ben's desk. "I know that other letters went out to all commanders, sir," he said. "I did not know the contents. Now I do. It is an honor to serve in your command, General."

"Fine, Tomas. Finish your coffee and relax for a few minutes. In one hour we're shoving off for a little town just north of what is left of San Antonio. Some of Hoffman's infiltrators have linked up with a group of assholes up there. We're going to wipe their butts with lead."

Tomas smiled. "I think I am going to enjoy serving in your command, sir."

"It gets interesting at times, Captain. I assure you of that."

After making sure that his husky, Smoot, was in good hands—it was; Thermopolis and Rosebud were taking care of it—Ben played with the animal for a few minutes and then climbed into the Hummer. He looked around at his team. "Tell Therm we're on our way, Corrie. Let's go, Coop."

Rebel engineers had reworked the interior of the Hummer, making it a bit more comfortable. They had bulletproofed the vehicle, and on Ben's staff Hummer a .50 caliber machine gun was mounted on top. Others were mounted with 7.62 machine guns or 40mm Big Thumper grenade tossers. Gun clamps had been installed inside for easier weapons carrying and a high-tech, state-of-the-art radio was built in under the rear seat.

Cooper slipped the Hummer into gear and the 2.5-ton vehicle rolled out, followed by several dozen more, including two Hummers assigned to Captain Tomas and his team. The Hummers bristled with weapons, both inside and out. In specially built racks in each Hummer were two Winchester model 1200 pump shotguns, which could be loaded with various types of rounds, including #00 buckshot, shells containing two steel darts, called flechettes, which could penetrate a steel helmet at 300 meters, and shells that contained a large lead slug that could cripple an engine or blow a door off its hinges from a distance of 100 meters.

On this mission, the personal weapon for each Rebel, including Ben, was the M-16 with the M-203 grenade launcher attached, nicknamed bloop tubes. The M-16 was chosen because of the ability of each Rebel to carry more ammo. If each Rebel personally carried ten pounds of ammo, he or she could carry 384 5.56 rounds as opposed to only 187 rounds of 7.62 ammo.

Fuel for the V-8, 6.2-liter GM diesel was no problem for the Rebels, since for over a decade they had been caching fuel, gas and diesel, all over the United States in secret underground locations. Ben had felt all along that someday the war would come home, someday a huge army would try to smash the Rebel form of government, and he had ordered materials cached all over the nation.

"Scouts are waiting just a few miles south of the ruins of San Antonio, Coop," Ben said. "It's an easy run from here. We'll hit Hoffman's finest just at dawn tomorrow."

The drive up Interstate 35 from Laredo was uneventful, but it was depressing for Ben. The Rebels saw absolutely no sign of life for over one hundred miles. Just desolation and silence. Ben commented on it.

"Of course," Beth spoke up. "After spending time in Hawaii, nearly any place would look desolate."

"You're right, Beth," Ben said. "But we are supposed to have a settlement up here in Pearsall, remember?"

She groaned. "I'm falling down on the job, General. Sorry."

"The scouts haven't reported on that outpost."

"It's about ten miles up the road," Coop said. "We'll know one way or the other in a few minutes."

The town had been destroyed, and done so some time back. In an alley, the Rebels found the bleached bones of dozens of people.

"Mostly men and boys," a medic said, after inspecting the skeletal remains. "Very few women, that I can tell."

He could tell. Lamar Chase's medics were not far from being doctors—most of them became doctors after several years in the field.

"How long ago?" Ben asked.

"Three months, maybe, sir."

"It is the same in my country," Tomas said, walking up. "And in all the countries Hoffman's troops overpower. They enslave as many men as possible and make *putas* out of the women and girls." He shook his head. "But here, it appears that the men and many of the women fought to the death."

"Rebels do that," Ben told him.

Maria and Victoria walked up to stand by Tomas. The two women in the Mexican detachment were very pretty ladies, and, Ben deduced, very tough ladies. "Then so shall we," Maria said. "For us, there is no going back. Vicki and me, we come from Villahermosa. We know that our parents and our brothers and sisters are dead. At the hands of Hoffman and his pigs." She spat out the last few words. "We have sworn to God and the Blessed Virgin that we will kill as many of Hoffman's soldiers as we can and will not be taken alive." Together, the ladies turned around and walked off.

A young Mexican sergeant smiled and made the classic Latin movement of shaking his fingers as if dispelling water and said, "Those two are *muy malo*, I tell you. Do not cross those ladies. I saw Vicki gut one of Hoffman's soldiers like a fish. She is ver' ver' quick with a knife."

"My kind of gal," Jersey said.

The sergeant looked at how Jersey fit her BDUs, rolled his eyes, and said, "Ai, yi yi."

"Stick it up your kazoo," Jersey told him, absolutely no diplomat in her at all, then walked over to Vicki and Maria.

Captain Tomas chuckled.

"I like that one!" the sergeant said. "Much fire in her."

Vicki, Maria, and Jersey looked back at the sergeant and all three giggled. It was somehow out of place considering how heavily they were armed.

"She likes me, too," the sergeant said, his eyes flashing.

"Come on, Casanova," Ben said with a smile. "We've got work to do. Beth, where are the caches in this town?"

The Rebels found the hidden arms and supplies and resealed the bunkers. Tomas was clearly awed.

"You have these all over the nation, General?"

"Hundreds of them. The water in those sealed containers might be stale, but safe to drink. The food is changed out every five years. It's fresh, now. Remember the locations we show you, Captain. I have a hunch we'll all eventually be forced to fall back on them."

"You sound like General Payon now, sir," the amorous sergeant said. "He believes that this war we fight with Hoffman and his army will be the one that will decide the fate of all the rest of the world."

"So do I, Sergeant," Ben told him. "So do I."

At the preset rendezvous just south of the ruins of

San Antonio, Ben linked up with the scouts. "We didn't want to use the radio to tell you about the outpost back there," the team leader said.

"We didn't check the caches either," another said. "Figured you'd want to do that."

"You both did well," Ben told him. "What have we got up ahead of us?"

"Large group of right-wingers who have linked up with about a hundred of Hoffman's dickheads," the team leader replied. "I figure a force of at least three hundred, all told." He took a map out of his case and opened it. "Right here, sir. Just outside of New Braunfels. Right on the edge of the hill country. And they're good, sir. Real good."

"Better than us, Sergeant?"

"I got to say as good, sir."

"Then this is going to be interesting," Ben said. He looked at Jersey and waited.

She smiled and said, "Kick-ass time!"

"What a woman!" the Mexican sergeant said.

Three

Ben waited in the darkness before dawn, sitting on the ground drinking coffee and eating from a breakfast pack. Like most Rebels, he preferred to eat breakfast in the dark so he did not have to see what he was eating. The prepackaged goop was highly nutritious, but looking at it could cause a sudden loss of appetite.

Scouts had moved out hours before. They would create a very loud diversion on the north side of the enemy's encampment a few moments before the main body of Rebels hit at the south end of the camp. The diversion would, hopefully, cover the sounds of the Hummers' fast approach.

Beth would be driving the staff car, with Cooper manning the .50 caliber. Once inside the enemy's perimeter, the battle would turn into a free-for-all. Surprise was the key to survival.

Ben finished his breakfast, buried the wrappers in the ground, and rolled a cigarette, smoking it while he drank the last of his coffee.

He checked his watch. A few more minutes before they moved out. These fast attacks were being conducted all over the southern half of Texas. Ben could not hope to smash all the right-wing groups who had surfaced all over the nation and aligned with Hoffman's infiltrators, but they could clear many of those in Texas and get them off their backs.

"Let's start getting in place," Ben said to his team. He ground out his cigarette and stood up. There was no need to go over anything. Everybody knew what was required of them.

The Hummers were already packed for the run and the Rebels began silently mounting up. In a dozen places all over the southern part of Texas, the same scene was being played out, getting ready for act one in this dangerous and deadly play between forces of decidedly different philosophies.

"Roll," Ben told Beth, and the teams moved out.

"All teams in place," Corrie reported from the rear.

The short convoy rolled through the night, headlights taped to permit only a slit of light, just enough for the drivers to see and no more.

After a few silent miles had passed, a tremendous flash of light laced the night sky ahead of them.

"Right on time," Jersey said.

"Pour the juice to it," Corrie radioed the lead vehicles. "Two miles from objective."

On the north end of the encampment, scouts were dropping rockets down mortar tubes as fast as they could, and the exploding 60mm rounds were more than covering the fast-advancing Hummers.

Cooper stood up through the hinged trap in the roof and jacked a round into the big .50. Ben lowered his window and Jersey and Corrie followed suit. The Hummers left the road and assumed a line, much like a cavalry charge. As soon as the Hummers' lights came into sight, the mortars stopped and the scouts grabbed up M-16s and charged to the edge of the encampment and jumped for cover.

Cooper began letting the heavy .50 caliber rock and roll and Big Thumpers began hammering out 40mm high-explosive grenades, the combined weapons dealing out misery and turning the early morning hour into a taste of hell for the enemy troops.

The Hummers slid to a halt and the Rebels bailed out, running for whatever cover they could find, but always forward. Ben threw himself through an open window of a house and rolled, Jersey right behind him. Coming up to his knees, he pulled the trigger of the bloop tube and gave a knot of men a fragmentation grenade. The shrapnel from the M-433 liner made a big sloppy mess in the den. Jersey's M-16 rattled and spat and two men wearing the death's-head insignia on their uniforms went down in a bloody heap.

"Bastards," Jersey said.

"Let's find the communications room," Ben said, and kicked in a door. Jersey rolled a grenade into the darkness and the two of them flattened against a wall.

"Grenade!" a man's voice called out in panic. One second later all that remained was the echo of his word of warning.

Outside, the firing was lessening. The suddenness and viciousness of the attack had worked . . . this time.

"One dead, two wounded," Corrie reported to Ben. "We have several prisoners."

"Make certain the camp is secure and let's see what we've got," Ben said.

This was the first time any of Hoffman's people had mixed it up with Rebels, and the surviving black-shirted followers of terrorism and the none-too-bright ultra-right-wingers who had joined with them were clearly shocked at the results. As daylight began streaking the sky, the prisoners sat on the ground in stunned and sullen silence, their hands tied behind their backs.

"Airstrip right over there, General," a Scout said.

"General!" one black-shirted man said. "Are you General Raines?"

Ben turned to him. "Yes."

"I am Major Garcia. I demand to be treated with all respect due an officer in the NAL."

"The what?" Ben asked.

"New Army of Liberation. That is Captain Grumman to my left, and Lieutenant Jammal Mubutu beside him."

"I know that son of a bitch," a black Rebel sergeant said, looking closely at Mubutu. "I went to school with him. Until he dropped out. His name is Jesse Williams. He was a member of a street gang in Chicago."

"My name is Mubutu." The lieutenant spat out the words. "I rejected the racist white name years ago."

"Yeah?" the sergeant said with a smile. "Well, I'm King Farouk. Screw you, Jesse."

The sky was still gray with the dawning. Ben looked at Major Mendoza. "I'll deal with you people the same way I deal with any damned terrorist, Garcia. You get no special favors from me."

"You, sir," the major spat back, "are no gentleman. And the weapons your people use are hideous. One of my officers is lying over there," he cut his eyes, "with a face full of steel darts from a shotgun blast. That is against all rules of the Geneva Convention."

"Conventions," Ben automatically corrected. "Those rules do not apply to scum like you." He turned his back to the major. "Corrie, get some big choppers in here to take back the wounded and the prisoners."

151

"Scum!" Garcia hollered. "You dare to call me scum?"

Ben slowly turned around and lowered the muzzle of his M-16 until it was pointing directly at the major's head. "Don't push your luck with me, Garcia." He smiled. "Or I'll turn you over to those two very attractive ladies standing right over there."

Garcia cut his eyes to where Maria and Victoria were standing, the butt of their weapons resting on their hips. They smiled at the major.

"And they'd like for me to do just that, Garcia," Ben said. "You and your pack of trash and filth and malcontents like Jesse there killed their parents, their brothers and sisters, and uncles and aunts down in Villahermosa."

"My name is Jammal Mubutu, you goddamn honky son of a bitch!" Jesse yelled.

The black Rebel sergeant looked at Ben. "With your permission, General?"

"Be my guest," Ben told him.

The sergeant stepped forward and kicked Jesse/ Jammal in the mouth and Jesse/Jammal didn't have anything left to say, or any front teeth, either.

"If they picked up arms against the great army of General Hoffman, then they deserved to die," Garcia said. "Heil Hitler!"

Ben laughed at him. "You dumb bastard. Hitler's been dead for about sixty years. And he would have shoved you in the ovens or the gas chambers right along with the Jews."

"That's a vicious lie," Garcia said. "We know the truth about Hitler. All that other was written and published by agents of ZOG to defile the great man's name."

"ZOG?" Beth said, looking at Ben.

"Zionist Occupation Government of North Amer-

152

ica," Ben told her. "There's a phrase from the past. That's the old Aryan Nations/KKK bullshit. The holocaust never happened, according to them. I am beginning to see what has been happening in certain sections of South America since the end of the Second World War. I couldn't understand this movement until now. But now, it all fits."

"Madre Dios! The swine have rewritten the history books and altered, or edited, old films," Tomas said. "They brainwashed their followers."

"Exactly, Captain. That is precisely what they did. And two or three generations of people have grown up believing it."

"Lies, lies, lies!" Garcia shouted. "All lies. Hitler was the savior of the world and the Jews killed him, just like they did our savior, Jesus Christ. The butchers, Roosevelt and Churchill, were the real villains, not the great and noble Adolf Hitler."

The black sergeant looked at Ben. "This is scary, General. Real scary."

"Tell me," Ben replied.

Cooper edged up to Jersey. "Jersey?" he whispered. "Who in hell are Roosevelt and Churchill?"

She cut her dark eyes to him. "Beats the hell out of me, Coop."

Those taken prisoner back at the Rebel outpost were freed and all immediately volunteered to join the active Rebels. They were welcomed in. Garcia and the other prisoners from the NAL were choppered back to Laredo, under heavy guard.

Ben prowled through the rubble of the devastated camp until he found what he was sure he would find. In Garcia's quarters he found the flag and took it outside. The Nazi swastika. He held it up for all to

153

see. Several of the older Jewish Rebels wore grim expressions on their faces at the hated sight. They knew the truth about that symbol. The Rebels of German ancestry shook their heads in disgust at the symbol invisibly stained with the blood of millions of Jews.

"This cannot be allowed to happen," Ben told the teams gathered around. "Not again. Not ever again. For those of you too young to know what this represents, when we return to base, I assure you all that you will know the truth." He threw the flag on the ground and kicked it away from him. "My older brother fought against that goddamn piece of shit decades back," Ben raged. "Somebody burn that damn rag!"

Ben stalked away, Jersey falling in step with him. "We got all their weapons, General. Real high tech stuff, too, some of it. Hoffman and his bunch must have been warehousing Heckler and Koch equipment for years. Over a hundred boxes of belted ammo. You know how our people love their light machine guns."

"The 7.62 HK11A1?"

"Right. And lots of replacement barrels and spare parts to go with them. We also found a lot of light stuff too. 9mm submachine guns."

"Before this is over, Jersey, we've very likely to be fighting with clubs and axes."

They walked a few more yards. "You think this is going to last a long time, don't you?"

"Yes. We're looking at some long and bitter and bloody months ahead of us."

"Hey, we'll make it, General. Bet on it."

He smiled down at the diminutive bodyguard. "It might go on for years, Jersey."

"We'll still make it. Can't nothing stop us,

General. And you know why? 'Cause we're right, that's why.''

Ben smiled. "All right, Jersey. So let's go give 'em hell!''

The teams pulled out and headed north, pushing hard. Hoffman's infiltrators along with American collaborators and sympathizers had struck at a small Rebel outpost located about seventy-five miles southeast of Abilene. The defenders had beaten off the attack, but only after suffering hard losses. They had radioed that the attackers had taken off to the north, toward the interstate that ran east and west. Ben had ordered eyes in the skies up and they had located the Nazi-loving bunch.

Now, as Jersey was so fond of saying, it was kick-ass time!

Four

The Rebels left the main highways and took to the secondary roads when they pulled to within thirty miles of the enemy camp. This group was reported to be much larger than the first bunch Ben and his teams had encountered down south and, according to reports, had taken over the deserted town with its two airports and looked to be settling in, probably planning to make it a major supply depot when Hoffman decided to make his push into North America. "Not if I can help it," Ben muttered to himself.

Corrie had received reports that teams of Rebels had kicked the hell out of Hoffman's people down along the border, pursued them back into Mexico, and wiped them out. Three battalions had been broken up into small search-and-destroy teams; the rest were stretched out at strategic crossing points along the border.

Therm had reported that small Rebel outposts all over North America had been attacked and, in some cases, overrun by Hoffman's troops and local guerrilla groups that supported Hoffman's wacko philosophy. Enough outposts had been seized to make it a worrisome matter. Ben had ordered the survivors of those attacks to regroup and wait to be resupplied, then to start harassment tactics against the post—just enough to keep the NAL on their toes and afraid to leave the protected areas.

Supplies were not a problem for the Rebels, since they had hundreds of thousands of tons of material cached all over North America. It would only be a problem should the war stretch into years. But it would be a bigger problem for Hoffman, who had to move his supplies thousands of miles, up from the south.

"Therm," Ben spoke to HQ commander. "Get Hoffman or his spokesman on the horn. Advise him that I have nuclear and chemical first-strike weapons all over Base Camp One in Louisiana. I think he is aware of that. Tell him that if Base Camp One is attacked, I will use those missiles against him."

Therm's sigh was audible over the miles. Therm knew Ben was not bluffing; he would launch those missiles. "That's ten-four, Ben. I will advise Herr Hoffman."

In his HQ, several hundred miles south of Mexico City, Hoffman read the communiqué and slowly laid it on his desk.

"Of course, he is bluffing," a general said.

Hoffman shook his head. "I don't think so. Raines put those missiles in place a long time ago. It's just simply a small matter of changing the coordinates. He would use them." He looked at an aide. "Advise this, ah, Thermopolis person that Base Camp One in Louisiana will not be attacked. And ask him what concessions we shall receive for this magnanimous gesture on our part."

The aide was back in a moment and handed Hoffman a single sheet of paper. One word was typed on it: NOTHING.

Hoffman grunted and handed the paper to the general. The general read it, cursed, then crumpled the paper and tossed it into a wastebasket. "The arrogance of that man is infuriating."

"But for now, he holds all the cards," Hoffman said. "No matter. Once Raines is defeated in the field, all we have to do is surround the base camp and starve them out. The nuclear devices will be useless, because by that time our people shall be all over North America and they will have no targets." He stood up, a tall and handsome man in his late thirties. His parents and his grandfather had seen to it that he was well-educated . . . and thoroughly brainwashed. The Holocaust had never happened. Hitler had been a great man, the greatest man who had ever lived. All the troubles the world had ever seen was the fault of the Jews. America was the enemy because it was controlled by Jews. Ben Raines was obviously a Jew-lover, so that made him the man to destroy, defeat, grind into the dirt.

Hoffman tolerated black people in his army because those who joined him hated America and were good fighters. Hoffman felt they were certainly inferior to him but managed to keep that opinion well-concealed. The blacks could be easily dealt with (meaning disposed of) at a later date. Right now, his primary concern was that goddamn Ben Raines.

"The first thing, the very first thing, we cripple is their communications network. They are using the community's old radio station just on the outskirts of town. That was very stupid on their part." He smiled that famous warrior's smile. "As we are about to point out to them. I want the old station taken intact.

My team will handle that. We might be able to pick up some valuable information by monitoring their frequencies. You've all studied layouts of the town and know what to do, so we go in on foot at midnight and start setting up for the takeover. The Hummers will come in fast with a driver and a gunner. Everybody else will already be in position. We've got a few hours before jump-off time, so get something to eat and try to get some rest. That's it."

The teams broke up and began checking equipment. Only after that was done would any of them eat, then lie down for a few hours of sleep.

The camp they made was a cold one, for their objective was only a few miles away. Ben woke at three o'clock and got his team up. The others in the dark camp were silently lacing up boots and slipping into body armor. Ben washed his mouth out with tepid canteen water and fastened the chin strap on his helmet. He picked up his M-16 and turned to Corrie.

"What do the scouts report?"

"We follow this little creek right to the back of the old radio station. No mines or booby traps. The first sentry post is by the side of the highway. The scouts have already slipped past it and are in position on the edge of town."

"Let's do it, people," Ben said. "By seven o'clock I intend for us to be eating a hot meal and drinking hot coffee, all compliments of Herr Hoffman."

His people grinned at him, then began slipping off into the blackness, heading for the dark outline of the Texas town.

Ben looked at the drivers and the gunners he was leaving behind. "You come in hard at the first shot, people. We'll see you in a couple of hours."

*   *   *

Nearly two hundred miles away, to the east, Buddy wiped the bloody blade of his knife on the dead man's trousers and sheathed the big blade. They had infiltrated a town about a hundred miles east of Austin and had left about a dozen careless and now dead sentries on the ground.

Buddy and his people began spreading out into the town, moving like silent and deadly wraiths in the quiet hours before dawn. They moved into position and waited.

Dan Gray and his people had tucked their Hummers away in a dry creek bed and silently entered the town on Interstate 20, north and west of Ben's present position.

"Map of Texas I got says there is a college here," a young Rebel said.

"We took all the books out years ago," Dan told him in a whisper. He smiled at the young man. "If you've got cheerleaders on your mind, forget it. The last game was played here back in '88, I think it was."

"I was about two years old, I think!"

Dan chuckled. "And I was in love with a fair English lady. Long ago and far away," he said with a sigh. "Heads up. Here comes a foot patrol."

The two black-shirted NAL men walked within three feet of the Rebels hidden in an alley. They were speaking in Spanish, and from the way they talked and walked, both of them were very bored. In a couple of hours, both of them would be very dead.

Dan's radio person said, "All people in place, Colonel."

Dan nodded his head. "Now we wait."

*   *   *

Striganov squatted by the side of the road and stared through the darkness at his objective for that morning. The Russian was about a hundred and fifty miles east and slightly north of Buddy's position. His team, most of whom were ex-Spetsnaz personnel, were lying in the ditches on either side of the old highway.

One of his men came slipping back from the edge of town. "Nothing to it, sir," he whispered. "One of them fired up a cigarette not five feet from me, puffed it a couple of times, then flipped the damn butt at me. When he turned his back, I grabbed it and stowed it." He reached into his pocket and pulled out the nearly unsmoked butt. "Look, sir. It's a real factory cigarette."

"Neither of you smoke," the voice came from the ditch. "So give it to me."

Striganov chuckled. "Fudov, you may smoke it when the battle is over. Toss it to him, Vladislav. A factory-made cigarette," he mused in a soft whisper. "I wonder where they got them?"

"They probably have factories that make them, unlike us," Fudov bitched.

Striganov again softly chuckled. "You even mention building a cigarette factory to Doctor Chase and he'll put you down for extended visits to Doctor Lang, the mad proctologist. Rest now. We strike in two hours."

West and his people had traveled the furthest north. They were now waiting to strike at a NAL encampment that had taken over the old Abilene airport. The mercenary and his men had moved to within spitting distance of a runway. There they lay in tall grass.

161

"I wonder why they chose the city airport instead of the old Dyess Air Force Base?" a team leader questioned.

"I'm just glad they didn't. Ben has tons of supplies cached out there. We do this fast and hard, people," West said. "We're taking five airports all over the state on this night. Ben is going to try to contain Hoffman's people in Texas long enough to train extra battalions. We have to have these airports." He looked at his watch. "We move in an hour."

Ben watched the hands of his wristwatch mark 0500 hours. He looked at his team. "Let's do it!"

Ben was the first to reach the old radio-station building. He was huffing and puffing but he'd be damned if he'd let the younger ones beat him there. He and his team tossed pepper-gas canisters in through the windows and waited for the occupants to come staggering blindly out. When they did, the Rebels conked them on the head and tied them up. In town, the teams had located many of the old homes and stores that were being used by the NAL and started blooping 40mm grenades in through the windows.

The attack came out of the night so suddenly and without even one second's warning, the NAL was literally caught with their pants down . . . or off might be better. They leaped from their warm blankets only to be blown apart by grenades and automatic weapons fire. The Rebel attack was so swift and so savage, most of the NAL never got to fire off a round in reply.

When the Hummers arrived about three minutes after the attack began, and the .50s and Big Thumpers began pounding out their war songs, the

162

battle really heated up in sound and fury.

By 0600, the Rebels were going house to house in a search-and-destroy mission. And they were not a bit friendly in their searching. If they suspected any NAL were in a house or building, they lobbed in WP and shot them as they tried to escape the flames. Hoffman's people only thought they were ruthless. Then they met Ben Raines's Rebels.

One of the black-shirted NAL was on his knees in the middle of a street as gray light began clearing away the night. He was sobbing and nearly hysterical in his pleadings for the Rebels to please spare him.

"Give me one good reason why we should?" Maria asked him.

"Because I am a human being!" he screamed.

"You have raped and tortured and killed, you pissy excuse for a man?" Victoria asked, contempt thick in her voice.

"Yes, yes! All those things. Many times. And I am so very, very sorry for them now. But if God will forgive me, why can't you?"

"Because I'm not God," Maria told him, and shot him in the head. She spat on his body and walked away.

"I tell you something, General," Jersey said. "Me and those Spanish gals are gonna get along just fine."

Five

At the radio station, Ben waited until the fumes from the gas had dissipated, then sat and listened for more than an hour to the transmissions being sent back and forth from North America to southern Mexico. From the number of transmissions, Ben then knew just how heavy was the infiltration of the NAL into North America. And it was enough to worry him.

Then, using encrypted burst transmissions, Ben talked to his batt comms. Every raid the Rebels conducted that morning had gone off without a hitch. Only one Rebel had been injured, and he had broken his ankle slipping on an oily spot on a runway.

"All bridges leading across into North America are wired and set to blow," Ike told him. "All we have to do is hook 'em up and flip a switch."

"Have you met much resistance?"

"That's ten-fifty, Eagle. It appears to me that Hoffman sent his people 'way north of the border to try to box us in."

"That's the way I see it. We've secured the Texas border, but that's only going to buy us a little time. California, Arizona, and New Mexico are still wide open. Any suggestions."

"Not at the moment, Eagle. Hoffman's boys can spill across those borders like ants to honey. I've sent people in to destroy the crossings, but that won't slow them much when they decide to spill over. You want me to start working on the bridges along the Colorado?"

Ben hesitated for a moment. "No," he finally said. "We're supposed to be rebuilding, not destroying. Once those bridges are gone, they'll not be rebuilt in our lifetime. And they're vital links. Let's play it by ear for a time."

"Okay by me, Eagle. We've got reports that a group of Hoffman's crud is operating about a hundred miles north of my present position. I'm going up to check that out."

"That's ten-four, Shark. Eagle out."

Ben was thoughtful for a moment. He knew Ike had been transmitting from Nogales. So if Hoffman had people about a hundred miles north, that meant that the outpost at San Manuel had more than likely been overrun. He told Corrie to bump Therm down at Laredo.

"Cecil's been hospitalized, Ben," Thermopolis informed him. "The doctors don't think it's anything more serious than exhaustion. His XO has taken over."

"All right, Therm. Keep me informed on his condition. What's the word from south of the border?"

"Hoffman has made no moves yet. I don't think he knows about his bases in Texas being knocked out."

"He will by noon. That's when they all check in. Advise General Payon of that and tell him to brace for an attack."

"Ten-four, Ben. Therm out."

165

"Pack up, Corrie. We're going to slide over toward Waco and see what's shaking along the way."

Ben's teams dropped down to Highway 84 and cut east, stopping at the ruins of Fort Hood when they saw smoke from many fires coming from the old military reservation. It was a squatters' camp, with about three hundred people existing there, and living conditions were awful. The human trash living there were all armed, but they knew better than to tangle with the Rebels. Some of them there had tried that before and had firsthand witnessed the awful fury of the Rebels.

"Radio for choppers to come in and get these kids," Ben said, after walking through the camp. "Just because their parents are walking garbage doesn't mean the kids have to be."

"You ain't got no rat to do 'at," a man shouted. "Them kids is ourn."

"They won't be by this afternoon," Ben told him. "If you want to live like pigs and sewer rats, that's your choice. But the children will be raised in a decent manner."

The man stood staring at Ben. But he wisely kept his mouth shut.

"These kids have lice, fleas, and all are suffering from malnutrition," a medic reported. "They've all been beaten and some have been sexually abused."

"Times is hard," a woman told Ben. "We grown-ups has got to have the best food so's we can hunt and fish and trap and the like. 'Em 'air kids is tough. They don't need as much food as we'uns."

Ben fixed her with a very dark and angry look. "Get this goddamn stupid person away from me before I shoot her," he finally said.

The woman paled under the dirt on her face and quickly faded back into the knot of unwashed and ignorant people.

"When we get over to the river, we'll all strip down and bathe," Ben said. "We can get the fleas and various other hopping and jumping insects off us that way. Jesus, how can people live like this?"

"You and General Payon are so much alike it is frightening," Tomas told him. "I have seen him weep at sights like this."

"No one has to live under these conditions."

"There ain't no work, General," a man said, stepping out of the crowd. "And don't none of us care to live under them rules of yourn. Way I see it, how we live ain't none of your goddamn business."

"The way you treat children certainly is," Ben said. "And you could live under Rebel rule if you tried. You just won't try."

"I tried," the man said. His hands were balled into fists and his face dark with anger. "I was at that outpost of yourn up near the Oklahoma border. Ever'time I turned around somebody was a-tellin' me to cut my yard or not to whup up on my old lady or the kids and all kinds of shit like that. I had me an old dog that wouldn't mind and wouldn't hunt. It wasn't no good for nothin'. I beat the damn thing to death with a 2x4 and a Rebel soldier boy come along and took it away from me and whupped my head to a fare-thee-well with it. I had a headache for a goddamn week. They throwed me and mine out of the community and told us not to come back. But they kept my young'uns. All you people is is a bunch of commonists."

"The word is *communists*. And you're very lucky it wasn't me that found you beating that animal," Ben told the man. "I'd have shot you."

"Your day's a-comin', Ben Raines," the man told him. "When Hoffman gits here we ain't gonna have the likes of you and your army tellin' us what to do."

167

Ben laughed at the man, and that seemed to make the misfit even angrier. "You really think Hoffman will tolerate the likes of you any better than I do?"

"At least he cares more about human bein's than he does animals!"

"Whup his uppity ass, Hugh," a woman shouted.

"Shet your mouth," Hugh told her without taking his eyes from Ben.

"Obviously I care about humans, Hugh," Ben said. "I'm taking the children to see that they are properly cared for, aren't I?" Ben knew he should just back off and leave the squatter camp. But he just didn't like the Hughs of the world. He had never been able to stomach men like Hugh, and they came in all colors and all sizes.

"Ah, hell," Jersey leaned close and whispered to Victoria. "I can see it coming. The general's gonna duke it out with this bum."

"You mean, fight him with his fists?" Victoria asked.

"Fists, boots, knives," Jersey said nonchalantly. "It really doesn't make that much difference to the general."

"But . . . generals do not fight with their fists!" Maria said.

"This general does," Beth spoke up.

Ben gave Hugh a closer inspection. The man was about forty-five, he guessed, and looked to be in pretty good shape. He obviously had not missed nearly as many meals as he had baths. Hugh was about six feet tall and at one time he'd been muscular. But the years had softened that. And Ben could guess with reasonable accuracy what was coming next out of Hugh's mouth. His type never varied all that much.

"You a mighty tough-talkin' man with all these

168

Rebels around you, ain't you, General?"

"Never varies," Ben muttered.

"What's 'at you said?" Hugh asked.

"I said you're a dickhead, Hugh baby. An unwashed, foul-smelling, semiliterate, smart-assed bully."

"Huh!" Hugh shouted.

Ben handed Coop his M-16 and unhooked his battle harness, handing that to Beth. He removed his pistol belt and tossed that to Tomas, standing by with a worried look on his face.

"No interference," Ben said, looking around him. "From either side." Then he stepped forward and busted Hugh smack in the mouth with a gloved fist.

The blow bloodied the man's lips and brought a roar from his throat. He charged Ben, both fists swinging, and Ben ducked under and planted a right into the man's belly. The air whooshed out and Hugh backed up, gasping for breath. Ben stalked him, giving the man no time to recover and get set.

"Stomp his sissy guts out, Hugh!" a man hollered.

"That'll be the day," a Rebel said.

Hugh, screaming wild curses, charged Ben and ran into him, the force of the collision knocking him to the ground. Ben rolled away from a vicious kick aimed at his head and jumped to his boots.

"Now I know the rules," he told Hugh. "And now I'm going to kick the snot out of you."

Hugh swung a looping roundhouse and Ben sidestepped and planted a fist onto Hugh's kidney. He followed that with another vicious blow to the other kidney and Hugh screamed in pain. Ben stepped forward and drove his closed fist down into the center of the man's back as hard as he could. Hugh screamed and fell to his knees, all the nerves in his body shrieking from the blow to his spinal cord.

169

So far he had not landed a blow to Ben.

Ben backed up and let the man slowly rise to his feet. Hugh's mouth was dripping blood and he was breathing hard. He cursed Ben as he walked toward him.

Ben stood silent, waiting, his fists raised. Hugh tried to fake Ben out but Ben wouldn't take the bait. Hugh shuffled and Ben noticed that when he did, his left dropped about six inches. The next time he shuffled, Ben plowed right in and hit the man a combination of lefts and rights that smashed Hugh's nose and pulped his already-battered lips. Hugh backed up, shaking his shaggy head. The blood flew.

"Bastard!" Hugh pushed the word past his swollen lips.

Ben's reply was a right fist to Hugh's nose. This time the nose spread out some. Ben snapped a left and further broadened Hugh's honker. Ben bore in now, slamming lefts and rights to Hugh's body and face. Hugh backed up, reached down, and jerked a knife out of his boot.

"Steady now!" Ben shouted, moving close to Jersey. "This is my fight. Give me a blade, Jersey."

Jersey handed him her long-bladed Bowie knife. "Gut him, General," she said.

Victoria and Maria both noted the expert way Ben held the knife, blade held to the side for a slash or a gut-cut, and the way his left hand never stopped moving, distracting Hugh.

"I'm a-gonna kill you, Raines!" Hugh spat blood with the angry words. "Nobody tells me what to do. I'm an in-dividualist."

Ben laughed at him. That was probably the longest word he knew. And he couldn't even pronounce it correctly. "I'm sure you were, Hugh. A beer-drankin', snuff-dippin', honky-tonkin', woodsroamin', coon-huntin', Saturday and Sunday afternoon armchair-quarterbackin' rugged individualist. And put all that together and you come up with a pile of shit."

"I hate your slimy guts, Ben Raines! I'm a-gonna cut 'em out, too."

"Well, come on, Hugh baby," Ben urged him. "Come on!"

With a snarl and a curse, Hugh came. He slashed wide, opening himself up, and Ben buried the blade in his gut, up to the hilt, and then ripped up, the blade slicing through and stopping when it caught on the V of his rib cage. Ben pulled the blade out and stood watching as Hugh dropped the knife and fell forward on his face. He screamed as the pain hit him and rolled over on his back, staring up at Ben.

"You see, Hugh baby," Ben told him. "All Rebels go through extensive close-combat training. They spend weeks just learning how to use a knife." He smiled, a hard curving of the lips at Hugh. "We do a lot of close-in work."

Hugh groaned and closed his eyes for a moment. He opened them and stared up at Ben. "Ain't you gonna let your medical people fix me up, Raines?"

"We don't provide medical service for people who do not subscribe to the Rebel philosophy," Ben told him very bluntly.

"You the hardest goddamn man I ever seen in all my life," Hugh said.

"Which is growing shorter much more rapidly than you would like, I'm sure."

"You a devil!" Hugh gasped very weakly.

Ben wiped the blade of Jersey's knife clean on a rag Coop handed him and returned the Bowie to Jersey. Hugh was jerking around on the ground making all sorts of disgusting sounds.

171

The others in the squatter camp stood silently, shocked by the ease with which the commanding general of the Rebel army, several years older than Hugh, had whipped the man.

"Let's go," Ben said, after slipping into his battle harness. "I'm rapidly developing the monkey-and-the-skunk syndrome about this stinking place."

"The monkey-and-the-skunk syndrome?" Victoria whispered to Jersey.

Jersey grinned, and whispered in her ear. The two women fell in behind Ben and walked off laughing.

Six

What was left of Waco was nearly deserted. A few people managed to survive in the ruins, living off only God knew what. They flitted out of sight upon spotting the Rebels. If they had children, they kept them out of Rebel view, knowing the Rebels would not hesitate to take them out of such a mean existence. There was no sign that the NAL had ever visited the city. The Rebels drove out to the old Waco airport. It was deserted and showed no signs of having been used in years. The Rebels pulled out, heading northeast on 31. They spent the night on the banks of the Waxahachie Creek, after taking a soapy bath, washing their dirty clothes and then changing into fresh BDUs.

On the road from Waco to Interstate 45 the Rebels had met several dozen people, struggling to survive. They knew all about this hard-eyed bunch of people called Rebels and did not wish to share in their way of life, preferring to go it alone. Ben did not understand that, but he respected it so long as any young were being cared for and not being abused.

"They're not eating high on the hog," a man who'd been standing by the side of the road told Ben.

"But they're eating well and the wife has taught them all how to read and write and figure and so forth. We got the books from a school down the road. We're doing all right."

Ben smiled at the kids who had gathering around their father. Their clothing was old and patched, but it was clean and the kids looked as healthy as any Rebel child.

"Is there anything we can do for you?" Ben asked.

"I don't reckon so. We rely on herbs and the like for medicines when we need it. I plow with mules and we have milk cows and chickens and hogs."

"You're not armed," Ben said.

"God will see us through," the man said.

"Uh-huh," Ben replied. "What happens when you run into vicious people who don't believe in God?"

"We have hiding places we run to."

"It's your ass," Ben told him, then motioned for Coop to drive on.

"And the asses of the kids," Beth said.

"They're loved and well cared for," Ben replied, as they rolled on. "How can we find fault with that?"

It was a question with no answer.

They followed the interstate to the ruins of Dallas/Fort Worth, buttoned up their Hummers and prowled the ruins of the once-great cities. The Rebels found signs of life in the ruins, but made no attempt to interfere, since the inhabitants were not hostile toward them. Ben knew that he and the members of his army were both admired and feared, envied and loathed, by many who resided in North America, and not just by those who chose to pick through the rubbled ruins of the cities to survive. If it bothered him at all, he rarely commented on it.

"No kids," Jersey said.

"They hide them when we approach," Beth said. "They're ignorant bastards and bitches and their kids will grow up to be the same. It's disgusting."

Ben remained silent, letting his team members vent their opinions. But it was rare for Beth to be so blunt. Jersey called it as she saw it, often shocking those around her with her bluntness, but Beth usually was not so outspoken.

"You think it ought to be against the law?" Cooper said with a grin.

"It is against the law," Beth replied. "Morally, at least."

"What the hell is this up ahead?" Ben blurted.

A large group of men and women, dressed in rags, stood on the sidewalks and stared vacant-eyed at the line of Rebels in their Hummers. They grunted and pointed at the Rebels.

"Check it out," Ben ordered. "But I think I know."

Rebels cautiously approached the large group and found them to be harmless. Ben got out and walked up to them. Many of them ducked their heads and raised their hands to cover their eyes. Others plucked at Ben's uniform. Ben pushed their hands away. They were all mentally impaired, as he had thought after he got over his initial shock.

"What the hell do we do with them, General?" Ben was asked.

"Let's get some planes in here," he told Corrie. "Bring medical teams in to tranquilize these people before we attempt to move them. Poor things can't help what they are. How in the hell they survived this long is a miracle."

"You soldier boys can take the men," a hard voice called from the rubble. "But you leave the women. We use them when we get hard-up for snatch."

The Rebels turned to face a knot of men, all armed.

Jersey said, "Those disgusting sons of bitches." She spat out the words.

Gunners had opened up the roofs of the Hummers and were in position behind the .50s and the 40mm Big Thumpers. If these dregs of humanity wanted a fight, it was going to be a damn short one.

"We take them all," Ben informed the group of men. "Back off or die. Those are your only two options."

The leader of the group of rabble looked at the awesome firepower facing him and his band of no-goods and slowly nodded his head. "Yeah. Well, I may be dumb, but I shore as hell ain't stupid. I knowed that someday you and your soldier boys and girls would come in here and fuck ever'thing up for us, Raines. Ah, hell, go on and take this pack of loonies. They's crazies wanderin' all over the place, Raines. We'll just find us another bunch."

"I don't like this," Tomas said softly. "We cannot allow them to continue abusing the mentally ill."

"I'm open for suggestions," Ben replied. "You want to open fire on them?"

"Truthfully, yes," the Mexican said. "But my conscience would not let me live with that."

"I do know the feeling."

The Rebels watched the men fade back into the ruins and disappear from view.

"There is an old parking lot just up the street, General," a scout called. "Plenty of room for choppers to land. But how the hell do we get these folks up there? They're scared to death."

"We herd them," Ben said with a laugh. "Just move them along easy-like. They'll go."

The Rebels watched the last of the mentally ill being placed on board Black Hawk choppers and then lift off.

"Let's get the hell out of here," Ben said. "Before those slime we ran off decide to make trouble."

"Too late," Coop said, looking around him. "Here they come."

"Hunt cover!" Ben shouted, and bellied down behind a rusted old car that had been abandoned for years.

"You want me to call for Apaches, General?" Corrie asked, just as the slime in the city opened fire. "They're not sixty miles away."

"We'll handle this, Corrie," Ben replied, loading his bloop tube. "I'm rather looking forward to it. Order all personnel to commence firing grenades."

No one among the Rebels could ever figure out exactly why the street slime wanted to pick a fight with them. But when the unwashed started it, the fight turned savage. Rebels began firing all types of 40mm grenades: buckshot, high-explosive, and fragmentation. The leader of the group managed to stand up at just the right time for the Rebels and the wrong time for him. He took an HE in the center of the chest and got himself splattered all over the rubble.

It seemed to take all the fight out of the rest of them. But they didn't know, or had forgotten, how Rebels fight. When they tried to run away and fade back into the depths of the ruined city, the Rebels cut them down. Then the gunners cranked up the big .50s and the Big Thumpers and really made life miserable for the thugs. Ben finally called a halt to it.

"Let's get out of here, people. Hell with this place."

West had shifted his teams up toward the Oklahoma border and Ben headed that way, while Buddy and Striganov linked up and Dan headed west on the interstate then cut south to Fort Stockton and eventually would head east toward San Antonio.

Down south, General Jesus Hoffman was getting fewer and fewer field reports out of Texas. At first he thought it might be due to his people shifting locations, then it began to dawn on him that just possibly Ben Raines was kicking the crap out of his invincible black-shirted army. That possibility became a reality when a messenger charged into his office, frantically waving a piece of paper and shouting.

"Calm yourself!" Hoffman shouted. "Sit down and calm yourself. What is it?"

The messenger fanned himself for a moment. "Our people just north of Fort Stockton are under heavy guerrilla attack. Only a small group are left alive and they are in the radio room. The message was cut off in midsentence."

"Read it to me," Hoffman said grimly.

"Garrison has been overrun by Rebels. Most personnel dead. Attack was sudden and vicious. Rebels rarely take prisoners. Have retreated to the radio room and there we will fight to the last. Heil . . .' It ends there, General Hoffman."

"Good man," Hoffman said. "He was praising the führer to the end. He was a true hero." He dismissed the messenger and stood up, facing the group of ranking officers there for a meeting. "A few defeats are to be expected. I want this to be remembered: We are facing a totally professional army. I'm afraid our sweep up through South and Central America, and our victories here in Mexico, have swelled some heads. I want this message read to all troops. That will take some of the air out of them. Gentleman, defeating the Rebel army will not be easy. We will do it, but it will not be easily done." He faced the huge wall map, and when he again spoke, it was with his back to his officers.

"Ben Raines is a skillful and ruthless commander. Remember that. He fights by no rules. You just heard the message: he rarely takes prisoners. All right, we must assume we have lost our bases . . ." He lifted his shoulders, let them fall, and then turned around. "Everywhere in Texas. There might be two or three still operational, but they'll fall. Then Raines will send teams out all over North America, hunting down our people. But the bulk of his people will be in Texas, waiting for us."

"Do we have a firm number of Rebel battalions?" he was asked.

"Anywhere from fourteen to eighteen," a Hoffman aide said. "There is no way of knowing how many of Payon's battalions will eventually join Raines in North America."

"So he has, shall we say, twelve to fifteen thousand Rebels. That's ridiculous!" a general said. "We outnumber him by thousands of men. Why are we waiting? Let's move now and smash them."

"I warn you all, again," Hoffman said, facing the group, "Ben Raines is not to be taken lightly. The Libyan, Khamsin, came here with thousands of men. Ben Raines and the Rebels destroyed his army. Down to the last man! We'll win this fight, have no doubts of that. But the battles will be fought not only with brawn, but with brains. I cannot stress that enough. Ben Raines is a wily fox, a dangerous wolf, a cunning tiger of a hunter, and as dangerous as the bite of a cobra. If you succumb to his siren songs, he'll lure you, trick you, trap you, and kill you."

Hoffman met the eyes of each man and woman in the room. "I was six years old when I joined my grandfather's youth movement. I have spent virtually my entire life preparing for this moment. I shall not see it wasted because of eagerness, carelessness, or vanity. We shall be victorious!" he shouted, slamming his hand down on the desk. "We shall not fail in our conquest of the world. We will win because we have God and the dreams of Hitler on our side. We will someday see the flag of the New Order fly over all the world. And the dreams of the greatest man who ever lived will at last be fulfilled. Heil Hitler!"

It was a strange and chilling moment as the room rocked with the stiff-arm and verbal salute as everyone jumped to their boots and shouted.

"Heil Hitler!"

Wichita Falls, Texas.

"As far as I can tell, Ben, we've pretty much cleaned out Hoffman's infiltrators—at least in this state," West said. "Dan's boys and girls just wiped a station down around Fort Stockton. The outpost up in Wichita Falls held and beat back several attacks. As soon as they're resupplied, they'll be in good shape. I've ordered supplies in."

Ben nodded his head and opened a map case. "I'm ordering the immediate evacuation of all Rebel-held outposts south of a Nacogdoches-Waco-San Angelo-El Paso line. I've ordered Ike and his teams to blow every bridge in this area. I'm going to make extreme southwest Texas impassable. Beginning here, just south of El Paso, everything south of I-10, from the Rio Grande east to 277, will be a no-man's-land. If that goose-stepping son of a bitch wants Texas, he's going to have to cross over down here." Ben hit the map. "Now, he might come up through California, Arizona, or New Mexico. If he does, he's going to find some damn rough and slow going. The roads and bridges running along the border from San Diego to El Paso will soon be virtually impassable. I—"

"General," Corrie stuck her head into the room. "Some . . . ah, people here to see you, sir."

"Who are they?"

"Cowboys, sir."

"Cowboys?"

"Yes, sir. Their colonel says they number about five hundred in all. I mean, they're not riding horses. But they're all dressed in boots and big hats. They're all in pickups and Jeeps. They are a, ah, formidable-looking force, sir."

"I have to see this," West said.

"Me, too," Ben said.

The men walked outside.

The first thing Ben noticed was the small group of men waiting for him were all dressed alike. Blue jeans and brown western-style shirts. And cowboy boots. He was relieved to see none were wearing spurs. A tall, rangy man broke from the group and walked over to him, holding out his hand. Ben shook it.

"Ned Hawkins, General Raines. Commander of the Texas Rangers. At your service."

"The . . . Texas Rangers?" Ben questioned.

"Yes, sir. We've been forming and training in secret for just about a year now. Around and just north of the Big Bend country." He smiled and Ben felt it was genuine. He took an immediate liking of the fellow. "We have all sorts of folks in this battalion, sir. We weeded out any who can't get along with other people 'cause of skin color. We had about fifteen hundred to start out. We have just over five hundred who made it through." His grin widened. "And I'm proud to say that we're all from Texas. The

181

only thing I'd ask of you is to allow us to fly our Texas flag alongside the new flag of the United States."

"How come my people didn't detect your movement north, Ned?"

"We came up here to north Texas just before you and your Rebels arrived, sir. We didn't want you to think we were a hostile force. We, ah, know that the Rebels often shoot first and ask questions later. And I'm proud to say that we do too."

Ben looked at the man for a moment. "All right, Ned. Bring your people in. Let's have a look."

"We'll all have a look," Jersey muttered.

Seven

Ben took one look and knew these men had come to fight. Ned Hawkins had not only trained them in combat skills, but also in military discipline. The men all stood at rigid attention. And while they were all driving pickup trucks, these trucks were not quite the garden variety.

The trucks were all four-wheel drive with high clearance. They had been repainted in earth tones to blend in. In the back of the trucks, heavy machine guns had been mounted and the sidewalls built up for maximum protection. The windshield had been replaced and could now be lowered on one side or the other, or both sides down.

"I knew a good ol' boy who used to bulletproof cars for a living," Hawkins said. "We went to his shop—'way out in the boonies—and reworked these babies. They won't stop a rocket, but they'll stop anything else fired from small arms. Except for a Haskins .50 caliber, incendiary-tipped. You got any of those, General?"

"Every one that was ever made, I believe," Ben replied.

Ned grinned. "I figured you would. You people

took everything that wasn't nailed down."

"Still doing it," Ben said, returning the grin. "But we also have a .50 caliber rifle that fires the same round but in automatic. Uses twenty-round clips. It's a real jewel."

"I bet it is! Come on. Meet the boys."

Ben met several Jim Bobs and Joe Bills, a couple of Bubbas, and Cooter and Scooter. There was not a single Tex in the bunch. Neb Hawkins's Texas Rangers—twenty-first-century style—were a combat-ready bunch. But they made it clear from the outset that they had plenty of respect for the Rebels.

"Any of your men married, Ned?"

"Some of them. What to do with the ladies is sort of a problem."

"They'll be safe at Base Camp One. We'll fly them over there. Providing you all polygraph or PSE in without a hitch."

Ned chuckled. "We all expected that, General. I'll personally shoot any man who flunks it. I can't abide a goddamned traitor."

Ben looked at the man. "I really believe you would."

"Oh, you can believe it. Like I told you, sir, we fight under two flags: Old Glory—or what passes for it now—and the flag of Texas. Any man who'd betray either one of them doesn't deserve anything but a bullet or a hangman's noose."

Teams of doctors and polygraph and PSE operators were flown in and every one of the Rangers passed the grueling tests. The Rebels all knew the Texas men would fit right in when Ned winked at Ben and called to a man nicknamed Slim. Slim looked like a strong gust of wind would blow him away. But Ben correctly assumed that Slim was all whang-leather, gristle and bone and rawhide tough.

184

"Yes, sir, Colonel?" Slim said.

"I hate to tell you this, Slim," Ned said with a straight face. "But I got to shoot you."

"Shoot me! What the hell for?"

"Or maybe you'd rather be hanged. They tell me that's a good, fast way to go."

"Hang! Hell, no!" Slim hollered. "What's happened, Colonel?"

"You failed all your tests, boy. That means you're a collaborator."

"Collaborator? Hellfire, Ned. I ain't no collaborator. I been a Baptist all my life. You can ask my sister about that."

Ned just couldn't pull it off. He took a long look at the expression on Slim's face and busted out laughing.

The last time anybody saw Slim and Ned for a couple of hours that afternoon, Slim was chasing his commander around the buildings of the old air force base, shouting curses and threatening to stomp his ass into the ground for pulling such a damn-fool stunt. While the Rebels and the Rangers stood around laughing.

Ben split up the Rangers into teams, then issued them body armor and other equipment he had flown in. "The cowboy hats are fine, until you go into combat," Ben told them. "Then you wear helmets just like everybody else. Macho is one thing. Stupid is another. I need all the live allies I can find. Dead, you won't be a bit of use to me. Or to Texas," he added, knowing that would encourage the use of helmets more than anything.

Ben approved of the way Hawkins had split his people up. Four men were assigned to most of the trucks. A driver and a gunner in the cab, and a machine gunner and helper in the padded bed of each truck. Others drove trucks loaded with food and ammo, cans of gas, and other equipment. Ben sent them westward at staggered intervals. When everybody was in place, from the New Mexico border to the west, and to the Arkansas border to the east, the teams would begin working south. They would inspect every town and travel every road in a search-and-destroy mission.

The Rangers had been assigned Rebel radios and a short course on how they worked was given by Corrie. There was no horseplay from the new men. They knew their lives might well depend on the radios and they paid close attention.

After wishing the new people well, and shaking hands with Ned, Ben and his bunch headed north, crossed the Red River into Oklahoma and cut east on Highway 70, taking the southernmost route across the bottom of the state.

They saw only desolation, despair, and ruin. For reasons that no one had ever been able to explain, Oklahoma had been the hardest hit by roaming gangs of thugs and punks right after the Great War and also during the later years. They had turned a large part of the state into piles of rubble. The Rebels did not have a single outpost in the southern part of the state.

"This drive is depressing," Cooper said, after they rolled through what was left of a small town. "Where the hell are all the people?"

"There are some out there," Ben said, gazing out the window. "See the plumes of smoke to the south?"

"Squatter camps," Beth said. "I was talking with a scout the other day. He told me this stretch along here has a lot of them. They don't do anything. Don't raise gardens or keep milk cows or do anything except hunt or fish. They've wiped out all the game in this area."

"We'll put a stop to that after we've dealt with Hoffman," Ben said. "Right now I don't have time to fool with the shiftless bastards. Although it would probably be prudent to take the time to do so."

"Why's that, General?" Cooper asked.

"Trashy-assed people like Beth just talked about are always looking for the easy way out. Anything that goes wrong is never their fault. It's always somebody's else's fault. Hoffman will recruit them to fight against us in one way or the other. If he's smart, that is, and I think he is."

"Scouts reporting a lot of chatter on CBs, General," Corrie said.

"Hold it right here," Ben said. "Let's see what's up ahead before we walk into something."

"Scouts are laying back and reporting a massive roadblock on the outskirts of the town," Corrie told him. "Heavily armed people are demanding that we pay them tribute before they'll let us use the highways."

Ben grunted. "Tribute, huh? Sure. It's a trap," he said, carefully rolling a cigarette. He was thoughtful for a moment. "Tell the scouts to give the terrain on both sides of the blockade a very careful going over. I think we're probably hard in enemy territory, gang. Pass that word, Corrie. I think Herr Hoffman's goose-steppers have been here before us."

"Scouts report seeing nothing out of the ordinary, General," Corrie said after bumping the forward people. "But they say if you want a gut feeling, something is wrong."

"Set up mortars," Ben ordered. "Fire only on my orders. When crews are in place, get on the CB channel and tell those people to tear down that blockade and get those hidden ambushers in plain sight or we'll open fire. Order the scouts back."

Corrie hesitated. "What if there are no ambushers, General?"

"Then I've made a mistake and those behind the barricades are in trouble."

Ben ordered Cooper forward. In sight of the barricades but well out of range, Ben stood outside the Hummer and watched and waited. For a few moments, it looked like a cold standoff between the Rebels and the locals. Then cooler heads prevailed among those behind the barricades and Corrie got the word.

"They say hold our fire, General. The ambushers are being called in and they're all backing off."

"Tell them to lay all weapons on the shoulder of the road and do it now." Ben watched through binoculars as the locals hurriedly complied. The barricades were torn down. The several-hundred-strong band of locals outnumbered the Rebels, but as it usually went, numbers meant very little. The reputation of the Rebels had preceded them. The locals wanted no part of the Rebels' fury when engaged in a firefight.

The scouts moved in fast and secured the locals. Two Hummers with top-mounted .50s had a very calming effect on the would-be ambushers.

Ben got out and stood looking at the shiftless bunch. They were dirty and unkempt. "Don't get too close," he told his people. "I think they've got fleas . . . among other things."

"There's a damn river right outside of town," Coop said. "Why don't they bathe?"

"They're losers," Ben said. "And nothing that anybody did would change that. If these were normal times, you could hand them a million dollars in cash today and they'd be dead broke in a year, or less, with nothing to show for it." He raised his voice. "Who's in charge of this pack of rabble?"

"I am," a man said, stepping forward. "And we ain't rabble."

"That is certainly a matter of opinion," Ben replied. "What did Hoffman's soldiers offer you to fight on their side?"

The man exchanged glances with several people left and right of him. "I don't know what you're talkin' about, Raines."

"Sergeant Morgan," Ben said, "if that man does not give a satisfactory reply to my question in five seconds, shoot him."

Morgan lifted his M-16.

"Wait a damn minute!" the local yelled. "Holy shit! All right. All right. Hoffman's people said they'd keep us supplied with food and clothing and the like. That's a hell of a lot more than you folks has done for us."

It was a never ending debate and Ben was weary of it. Back in the 1960s, the federal government had created programs to ease the burden of the poor. It looked good on paper. In effect it destroyed the work ethic and ruined the pride of millions of people. Why work when the government (using the tax money from millions of hard-working citizens) would feed, clothe, and house those who didn't choose to work? Like nearly every government program ever devised by those ninnies in Washington, it swelled out of control and those in power didn't have the courage to stop it.

"There are no free rides in Rebel society, mister," Ben told the man, knowing damn well the citizen already knew it. Ben also felt this man was not from

Oklahoma; the accent was all wrong.

"We're American citizens," the man said sullenly. "We got a right to food and a decent life."

"There is no America," Ben told him. "Not like anything you or I knew before the Great War. At least something good came out of that tragedy. And the states are united, held together, only by Rebel outposts, populated by men and women who work their butts off from daylight to dark in an attempt to build a better way of life. You people know all this. You're just too goddamn lazy to pitch in and help. Every one of you know the rules. If you want Rebel help, we'll give it to you. All you've got to do is follow a few rules."

"Your rules is too harsh, General," a woman called out. "They're unreasonable."

"I've seen buildings all over the country jam-packed with law books," Cooper said to Ben. "Billions of words that the average citizen couldn't make heads or tails of. Our rules don't even fill up a little notebook. What the hell's the matter with people?"

"It's too simple for them," Ben said. "Sergeant?"

"Sir!"

"Gather up all the weapons. Prepare to move out."

When the citizens didn't protest, Ben knew they had more weapons cached somewhere. And if there were any children, the people had hidden them from Rebel eyes. The Rebels put the town behind them and rolled on. They traveled through fifty miles of nothing. Absolutely nothing. This time there was not one sign of human habitation. No smoke, nothing.

"Spooky," Jersey said. "I'll be glad when we're clear of this stretch."

The next town they rolled through was deserted,

and had been for a long time. Years of looting had left it very nearly in ruins.

"Let's spend the night here," Ben said. "We know there are people in the next town. What we don't know is how they'll receive us. We'd better be fresh when we find out."

Ben walked the deserted main street of the town. In what had once been a drug store, he stepped into the gloom and prowled around. The place had been picked over so many times even the rats had finally left it.

He didn't bother to check the pharmacy, for he knew he would find far-out-of-date medicines on the floor and on the shelves. The only things taken would be the drugs that would give someone an artificial high or low. Drugs that would save lives and fight infection would be largely ignored by the ignorant assholes with a looter's mentality.

He stepped out of the gloom and into the late afternoon sunlight, his team right with him, and walked on.

"Scouts report the small library was burned," Corrie said. "All the books destroyed."

"Naturally," Ben replied.

"Somebody sure did a number on this town," Cooper said.

"Our people were probably among the first to strip it," Ben said with a smile. "Back when we were building the old Tri-States."

They passed what had been a small cafe. "I bet you a lot of coffee was sold in there and a lot of gossip shared," Beth said. "If that place could only talk."

"Memories," Ben spoke softly. "Memories of a time that will never come again."

A Hummer rolled up beside them and stopped. The Rebel said, "General, there isn't anything in this town. We haven't seen a dog, a cat, a rat, nothing."

Ben stood for a moment, listening. There were no birds flying or singing. Without moving his head, he cut his eyes to the second floor of a building across the street. "At my orders," he said very softly, "we jump into that cafe. When we jump, you people in that Hummer get the hell off the street and find cover. We just walked blindly into an ambush. *Now!*"

Eight

Ben's helmet was knocked from his head by a slug. Luckily, his chin strap had not been fastened. From the second-floor windows of the buildings on both sides of the street, automatic weapons opened up. For a few seconds, the fire was so intense all the Rebels could do was keep their heads down and hug the floor.

"We've got people down," Corrie shouted over the rattle of combat.

"Start firing grenades into the second floor of the buildings," Ben returned the shout. "Get those bloop tubes working and the Big Thumpers going. Get some cover smoke into the streets, people. Cooper, check the back door. We've got to get out of here."

Cooper scrambled through the litter and bellied down on the back-room floor. He had just spotted movement across the alleyway as Beth joined him. "People in that building just across from us, Beth. They're all dressed differently, so that lets our people out."

"Grenades?"

"Why not?" Coop said with a grin, leveling his

M-16. "You loaded?"

"Let's do it."

They fired as one, and the 40mm grenades sailed through the windowless frames of the building and exploded. Screams of pain from the shrapnel from the fragmentation liner reached them just as they reloaded and fired again. Out in the street, .50s were yammering and Big Thumpers snorting as they hurled their grenades. M-60 machine guns, called The Pigs, began grunting out firepower.

Ben slid on his belly on the littered floor and almost sailed right out the open doorframe. Beth grabbed him by the ankles and held him back only after Jersey grabbed her by the belt and held on.

"Larry, Curly, and Moe," Ben muttered. He looked out into the alley and could see no one. "Put a couple more grenades into that old building and then let's get the hell gone from here."

Cooper and Beth blooped a couple more grenades across the alley and the team took off, cutting to the right and running up the alley. Ben jumped into a building near the end of the block, his team right behind him. They stood for a moment, listening. Boots thudded on the old floor above them, sending dust down on their heads. Ben grinned and pointed the muzzle of his M-16 toward the ceiling. His team followed suit.

Five M-16s rattled, and one hundred and fifty 5.56 caliber slugs created a duststorm in the room and turned the room above them into a death trap. The falling bodies created another dust storm and Ben stepped into what had once been a showroom for something.

"Corrie, order all personnel to start using incendiary rounds. Burn the bastards out. Let's fall back to the vehicles."

Back into the alley again as the Rebels began lobbing special-purpose ammo. Big Thumpers were knocking out thirty-five to forty rounds a minute and the town was soon burning. Those as-yet-unknowns who had almost succeeded in effectively ambushing the Rebels began running out of the inferno.

"Take some alive," Ben ordered. "I want to see who is behind all this."

Three people were brought to Ben. Two men and a woman. It surprised him when he saw they were Oriental. "Who the hell are you?" he asked.

They stared at him, sullen and silent.

"Maybe they're shy?" Cooper suggested.

The woman looked at him. "Stupid American bastard!"

"I can see right now that you and me are never going to be real close," Coop replied.

She spat at him, then cut her eyes to Jersey. "What are you here for, ornamentation? The American army has always been unfair in their treatment of women."

"Not in this army, sister."

The woman snorted, quite unladylike, and said to Ben, "I suppose you are going to rape and defile me. Well, go ahead. It's what I expect of barbarians."

"Lady," Ben said, "and I use that term as loosely as possible, I wouldn't screw you with Herr Hoffman's dick." She narrowed her eyes at that and Ben knew he'd hit home.

Buildings in the town began collapsing as the flames consumed them. Somewhere, someone was screaming hoarsely. Ben waited until the crashing abated, then said, "I won't even ask what nut group you were with before the Great War, but I could

195

probably make a very accurate guess. When you get to operations central, I would suggest you answer any question asked you truthfully and quickly. You won't be physically tortured, but the drugs we use can be pretty grim. Keep that in mind."

"You will never, ever get anything out of any of us, General Raines," she boasted.

"That's what they all say, sister."

The Rebels did not take the time to bury the enemy dead. They left them where they lay sprawled and pulled out after burying their own dead. They turned north a few miles outside Ardmore and made a cold camp in a ghost town. The prisoners were kept under heavy guard.

"You'll kill us if we attempt escape, I suppose?" the woman asked.

"Nope," a guard told her. "We want you alive. We'll just blow your kneecaps off."

The prisoners glanced at one another; there would be no attempts made at escape. They had quickly learned that the Rebels meant every word they said.

The following morning, coffee was heated by using smokeless heat tabs and the Rebels were on their way. The Rebels had buried five of their own and several more were badly wounded, so it was imperative they reach a spot where planes could land and take out the wounded, resupply the teams with gear, and bring them up to strength with personnel.

"Tell operations we're going into what's left of Ardmore," Ben told Corrie. "One way or the other, we'll take the airport. Tell them to get birds in the air with personnel and equipment."

"I'm north of Gainesville, Texas, Father," Buddy

196

radioed. "I'm moving out now with two full teams and will be ready to assist you in one hour. Two more full teams are thirty minutes behind me and will be crossing the river a few miles east of my position and approaching on Highway 70."

"That's ten-four, son. What do you have on the situation in our objective?"

"Nothing, sir. Except most of the city is in ruins. And we don't have gunships anywhere close. We're going into the unknown."

"We've done it before. See you shortly." Rolling out, Ben said, "We're just about one hour away. We should be arriving at about the same time."

But the worry was groundless. The small city lay in deserted ruins. With all Rebels working feverishly, a runway was cleared and the planes touched down. Rather than wait any longer, Rebel doctors went to work and operated on the wounded right there.

"Our worries were for naught, son," Ben told Buddy. "You and your people can take off anytime, and thanks for your help."

Buddy didn't move.

Ben eyeballed him curiously. "Did you hear me, son?"

"I heard you. We're staying."

"As far as I know, boy, I still give the orders around here."

"That is correct, sir. But your orders can be overridden if all other commanders voice strong objections. I believe you set that up yourself."

"Ummm," Ben said. "Yes, I did. I wondered what you were doing so far north. The batt comms sent you and these other teams to birddog me, huh?"

"In a manner of speaking." Buddy braced for a verbal assault.

It didn't come. His father smiled and patted the son's muscular arm. "I guess I'd better get used to it. All right. With this much firepower, we'll penetrate deeper into this state and see what we can find. As soon as the wounded and the prisoners are airborne, we'll pull out for a look-see."

They didn't see much in the way of life. There were survivors, for plumes of smoke were always in evidence. But the people weren't coming forward to be seen. Only a few survivors had come forward, and those few had seen no enemy troops. And they wanted no part of the Rebel way of life. They didn't ask for any help, and Ben didn't offer any. The teams rolled on up the interstate.

"This reminds me of the way it was years ago," Jersey said. "I feel like we've been pushed back into time."

"Call me dumb if you want to," Cooper said. "And no smart cracks from you, Jersey, but I don't understand these people. We offer education, medical help, safety, community activities, all sorts of things, yet so many will not take advantage of it. I don't understand it."

"Join the club, Coop," Jersey said. "But I've about made up my mind not to worry about them anymore. I'm sorry for their kids. But we can't shoulder the troubles of everybody and damned if I'm going to try. If they won't help themselves, they can just go to hell."

"We'll have to fight them someday," the usually quiet Beth remarked. "It's been that way since recorded time. The haves versus the have-nots. Right, General?"

"You're right, Beth. It's sad, but true. We will have to fight them someday. Coop, We'll cut east on 19 at

Pauls Valley," Ben said, sticking the map back into the case. "I think we can pretty well call this area clean."

"But it's not like we're wealthy," Corrie got into it. "I mean, we have a monetary system. But without a Rebel ID card the money is no good. The few Rebel outposts that the outsiders have managed to overrun look like a squatter camp in a few months. When they get nice things, they always screw them up and turn everything into trash."

"Look over there, General," Coop said, pointing to a shack set well back off the interstate. Smoke came from the chimney. "They have no running water, no electricity, outside toilets. The kids are dirty and in ragged clothing. It's disgusting!"

Ben let them talk. How to tell them that before the Great War, with billions of dollars being spent yearly on social programs, the same shack had been occupied by people of basically the same caliber as those now in it. Ben knew, of course, that there were exceptions to that, but he also knew that basically he was correct. No matter what you did for certain types of people, no matter how much you gave them, it was never enough; they always wanted more.

Ben almost ordered the convoy to stop and go back to the shack by the road and call out the occupants and question them. But what would be the point? Ben had been doing that very thing for years and had never been able to get through to any of them to this day. He had talked himself to the point of anger trying to convince people to get off their asses and do something to improve their quality of life. It was the same old story: give me something for nothing.

Of late, most of the time, he had just been saying to

hell with it and letting those types go their own way. But Beth was right: someday the Rebels would have to fight them. And that was a day that Ben was not looking forward to. It had almost happened when the nation was whole. Had not the Great War shattered the nations of the world and brought everyone to their knees for a time, a class struggle had certainly been looming on the horizon.

"Scouts report trouble up ahead, General," Corrie said. "Interstate is blocked and armed men behind the barricades."

"Bring the convoy down slow," Ben ordered. "How are the men armed and dressed?"

"Rifles and light machine guns. All kinds of clothing, General. The scouts say it's more a mob than an army."

"Guess what, gang," Ben said. "The day we've been discussing is here. At least in this part of the country."

"Wonderful," Cooper muttered.

"Line the spearhead vehicles abreast on the road, Corrie. A .50, Big Thumper, Big Thumper. I don't want to do harm to these people. But I will not kowtow to them. This nation is not going to be dictated to by rabble."

"You want Beth to drive and me on the .50, General?" Coop asked.

"I want you right where you are, Coop. Take us up to the spearhead vehicles."

It was one hell of a barricade, stretching across both sides of the interstate. Old trucks and cars, railroad track and ties, roadside barriers, and piles of junk quite effectively blocked the highway. Only the right shoulders were kept free.

A scout trotted back to Ben. "They call themselves

CROTCH, sir."

"I beg your pardon?" Ben said.

"The Coalition for the Rescue of the Oppressed, Terrorized, Common Homeless. CROTCH."

"I think I could have come up with something a little better than that," Ben said.

"CROTCH?" Jersey questioned.

"That's what the man said. What do they want, as if I didn't know?"

"Housing, clothing, food, and safety."

"They could easily have it," Ben replied. "All they have to do is swear alliance to the Rebel philosophy and stick with it."

"They say they won't do that. They don't have to, and they're not going to."

"Well, they are slap out of luck."

"Are we going to fight these people, General?"

"No. We'll just turn the column around and take another road east."

"Ben Raines is a racist pig!" the voice came over a bullhorn from behind the barricades.

The scout, who just happened to be black, ducked his head and tried to hide his grin.

"Are all those folks up there black?" Ben asked.

"Oh, no," the scout replied, struggling to keep from laughing. "It's a real rainbow up there."

"Ben Raines is a Republican racist honky pig!" the voice boomed.

"Is this a side of you that I don't know?" Tomas asked.

Ben cut his eyes. The Mexican officer was having a hard time keeping a smile from showing through. Ben shook his head. "Well, he's right about one thing: I was a Republican."

"The members of, ah, CROTCH, are shifting

people around, sir," Corrie said. "They're flanking us."

"I don't want to fight these people," Ben said. "Let's get out of here. Turn the column around and head out."

"Barricades are being thrown up south of us, sir," Corrie said.

"Billions for defense and nothing for the CROTCH!" boomed the voice.

"What billions for defense?" Ben bitched. "Hell, we stole nearly everything we have."

"The way south is blocked," Ben was told.

"You cannot escape us now," the words were pushed out of the bullhorn. "The time for CROTCH is here."

"Somebody tell that silly son of a bitch not to open fire on us," Ben said.

"What if they do?" Cooper asked.

"We return it. I don't want to hurt any of them. But I won't stand by and become a willing target. Somebody get me a bullhorn. I know we brought one."

Beth scrounged around and found a bullhorn, handing it to Ben. Ben clicked it on. "This is General Raines. Tear down that barricade and we'll talk about your situation. Do not open fire on us. Repeat: do not open fire."

The reply was a barrage of bullets from behind the barricade. "Death to those who would enslave us!" the voice of CROTCH boomed.

"Mortars are in place," Corrie told him.

"Do we scratch CROTCH now?" Cooper said with a grin. All of them were kneeling on the pavement, behind their vehicles.

Jersey groaned. "I swear, Coop. You get worse

with each passing day."

"Start walking the mortars in," Ben said, as gunfire from the barricades increased. "I've had this."

Victoria and Maria grinned at each other. "The monkey-and-the-skunk syndrome," they said together.

Nine

Mortars, rocket launchers, and Big Thumpers took all the fight out of CROTCH, and it didn't take long to accomplish that. Members of CROTCH threw down their weapons and stood in the median, their hands in the air.

"Barricades south of us have been abandoned," Corrie said.

The leader of the now-defunct movement was brought to Ben. The man had a knot on his head about the size of a hen's egg where he'd been conked on the bean by falling debris. He was sullen as he stared at Ben.

"You still got an itch to scratch?" Ben asked him.

"No point in discussing anything with a white racist government," the man said.

"Look around you," Ben told him. "You'd be hard-pressed to name a nationality that isn't represented in this army. If I was a racist, do you honestly think these men and women would be fighting alongside me?"

"Uncle Toms and Apples," the man said.

"Apples?"

"Indians who are red on the outside and white in

the middle." He suddenly shouted, "Arise, brothers and sisters of color! Throw off the yoke of slavery and turn your guns against this man. Kill the honky pig!"

The rebels of color looked at each other. "That son of a bitch is as nutty as a pecan pie," a Cheyenne Indian said.

"We must have housing and food and clothing and medical care," the CROTCH leader shouted.

"Well, hell, man," a black rebel said. "Go find you a house and live in it. There are hundreds of thousands of abandoned homes all over the country. Grow a garden. Get some cows and chickens and hogs and goats. There are millions of them wandering around. They don't belong to anybody."

"You're missing the point," Ben told the Rebel.

"I'm sure missing something, General," the Rebel admitted. "Can you fill in the blanks?"

"He wants us to do it for him."

"Does he want us to sit him in a highchair and hand-feed him, too?"

"You're nothing but a white-man's nigger," the leader of CROTCH told the Rebel.

The black sergeant walked over to him. "You're gonna be a dead nigger if you don't watch your mouth, boy."

"You have a name?" Ben asked him, before the black sergeant decided to end the conversation by a fist to the mouth.

"Freedom and liberty and justice for all!"

"This is pointless. Buddy, where are the rest of this idiot's followers?"

"Scattered like the wind," his son replied. "We're holding about fifty of them. The medics are working on the wounded."

"At least they're getting medical care," Freedom

and Liberty and Justice For All said.

"I just don't know what to do with you," Ben admitted. "I think you're around the bend and dangerous. But being crazy isn't a crime."

"Power to the people!"

Ben shook his head and turned to Buddy. "Make sure all the weapons are gathered up and turn this nut loose as soon as the convoy has passed. We've wasted enough time here."

"Food not guns!" the man shouted.

"Oh, shut up," Ben told him.

Then the man made the biggest mistake of his life when he said, "When Hoffman gets here we'll see you dead, Ben Raines."

Ben hit him. It was a hard blow and it caught the man flush in the mouth and knocked him sprawling on the cracked concrete. The so-called homeless advocate rolled to his feet, a knife in his hand. A Rebel clubbed him on the back of the head with his helmet. The CROTCH leader crumpled to the road.

"Hoffman's troops have been up here and are probably still here," Ben said. "Get this bastard into a vehicle and we're gone to the next town. Just make sure it's off the interstate to the east. Scouts out and check it over carefully. We just might have to fort up there. I have a hunch this homeless crap was a delaying tactic and they're waiting for us up at Pauls Valley. We'll interrogate this jerk there."

"That would be about fifteen miles east of here on old Highway 29," Beth said.

"Let's go. I got a bad feeling about this."

Before the Great War the town had a population of about seven hundred and fifty souls. No one had lived in the town since that momentous event. Scouts checked it out carefully, every house and every store, top floors, ground-level floors, and basements. It was safe.

"Back your Hummers into those stores so the .50s and Thumpers can be used," Ben ordered. "Back them all the way in so they can't be seen from the street. Buddy, spread your teams out on the second floors of those buildings and on the rooftops. I'll be over there in that old feed store. Extra ammo for everybody. Let's move."

Ben watched as the Hummers were backed into the buildings. The storefront glass had been knocked out years back. "Cover any oil spots with dirt," he ordered. "Wipe out all sign of tire tracks."

"You think this is a large force after us, don't you?" Tomas asked.

"Yes. I do. I have a hunch it might be several hundred, or more. We'll know more after Mr. Crotch is pumped full of injectable Valium."

"That is a truth serum?"

"In large doses. Come on. Let's get into position to make boom-boom with the bad guys."

Tomas laughed. "You have a very dark sense of humor, General."

"Gallows humor, Captain. You'll develop it if you stay around us long enough."

They began walking across the street. "After the government smashed the old Tri-States, General, how many people did you have left in your movement?"

"Just about three hundred. The government came close to wiping us out. But many men, whole units, of the U.S. Army and Marine Corps deserted to join the Rebels. From generals to privates. Many of them are still fighting with me. Some of the senior people grew too old for the field and took over outposts. Others died." They walked into the store and paused in the door. "Ike and Cecil and Tina and Chase. James Riverson. Jerre." His voice trailed off.

Tomas did not pursue that. He had learned the story from Tina and let affairs of the heart remain private and personal.

"And it grew and grew and grew," Tomas said, his voice filled with awe. "Then it spread down to my country and Payon was convinced to lead the movement there."

"We're going to take some losses up against Hoffman, Tomas. Be ready for that."

"I have already lost my wife, my children, my parents, and many friends. I have but my life to give. And I shall gladly give that toward victory." He spoke the words softly, but with emotion behind them.

There was nothing Ben could add to that, so he made no attempt. The men walked into the gloominess of the old store, which still smelled faintly of feed and seed and fertilizer.

"Mister Nutty is just about ready to be questioned, General," Ben was told. "That spook from intelligence is with him."

Ben smiled. It didn't take long for the old words to reappear about the men and women who worked in the intelligence section of the Rebel army.

"I say something funny, General?" the young woman asked.

"I used to be a spook, Leslie."

"You're not that weird, General."

Ben laughed as he and Tomas moved on to a table and chairs that had been righted and sat down. "I can't offer you coffee, Tomas," Ben said. "The coffee smell lingers, and that would be a dead giveaway if I'm right and NAL does attack us."

Outside, Rebels were carefully seeking out and

covering any tire or oil sign that might have been left on the street. When they had finished, the town appeared to be as deserted as when the Rebels had found it.

If the NAL did walk into town, they would find a very deadly trap waiting for them.

The spook from intelligence, who had joined Ben's team back at Wichita Falls, walked into the big main room of the old store. "You were right, General," he said, sitting down. "Hoffman has a large force up here attempting to recruit the malcontents. That fruitcake in there says about seven hundred and fifty people. And I believe him."

"Jesus," Ben breathed the word. "I thought maybe two companies at most."

"They were set up to cream us at Pauls Valley. I figure they'll pick up our trail and be here sometime around midnight tonight."

"Have the people get some rest, Corrie," Ben ordered. "Stagger the guard details so everybody is ensured some sleep." He walked into a back room, the spook right behind him, and looked at the leader of CROTCH.

"He's alive," the spook assured Ben. "But he's going to be out of it for quite a few hours."

Ben chuckled with a soldier's humor. "Be interesting if he slept right through the battle and woke to find himself surrounded by bodies."

"It's likely he'll do just that."

"Won't he be surprised," Ben said, and walked away.

There were four ways into the tiny town, and Ben had sentries posted on all four roads, about three miles outside of the town. Ben rested for a few hours, and by nine o'clock, he was up and ready to go. He restlessly prowled the store, waiting for the word, his M-16 slung.

"A large force coming straight at us down Highway 1, General," Corrie's voice came out of the darkness. "Approximately five miles out and moving about twenty miles an hour."

"Alert all troops," Ben said softly. "Everybody in position. If we pull this off, it will really jar Hoffman down to his toenails."

Ben had shuffled troops around to be in position to bottle up the NAL on both ends of the town. The Rebels were spread very thin, but Ben was counting on complete surprise to make up for their being outnumbered. Springing deadly ambushes was just one of the Rebels' specialties.

"Column has stopped," Corrie said. "Sending out recon."

"All troops observe noise discipline," Ben ordered. "Have a Rebel with a silenced pistol standing over Sleeping Beauty in the back room. If he starts to snore, shoot him in the head."

The man from intelligence moved quietly to the back room, a canned Colt Woodsman in his hand. One snort and Mister CROTCH would sleep forever.

"Starting to sprinkle outside," Jersey whispered.

"That's good and bad," Ben said. "The rain will deaden any smell of gas or oil. But we don't need lightning to go with it."

"Enemy recon entering northeast edge of town," Corrie whispered. "Fanning out."

Thunder rumbled in the distance. Every Rebel was silently praying that any lightning would hold off for a few minutes. Illumination was one thing they did not need at this time.

The recon advanced to the middle of the deserted

old town, on both sides of the street. It puzzled Ben why they didn't advance on the sidewalks, hugging the shadows. But he was certainly glad they didn't.

One Rebel sneeze, one cough, one dislodged pebble, or one creak of an old board would give them away and possibly spell death for all of them. The Rebels waited.

They watched the recon leader lift a walkie-talkie. Seconds later, the recon team began walking back toward the edge of town. All could tell by the way they walked that all tension had left them. They believed the town to be deserted. The Rebels had pulled off phase one.

"They have to come right through town," Ben whispered. "Unless they decide to backtrack."

Suddenly one of the NAL recon team stopped, holding up his hand. The others dropped to the street. The suspicious member walked to the sidewalk and peered into the gloom of what had once been a cafe. He stepped closer and looked hard. Finally he shook his head and stepped off the sidewalk. "Nothing but a damned hatrack," he said to the others. They laughed and stood up from the street.

"You're getting jumpy, Melendez," the words came softly through the rain, which was getting heavier.

"Screw you, Barnes," was Melendez's reply. "You better stay jumpy when dealing with the Rebels."

"They're just flesh and blood like anybody else," a third voice was added. "They're not supermen."

"Or superwomen," a female said.

"Yeah, yeah, yeah, Hilda," another recon member said. "Must not forget the weaker sex."

The men of the team laughed.

Hilda said something in reply that Ben could not

211

catch. He assumed it was not at all complimentary.

"I'm whipped out," the words drifted to the Rebels. "I hope we hole up here for the night. I could use some sleep."

I hope you do, too, Ben thought. Then I can assure you that you will all sleep forever.

The recon members pulled on raingear and sat down on the sidewalk, under an awning. They smoked and talked as they waited for the convoy to pull in.

They're all speaking English, Ben noted with some surprise. Some of it heavily accented, but English is obviously the language of choice.

Trucks began pulling in, filling the street, and soon the line of vehicles stretched from one end of the town to the other, parked side by side on the wide street. The vehicles pulled in tight, nearly touching bumpers, which Ben thought was strange, since it hampered the troops' exit from the carriers, but he was glad for it. Stay bunched up, people, he thought. The closeness will be a comfort to you as you die.

The rain intensified as the storm moved closer. Lightning began dancing across the skies.

Corrie had moved close to Ben. She whispered, "That's all of them. Our people on both ends have moved into position."

"Give the orders to fire," Ben said.

"Hey!" an NAL soldier shouted. "That's a god-damn Hummer in that building over there."

The stormy night suddenly turned deadly.

Ten

The littered street was a roaring battleground as the Rebels opened fire, giving the New Army of Liberation every ounce of grief they could hand out. And that was more than sufficient. The gas tanks on the vehicles of the NAL caught on fire, some of them exploding, sending shrapnel howling into flesh. Boxes filled with small-arms ammo started popping and mortar rounds heated up and blew. The men and women of the NAL never had a chance to do anything but die, and they did that in droves. Those who made the sidewalks were chopped down by automatic-weapons fire. Those who ran into alleys found them sealed off by rusting old hulks of vehicles that had been dragged into place by Rebels during the daylight hours, and they quickly and painfully discovered the hulks had been booby-trapped. They had nowhere to run except back into the battle and nothing to do when they got there except die.

For several moments the small town in Oklahoma resembled hell as the night was set on fire by the blazing vehicles and the screaming of the mortally wounded.

The gunsmoke and the smoke from the fires that stretched from one end of the town to the other caused Rebel throats to burn and eyes to water. Still Ben did not give the orders to cease fire. The Rebels continued to pour their lethal fire into the packed streets. After five minutes of hell had passed, Ben shouted to Corrie to cease fire.

The Rebel guns fell silent as the rain picked up in tempo, the storm gradually putting out the fires in the street. The stench of death was heavy and sickening, the fires having consumed many bodies. Rebels began gathering up all usable NAL weapons. An occasional shot cut the night as Rebels put the horribly wounded out of their misery and sent them into the arms of whatever God they worshipped. Rebels began blowing passageways in the rear of buildings to get their Hummers out, since the main street was impassable due to the torched and scorched hulks of burned vehicles.

The Rebels left the still-burning main street and pulled back to the edge of town, seeking shelter in old homes to wait out the stormy night. When dawn came, they would more thoroughly investigate the death site.

The Rebels caught a few hours' rest and were prowling through the still-hot rubble in the grayness of dawn. Anything that anybody might be able to use was salvaged.

"Put the bodies into that stretch of buildings," Ben said, pointing. "Then we'll saturate it with gasoline and burn it to the ground. We don't have the equipment to scoop out a mass grave. I want a body count."

When the distasteful business was finally concluded, and the buildings were blazing, the Rebels pulled back to escape the intense heat. The collaborator had finally come out of his drug-induced sleep and was clearly in shock at the battle site. He was so badly frightened he could not stand. Ben looked down at him.

"There is what remains of the troops who were to be your salvation, Mister CROTCH," he told the man. "Now what do you have to say?"

"My name is Wilbur Harris," the man replied, his voice no more than a whisper. "I feel terrible. What have you done to me?"

"I think what is more important is what I'm going to do to you."

"Hoffman's advance people promised the homeless and the destitute jobs and food and medical care," Harris said. "You can't blame us for taking them at their word."

"Oh, really?" was Ben's reply. He turned his back to the man. "Corrie, give the word to mount up."

"What are you going to do with me?" Wilbur asked.

"Absolutely nothing," Ben said. "You're on your own now."

"You're just going to leave me here?"

"That's right."

"I'm hungry."

"We piled the field rations of the NAL on the sidewalk in front of the old drugstore in town," Ben told him. "Help yourself. There should be enough to last you for weeks. I hope I never see you again, Wilbur. Because if I do, I just might decide to shoot you on the spot. Let's go, people."

The Rebels pulled out, leaving Wilbur Harris still sitting on a log in a wooded glen on the edge of what remained of the town.

"Wiped out?" Hoffman asked, his voice clearly mirroring his shock. "Seven hundred and twenty of my troops wiped out?"

"To the last person, General. One of the North American groups sympathetic to us reported not ten minutes ago. The four companies were ambushed and their bodies burned." He pointed to a map of the United States. "Right here in this small town in Oklahoma."

It was difficult to shock Jesus Hoffman. But this news paled his face and silenced him for a moment. Finally he rose from his chair and walked to a window. "The First Expeditionary Force was one of our finest units. Skilled combat veterans all. They must have faced several battalions of Rebels for something like this to have happened."

"About a hundred and fifty Rebels, sir," the aide spoke the words softly.

Hoffman turned slowly. His mouth opened and closed soundlessly several times. "What . . . did . . . . . . you . . . say?" He finally found his voice.

"About a hundred and fifty Rebels, sir."

"Impossible!" Hoffman shouted. "One hundred and fifty Rebels could not defeat even fifty of our people."

"No, sir. It is not impossible. The American who reported this saw the units leave the town. He was watching from a wooded knoll outside of town. He then personally interviewed a man named Wilbur Harris. Harris was the man the Expeditionary commander enlisted to stall General Raines while they were setting up an ambush site on the interstate. Harris said the Rebels injected him with some sort of

216

truth serum and questioned him. The American then inspected what remained of the town and concluded that Harris was telling the truth. Tire tracks confirmed the Rebels' small force."

"Do we have any force left in that area?"

"Yes. But they are broken up into small units and scattered. They are over near the Arkansas/Missouri line. We do have numerous small units of Americans who believe as we do."

"Texas?"

"So far as we have been able to tell, only a handful of our people remain in that area. A group of Texas Rangers smashed the last major outpost of ours over near the New Mexico line."

"Texas Rangers? You mean, like in the old cowboy movies?"

"Something like that, sir. From all that we can gather, the, ah, Rangers approached the outpost on horseback. They appeared friendly . . . at first."

"Horses?" Hoffman said weakly.

"Yes, sir. It appears these men planned this out very carefully. They showed up very bedraggled looking, requesting food and medical assistance. Once inside the compound they pulled their, ah, six-guns and opened fire."

"Six-guns!" Hoffman roared. "You mean like in John Wayne movies?"

"Ah . . . well, yes, sir, I suppose so. But their companions were waiting about a mile outside the compound. They then attacked using very modern equipment. It was a, ah, trick."

"I have the finest attack helicopters in all the world," Hoffman said, sitting down behind his desk. "I have the most modern of equipment. My people are the most highly trained of any army known to

217

exist anywhere. And you are now telling me that a bunch of Texas good ol' boys came loping up on ponies and started a shootout like the O.K. Corral and defeated my men? Ramon, do you take me for an idiot?"

"I am only repeating what came over the radio, General. Nothing more, nothing less. The main Texas force came in with .50 caliber machine guns and mounted grenade launchers."

"All right, all right, Ramon," Hoffman said wearily. "I am not blaming you for this report. Sometimes the messenger must endure a verbal onslaught for being the bearer of bad news. I apologize for my behavior. You may go, Ramon."

Hoffman sat at his desk, alone in the room. "Six-guns and horses? Good God!"

Ben and his teams rolled through southeast Oklahoma and encountered no hostile forces. They saw people, but no one raised a hand against them. Ben correctly guessed that the news of the ambush had preceded them and that anyone who had aligned themselves with Hoffman was making themselves scarce. All Rebel outposts in this part of the state had either been overrun and wiped out or the people had packed up and fled north, or some other direction, when the enemy troops approached.

At the Arkansas line, just south of Fort Smith, Ben ordered the column to cut south and head for the Texas line. Just above the junction of 59 and 259, the column shut it down for the night, bivouacking along the main street of what appeared to be a deserted town.

Sitting on the curb drinking a cup of coffee, Ben

said to his son, "Those people who have been following us all day should be making an appearance soon."

"Yes. Probably right at supper. You think this is one of those ultra-right-wing survivalist groups, Father?"

"Probably. This area had a lot of them just before the balloon went up."

"These groups, they hated blacks and Jews and all minorities, did they not?"

"Some of them did. Some of them were just made up of men who never got over being a boy and playing children's games, only this time with real guns. Most of them were harmless. Meet every other weekend or so and shoot off a lot of ammunition and then go back to their nine-to-five jobs on Monday."

Buddy smiled. "Did you ever belong to one of those groups, Father?"

"Hell, no! For a lot of reasons. I got shot at enough in the army and doing spook and merc work later. But the main reason was that writers don't have time for anything except writing."

"It's a full-time job?"

"If you want to make any money at it."

"How much money did you have in the bank when the Great War struck?"

"Oh . . . about forty thousand dollars."

"That's a fortune, Father!"

"Not really. Inflation was killing the nation. Really, the money was worthless. There wasn't anything to back up the paper money, as far as I was concerned. Except faith."

"I do remember money, of course. But all I knew was Mother gave it to me and I spent it. About this survivalist group, Father? . . ."

"The main bunch will lay back. We should be hearing from the scouts we dropped off along the way any time, now. A small bunch will come in to size us up. Then, if they think they can take us, they'll hit us full strength when we're all asleep. I have a hunch they were watching us when we ambushed the NAL. Or came up on us while we were gathering up the dead. Wilbur told us that a lot of groups had gone over to Hoffman's side."

"It doesn't make any sense, Father."

"I know. Hoffman's army is made up of people of all nationalities. Ultra-right-wing groups are traditionally made up of people who dislike minorities. Buddy, nothing about this thing makes any sense."

Ben was silent for a moment as he opened his field ration pack. Dinner was usually edible and sometimes even tasty. Lunch was tolerable . . . at least you could look at it without barfing. Breakfast was always one big yukk. Ben ate what his troops ate. All Rebel commanders did, from squad leaders to battalion commanders. That was a hard and fast rule.

"What is this stuff?" Buddy asked, looking at the contents of his dinner pack.

"It says it's hash."

Both Father and son reached for the hot-sauce bottle. That was something all Rebels carried. Put enough on and it kills the taste.

"The lookout on the water tower reports a small force of men heading our way," Corrie said, sitting down and opening her dinner pack. Jersey had thrown hers away and was gnawing on a day-old peanut-butter sandwich.

"I'll trade you a dessert pack for that sandwich, Jersey," Cooper offered.

Jersey stopped eating. "What is the dessert today?"

Cooper shook his head. "I don't know, Jersey. I've looked and looked at it. But I can't figure it out. It's dark."

"Forget it."

"How large a force, Corrie?" Ben asked.

"Ten people."

"I wonder how large a force they really are?" Beth questioned, sitting down on the curb and opening her dinner pack. She looked at it and groaned. Everybody was striking out on dinner this afternoon.

"What do you have?" Jersey asked.

"Pork and noodles."

"See if you can find a hungry dog."

Beth looked at her. "I thought you liked animals."

"Probably a couple of hundred," Ben answered Beth's original question. "Enough to cause us problems."

The rattle of vehicles reached the group. Three old Broncos rolled up the main street.

"Real professionals," Jersey remarked. "All their vehicles are painted green cammie. Wonder what they do in the wintertime when it snows?" Without waiting for a reply, she said, "First one of these jokers that call me little darlin' or honey is gonna get a boot in the nuts."

Victoria said, "These people coming, they don' like Mexican people?"

"Not much, Vicki," Jersey told her. "At least, not the ones we've ever come in contact with."

"What is their problem?" Maria asked.

"Mainly they're just stupid," Corrie said.

"Come on, ladies," Ben said. "You all know we've got a lot of ex-survivalists in this army. They're fine soldiers and don't have a bigoted bone in their body."

221

"You mean you think this bunch coming in is doing so to join up?" Jersey asked.

Ben laughed, and placed his M-16 within easy reach.

"Yeah," Jersey said with a grin. "That's what I thought."

Eleven

"Howdy there, folks!" the cammie-clad man called with a wide grin, stepping out of his pickup. "Y'all got to be the famous Rebels, right?"

"A very small part of them," Buddy replied, sitting beside his father on the high curb.

"Well, I sure am glad to make your acquaintance. I'm Peter Banning. Me and the boys here sort of keep things under control in this part of the country. Been keeping the riffraff out of here for years."

Ben finished the last of his dinner and carefully folded the wrappings, putting them in a container. When all the Rebels had eaten and placed the wrappers in the container, it would be buried. The Rebels used very little that was not biodegradable.

Only then did Ben start sizing up Peter Banning. He was not impressed. Banning was a bully. Ben had made a study of bullies over the years and could peg one at a distance. At first glance, Banning would come across as a very affable sort, with an easy grin. But his eyes and body language gave him away. Ben cut his eyes to Jersey. The woman was tense, and Ben knew that she had taken an immediate dislike for the man. He could feel the tension among the Rebels.

Peter lifted his gaze to the water tower and his expression tightened when he saw the Rebel on the catwalk around the tank. The man began to pick up on the subtle shifting of Rebels. He began to realize that while he had played at war for years, and even won a few pitched battles, here he was dealing with solid professional soldiers. Nothing was left to chance. Banning and his men had placed themselves in a box, and one wrong move would mean their being shot to ribbons in seconds. He doubted his people could even get off a round. He feverishly hoped that none of his boys got hinky. He cut his eyes back to Ben and looked at the man with grudging admiration.

"You'd be General Ben Raines."

"That's right." Ben began rolling a cigarette. "What's on your mind, Mr. Banning?"

"We saw you passin' through back up the road about an hour ago and just thought we'd check you out, that's all. Can't be too careful, you know."

"You're a liar, Banning," Ben said. "You and your people have been following us all day. Your main force is about eight miles up the road. Now state your business."

Banning lifted his eyes and paled. Three Rebels had appeared out of the store behind where Ben and his team sat on the curb. The three Rebels were each carrying Heckler and Koch light machine guns. The H&Ks fired a 7.62 round that could make a mess out of a man in a heartbeat.

"I guess you caught me in a lie, General," Banning said.

"I guess I did." Ben lit his hand-rolled and waited. "What happens now?"

"You answer a few questions."

"Maybe I don't feel like answering questions."

"Neither did a man name of Wilbur Harris. But we convinced him to talk to us—in a manner of speaking. Where is Wilbur now, Banning?"

"He's with us. Back up the road."

"I thought as much. What did Hoffman's people promise you, Banning?"

"Hoffman? I never heard of him."

"You're lying again, Banning. It's not nice to tell lies. Your nose might start to grow." Ben smiled. "Or I might decide to cut it off."

Banning started to sweat. This wasn't going well at all. Raines had seen right through him from the start. "We ain't done nothing to you, Raines. Nothing at all. It's a free country. Me and my boys can travel wherever we damn well please to go."

"I'll ask you again: What did Hoffman promise you? And before you reply, bear in mind that we know everything that was in Wilbur's head."

"We'll be leaving now, General," Banning said.

"Go ahead," Ben said, surprising the man. "We won't stop you."

Banning and his men started backing up slowly toward their vehicles, keeping their hands away from sidearms. The Rebels watched them drive away.

A Rebel said, "The bumper beeper's in place. 40.22."

Corrie punched in the frequency on a hand-held scanner and it came in loud and clear.

"You think they'll shake down their vehicles, Father?" Buddy asked.

"I doubt it. Right now they're so thankful they got out of here alive they're not thinking about anything else. Give them an hour and they'll get mad. Then they'll start planning an attack. Corrie, check with the tower lookout. Make sure they don't drop off anybody to spy on us."

225

"Tower reports no one has left the vehicles."

Ben lifted a state map and studied it for a moment. "They have two ways they could come in from the north. But only one way in for about two miles after the junction. Buddy, take your teams up the road and set up just south of the junction. I really don't want to have my sleep disturbed by a firefight here in town."

His son grinned. "Sleep well, Father." He stepped out of swinging range. "I know that a man of your advanced years needs lots of rest."

The running Buddy almost got conked on the head by Ben's thrown helmet. Luckily, he sidestepped just in time.

"Wonder how Buddy is going to handle this one?" Jersey asked. The team was again sitting outside on the curb. The night air was cool and the Rebels were enjoying the rest, having broken up into small groups, talking and gossiping a bit before turning in for the night.

"I'm sure he'll be very inventive," Ben replied. "The boy has a devious mind."

"I wonder where he got it?" Tomas asked dryly.

"Certainly not from me," Ben said with a straight face. "There isn't a vicious or deceptive bone in my body."

"I'm going to bed," Beth said, standing up. "It's getting a little deep out here."

Buddy and his teams had planted claymores alongside the road. The spot they had chosen was where the road dipped down, with high embankments on either side. That area ran for about five hundred feet. The claymores would explode about three to four feet up, throwing the lethal charges directly into the side windows of the Broncos and pickup trucks. After the charges blew, Buddy and his teams would hose the area down with H&Ks taken from dead NAL troops. And that should take care of Mr. Peter Banning and his turncoat followers.

Buddy and his teams settled in to wait.

"I'm tellin' you, Pete," one of his men said, "I think we all ought to haul ass outta here. Maybe all the way to Canada. Forget about fightin' Ben Raines and the Rebels. I got a bad feelin' about this, Pete."

"No way, Burt," the still-angry Pete said. "That man made a fool outta me. And no man does that to Peter Banning and lives to talk about it. It wasn't done back when we had a government, and it ain't gonna happen now."

"You best leave him alone," Wilbur Harris spoke softly in the night. "Remember, I've seen first-hand what the Rebels are capable of doing."

"Keep your mouth out of it, Will," Peter told him. "You ain't got no say in none of this."

"Then I'll pass on this," Wilbur said. "I take my orders from Hoffman, not from you."

"You took your orders from Captain Brunner. He's dead and his body burnt. Thanks to you and your flappin' mouth."

"That sure as hell don't make you in command. Besides, if you was shot full of dope like I was, you'd probably tell them more than I did."

"I doubt it. I ain't gonna stand here and argue with you, Will. Do whatever in the hell you want to do. Mount up, boys, We're moving against Ben Raines and them uppity Rebels."

"What do you want on your tombstone, Peter?" Wilbur asked.

"Screw you, Wilbur. I hope I never have to look at your ugly goddamn face again."

You won't, Wilbur thought. In about an hour, the only thing you'll be seeing are the fires of hell.

Wilbur sat and watched the men climb into their vehicles and pull out. He listened until he could no longer hear the sounds of their engines and then stood up, picking up his pack. He was going back up the road where he'd stashed the radio he'd found intact by the side of the road back in that death town and call into his contact up in North Oklahoma. Captain Ohida was just about the only one left that Wilbur knew of. He knew there were more, but didn't know how to contact them. He'd tell Captain Ohida that he could scratch Peter Banning and his bunch. They were as surely dead as the night was dark.

"One mile away," Buddy said, after his forward man bumped him. "Get set. Damn!" Buddy cussed. "They're leaving their vehicles and walking the rest of the way."

"Staying in the road?" a team member asked.

"So far. Let's see if they're as stupid as they are ugly."

"That's asking a lot," a woman said, her grin evident in the darkness.

"It's going to be a real mess in the road when those claymores go," a team member said. "Like yukk city."

"Yes," Buddy agreed. "But at least we'll have some more four-wheel-drive vehicles. Pass the word, observe noise discipline from now on."

The Rebels waited on the cool dewy grass. All were startled when the sounds of voices reached them. Peter Banning certainly had loose discipline. But the

Rebels were hard-core professional fighting people, not play soldiers.

"I need to take me a piss 'fore we start killin' Rebels," the voice reached them.

"Well, piss then and catch up," Banning told the man with a full bladder. "Jesus Christ, can't you guys do nothin' right?"

The Rebels waited in silence and without any movement except for their eyes.

"Hey, you guys," the urinating man called. "Wait up, will you?"

The night was suddenly split wide open by explosions, and before the booming echoes had died away, the wild screaming of dying men shattered the stillness. Shrapnel from the claymores virtually shredding most of Banning's men. The few who were left alive were quickly disposed of by automatic-weapons fire. Seconds later, the only one left alive stood in shock in the middle of the road, his M-16 slung on one shoulder and his dick in his hand. He looked up to see several Rebels standing on the top of the embankment, looking down at him.

"Hi, guys," he said weakly. "Can we talk about this?"

"Put your dick back in your pants," a woman told him. "It is definitely not a turn-on."

"Yes, ma'am," the would-be survivalist said meekly.

"This is all he knew?" Ben asked, after listening to the cassette tape of the interrogation.

"That's it," the spook from intelligence said. "And he wasn't lying. He was so scared he'd have turned in his own mother . . . if he had one that would claim him."

"Bring him in to me."

The only survivor of the previous night's ambush stood in front of Ben and shook with fear. He'd been forced to walk, and sometimes wade, among what was left of his buddies in the road before the Rebels brought him into town, and that sight had just about done him in.

"Now, what am I going to do with you?" Ben asked, leaning back in an old cane-bottomed, straight-backed chair.

"General Raines, sir," the man said. "My name is Chester Higgins. I run a grocery store 'fore the Great War. And I never was in any trouble with the law. I—"

"Shut up!" Ben told him. "I am not interested in your personal history. What I want to know is this: Should I shoot you or turn you loose?" Actually, Ben had already made up his mind to turn him loose.

"Lord God, General, don't shoot me. You turn me loose and I swear you'll never hear no more from me again. And that's a promise."

"You won't join up with another group who have plans on fighting me?"

"I might join a church, if I can find one! After what I seen and walked through last night, I don't need no army to join. What I need is salvation in the worst kind of way. I need to talk with the Lord."

"You just about met Him face to face last night," Ben reminded the man.

That got Chester's knees shaking so bad he had to sit down before he fell down.

"So you have religion now, is that it?" Ben asked.

"It's about time, don't you think?" Chester put his trembling hands under his legs to contain them.

Ben chuckled. "All right, Chester. Get out of here. And if I see you again, you'd better be the most peaceful man in all the world."

Chester hit the door and was gone.

Buddy walked in, poured a cup of coffee, and sat down in the chair Chester had recently vacated. He smiled at Ben. "That, Father, is one scared man. You should have seen him tiptoeing through the gore last evening, alternately barfing and praying. If we'd have had music it would have been a ballet . . . of sorts. I thought that was a nice touch to cap off a very successful evening."

Ben looked at his son and shook his head. "You, boy, are going to be harder than I am."

"I certainly had a good teacher, Father. Where do we go from here?"

"Let's go check out those other groups that Wilbur and Chester told us about."

Corrie called from the other room. "A company-sized force has just been reported down in the Ouachita National Forest. Ten miles south of here."

"Hostile?" Ben asked, walking over to stand in the open door.

"Scouts don't know, sir. They did not make their presence known."

"Get the people mounted up, Buddy. Let's go see if they're friend or foe."

A few miles to the north, Wilbur Harris was radioing in.

Twelve

Ike and his people stayed busy rendering large portions of roadway impassable and blowing every bridge in their sector. The area assigned to Ike and his people was so large that planes and helicopters were in use transporting the teams from place to place. Ike and his people had encountered very few hostiles. The word was spreading among those in North America who had aligned with Hoffman that they had better stay the hell away from those prowling teams of Rebels. To mix it up with the Rebels was not a wise thing to do.

South of the border, teams of Mexican soldiers sent out by General Payon were herding those who wished to go north across the border. Many did not wish to leave their homes. The soldiers didn't argue the point with them. There just wasn't time.

Once across the border, the people were interviewed, given medical exams, and those fit to fight were asked if they wished to do that. Not a one refused.

Tina and Raul had their hands full setting up training schedules for the new people.

Back at Base Camp One, Cecil had the factories

working twenty-four hours a day, making everything from uniforms to ammunition.

In the HQ Company building, Thermopolis often wished he was back in the field. Things were a lot less hectic.

South of the border, Hoffman's forces mustered to move against General Payon's troops and found very quickly that nearly everything they drove across, touched, or put their boots on was going to blow up. Hoffman had not counted on this. And he was not prepared for any type of assault from the sea. He ordered his troops back across the line, and the push toward Mexico City was halted, for a time.

At the edge of the Ouachita National Forest, Corrie acknowledged the message and said, "Hoffman just tried a push across the no-man's-land. He obviously thought it was a bad idea, for he immediately pulled his people back."

"Buying us a little more time," Ben said. "Every additional day makes us stronger and better prepared to meet him when he does try to cross our borders."

"Scouts up ahead," Cooper said.

"We think they're hostile," the team leader told Ben. "They know we're here but have made no aggressive moves toward us. About a hundred and fifty of them. They're well-armed and seemed to be very well trained. Nothing like that shit group Banning ran. Their camp is clean and so are they."

"You have a fix on radio frequency?"

"That's a ten-four, sir."

"Give it to Corrie, please." Ben turned to another scout. "You find us a good defensive position?"

"Yes, sir. We could stand off a battalion in the place I picked."

Ben saw his teams get into position for the evening and told Corrie to contact the group camped in the forest. "Let's see if they want to talk with us."

"We're minding our own business, General," came the reply. "We don't want anything to do with you or your army. So just leave us alone."

"Want to come over for coffee?" Ben asked, a strange smile on his lips.

"No."

"Downright unfriendly," Cooper said. "I smell a stinking rat, General."

"Yeah. So do I, Coop. But if they are linked with Hoffman, why didn't they pull out? Surely they knew we were coming in this direction."

"They knew," Beth said, walking up. "Corrie just got a fix on some of the frequencies they're using. They're transmitting in code. That spook says he wasn't trained in cryptology and can't break it. That guy is weird!"

Ben smiled at that. He knew it went with the territory. He turned to the leader of the scout team. "How good are these people?"

"Real good, sir. They've got the forest around their camp covered with trip wires. I went a little ways, but it's a real maze in there. I didn't go in far. Just far enough to know these guys are plenty good. They're not cornballs."

Ben looked off into the distance for several moments. "Why?" he finally tossed the question out, to no one in particular. "Why would they go to such lengths knowing that we were on the way here and would surely stop and check them out? And more than that, once we did check them out, and received such an unfriendly reply to any questions, we would immediately become suspicious of their motives."

"Because they want us to linger for a couple of days," Buddy said.

"That's correct, son. Now tell me why they want

us to do that."

Buddy looked puzzled for a moment, then said, "So they can contact a much larger force and wipe us out."

"Very good, son. But you're forgetting something. What about the statements of Wilbur Harris and Chester Higgins? They both stated that there were no large forces anywhere near here. Wilbur was drugged and Chester was so badly frightened it was impossible for him to tell a lie."

"Those two were low-level personnel," Jersey said. "They wouldn't know all about the placement of Hoffman's troops."

"Right," Ben said. "So now we are facing a dilemma. What to do?"

"We would have no trouble against this bunch here," Buddy said. "Or very little trouble. But against a much larger force, with no hope of ambush . . . I don't know, Father."

"I don't either. So until we make up our minds, I think that we shall behave as Riffs and fold our tents and slip quietly into the night."

"It isn't night and I don't know what in the hell a Riff is," Cooper said.

"Your education is sorely lacking, Coop," Ben said, putting an arm over the young man's shoulders. "You'll have to listen to *The Desert Song* sometime. It's really quite an entertaining light opera."

Cooper looked up at Ben. "What's an opera got to do with us hauling our asses out of here, General?"

"You'll have to listen to it to discover that, Cooper."

"Cooper and opera," Jersey said, shaking her head. "This I got to see."

"And hear," Ben added.

"Wonderful," Jersey said. "Me and my big mouth."

* * *

The Rebels slipped out just after dark. Since their encampment was several miles from the other camp, and Ben was reasonably sure that they were not being spied on, the pullout was done easily enough. They backtracked several miles and then turned west, pulling over in a town that was so small it wasn't even on the old state maps they were using. There were just enough old homes and stores in the town to hide the Hummers and the newly acquired Broncos. Even then it was a tight fit.

"Encoded burst transmissions, Corrie," Ben said. "Just give HQ our location for the time being. I've got to think about this situation."

Scouts came in about half an hour later. "We weren't followed, General. We pulled it off."

Ben smiled. "Won't they be surprised in the morning. I want constant scanning of the frequencies we know they're using. Give them to Therm so the decoding boys and girls down there can go to work. I want to know what these people are up to."

The Rebels ate and went to bed, got a good night's sleep, then ate and rested until noon of the next day. Corrie received word from HQ that the code had been broken.

"There was a large force of NAL people up in the northwestern part of Arkansas," she said. "They were only about ten miles away from our location when we pulled out last night."

"We just made it," Ben said. "And you can bet they're looking for us right now. This little town is so far off the beaten path it isn't even on some maps. On the other hand, we could very easily be trapped in here . . ."

"Sentries report a dozen vehicles coming our way,

General," Corrie said. "From the east. Mixed bag of light and heavy trucks. Three miles out and coming in fast. Approximately one hundred troops. It's the black-shirts." She held up a hand. "Vehicles coming at us from the west. Just about the same number. We're boxed."

Ben picked up his M-16. "As they say in the navy, battle stations, folks."

The Rebels moved quickly, but without panic. They had done this so many times it was very nearly automatic. They all knew they could not hope to pull off another deserted-town ambush trick, for the NAL knew they were here. How they knew was unimportant at the moment. They probably had been spotted by locals who had been recruited into Hoffman's movement.

The two sentries posted three miles out east and west of the town would know to keep their heads down and out of sight. Four people against a large force would make very little difference and would, in all probability, only get the Rebels killed if they exposed themselves.

Ben did a little fast headwork. His people were probably outnumbered, but not by many. Hoffman's troops were coming in fast, so that meant they could not be pulling artillery. In terms of firepower, both the Rebels and the black-shirts were pretty well evenly matched up. But this battle had to be over and finished as quickly as possible. If it dragged on, that group of turncoat Americans camped in the Ouachita would soon join the black-shirts, and then the Rebels could be in real trouble.

"Corrie, nobody fires until I give the orders. We've got to let them come in and face them nose to nose. We can't let this turn into a prolonged affair. You can bet reinforcements are on the way right now. Pass the word to prepare for hand-to-hand combat."

Victoria and Maria checked their long-bladed knives for sharpness. Both of them had been stropped to a razor edge. Rebels checked pistols, for this was going to be very in-close work. All made sure the helmet-strap cup under the chin was tight and in place. This could very likely turn into a clubbing type of warfare, and a helmet could prevent a cracked skull.

Ben could see the black-shirts entering the edge of town, from the east, and he assumed also from the west. "Corrie, get the drivers in the Hummers and the gunners in place. Everybody else on their feet. Make the first rounds count," Ben said. "Then we're going to do the only thing we can to save our asses."

Those in the room with Ben looked at him.

Ben smiled. "Charge." He lifted his M-16 and sighted in a black-shirt. "Fire at will," he said, and shot the Nazi right between the eyes. "Charge!" he shouted, and was out the door.

As Ben had been counting on, the move caught the black-shirts totally by surprise. Whatever they had been expecting, this was not it. The Rebels rushed them, screaming and shouting and cursing at the black-shirts.

"They're mad!" a black-shirt platoon leader yelled. The words had just left his mouth when a Rebel shot him in the face with a 9mm subsonic round at nearly point-blank range.

Ben slammed into an officer and rode the man to the ground. He jammed the muzzle of his pistol into the man's neck and pulled the trigger. The slug tore a huge hole as it went through, then bounced off the pavement and reentered the man's skull just above the eye.

Ben rolled and kicked out, his boot catching a

black-shirt on the knee and felling the man. A Rebel shot the man as he was falling. Ben rolled away and came up on his boots.

Ben smashed his pistol into a man's face and felt the bones crunch under the impact. Jersey jammed the muzzle of a short-barreled CAR into the man's ribs and gave him lead. The slugs knocked the black-shirt backward, down and dying.

Vicki and Maria were using their knives, the blades shiny and red with blood as they slashed their way through the milling and sweating melee.

The black-shirts went into a panic. They were seasoned soldiers and had been ready for combat, but they were not mentally prepared for this type of nearly insane fury they were meeting from the Rebels.

Buddy faced two men who had either dropped their rifles or had them smashed from their hands. One clawed for a pistol, and Buddy shot him in the face with a .45, then turned the pistol on the other man, the slug taking the black-shirt just above the nose and nearly taking off the top of the man's head. Buddy was clubbed on the helmet by a black-shirt swinging an empty rifle, and the blow knocked him to his knees. Buddy grabbed the man by one leg and brought him down to the street. Using his enormous strength, Buddy savagely twisted the leg and the bone popped, tearing out through flesh and cloth. The black-shirt screamed once and then passed out.

Buddy picked up the man's rifle and set about busting necks and heads of black-shirts. It was so close that firing would put Rebel lives in danger. It was down to knives, clubs, entrenching tools, and hand axes.

"Spare me!" one black-shirt screamed at Jersey.

"Not likely, prick," the little bodyguard said, and

smashed the man's face to blood and pulp with an entrenching tool. She turned and split another skull with a shovel. Beth rolled out from under the broken body and jumped to her feet after grabbing the small camp hatchet from the Nazi. The women shoved through the crowd, looking for Ben.

Tomas jumped on the back of a black-shirt and rode him to the ground, then jerked his head back and cut his throat. He caught a glancing blow from a rifle butt that knocked him to one side just as one of his men stuck a pistol to the Nazi's head and blew his brains out.

"Gracias," Tomas panted, then watched in horror as his friend was decapitated by a machete-swinging black-shirt. The head bounced on the street. Ben stepped up and buried an axe he'd taken from a downed Nazi into the man's back. The black-shirt shrieked and fell to the bloody pavement.

A black-shirt, screaming his hate and rage and frustration, ran up to Ben, a tire tool in his hands, held high over his head. Tomas kicked the man in the balls, and as he went down to the old pavement, doubled over and puking, Ben kicked him in the face with a boot.

A burly Rebel finished it by shooting the man in the head.

It was over as suddenly as it had begun. The single street of the tiny town was littered with dead, dying, and badly wounded, not all of them black-shirts.

An Oriental man, both legs broken and twisted after having been run over by an almost-five-thousand-pound Hummer, lay on the street crying. "Devils," he sobbed. "Devils and madmen. You do the impossible."

"What kind of shape are their vehicles in?" Ben called.

"Fine shape. Like new," Buddy returned the shout.

"Load up all their gear and weapons and assign drivers. We're getting the hell gone from this place. Pick up our dead for later burial."

A black-shirt lay on the pavement, badly wounded by a knife blade in the belly. He watched as Ben leaned against a Hummer and started to roll a cigarette. "That won't be necessary, General Raines. I have a full package . . . in my pocket," he groaned out the words. "And a carton in a Jeep at the end of town. Take them. I will have no further use for them."

Ben knelt down beside the man and fished out the cigarettes, enclosed in a metal protective case. The silver case had a swastika embossed upon it. Ben started to throw cigarettes and case away.

"The container does not diminish the quality of the product within, General," the black-shirt said.

Ben thought about that for a moment, and took out the pack of smokes and put the container in his pocket to keep as a souvenir. He lit two cigarettes and placed one between the dying man's lips.

"*Obrigado*, sir."

Ben stared at the man. "You're Portuguese?"

"*Sim*. I mean, yes."

Ben waved a medic over. "Give this man a shot for the pain."

"Yes, sir." He knelt down and inspected the wound. "You're not going to make it, soldier."

"I know. The blade tore through . . ." He groaned in pain. ". . . my stomach and into my guts."

The shot given, the black-shirt inhaled deeply of the smoke and said, "You and your people are truly unbelievable, General. You fight like demons."

Ben noticed the man's wedding band. "You're married?"

"I was. She is dead."

"Sir," a Rebel called. "Can we keep these hand-rolled cigarettes we're finding?"

There were a lot of smokers among the Rebels, even though Doctor Chase bitched and growled and howled about it.

"Sure," Ben called. "Just leave that carton in the Jeep down the road. Those are mine!"

"Yes, sir!" the Rebel called.

The dying black-shirt managed a chuckle. "Soldiers are soldiers the world over, are they not, sir?"

"In many respects, yes. Although some of our objectives and philosophies certainly differ."

"Confusing times, General."

"Not for me, soldier."

"Nor for General Hoffman, sir. I assure you of that. You both have very firm beliefs and will both go to the grave believing you are right."

"How is your pain?"

"Gone. I thank you for that. How many of my group survived the attack?"

"Not many."

"You will shoot them?"

"No. We'll take them back for interrogation."

"Then you will shoot them?"

"No. They'll be kept alive and treated well."

The soldier frowned. "Then we have been lied to about how you treat prisoners. We were told that you did not take prisoners."

"We don't take many. Or we try not to. But we're not savages all the time."

"Is the sky becoming dark, General?"

The sky was bright and blue and clear. "Yes," Ben lied.

The black-shirt did not reply. Ben looked back at him and the man was dead. Ben took the cigarette from his lips and ground it out under a bootheel. He stood up.

"Everybody ready to roll?"

"All set, Father," Buddy said. "Where to?"

"To a secure airport so we can get planes in for our wounded."

"What about us, General?" a wounded black-shirt called.

Ben looked at him. "We're not going to shoot you, soldier. Be thankful for that. So don't press your luck."

The black-shirt cussed him in a language that Ben was not familiar with, but could tell the words were not complimentary. "Mount up," Ben said. "Before I change my mind."

Thirteen

The Rebels pulled out and took a southwesterly route, heading toward a small town near the border that reportedly had a landing strip large enough to handle twin-engine cargo planes. In addition to the Rebel wounded, the Rebels brought along two officers and four sergeants of the NAL. They brought no NAL wounded with them.

They made the one-hundred-mile run in good time and encountered no hostiles. But scouts kept a wary eye on their backtrail, knowing the force of American turncoats was more than likely following them, waiting for a chance to strike.

Intercepting the radio messages, Striganov sent teams from his command racing up across the border, and the small airport was clean and the planes waiting by the time Ben and his unit arrived. The Rebel wounded and black-shirt prisoners were airlifted over to Base Camp One in Louisiana.

"That force just behind us has got to be dealt with," Ben told the Russian's men. "Sooner or later, and it might as well be sooner. As soon as we are resupplied, we're heading back."

Soldiers will gossip among themselves, and it

wasn't long before all of Ben's batt comms were on the horn, raising hell with Ben for leading the reckless charge into the streets of the tiny town on the edge of the national forest.

"And you got the nerve to jump on my ass for being aggressive," Ike fussed at him from his position in New Mexico.

"Very foolhardy, General," Colonel Gray radioed. "Your place is back at HQ, not racing willy-nilly about the countryside endangering yourself."

"You know better, Ben," Colonel West admonished him. "Too many people are depending upon you for you to place yourself in that much danger."

And so on and so forth from all his senior batt comms.

Ben listened, acknowledged the transmissions, then promptly forgot all about them. The only way he was ever going to leave the field was in a body bag. His batt comms knew that; they just wanted to press home the point occasionally.

Before dawn the next morning, Ben and his teams were on the road, freshly supplied, rested, and well-fed, chasing after the turncoat force of Americans north of them.

South of the no-man's-land in extreme southern Mexico, Hoffman listened in dismay and disgust as Ramon read him the latest reports from North America.

Hoffman finally lifted a hand and said, "Enough! I've heard enough. Thank you, Ramon. That will be all. Keep me informed, please." When the aide had left the room and closed the door, Hoffman turned to several of his field commanders and said, "We will radio our people in the midwest to stay low and not

245

to engage the Rebels unless forced to do so. My God, people, think of it. We had six battalions in Texas and Oklahoma. We now have approximately two thousand personnel left in those areas."

"That is not taking into account the American groups who had come over to us," a field commander pointed out.

"Well, so far, they haven't shown themselves to be any better against the Rebels than our own highly trained and motivated troops," Hoffman replied. "The commanding general of the Rebel army, charging out into the streets with his troops and all of them fighting like a pack of common hooligans. I've never heard of such a thing. The man must be losing his mind."

"If he is," a field commander said dryly, "I, personally, would like to be infected with the same disease."

"What manner of man is this?" another asked. "To kneel in the bloody streets and chat with one of our dying soldiers; lighting a cigarette for him. Ben Raines is a complex man."

"I wonder if we are not like the dog, chasing its tail," Hoffman mused aloud.

"What do you mean, Field Marshal Hoffman?"

Some of the older officers insisted on calling Herr Hoffman by that title.

Hoffman shook his head. "It's just a germ of an idea, General Cortez. But it may be a good one."

"If you thought of it," another field commander verbally stroked the field marshal, "of course it will be a good one."

That pleased Hoffman and he sat down, smoothing his hair with one hand. Hoffman was very vain about his looks. "I will think about it and let you all know when I reach my decision. If we could pull it off . . ." He let that trail into silence. "It could mean instant victory for us. Yes. It certainly could."

"Thermopolis says Hoffman is up to something," Corrie said, after receiving a message from HQ. "Everything is too quiet south of the zone."

"Is that the opinion of our intelligence people or Therm's own opinion?"

"Therm's opinion."

"Then there might be something to it," Ben said with a smile. Sometimes G2 got a little weird in their thinking.

"Therm thinks the NAL may try to make a grab for you, General."

Ben was silent for a mile or so. "I wonder where, why, and how he came up with that?"

"I don't know. He didn't say. He did say he was going to share those thoughts with the other batt comms."

"Oh, that's wonderful," Ben said. "Ike will probably insist upon me being surrounded by several battalions. In a castle with a moat."

Ben and his Rebels had inspected the now-deserted camp of those turncoats in the national forest. They were long gone, but there was no question about it, the men were professional soldiers and woodsmen. They left no trace of themselves behind.

"Nothing, General," a scout reported to him. "It rained here last night and wiped out any tracks that might have given us a clue."

Ben leaned against his Hummer for a moment. There was no point in going off in a blind search. That was a good way to get killed. He needed to talk to Therm and find out more about Thermopolis's theory, or hunch, that a snatch attempt might be made.

"All right," Ben said to the scout. "We'll head over toward McAlester. The route will be 1 and 63. Take off."

"Right, sir. Give us a thirty-minute head start."

"Will do."

At a tiny hamlet about fifteen miles outside McAlester, they saw an elderly man mowing his lawn with an old push mower, and Ben halted the short convoy and walked over to the picket fence. The man stopped his mowing and walked to the fence. Ben noticed the man was wearing a pistol. And by the way he walked, he definitely wasn't afraid of them.

"We're friendly," Ben assured him.

"That bunch that come through here the other day damn sure wasn't, soldier boy."

It had been about four decades since Ben could accurately be called a boy, and he had to smile at the old man's words. "Oh. Did they do you any harm?"

"Oh, no. They were just rude and sort of arrogant acting. Very demanding bunch of assholes."

Ben laughed. "I don't think they intimidated you one bit."

"Damn sure didn't. Me and wife been here for over fifty years. And we plan on dying right here. No bunch of so-called survivalists will make me take water. You're General Ben Raines, aren't you?"

"That's right."

"Francis!" the old man bellered. "Come on out here, old girl. You can get out from behind that machine gun now. It's Ben Raines and the Rebels."

"Machine gun?" Ben questioned.

"Yep. Got five of them. Three M-60's and two .50 caliber babies. When I saw what was happening to this nation, I bought them on the sly, I did. Not all at once, mind you, but one at a time. Back when money was worth about something. I was with a special unit

248

in Korea that later came to be called the Green Berets. Special Forces. I stayed in the National Guard for thirty years after I got out of the regular Army. I do know something about weapons," he added with a smile.

"I imagine you do."

Ben met Francis and noticed that she was wearing a pistol. That produced no feeling of sadness or sorrow for the elderly couple. The old couple was probably safer now than back when the world was whole and governments were still mucking about screwing up everybody's lives. They could at least defend themselves now without fear of going to jail for protecting themselves or being sued by a criminal.

"This bunch that came through here, did they say where they might be heading?"

"Not really. But I heard them say something about Lake Eufaula. But that's one hell of a big lake."

Ben nodded his head. He'd been there, years back. Had a firefight there, as he recalled. "That bunch is in league with a South American Nazi general who has plans on taking over all of North America."

"I heard on our shortwave radio about that jackass. You going to stop him, General?"

"We're going to try. But I'm very much afraid that the fight will eventually be all over North America."

"Well, me and Francis here are in our eighties. We're in good health, and plan to live on a few more years. If any Nazi son of a bitch comes knocking on our door, he's going to get a whole hell of a lot more than he bargained for. I'll tell you that."

"You want my medical people to look you both over while we're here?"

Francis shook her head. "I was a registered nurse and a surgical nurse, General. So far, for a couple of

249

old poots, we're creeping around feeling pretty darned good."

"God bless you and your troops, Ben Raines," the old man said. "I just wish that someone like you had come along before the whole damn world blew up. We'll include you in our prayers."

"Thank you."

The man cut his eyes to Jersey, standing with the stock of her CAR on one hip. "You a little-bitty thing, but you look like you know how to use that M-16."

Jersey smiled at him.

"She's my bodyguard," Ben said.

"You got good taste in women."

Jersey was blushing down to her toenails as they pulled out.

Ben directed the forward scouts to head toward Lake Eufaula while the column would pull up and wait just a few miles south of McAlester.

"If that bunch is holed up somewhere around the lake," Ben said, "we could spend days looking for them and never find them. But we can't let them slip away. We don't want that bunch at our backs when Hoffman tries for the border."

The scouts reported back that they could find no trace of the elusive bunch. "They've got to be making cold camps, General. We checked out every smoke, and found only locals, trying to make it."

"The outpost at the head of the lake?"

"Wiped out. A local told us this bunch we're after did them in."

"All the more reason to find them," Buddy said.

"We'll find them," his father said. "Or they'll find us, if Therm is correct in his thinking."

"You think they're a major part in this kidnapping theory?"

"Yes. But I don't know what part they play. Corrie, get some choppers up here and let's do an air search. Buddy, clear off an LZ over in that meadow."

"You be careful, Ben," Therm told him in coded messages. "All regular traffic from Hoffman's area has ceased. We think the plans have been sent and received and everything is now in motion. It all adds up to a kidnapping attempt."

"I can't see it, Therm," was Ben's reply. "This may be only the lull before the storm."

"Negative, Ben. But it's too risky for you to try to make a run for home base. Too many miles separate us. G2 and all batt comms say for you to dig in and sit tight. We have solid info that Hoffman's people have SAMS, so we don't want you in the air. The batt comms don't want to have to override you, Ben. But they will in this case."

"All right, Therm. I'll sit tight."

"It would take a hell of a force to overrun us, Father," Buddy said. "This little crossroads village is ideal for defense. What do Therm and G2 base their worries on?"

"I don't know. It's something they picked up and don't want to go on the air with. I've got a hunch that Payon has people placed deep in Hoffman's organization. I'd make a bet they got word out to him and he sent Therm the message by courier. That's the only thing that makes any sense to me."

The tiny hamlet was made up of three buildings— an old service station and bait shop, a small grocery store, and a bar—and about a dozen homes. It was not on any map that Ben had looked at. The Rebels surrounding him were well-equipped and well-supplied. Ben figured they could withstand a light to moderate attack. Any heavy force could overrun them easily, simply by sheer numbers. But he didn't think

251

Hoffman had that large a force in this area.

Teams of Rebels were racing toward his location at this moment, so if a kidnapping attempt was to be made, it would be within the next twenty-four hours. After that, the place would be crawling with Rebels.

"Heavy rain and high winds to the south of us," Corrie reported. "The choppers have been grounded and this storm is expected to last at least twelve hours. It's slowing up everybody."

"What do you think, Father?" Buddy asked.

"They'll hit us tonight," Ben said. "Bet the farm on it."

Dark and savage-looking storm clouds were gathering to the south and the west. This part of Oklahoma was going to get a real weather pasting in a few hours.

The storage tanks of the old service station had long been drained of fuel—no danger of anything blowing up—and the building was solid, constructed of concrete block. Ben was using it as his CP and living quarters.

The Rebels were tense as the storm approached them. Lightning danced in the skies, and several times funnel clouds appeared, but did not touch down.

"Steady, folks," Ben told his people. "Just settle down. If a funnel cloud touches down, we'll jump in those old bays in the service area."

"The storm isn't what's making them jumpy, General," Jersey told him.

"I know, Jersey. I know."

Just before dark the rains came, the sheets of water so intense they limited vision to only a few yards.

"Here they come!" The shout was faint above the roaring of the storm. "They . . ." The wind blew his words away into the darkness.

The attack was well-planned, and it was fast.

We're not going to hold them, Ben thought, lifting his M-16. We finally ran out of luck.

"General!" Jersey screamed.

Ben turned and took the butt of a rifle on the chin. The last thing he remembered was falling into a black pit.

Book Three

They were going to look at war, the red animal—war,
the blood-swollen god.

Stephen Crane

One

When Ben finally regained consciousness, he did not move or open his eyes. He lay as still as possible in the covered bed of the moving truck and tried to ascertain whether he was alone in the rear compartment. He couldn't tell. If he was being guarded, the guards weren't very talkative or they were asleep. His hands were bound behind his back, with rope it felt like, but his feet were free.

Bad mistake, people, Ben thought.

The truck slowed, then pulled off the road and onto the shoulder. Ben lay with his eyes closed and heard the canvas flap being jerked open and the tailgate lowered.

"I guess Sternholder got it all in him," a voice said. "He said to check him in about six hours. If he was still out, he'd be out well after we hit the Arkansas line."

The Arkansas line? Ben thought. The Arkansas line was no more than seventy miles from where the Rebels had been holed up. Must be a slow-assed truck.

"We'll check him again when we get to Siloam Springs. That's about an hour off."

Extreme northwest Arkansas, Ben thought.

Ben felt the man crawl up into the bed of the truck and then a sharp tug on his hands. "The tether rope is strong. He's not going anywhere. Let's take a piss and get gone. Mountain Home is a long ways from here."

"It's only about a hundred and sixty miles from Siloam Springs to the base camp. And these roads are pretty good."

"Come on, you guys!" another voice added. "Let's move!"

"Keep your pants on, Cord. You just stay behind us and keep your eyes open."

So a vehicle was following them. That made it even worse, Ben thought.

The tailgate was slammed closed and the canvas flap tied in place. Seconds later, the truck lurched forward.

Ben opened his eyes and let them adjust to the dim light coming from the cab. His hands were numb from the tight ropes that bound his wrists. He pulled his legs up and felt for the sheath knife that he wore buckled to his right boot. Naturally, it was gone. He expected that. That's why he wore it there. So they would take that and not look any further.

He pulled his trouser leg out of his boot and felt for the top of the thin stiletto blade he carried in a pocket sewn inside all his boots. No handle, just a very thin, razor-sharp blade about three inches long. It was there. He worked his fingers to get some feeling back in them just as he felt he might pass out again. Whoever Sternholder was, he had gotten enough of the juice in him to screw up Ben's thinking. He fought the feeling of falling into blackness, and after a moment, it passed. He deliberately put all thoughts of his team from his mind. This was no time to think about them.

He pulled the blade from its pocket, being careful not to cut himself, and tucked it under one leg, laying on it. He was so damn weak. Then the knockout shot began working on him again and he faded.

Voices woke him. "Goddammit, I said to check him at the line, you asshole!"

"I forgot and you were asleep. Hell, man, look at him. He hasn't even moved." Ben heard something click; probably a flashlight. "See, the ropes are still tight and the tether rope is secure."

"All right, all right. We're about seventy-five miles from home. You sleep and I'll drive. Two hours from now, we'll have hot food and a warm bed."

Ben did a slow three hundred and sixty count after they were once more rolling. Time enough for the passenger to fall asleep and for Ben to make sure he was thinking clearly and wasn't going to pass out again.

Then he couldn't find the goddamn blade.

He carefully searched all around him, then shifted and searched that area. Nothing. He heard something click and in the dim light saw the blade. It had bounced off the side of the bed as they rounded a curve.

Ben went to work on his ropes, cutting his outer wrists and hands half a dozen times in the process. It took him about half an hour to cut through his bonds. His fingers were so numb the blade kept falling from his grasp. A half hour had passed. Ben knew this country, had once seriously considered buying property in this neck of the woods. They should be close to Harrison by now; maybe even past it. He didn't have to open the canvas to see if the truck behind them was still there. The lights were bright enough for Ben to tell it was. He looked at his watch. Two o'clock in the morning. He put his blade back in its pocket and stretched out on the bed floor to think about his situation.

Then he noticed that the lights of the truck behind him were gone. You idiot! he thought. Of course. The damn road is a winding one. There are many spots where you'll have ten or fifteen seconds to jump without being seen.

He rubbed his sore wrists and numb fingers until the feeling returned.

He parted the rear curtains just a fraction of an inch and saw that the truck following them had backed off. It appeared to be heavily loaded as it labored up the steep grade. The truck in which he was riding was slowing down too as it made its way up the grade. Then Ben felt them entering a curve. The truck following them was out of sight. He jerked open the curtains, held on as he fastened the rope back in place, and jumped, hitting the ground hard and rolling off the shoulder. He was in brush immediately, for the area was grown up all around him.

The fall knocked the wind from him, bruised his leg, and cut his hand. He lay still as the last truck rolled past him, then painfully stood up and limped to the edge of the road. He almost ran into a road sign, now all rusted and almost impossible to read. YELLVILLE, 1 MILE.

As close as he could remember, he was about twenty-five miles from Mountain Home. And one mile from Yellville. He started walking, staying close to the edge of the brush. He still wasn't thinking as clearly as he would like to, but he knew his mind was slowly returning to normal.

There were things he could not understand about

his capture. Why hadn't they flown him up here? Why had he been so loosely guarded? And what the hell was he going to find when he got to Mountain Home?

He heard a vehicle coming toward him from the east and slipped into the brush. The old truck rattled past and Ben began looking around, feeling around, for a staff. He found a wrist-thick limb about four feet long and once more stepped out onto the shoulder of the road. Soon the dark shapes of buildings came up on him as he approached the small town. The cool mountain air and the walk had helped to clear his head and Ben felt he was very close to one hundred percent.

Voices stopped him, froze him, and then sent him stepping into the shadows of an old building. He waited.

"I wonder what the big news is?" the voice drifted to Ben.

"I reckon we'll know in a few hours," the second man said. "Rumor is they grabbed Ben Raines."

"I'll believe that when I see it. You gonna get some rest 'fore we pull out?"

"Naw. I got a few hours' sleep. I think I'll have me a smoke and wait til the mess opens for coffee."

"Be fun watchin' Jackman torture Raines, won't it?"

"It will be for me. I hate that son of a bitch. He run me out of Louisiana few years back. Killed my en-tar family."

"Wake me up at dawn and we'll ride over together."

"I'll do 'er."

The man walked away and disappeared into the darkness. Ben could see that both men were armed.

Step over here, you half-wit, Ben thought. I'll bend

this pole around your red neck.

The man who hated Ben Raines walked toward the building. He squatted down and rolled him a smoke. A match flared and Ben moved, knowing the man's night vision had just been destroyed. He brought the staff down on the man's head, and redneck #2 hit the pea gravel without making a sound. Ben dragged him to the side of the building, jerked out the man's sheath knife, and cut his throat. He took the man's weapon, an Uzi, and stripped off the web belt, which held a Beretta 9mm pistol and clip pouch. The man carried five full clips for the Uzi in a canvas pouch. Ben slung that.

He dragged the body around to the rear of the building and dumped it in a ditch, then returned to the side of the building and kicked dirt and gravel over the dark bloodstains. Then Ben got the hell out of there.

Ike's face was tight with grief and anger as he inspected the battle site south of McAlester. They hadn't lost this many Rebels in the taking of the Hawaiian chain. Over fifty dead. Corrie, Jersey, Beth, and Cooper, all wounded. Buddy had taken a slug through the shoulder.

And Ben had been captured.

To further complicate matters, the heavy rains had prevented any of the survivors from knowing which direction the kidnappers had gone, and there had been no radio messages from Hoffman's America-based allies. It was going to be like looking for a needle in a haystack.

But the news of Ben's capture did not have the effect upon the Rebels that Herr Hoffman had planned. It didn't demoralize them. It just pissed them off to the core.

"Goddamn you, Hoffman," Ike swore. "I swear if there is a God in Heaven, I'm going to stick the muzzle of my CAR up your Nazi ass and empty a clip."

"Thermopolis on the horn, General," Ike's radio-operator called. "He wants a damage report."

"Tell him it's bad," Ike replied. "Real bad." Hang on, Ben, Ike thought. Hang on, man.

At first light, Ben found a small cave, and after checking it carefully for bears or snakes or panthers, he crawled inside and lay down. He was exhausted and hungry. He had found a small spring and satisfied his thirst with the cold water, but he was very hungry. He closed his eyes and let his tense and sore muscles relax.

When he opened his eyes, he was startled to find he had slept more than eight hours. His strength had returned, but he was hungry enough to eat just about anything. He crawled to the mouth of the small cave and lay still, listening for any alien sound. Birds were singing and squirrels were chattering.

Ben crawled out into the middle of the afternoon and checked his bearings.

He had been following a meandering creek (Crooked Creek) as it wound eastward, and assumed the creek would eventually empty into the White River. He would follow it as long as he could, or until it made no sense to continue the twisting and turning.

He walked for half an hour until coming to a gravel road. He knelt by the road and watched and listened. The old road ran north and south. North would take him back to the highway. He turned south, staying in the woods. He was covered with chiggers, and knew the little burrowing bastards would begin to give him fits in a few hours, but it couldn't be helped. He bellied down at the sounds of a vehicle coming up the road fast, from the south. Three men and a woman in an old Cadillac roared up the road, kicking up clouds of dust.

Had to be a house down this road. Ben walked on. Ten minutes later, a home came into view. Please, no dogs, Ben sent out a silent prayer. And no one at home.

He got one out of two. Well, he thought, as the dog started barking, I'm batting five hundred. It was a black lab, and Ben softly called to it, holding out one hand from the edge of the timber. The dog looked at him suspiciously, then wagged its tail and came to Ben.

"How you doing, feller?" Ben asked, petting the lab. The dog licked his hands and face and then went trotting off into the woods to play.

Ben eased up to the rear of the house and paused, listening. He could hear no sound from inside. Taking a deep breath, he stepped up onto the back porch and opened the door. The house was silent. Quickly inspecting the rooms, Ben found a cache of survival food and in another room, an arsenal. He picked up one of half a dozen backpacks and two canteens. He found 9mm rounds and clips for an Uzi. He took a blanket and a ground sheet and a box of waterproof and windproof matches. He carefully selected survival packages of food and a small first aid kit from a box that contained dozens of them. He took fresh socks from a cardboard box and clean underwear still wrapped in plastic. Fruit of the Loom. He found soap and took a fresh bar.

He prowled the house, being careful not to disturb

anything. There were pamphlets about Hoffman's NAL and white supremacy. Ben wasn't that hard up for reading material.

There were several loaves of fresh-baked bread on the table, covered with a clean white cloth, and the bread smelled so damn good Ben wanted desperately to take one, but he knew better. He did pause long enough to eat a bowl of stew from the pot on the stove, and carefully washed out the bowl and spoon, replacing them exactly where he had found them.

He left the house, closing the back door, and headed for the creek. Now he would make it. Now he would get cleaned up, eat some more, clean out the cuts on his wrists and hands, and then he would go raise some hell with this Jackman person. He had found cases of grenades and hooked half a dozen onto a battle harness and put half a dozen more in his pack.

He looked around for the dog, but the lab was off in the woods, having fun. "Luck to you, boy," Ben muttered. He still had refused to think about his team back in Oklahoma. There would be time for that later.

Ben returned to the creek and followed it for a couple of miles. He found a dandy spot for a camp and after carefully checking it out, took a quick bath and changed into fresh clothing, from the skin out. He had found sets of tiger-stripe and had taken one. He filled his canteens and dropped in water-purification tablets. Then he treated the cuts on his hands and wrists. He filled up the extra clips and took down his Uzi, cleaning it carefully. He checked the knife he'd taken from the dead redneck and found it to be honed to a razor edge. Only then did he eat and stretch out, unfolding a map of Arkansas he'd found in a pile back at the house in the country with a friendly lab guarding it.

He would leave the creek south and west of Gassville and work north, crossing the highway and staying on the north side of it until he reached Mountain Home. There had been a Rebel outpost at Mountain Home. Obviously it had been overrun and now served as a base, or CP for this Jackman person.

"You screwed up, Jackman, Hoffman, or whoever put the grab on me," Ben muttereed. "You screwed up bad."

Ben was free, in a manner of speaking, but still in a hard bind, and knew it. Even if he could get to a radio powerful enough to transmit hundreds of miles, he couldn't afford to call in to HQ, for Jackman's men would be scanning all frequencies. Once he gave out his location, Jackman's men would hunt him down like an animal.

He heard the sound of a low-flying plane and slipped back under the overhang a few yards from the creek. He waited under the plane was gone before again stepping out. The search was on, but Jackman had a lot of territory to cover.

Ben rolled up in his blanket and went to sleep.

He was up long before dawn and restless, wanting to get moving, but knowing that stumbling around in the dark would be a stupid thing to do. He used a heat tab under his canteen cup to heat water for coffee and drank the hot bitter brew that had been packed for the U.S. Army years back. It tasted like shit smells. And the tablet-purified water didn't help any. But it was hot and Ben supposed it still had caffeine in it after all the years.

He was moving at first light, following the creek and staying in the brush or very close to it. He stopped often to listen and carefully check his

266

surroundings. So far, Ben knew, he had been very, very lucky. But the closer he drew to the road, the more cautious he must become.

The closer to any artery, the more people he would have to avoid. He came to an old blacktopped road and squatted in the brush beside it. Directly across from his position was a home made of native stone. The lawn was all grown up into weeds, and one porch support post had given way and collapsed. He stepped out of the brush, then ducked back quickly. He had almost made a fatal mistake.

About five hundred yards north of his position he had spotted a roadblock. He headed south toward a long curve in the road, which would prevent those at the roadblock from seeing him, and checked it out. All clear both ways. He darted across the highway and into the brush. He followed the creek several more miles and then cut straight north.

That night he camped in timber on the side of a hill overlooking a lovely meadow. He felt pretty good; smug even. He had crossed Highway 62 just after dark and had crossed the White River bridge in the back of a bob truck full of vegetables. He had ridden the truck for miles until the driver had slowed for a turn on Highway 126 north. Ben left the truck carrying a watermelon under each arm.

He was about four miles from Mountain Home and full of watermelon.

Ben was in his fifth day of not shaving, and was beginning to grow a respectable beard. He had discarded his tiger-stripe uniform for a pair of jeans and dark shirt he had stolen from a clothesline early that day. He had found a terrible-looking old hat with a wide floppy brim and, after giving it a good dunking in a creek, now wore that. At a distance, he looked like just a down-on-his-luck bum.

He watched the lights come on in Mountain Home. The Rebels had gotten the electricity back on and now Jackman and his crud were using it.

Ben chuckled darkly in the night. "Have fun, Jackman," he whispered to the darkness. "Tomorrow I start pulling your plug."

Two

Ben had worked close to town and knew without any doubt that Jackman's men had taken over the place. It was real easy to tell: the Nazi swastika could be seen everywhere one looked. There were a lot of black-shirts in evidence as well, and only those troops and the cammie-clad men of Jackman's carried weapons.

"Fair game," Ben muttered. "Now I start having some fun." He was crouched inside an old fast-food restaurant and peering out through a crack in the boarded-up windows. He smiled, a grim curving of his lips. Come the night, darkness was not the only thing that was going to fall.

A walking patrol of two heavily armed men stopped in the shade of the building to smoke and talk. Ben listened.

"I ain't never seen Jackman so pissed. I thought he was gonna shoot them ol' boys who was bringin' Raines in."

"Me, too. At least I heard he was pissed. I'm glad I wasn't around."

"You think Ben Raines is around this area?"

"Hell, no. Man, he's workin' south toward his own

people. He's a hundred miles from here by now."

"That's what I think, too. You going to the citizen-hangin' tomorrow?"

"Wouldn't miss it for the world. Folks got to learn if they collaborate with the enemy, they gonna get hung."

"Damn shame to hang that fine-lookin' piece of ass. Jackman could have give her to us."

Laughing, the men moved on.

"Ummm," Ben said.

For reasons that were still unknown to Ben, years back, when the plague had run its course and the final collapse of governments came about shortly afterward, many jails and prisons were destroyed. Most courthouses were blown up or burned. Perhaps it was to destroy public records and erase past crimes. Ben never had been able to figure that out. But on this night, it would prove to be a good thing, for the six people who were to be hanged the following morning were being held in an old motel on Highway 62. Ben had learned that by listening to people talk as they walked past his hiding place during the day. Two women and four men.

By nine o'clock that night, Ben was lying in the tall grass about a hundred yards from the motel.

It was easy to see which rooms were being used as cells. The big windows had been removed and bars were in their place. Directly in front of the holding rooms, about fifty yards out, was a sandbagged machine-gun nest, manned by two men. Three armed guards patrolled the walkway in front of the converted rooms.

"I got to piss," one of the machine gunners said. "Be right back."

"Take your time," his buddy told him. "Bring us back some coffee and a doughnut, will you? After you wash your hands," he added with a laugh.

His buddy gave him the bird and walked off into the gloom.

Ben slipped through the soft wet grass and wormed his way down the embankment and snaked his way to the rear of the sandbags. With one quick movement, he grabbed the man's long hair, cut his throat, and gently let the chin go forward until it was resting on the man's chest.

The next part was going to be tricky.

The second machine gunner came walking back, both hands full of coffee cups. Ben hoped he could salvage at least one of the cups. He needed a cup of coffee.

The sandbags were about three feet high and Ben lay close to the rear bags. The guard came up and stood for a moment.

"Jesus Christ, Denny. Jackman come by here and see you sleepin' it'd be your ass in a sling. I told you to stop layin' out with that damn woman. She's sappin' all your strength." He sat the cups on the top of the bags and stepped into the square. "Go on and sleep. I'll jab you if I need you."

Ten seconds later, all he needed was a good record with the Lord. Something Ben doubted he had.

Ben lay behind the bags and ate the doughnut and drank both cups of coffee, even though one had cream in it and Ben liked his coffee black with one sugar.

Working very carefully, glancing over at the walking guards every few seconds, Ben removed the pistol belts from each man, their battle harnesses, and took their M-16s.

Now it was going to get dicey.

He slipped back into the tall grass and worked his way to the end of the motel grounds. He stashed the gear and squatted in the darkness behind a car, wondering what in the hell he was going to do now.

"I got to go shit," one of the guards said. "That greasy crap that my wife fixed for supper is workin' on me hard."

"Go crap over yonder behind my car. If Jackman comes up, we can say you was checkin' out a noise."

Ben smiled. Come on, come on. He was pleased to see the man was about his height and had a dark stubble of beard. It might work. It just might work.

The guard was moaning and holding his stomach as he approached the car. He fumbled with his battle harness and laid it aside, then tore open his belt and dropped his trousers. The only relief he got was the blade of a knife tearing into his back and ripping upward as a hard hand clamped over his mouth. Ben picked up the man's fallen beret and plopped it on his own head. He waited a few minutes, then stood up, walking slowly toward the motel. Several cars drove past and the last one pulled in.

As the car was pulling in, the driver called, "Hey, Fuller. Come over here. I got a message from Jackman." He pulled the car past the corner of the building and out of sight.

Go on, Fuller, Ben silently urged. Go on.

Fuller went, leaving just the one guard.

"'Bout time you got back," the guard said as Ben walked up. The man's eyes widened and he opened his mouth to yell.

Ben's knife, which he had been holding close to his right leg, flashed in the dim light and the guard went down, blood spurting from his torn throat. Ben tore the ring of keys from the man's belt and fumbled with the keys for precious seconds until he found the right one. He pushed open the door and stood for a few more seconds looking at a very lovely woman. He blinked and tossed her the keys.

"Get the others and get down to the end of the parking lot," he told her. "Move. Quickly now. There are guns at the front of that old Mercury. Move!"

"Who are you?" she breathed. Then her eyes widened. "My God. General Raines."

"Move, darling," Ben said. He heard a car pulling out. "We're all out of time. Move, goddammit!"

He ran to the edge of the building and knocked Fuller sprawling to the concrete. A kick to the head put Fuller out of it for a long time. If his skull wasn't fractured, he'd have one hell of a headache for a day or so.

Ben ripped the battle harness from him and took off the web belt containing pistol and clips. He ran back to the holding rooms. The woman had unlocked the doors and the prisoners were standing outside, all of them looking dazed and scared and slightly confused.

"Move!" Ben called in a hoarse whisper. "Let's get the hell out of here." He tossed the M-16, web belt, and ammo pouch to a man and pushed the others toward the far end of the parking lot.

Then Lady Luck lifted her skirts and crapped all over everybody.

A car pulled in, the headlights highlighting them all. "Hey!" a man yelled, and floorboarded the old Cadillac. Ben leveled the Uzi and gave the windshield half a clip. The car slewed to one side and went crashing into the lower level of the motel.

"Go!" Ben yelled. "Into that field and keep going straight."

"No," the woman said. "I know where to go."

"Lead the way, then. But for God's sake, move!"

They ran into the field just as sirens began splitting the night air and headlights of fast-moving cars and trucks were darting in all directions behind them.

They ran until Ben thought his sides would bust open. When they reached a deserted and nearly burned out old subdivision, the woman stopped and they all bent over, gasping for breath.

"I can't do it, Ann," a man about Ben's age said, bending over and holding his sides. "I can't go on."

"Come on, Larry," the woman urged. "It's not that much further."

"Let's go," Ben said. "So we all drop dead of a heart attack. Beats hanging any day. We'll walk for a minute then run for a minute. Lead the way, Ann."

She led them through a maze of burned homes and rubble. They crossed a creek and rested for a moment.

"Names," Ben said.

"I'm Ann," the woman whose beauty had stopped Ben for a few seconds back at the motel. "That's Larry, Paul, David, and Frank. This is Carol. We heard you were dead, General."

"Greatly exaggerated and very premature," Ben said with a smile. "Did Hoffman find our weapons cache here?"

"What weapons cache?" Frank asked.

Ben chuckled. "Come on. Let's find us a place to hole up for the night and then we'll really start doing some damage. Lead the way, Ann."

They skirted another line of darkened houses and crossed an open meadow, all of them keeping low. They crossed another creek and then heard the baying of bloodhounds behind them.

"Shit!" Ben said. "I might have known these ol' boys would have those. We find us some transportation and throw them off. Where's the highway?"

"Secondary road just up ahead," David said. "But how will you get a vehicle?"

"Is there a curfew on?"

"You bet. No one but Jackman's people are allowed out after dark."

"That makes it easy then," Ben told the small group. "We just kill the driver."

At the road, Ben motioned the others down into a ditch and he squatted beside the road in brush. The first vehicle was a small car and he let that go past. Then a pickup truck came driving slowly toward them, traveling no more than five miles an hour, a spotlight on the passenger side searching the ditches. When the vehicle drew even with Ben, he put half a dozen slugs through the open window. The driver must have had his left foot on the brake pedal, for the truck stopped abruptly, then started moving forward slowly.

Ben jumped out of the brush and jerked open the door, dragging the dead driver out and dumping him on the blacktop. He got behind the wheel and stopped the truck.

"Get their weapons," he told the group. "And get in."

Ann and Frank got in the cab with Ben, the others in the open bed of the truck. "Lay down," Ben told those in the rear. "This could get wild before it gets better."

"You're a cold one," Ann told him, her hazel eyes on Ben.

"I'm alive," Ben replied, then dropped the transmission into drive and took off. "Which way?"

"Stay on this road until I tell you to turn. We'll head out into the hills. It's a no-man's-land out there. That's where the resistance is located. Jackman's people don't venture out there."

"Does this take us out to the airport?"

"Right past it. But the airport is no longer in use. Jackman uses another strip south of here."

"Good," Ben said with a smile. "The airport is where the supplies are cached. They were modernizing it when the Great War hit. After the collapse of Tri-States, we hid supplies all over the nation."

"How come we weren't told of that?" Frank asked.

"If you didn't know, you couldn't have talked under torture."

"Makes sense," Frank said. "I guess."

A vehicle roared past them, the driver slammed on his brakes, and spun around in the road.

"Open fire on that vehicle," Ben shouted to those in the rear.

The night roared with automatic-weapons fire and the car behind them left the road and crashed into a huge old tree. If there were any survivors, they posed no immediate threat. Ben drove on into the night. At the old abandoned airport, Ben whipped in and drove to a hangar, parking inside.

"Are you insane?" Carol yelled from the rear of the truck. "We've got to get away!"

"Running away is not something I do well," Ben told her and the others. "You people find something to dig with. Move!"

Ben ran to the old office building, which had been gutted by fire years back. Ben centered himself at the building and walked ten steps.

"We'll dig here," he said, as Larry handed him a shovel with half its handle broken off.

A few frantic minutes later, Ben's shovel hit metal. He pried open the cleared lid and started handing out boxes to the group. "Load the truck and then meet me back at the road." He opened a long box. "Ann,

276

grab as many of these as you can carry and come with me."

"LAWs?" Paul questioned.

"You got it," Ben said. "Come on, Ann."

"Well, I'll just be damned," Paul said.

"Some of Jackman's people soon will be," Ben told him, and took off at a run for the road. He could see fast-approaching lights in the distance.

"It's going to be close," Ann panted by his side.

"Close only counts in horseshoes and hand grenades," Ben replied, kneeling down in the center of the highway. He pulled the safety pins and extended the inner tube, cocking the LAW. "Stand clear and have another one ready for me," he told Ann, shouldering the LAW and sighting in.

"Jesus," Ann said. "Fire the damn thing!"

"Too far away. They'll be in range in about five seconds."

Ben did a slow count and fired the 66mm rocket. The lead car exploded in flames and the driver of the car behind it jammed on his brakes. But it was too close. The second vehicle slammed into the burning mass of twisted metal just as Ben fired the second rocket. The roadway was turned into a blazing death trap, the explosion blowing part of a body through the shattered windshield. A third vehicle tried to get the hell gone from that area, the driver attempting a state trooper turnaround in the road, and the vehicle stalled out, exposing its right side for a moment. That was all the time that Ben needed. He fired a third LAW. No one would be using that highway for a while.

"Bye-bye, assholes," Ben said, standing up just as the now-heavily-laden truck pulled up.

"We got most of it and piled lumber and other stuff over the hole," David said. "I don't think they'll find it."

277

"We have other caches around the area," Ben said, getting into the back. "Let's go find someplace safe to rest and have something to eat. Excitement always makes me hungry."

Ann shook her head at his words. "Everything I ever heard about him is true."

Three

They smelled the smoke before they saw the flames. Then they heard the explosions. Frank turned off on a weeded-up country road, drove a couple of miles, and pulled onto what had once been a logging road and brought the truck to a halt.

"Jackman's people have hit the resistance camp from the north," Ann said. "We told them it wasn't safe. We suggested they move their operations further north, up into Missouri. They wouldn't listen."

Ben nodded his head, then realized the nod could not be seen in the night. "Doesn't matter now. We're on our own and we'd better accept that."

Carol sank to the cool earth. "Sometimes I just want to give up."

"When you decide to do that, Carol," Ben told her, "do it without me. You're all just tired and scared and desperate and probably hungry, too. I know I am. Hell, folks, I've been in a lot worse jams than this. Now get a flashlight out of one of those boxes and show me on a county map where we are. There are maps in with the other stuff."

A map and flashlight were found and Ann pointed

to a spot. "See this maze of county roads? We're right here."

"Oh, well, good," Ben replied cheerfully. "About a mile from here is an old long-abandoned sawmill, right?"

"That's right," Frank said. "How did you know about that?"

"That's where we put the largest cache of supplies long before we resettled the town."

"Radios?" Paul asked.

"No. The batteries would be worthless after this long a time, anyway."

"The food?"

"Maybe. I think so. We'll soon know. Come on. Let's unload this truck and hide what supplies we can't carry. After that's done, move the truck up the road a good mile or so. Who'll volunteer to do that?"

Larry raised his hand.

"Fine. We'll wait for you right here."

When Larry rejoined the group, Ann took the point and they moved out down the now barely recognizable old road. At the old sawmill, Ben told them all to relax, eat, and get some rest. They would dig up the second cache in the morning. They all wondered why he was smiling as he patted one of the boxes from the truck.

"Plastic explosives," Ben said. "C-4. With all the necessary dodads to make it go boom whenever we want it to."

"What's that thing?" Ann asked, pointing.

"Radio-controlled detonator."

"I thought you said we didn't have any radios," Carol said.

"We don't. Not the kind you're thinking of. But we

have the equipment to send a signal to one of these things that will make it go bang." He grinned like a little boy who had just found a whole box of Oreo cookies.

"You're just not a bit worried," Ann said, looking strangely at Ben. "This is . . . you're actually looking forward to this, aren't you?"

"Sure," Ben said brightly. "Why not? We're free. We're just as well-armed as those we're facing. We have food, water, plenty of weapons, lots of ammo and explosives, clean clothes, soap that I'm going to use in a little while to take a bath down at the creek, and medical supplies that I'm going to use to help kill all these goddamn chiggers on me!"

"General," David said, "we are surrounded by several thousand enemy troops. Troops of Jackman and black-shirts from South America. I mean, we are completely surrounded, General Raines. We're in a really lousy position."

Ben smiled and patted him on the shoulder. "Relax, David. After we dig up the other supplies, then we'll take a bath, and get the grime off us, and then I'll show you how seven people can successfully take on fifty times that number and win."

"Win," Ann repeated. "You really think that seven of us are going to win against five hundred times that number?"

"Oh, sure," Ben said. "Piece of cake."

The others, none of them trained Rebels, looked at him as if he were totally bananas.

Ben worked on the M-16s, attaching 40mm aluminum bloop tubes in place of the forestocks, the modification on each weapon taking about twenty minutes. "This lever here on the left side releases the

281

launcher's barrel," Ben told them. "It slides forward for loading. The magazine is your handgrip when using the bloop tube. With the M16A2 rifle the bloop tube has an effective range of about 460 meters. This Uzi here is just a dandy weapon, but from now on, I'll be carrying a rifle with a bloop tube just like the rest of you. Believe me when I say that when the seven of us pull out of here, we will have among us some awesome firepower. We're going to be traveling light on food and heavy on weapons. For the next several nights, we're going to be caching equipment all around Mountain Home and mapping out locations where we can duck in and hide. Now then, enlighten me. I knew that back before the Great War there were a lot of survivalist groups in this area, but I didn't know the majority were Nazis."

"They weren't," Ann said. "Most were just guys who liked to dress up like soldiers and shoot guns. All of us grew up in this area. When the Rebels declared it an outpost, we all returned and life was good for several years." She looked at Frank.

"Then it turned to shit," Frank said. "Very quietly and very subtly, Hoffman began sending people in. They were smooth and likable and worked hard. We had no idea of the number and certainly had no idea that they were planning a takeover. One day we looked up and Jackman and his bunch just began slaughtering the few Rebels who were stationed here. It's like you said, General: we're not trained professional Rebels. We're teachers and carpenters and pharmacists and so forth. We've all had a little training with weapons. We know how to use them, have used them, and will again. We're a . . . little bit more expert now. But Jackman just rolled over us."

"Well, folks," Ben said. "We're about to start doing some rolling ourselves. Rock and roll."

282

The team worked for three nights, caching supplies and checking out possible hidey-holes. Several times Jackman's patrols came within a few yards of where they lay, but always they walked on.

"They're scared and being overcautious," Ben told the small group. "But I don't understand why they're not using the dogs."

"They're probably using them over in the lake area, east of us," Larry said. "That would be my guess. They've caught a lot of people who tried to hide over in that area."

Ben nodded and returned to his map. They were going to strike this night.

"Intelligence has broken the code!" Ike was informed. "Ben's alive and is reported working with resistance groups somewhere. But we don't know where. Why doesn't the general radio in to us?"

"I'll tell you why," Chase grumbled. "Because he's having a ball, that's why. He's running around somewhere playing a middle-aged Rambo, blowing things up and taking chances, and shooting people and enjoying the hell out of it. He doesn't have to listen to us bitch at him about it."

"He wouldn't do that," Rebet protested.

"The hell he wouldn't," Thermopolis said. "That's exactly what he's doing."

"Well," Ike said, surprisingly easy on Ben. "There is this, too: Ben might not have access to a radio. And even if he did, if I was in his boots, I wouldn't use one for fear of being tracked. I think I like my version better, folks." Ike smiled. "But you're right, Lamar. Ben is having fun."

*　　　*　　　*

"Here they come, gang," Ben said, bellying back down on the cool grass. "A nice short and fat column. Spread out and get ready. You say they move a lot of ammo and gear up north, Ann?"

"Yes. Beefing up their friends who are in the timber just across the line. Getting even a light plane into those areas is just about impossible."

Ben smiled and screwed the cylinder containing rocket propellant into the warhead section of the 40mm rocket. He loaded the round, uncovered the nosecap, and pulled the pin. He lifted the old RPG-7 to his shoulder and sighted in. "Come on, you goose-stepping bastards. Come to the Eagle."

There were eight trucks in the column, and they were running close together. "Stupid," Ben said, and pulled the trigger.

The rocket impacted against the side of the slow-moving lead vehicle and it blew. The truck must have been carrying high explosives, for the explosion rocked the ground. The rest of Ben's team began firing their bloop tubes, with surprising accuracy, Ben noted, and the entire convoy was blazing and blowing within seconds.

"Let's get the hell gone!" Ben said.

They ran back into the brush, and as they left the brush heading for a hidey-hole, a patrol of black-shirts rounded a curve in the old animal trail. They were as surprised as Ben's team, but slightly slower in reacting.

Ann, Carol, and Frank fired 40mm rockets at the now-bunched-up patrol as Ben, Larry, Paul, and David opened up with automatic fire. They left the patrol dead and dying on the cool ground and vanished.

*   *   *

Jackman was furious. He paced his office and shouted and cussed. Back and forth before the swastika hanging on the wall. "Goddammit, you mean to tell me that six or seven people are out there screwing up this entire operation and you trained soldiers can't contain them?"

His commanders sat in silence. They could do little else, for Jackman was telling the truth.

Jackman paced back and forth before the Nazi flag. "We capture the commanding general of the Rebel army and my people don't have sense enough to place an adequate guard on the man. That same man then frees six prisoners from holding pens and in the process kills every guard at the facility. What the hell were the guards doing, standing around with their thumbs up their asses? Two nights ago they attack a convoy ferrying supplies to the north. Wiped out. That same night they ambush a black-shirt patrol. Wiped out. The next day they destroy a sentry post, blow up a storage area, and ambush one of our patrols. That night they launch a rocket attack against a barracks. The next day this pissy-assed little band of malcontents, being led by a middle-aged man, shoot down a plane as it was taking off and then proceed to shell the new airfield. Then that night they kill more than fifty of our people. Goddammit, do something!"

"Do what, Mr. Jackman?" the commander of the black-shirts stationed in that area asked. "They are successful because of their small size. And they are being led by a man who is probably the foremost expert in guerrilla warfare in all the world. I was surprised that Ben Raines did not call his forces in to crush us here. Then it dawned on me why he had not done so. The man is having fun."

Jackman's eyes bugged and his face reddened with

new anger. "Fun?" he shouted.

"Yes," the black-shirt commander said calmly. "Fun. We know from many, many intelligence reports over the years on Ben Raines that his own people place restrictions, or at least attempt to place them, on his movements. He is a true combat soldier. He long ago found the 'high' that comes with intense combat. The rush that hottens the blood when faced with danger. And a great many of his troops are like him in that respect. That's what makes the Rebels such a formidable force. Yes, Mr. Jackman, General Ben Raines is having fun."

The field phone jangled, and Jackman grabbed it and listened for a moment. Then he held the phone out at arm's length and stared at it. He looked as though he wanted to smash the instrument. With a great deal of effort, Jackman managed to restrain his baser emotions and gently slipped the phone back into its base. He looked at the black-shirt commander.

"Raines and his . . . team just attacked a twenty-man patrol up at Pigeon Creek. Wiped them out except for one man. Ben Raines gave that man a message to be personally and verbally delivered to me. He's being brought here now."

The black-shirt chuckled. "Now that is a message that should be interesting."

"You think this is funny?" Jackman asked.

"In a grim sort of way, yes. I hope you are all taking notes on this campaign. It's a valuable program that Ben Raines is conducting."

"Taking notes," Jackman repeated. Before he could blow up in a rage, the sole survivor of the ambush was ushered into the room. Jackman faced the still-badly-shaken man. "You have a message for me?"

"Yes, sir. But you're not going to like it."

"Tell me."

"Ben Raines said for me to tell you that, first off, you are a quasiliterate redneck asshole with shit for brains . . ."

The black-shirt commander contained his chuckle. Ben Raines was certainly right about that.

Jackman's eyes bugged again.

"Ben Raines says that you haven't got the sense to lace up your boots without an instruction manual."

Jackman sat down.

"Ben Raines says that he's going to cut off your head and stick it up your butt, which you probably haven't wiped since it's obvious to him that your mother failed to teach you proper personal hygiene."

Jackman's mouth dropped open.

The black-shirt had to cover his mouth to hide his grin. Raines was baiting Jackman and it was working.

"Raines said that you were so stupid you were a walking reason for anyone with common sense to support abortion."

"That's enough!" Jackman said, slamming a hand down on his desk.

"There's a lot more, sir."

"I don't want to hear it. What is that in your hand?"

"A package from Ben Raines."

"It's a bomb!" a commander shouted.

"No, sir," the messenger said. "It's Ben Raines's underwear."

"His underwear?" Jackman said.

"Yes, sir. Ben Raines said that you were so perverted you probably got off sniffing dirty underwear so he sent you his and told me to tell you—"

"I don't want to hear anymore of this!" Jackman

shouted, jumping to his feet. "Goddammit, get out of here."

"Yes, sir."

"Wait a minute," the black-shirt said to the messenger. "Let's hear it all. What else did Raines have to say."

"I said I didn't want to hear anymore!" Jackman shouted. "Get out of here."

"Stay," the black-shirt said. He sat silently and stared at Jackman for a moment.

Jackman got the quiet message and sat down. "Oh, go on," he said.

The messenger, obviously very uncomfortable, looked at Jackman and said, "Ben Raines said he is going to bust up your little playhouse and grind you under his bootheel."

The messenger went on and on, with Jackman getting angrier and more red-faced. It was one personal invective after another. Finally the black-shirt realized he was not going to learn anything of substance from the messenger and dismissed him.

"I'll send Ben Raines to hell!" Jackman said. He pounded big fists on the desk. "I'll capture him and strip the flesh from him. I'll—"

"Calm yourself," the black-shirt said. "Now just calm down. You're doing exactly what Raines wants you to do. Losing control. You can't afford to do that. You—"

"I run this area, Major," Jackman's words were cold. "Me. Not you. You're here by invite only. I suggest you don't forget that."

The major smiled—thinly. "If those are your final words on the matter, I think then, Mr. Jackman, that I shall take my contingent of troops and move further north. I might find a more congenial atmosphere among those stationed north of the state line."

"Take your goddamn troops and leave, then." Jackman's words were thick with anger. "I'm tired of you lookin' down your nose at me."

The major stood up. "I shall be gone within the hour, Mr. Jackman."

"Good. Take your goddamn uppity attitude with you."

"Oh, I shall. Good-bye, Mr. Jackman. I wish you much luck in your campaign against Ben Raines . . . you're going to need it."

"Fuck you!"

The black-shirt smiled and closed the door behind him.

"Now then," Jackman said. "Listen up, people. We destroy Ben Raines and his little band—tonight!"

Four

Ben and the others lay some one hundred yards from the road and watched the lights of the trucks draw closer. "Pass the word," Ben said to Ann. "Hold positions, but do not fire. Do not fire. Let them go on by."

The convoy rumbled past.

"What's the matter, Ben?" Ann asked.

"It's too easy. It stinks. It's a setup." He looked down the road and smiled. "See them?"

She stared but could see nothing.

"They're running without lights," Ben told her. "Staying about three miles behind the sacrificial lambs. I'd bet every cent I ever owned those are townspeople who were forced to drive the convoy trucks."

She hissed her disgust at that.

"Arm the LAWs," Ben said. "We're going to give Mr. Jackass a hard lesson on why it's not nice to play with innocent human lives."

The LAWs armed up and down the line, Ann asked, "Why did you move off the ridges on this particular night?"

"When you're fighting a guerrilla war, Ann,

readable patterns can get you killed. Here they are. Steady now."

The trucks were filled with heavily armed soldiers of Jackman.

"Fire!" Ben yelled, and the trucks exploded in front of them. The high-explosive warheads blew the gas tanks and sent body parts flying all over the road.

Ben and his team of survivors opened fire with automatic weapons and finished off any who might have survived the blasts. Then the seven of them melted back into the night and circled around, trying to catch up with the first convoy. The drivers had stopped in the road when the sky behind them lit up from the attacks.

"Jackman is holding our families hostage, Ann," a man said. "He says he'd shoot them if we refused to drive the trucks."

"What you carrying back here?" Ben asked.

"I don't know. Boxes of something. General Raines, you've got to clear out. Jackman says that from here on in, for every day you stay attacking his troops, he'll kill ten townspeople."

"That's the breaks of the game, Ted," Larry told him. "They killed my wife and kids when I joined the resistance, remember?"

"David, Frank," Ben said. "See what's in those boxes."

"You've turned hard, Larry," Ted told him. "I don't know you anymore. I want all you people to clear out. All of you. I'm thinking that maybe living under Hoffman's rules wouldn't be so bad."

Larry lifted his pistol and shot the man between the eyes. The local tumbled from the cab of the truck to fall in a heap on the blacktop.

"Jesus, Larry," another man said.

"You want some of it, Burt?"

"No, man. No. But my wife and kids . . ."

"You think Jackman won't kill them and you when he learns the ambush failed?" Ann told him. "If you think he won't, you're very badly mistaken."

"Get out, Burt," Ben told the man. "You're in the army now."

"Radios, General," David called. "And food and clothing and all sorts of gear."

"Get in the trucks," Ben ordered. "We'll drive to that safe area and see what we've got. Move, people."

"What about Ted, General?" another man asked.

"What about him?"

The man looked into Ben's hard eyes and shrugged his shoulders. "Nothing, General. Nothing at all."

Ben and his people had gathered many, many weapons over the past week, all from dead or dying troops of Jackman. The five new men were outfitted and told to get some rest. Ben went over the gear. Much of it was material they had no use for, but the radios and field rations and some of the clothing they could certainly use. They had loaded what they could use on one truck and burned the others, then drove miles away to a reasonably safe section of the county. The drove the truck under a part of a falling-down old barn.

The radios were top-quality, and at dawn, Ben strung an antenna and sent out a three-second message on a frequency he knew was constantly scanned by every Rebel patrol and outpost in North America.

EAGLE ROOSTING MOUNTAIN HOME. Then he quickly cut the radio off.

The message was picked up by a patrol in southern Missouri and immediately related to HQ in Laredo, Texas.

"Mountain Home, Arkansas!" Thermopolis

292

houted. He grabbed up a field phone and rang up ke. "Ben's in Mountain Home, Arkansas, Ike. Confirmed."

Five minutes later, Dan and West had their battalions forming up and recon teams were struggling into parachutes and loading into aircraft.

"Did you try to reestablish contact with him?" Tina asked Therm.

"No. Since we didn't pick up the signal, his radio isn't strong enough to reach us. Ben probably cut the radio as soon as he sent his message."

"If he lasted this long, he'll make it another twenty-four hours," Striganov said. "By this time tomorrow, there'll be several thousand Rebels in that area." He looked at Ben's team, all standing around bandaged up from gunshot wounds. "And no, you cannot go with the assault teams."

Buddy opened his mouth to protest and Striganov fixed him with a hard look. Buddy closed his mouth. "Perhaps when the area is secure, boy," the Russian softened his look with words. "Be content for the time being with the knowledge that your father is safe."

The black-shirt commander and his contingent got out of Mountain Home just in time. Had they waited another twelve hours to depart, they would have found themselves surrounded by grim-faced Rebels with the blood running hot with killing fever.

The Rebel recon and assault teams landed south and west of the town and quickly formed up. Jackman received the word about paratroopers landing and foolishly dismissed it.

"Oh, yeah?" one of his commanders said sarcastically. "Well, tell that to Brownie. He's gettin' treated now at the medics. The Rebels wiped out his whole damn platoon!"

Every team that was roaming around the borders of Oklahoma, Texas, Arkansas, and Missouri shifted gears and headed for Mountain Home, and they were in no mood to play word games with anybody who even mildly supported Hoffman or Jackman.

The man who had brazenly displayed the Nazi swastika on a flag pole in his front yard looked down in horror at his second cousin, now sprawled on the ground with a bullet in his head. Then he cut his eyes to the Rebel officer holding a Colt army issue .45 caliber autoloader in his hand.

"Now, motherfucker," the officer said. "If I have your full attention, you will answer my questions or in five seconds you can join this dead prick in your front yard."

"You got it, man!" the Nazi-lover blurted the words. "Whatever you want to know, I'm the feller who'll tell you. Oh, yeah. You just ax your questions and I'll tell you whatever is it you want to know."

"You already know the questions," the Rebel officer said coldly.

"Oh, yeah. That's right. Shore is. Well, you gonna hang a right on 201 just down the road here. Hit's about twenty-eight or thirty miles to Mountain Home. Not far. Jackman's got roadblocks in three places, he does, beefed up with machine guns." He looked around at the gathering teams of hard-eyed, grim-faced, and heavily-armed Rebels and swallowed hard. "But I don't 'spect y'all will have no trouble bustin' through. Jackman's got maybe two thousand or more men down yonder. A whole bunch of black-shirts just passed through here not more than two hours ago. Headin' north. But I 'spect they didn't go far. Maybe up into the old national forest north of here. That's where another bunch like Jackman's is holed up waitin' for the liberation. Oh, Lord! I done said the wrong thing, didn't I?"

"You didn't win any points," the Rebel officer told him. "Now I'll tell you what you're going to do. You're going to haul down that Nazi flag, piss on it, and then you're going to burn it. You got that?"

"Oh, yes, sir. I need to go real bad like right now."

"Do it."

"But y'all got wimmin in the bunch. I can't pee in front of no wimmin."

The officer lifted the .45 and cocked it.

"Oh, yes, I can! Earline," he bellowed. "Haul down that fuckin' flag, woman. And fetch some far."

The Rebels watched as the man peed on the flag and then set it blazing.

"What country are you in?" the Rebel officer called to the man.

"America!" the former Nazi squalled. "God bless America. Liberty and justice for all. Whooeee, Lord, yes. You want me to sing 'The Star-Spangled Banner'?"

"Spare me that. We'll be checking back from time to time, partner. I really hope this sudden rebirth of patriotism isn't temporary."

"Oh, it won't be!" the citizen assured him. "To hell with Hoffman and Jackman and all them Nazi bastards. You boys and girls is lookin' at a borned-ag'in Christian and a true red, white, and blue American."

"Uh-huh," the officer said. "I sure hope so. Let's roll, people."

The same scene was being replayed all over the area as supporters of Hoffman and Jackman suddenly found themselves looking down the barrels of guns in the hands of Rebels. Other citizens dug up weapons they had buried when Jackman took over and were busy rounding up and hanging sympathizers and collaborators. The Rebels did not stop them.

The Rebels blocked all roads leading into and out of Mountain Home.

"Looking for me, Dan?" Ben called from the timberline.

The Englishman turned and a huge grin cut his features. "General!" He walked over and shook hands with Ben. "You certainly gave us a dreadful fright there for a time."

"How's my team, and how many people did we lose down in Oklahoma?"

"Your team came out just fine. A few minor wounds. Fifty-seven dead at last count and two that the doctors don't think will make it." He looked at the men and women coming out of the timber. "New recruits?"

"About half of them, yes. What's the word south of the border?"

"Just after you were reported alive and active, Hoffman started radio traffic. The man is furious. He then tried a push against Payon's troops, and the Mexican Army held firm and threw them back."

Ben waved his new team to his side. "Ladies and gentlemen. This is Colonel Dan Gray. All right, people. Let's go retake the town."

Jackman was physically ill. After returning from the bathroom, where he had vomited up his churning fear, he gathered his commanders around him. "We don't have a supporter left alive in the county. The goddamn locals are hanging our people from lamp posts and tree limbs and power poles. We're cut off. The town is surrounded. It's got to be every man for himself."

"Bust-out time, sir?" a commander asked.

"That's right. Break the men up into small teams and before they go out, dress in civilian clothing. If they're spotted by Rebels, they can always drop their weapons. We've got weapons up the butt cached up north. Right now, getting out is the main problem. Shit!" he shouted.

The original six that Ben busted out of the holding room stayed on with the Rebels. The men from the convoy just wanted to go home and see if their wives and children were safe. They were not safe. Jackman had ordered them executed the same night as the ambush.

"You feel bad about that?" Ben asked Larry, as they sat drinking coffee and eating their first really hot meal in days.

"Not really. I should, I know, but after my wife and children were slaughtered, I . . . went numb. In a war, people are killed. That's the nature of the beast." He took a sip of coffee. "It's going to get real bad before it gets better, isn't it, General?"

"Yes. And we're going to need every man and woman who can hold a gun."

"Count me in. But we'll need more training than we received up to this point."

"It's going to be OJT for most of you, Larry. Don't worry. You and this team have done just fine."

Ann and Carol joined them. The ladies were freshly bathed and shampooed and had on clean BDUs. They both had changed during the days spent with Ben. They both were lovely women, but both had changed into warriors. Ben had seen it happen many times. He smiled at them and picked up his M-16.

"You ladies ready to go kick some ass?" he questioned.

Ann returned his smile. "Do you ever get tired of it, Ben?" She and Ben had been on a first-name basis almost from the start.

"Occasionally," Ben admitted. "Just like mechanics get tired of having their hands greasy all the time and truck drivers get tired of shifting gears. Then I tell myself it's just a job that needs doing."

"But there is more to it than that. You really like what you're doing. And now I suddenly find myself experiencing all new emotions. It's . . . somehow frightening."

Ben knew the feeling all too well. "Ann, this country wallowed for several decades in lawlessness. Decent people had their hands tied in what they could do in defense of home, self, loved ones, property, and so forth. The punks and crud had more rights than their victims. The Rebels are changing that. We're bringing law and justice and order back to this nation. Do I enjoy being a part of that? Yes. I do. Do I enjoy the killing? Sometimes. Yes. Does that bring me down to the criminals' level? No. I don't think so."

"The crap in the town are beginning to make their run for it, General," a Rebel wearing a backpack radio called. "They're busting out in small groups, all wearing civilian clothing."

"Let's go to work," Ben said.

Five

As Jackman's people were leaving the town, Rebels entered it. They did not, at first, use the roads and streets, choosing instead to cross fields and meadows and walk the ditches and creeks in their advance. They ran into a lot of Jackman's men. They left a lot of Jackman's men dead.

As they entered the town, scores of weary locals came out of their homes to stand and watch the well-fed, well-armed, and combat-experienced Rebels walk past.

"We'll be reopening the hospital," a Rebel called to a group of people. "Anyone needing medical treatment can go over there now. It's clear."

Ben and his team went first to the motel that served as a jail. The scene that greeted them was not totally unexpected.

Jackman's men had killed all those being held.

"Get somebody to ID the bodies and bury them," Ben ordered. "I'll use that old real estate office across the street as a CP. Get it cleaned up and staffed."

"Yes, sir."

"Dan, find the building that Jackman used for a CP and go over it carefully. Watch out for booby traps. Bring me any papers and maps you think are pertinent."

The sounds of small, very intense firefights cracked around the edge of town all that day as Jackman's men tried to slip through the Rebel lines. But as more and more patrols came in from all over a five-state area, the Rebels had not one noose circling the town, but three. The first noose lay just outside the city limits. The second one was three miles out from the first. And the third noose was the sealing off of all bridges to the south, east, and west, and a narrowing pyramid of troops to the north. Some of Jackman's people made it out. But not very many. Most chose to die fighting rather than face harsh Rebel law. For this town had been a designated outpost, and any violation to its sovereignty meant hanging under Rebel law. And Rebel law left few shaded areas for discussion.

A lot of rope was stretched those first few days after the Rebels reclaimed the town.

Four days after the reclaiming of the town, Ben put together rod and reel and a tackle box of lures and went fishing on Norfork Lake. The siege of Mountain Home was over.

Ben's original team was waiting for him when he returned to his CP.

"Ugh!" Jersey said, after hugging Ben. "You're all wet!"

"I don't want to talk about it," Ben replied.

"It's customary to remove your clothing before swimming," Dan said with a definite twinkle in his eyes.

"Funny, Dan. Very funny."

Buddy was sitting in a chair, his left arm in a sling.

"Father, did you fall out of the boat?"

"Yes, dammit. I fell out of the boat. And I lost the fish, too. That bass must have weighed a good eight pounds. When I tried to get back in the boat, I tipped it over and dumped Lieutenant MacDonald in the drink. We finally said to hell with it and swam ashore." He laughed at the recalling of it. "Talk about a comedy of errors. I'm just glad no one was around with a video camera. I'd never live it down. Somebody find me a dry shirt."

Ben took the kidding good-naturedly. When it had died down, he asked, "Tell me what happened back at the crossroads. How the hell did we get overrun?"

"The heavy downpour of rain certainly contributed to it," Buddy said. "Other than that, I haven't talked to anyone who had a clue."

"I think it was a suicide charge, General," Jersey said. "Make-or-break time for them."

"I'm thinking you may be right," Ben said, slipping into a dry shirt. He had flagged down and bummed a pair of trousers off a supply-truck driver and had not worn boots while fishing. "The latest estimates are that about four hundred to four hundred fifty of Jackman's men got out. Including Jackman. So we'll be meeting him again. And I hope he gives One Battalion the honor. I have some things I'd like to discuss with Mr. Jackman. Now then, what glad tidings did you people bring me from south Texas?"

"Doctor Chase is very angry with us," Buddy said, waving at the team. "We left without his officially releasing us . . . in a manner of speaking."

"Actually," Jersey said, "what we did was, we bribed a pilot into holding a plane for us and slipped out the window of our rooms. You should have heard Doctor Chase on the radio. That man sure knows how to cuss and holler."

"Yes," Ben said dryly. "I am well aware of that particular skill of the good doctor. I want you all to check with the doctors at the hospital so they can report back to Chase. Let's smooth this over and be nice boys and girls."

For the next ten days, Ben did nothing except look over reports and sleep and eat and watch his team regain their health until they were all so restless they were snapping at each other. Ben had watched other Rebels move into the area around his CP, and he knew Ike had sent them in and ordered them to stick to Ben like glue. There would be no more lone-wolfing it for Ben was the idea.

Ben smiled and thought; Unless I take a notion to do it.

On the eleventh day after Ben fell out of the boat, he told his team, "Get packed up. We're pulling out in the morning and paying that pack of goose-steppers north of us a visit. We might as well get that over with while we're up here."

"My people would be happy to take that task off your hands, Ben," West said.

"I think Ike has sent enough personnel along to ensure my safety, Colonel. Don't you?"

The colonel concurred.

At a meeting of platoon leaders, Ben pointed to a wall map. "Our objective is these five areas I've highlighted. "It's an old national forest area that is spread out for about a hundred miles west to east and north to south. We're going to have to go in and dig the bastards out. They are at least twenty-five hundred strong. They know these areas and we do not. Watch out for all kinds of nasty surprises once we get in there. Be ready to shove off at dawn."

His team was up and ready to go even before Ben's feet hit the floor. They had coffee ready and had been to the mess hall and brought back biscuits and gravy.

"You people must really be anxious to get going," Ben told them, accepting a plate of biscuits and gravy and a mug of coffee. "Tell you the truth, so am I."

About sixty miles to the north and east, Jackman was anxious to get going as well. If he had his wish, he'd get going about as far as Canada and then bury himself in the woods. But that was not to be.

"Come on, Jackman," the leader of the Nazi movement in what had once been known as Missouri told him. "Snap out of it. We'll rebuild, that's all."

"The man's charmed, Robert," Jackman said, looking down into his coffee cup.

"He's lucky, I'll give him that much. But charmed, no. Look, Jackman, we can duck and dodge until Hoffman crosses the border. After that, Raines will have to commit all his troops in Texas. We're just going to have to stay one step ahead of him."

Jackman looked at the man. "Robert, I lost seventy percent of my people to Ben Raines. The man takes unbelievable chances. Bullets don't hit him. I'm telling you, the man is spooky."

"Knock off that kind of talk, Jackman. You and your boys are beginning to make my people jumpy with all this voodoo crap."

"Then how come no one's ever been able to stop him?" Jackman met the man's eyes. "Do you know how many times Ben Raines has been shot, stabbed, run over, blown off of mountains, beaten half to death, gassed, tortured, and only God—or the devil—knows what else? Huh? Do you?"

Robert DeMarco sat down across the table from his longtime friend and fellow follower of Hoffman.

"Do you know what you're saying, Jackman?"

"Yeah. That Ben Raines is either in league with the devil, or he's got God on his side. That's what I'm saying."

For the first time since Jackman and his men came into camp, DeMarco felt a tinge of worry. He'd heard all the rumors about Ben Raines; heard about the old man with the robe and staff who was sometimes spotted near Ben Raines. What was he called? Yeah. The Prophet, or something like that. The old man could be in half a dozen places at once, so it was rumored. DeMarco frowned and shook his head in disgust. "Jackman, listen to me. Ben Raines is not a supernatural figure. He's flesh and blood just like you and me . . ."

But Jackman wasn't having any of that. He waved DeMarco silent. "You haven't fought him, Robert. I have. The best thing for us to do is pack it in."

DeMarco couldn't believe what he was hearing. Jackman was a tough and resourceful man who had survived over the long years and built quite an army of followers. Of course, that army had recently been thoroughly smashed and routed by Ben Raines and his Rebels, DeMarco was forced to admit. And that had obviously shaken Jackman down to his boots.

He looked at the man. Jackman, at least for the moment, appeared to be a beaten and demoralized man. And his men were just as bad if not worse. Since Jackman and his men had appeared, DeMarco had put his encampments on full alert. He had always risen long before dawn. The first morning, it had surprised him to walk into his kitchen and find Jackman up and drinking endless cups of strong coffee. Now he was used to that sight, but not at the rapidly deteriorating condition of Jackman. The man had trouble sleeping and he was drinking far too much. His eyes were constantly red and his face was getting puffy from the homemade booze.

DeMarco left him at the table and walked through the encampment in the woods to his communications building. The buildings in the forest were constructed of wood and painted earth-tone colors which looked startlingly like tree bark. No trees had been cut down in the building of the cabins, and because of that, many of the cabins were of varying size. But damned hard to spot. DeMarco was much more a realist than Jackman, and ten times the woodsman.

He almost collided with a man leaving the snug little cabin in the woods. The man backed up and Robert DeMarco closed the door.

"Raines is on the move, right?"

"Yes, sir. Crossed into Missouri about twenty minutes ago and continued north on 101."

DeMarco moved to the map. "That's Holcomb's territory. Did you bump him?"

"Yes, sir. Told him to get ready and stay low."

"How big a force?"

"They're still crossing over, moving at about thirty miles an hour."

"Damn!" DeMarco said. "We're in for a real shitstorm."

"Looks that way," the man said glumly.

DeMarco cut his eyes. "Don't tell me you're getting spooky, too."

"Spooky, no, Colonel. Concerned, yes. All those groups in Texas and Oklahoma and Arkansas were sent up to cause the Rebels trouble while Hoffman and his people pushed north. The Rebels kicked the crap out of them and kept right on comin'. And Hoffman is bogged down in southern Mexico. Now we're left holding the bag up here and the Rebels are closin' in on us. Yeah, I'm concerned, Colonel. You bet I am."

DeMarco did not take offense at the communication sergeant's remarks. They were all in this together. They had voted to join Hoffman's movement and not a single hand had been raised against that decision.

"I'm concerned, too, Reg. From this moment on, only emergency messages go out on the air. There is a pretty good chance the Rebels won't find us in here." He paused and smiled. "Well, not a pretty good chance, but a chance. If we have to die for the things we believe in, so be it. We all took the oath and I expect all to stand by their word."

"I'll stand, Colonel. You know that."

"I know, Reg. I know." His right arm shot out, stiffened. "Heil Hitler! Long live his glorious name."

"Heil Hitler!" Reg said.

"They're split up into five groups," a senior scout told Ben, unfolding a map and spreading it out on the hood of the Hummer. "Before they stopped transmitting, our communications people pinpointed the five locations. We believe the largest force, and the HQ of the group's leader, is up here in this area, just a few miles south of I-44. It would be difficult to say just how many we're facing. Of course, they outnumber this group, but what else is new?"

"You have had no contact with any of them?"

"No, sir. They're staying low and quiet. No smoke. I guess we're going to have to go in and dig them out."

The sun had just burned the early morning mist

away from the land. It was quiet and peaceful and lovely. Rolling hills country, thickly timbered and overgrown with brush. Some of the best ambush country to be found anywhere.

"Corrie, pass the word that anybody still in tiger-stripe change into regulation camouflage. Body armor and helmets on. We'll enter from the south end and push straight north, one section at a time. We'll do it slow and easy and right. We enter the timber in one hour."

Buddy and one company of his Eight Battalion entered the timber on the west side of the North Fork White River. Ben and his contingent pushed in on the east side of the river, and West took his teams in heading straight north toward the end of County Road AP just past the ghost town of Siloam Springs. Every team hit trouble immediately.

DeMarco's men had dug in deep and were well-concealed, having had months and even years in some cases to prepare for this. A heavy machine gun pinned Ben and his team to the ground behind a small rise.

"See it?" Ben called.

"I got it,' Jersey called, lying about five yards from Ben. "Too damn close for mortars."

"On three we'll bloop some grenades in," Ben called. "Pass the word."

Ten .40mm grenades later, the machine-gun emplacement was silenced and the trees surrounding the nest were splattered with blood. The Rebels moved on, scouts leading the way.

"Freeze!" Ben called softly, looking down and seeing the thin black wire stretched about eight inches above the ground. "Everybody stay exactly where they are. We've walked into a booby-trapped area. Look around you and check your area, then backtrack out. Check for grenades taped to trees and be careful where you put your feet. Easy does it now. Everybody turn carefully and let's get the hell out of here."

When the Rebels were well back of the thickly timbered death trap, Ben called for mortars. The 60mm mortars began sailing in, and the area shook with their impact and the roaring of the booby traps going off.

"Walk them up for five hundred meters," Ben called. "When that area is clean, we'll advance."

Corrie called in coordinates and the mortar crews adjusted and began dropping the rockets down the tubes. Ben and his section started a slow advance into the smoking and hole-pocked area. One mortar round had landed directly on a machine-gun nest, exploding the grenades and the ammo in the hole. The passing Rebels could tell the occupants had been human, but just barely.

Ben kicked a blown-off arm back into the hole and walked on. Jersey looked over at the stiffened, bloody arm, shrugged her shoulders, and said, "Heil Hitler to you, too, jerkoff!"

Six

Dan sent several of his platoons racing north on the west side of the forest, while Striganov sent several of his platoons hard-charging up the east side. Every few miles a squad would be dropped off, with plenty of food, water, and ammo. They spread out, quickly dug in tight and right, and kept their heads down. They would not be used unless any of DeMarco's men inside the old national forest tried to make a run for it. Those trying to flee would be in for a very unpleasant surprise. Each squad had at least one M-60 machine gun, a mortar, and all M-16s were equipped with bloop tubes.

Inside the thickly-grown-up forest, with its sometimes impenetrable brush, the Rebels were advancing very slowly, and meeting stiff resistance every foot of the way.

Ben spat out a mouthful of dirt and twigs and rotted leaves, and cussed as the bullets sang deadly songs over his head. "I am getting just a little bit tired of this," he said, then bellied down tight against the ground as another burst of heavy machine-gun fire cut the air.

Several Rebels tossed grenades and the machine

gun was silenced. Moaning filled the air. "Oh, God, help me! Somebody come help me!"

No Rebel moved or spoke.

"I'm a soldier. I got rights accorded me," the voice called.

Ben looked over at Jersey, lying a few feet from him. "Nobody said it was going to be easy," the little bodyguard cracked.

"I heard that," the wounded turncoat said. "It ain't right for you to make jokes while I'm bad hurt."

"Who's making jokes?" Jersey asked.

"Bitch!"

She yawned. "I think I'll take a nap, General. It's so nice and cool here."

"You come help me!" the wounded man shouted. "I'm bleedin' real bad."

"It has been a long day," Ben said.

"If you don't come help me pretty damn quick, I'm gonna die!" the man yelled.

"I wish you'd do it quietly," a Rebel called.

"He's up to something," Cooper whispered, crawling up to Ben's side.

"I agree. Pass the word to watch for a grenade."

Coop looked at Jersey. "Are you asleep?"

"If I was, Coop, you just woke me up."

"I hate all you bastards and bitches," the wounded man called. "You'll win a few battles, but you won't win the war. Not this one. You're dead and beat and you don't have enough sense to realize it."

"He doesn't sound wounded to me," Corrie said.

"Nor to me," Beth said. She took a grenade from her battle harness and pulled the pin. She released the spoon and tossed it. It was a good throw, landing right in the center of the gun emplacement.

There must have been two or three hundred pounds of high explosives the wounded man had wired to go in the hole, for when the grenade blew, the following blast knocked birds' nests out of trees, nuts off branches, and shook the ground for a five-hundred-meter radius.

"Jesus Christ!" Ben said, shaking his head and getting to his knees, peeping over the small rise of earth. There was a huge hole in the ground and bloody pieces of people scattered all over the place. The twisted metal of a machine gun lay about fifty feet from the hole.

"He was waiting for some of us to come to his aid and he was going to take a few Rebels with him," Jersey said, sticking a finger in one ear and wiggling it around.

"Buddy on the horn," Corrie said, handing Ben the receiver.

"Go, boy."

"What the hell was that explosion?" his son asked. "We heard it clear over here."

"A human bomb. How's it going in your sector?"

"Slow. We've reached a good spot to call it a day and I've got people digging in."

"Sounds like a good idea to me. I think we'll make camp here. Bump you later. Eagle out."

Ben looked over at Jersey. Her face was streaked with dirt and she looked more like a very pretty wayward street urchin playing at being a soldier rather than the extremely dangerous and highly skilled combat veteran Ben knew she could be. She was also sound asleep.

On this, the first full day of fighting, most of the Rebels advanced slightly more than three miles. Others units could have gone further, but did not want to outdistance their own and get cut off and in a hard bind. Those waiting outside the forest maintained their silent vigil and stayed down.

Ben had perimeters laid out, rigged up booby-trapped trip wire, strung up perimeter bangers, and posted sentries, making the encampment as secure as possible. Both sides knew where the other was, so there was no point in not heating rations and having coffee. The food was bad enough even when heated, and after eating the goop, while relaxing and feeling the battle tension slowly leave one's body, coffee or hot chocolate was like a good friend come to call after too long an absence.

Corrie's highly sophisticated radio was easily capable of picking up transmissions from Mountain Home—and much further than that with properly strung antenna—so Ben spent several minutes that evening going over and sending replies to the messages for him from Therm, down in Texas.

The huge hole in the ground had been cleaned up of the gore and twisted metal, and Ben used that for a roost for the night. It was plenty big enough for him and all his personal team members. Before supper was over, the skies opened and a light rain began to fall. Shelter halves were buttoned together and poles were quickly cut to make braces for the waterproof tarps.

"I am certainly glad we know each other well," Beth said dryly, as the rain pelted the tarp.

The team was all stretched out, side by side, all against one wall of the hole.

"I think it's romantic," Cooper said, knowing that would provoke an acid response from Jersey.

Ben, sitting between Beth and Jersey smiled in the night and waited for Jersey's reply.

"Cooper," Jersey said. "We are sitting in the middle of a battleground, in a blasted-out hole in the ground, with our butts wet, and you think it's romantic? I worry about you, Cooper. I really do. And if you don't get your hand off my leg, I'm gonna smack you right in the mouth."

"Isn't it great to be back together again?" Corrie asked. "Gee, what fun!"

Ben chuckled as the rain pelted the tarp.

"I'm warning you, Cooper," Jersey said. "I'm gonna hurt you."

"I'm only trying to find a comfortable place," Coop said.

"Why don't you go sleep with Dankowski and Simmons?" Jersey suggested. "You can read yourself to sleep with their Superman comic books."

"I heard that," Dankowski called from a few tents away. "It's Batman, not Superman."

"Whatever," Jersey said. "Now everybody shut up, I'm tired."

Ben closed his eyes and drifted off to sleep with the east of the professional soldier, wet butt and all.

The morning was unusually cool for this time of the year and the rain continued coming down. Those factors did not improve the mood of the Rebels as they prepared themselves for another day's battle with the turncoats. Seven o'clock that morning found the Rebels facing DeMarco's men across the cracked blacktop of an old road in the southern part of the forest.

"They'll be anticipating smoke and expecting us to come across head-on," Ben said. "So we'll give them lots of smoke and cross on their flanks. I want ten people spread out right here lobbing lots of smoke. The rest of us will split up and cross at my signal. Move out."

The cool wet morning was suddenly shrouded in swirling, vision-limiting grayness as smoke grenades

313

began spewing out cover for the Rebels. Rebel machine gunners on the south side of the road began spraying the area immediately in front of them with lead, keeping their fire directed into the thick smoke while Rebels crossed the road and set up east and west of the enemy's positions.

Across the river, Buddy and his people had crossed the road and were advancing steadily, pushing the troops of DeMarco back. Buddy's plan was to shove them north until they reached a long bend in the river, where only a few hundred yards of forest remained for concealment. He had already bumped part of Dan's contingent and they were waiting on the west side to spring an ambush.

Holcomb had already radioed DeMarco that it appeared they were cut off and could only fight a last-ditch stand in the timber. Some of his people had already attempted to flee the timber, only to be cut down by hidden teams of Rebels.

"I told you," Jackman said in a dull voice. "I tried to warn you about the Rebels. They're the sneakiest bunch of bastards and bitches I have ever seen. They don't fight by rules, Robert. They fight to win and they don't give a damn how they do it."

DeMarco was getting tired of Jackman's constant bitching and complaining, but he was forced to agree with the man's assessment of the Rebels. Everything he had thought the Rebels would do, they didn't do. They didn't fight in any way he had ever studied. Raines seemed to delight in breaking all the rules.

"Sir, large groups of Rebels are moving into position along the south end of Davis's territory," DeMarco was told. "They're spreading out from Alton to Doniphan, all along Highway 160."

"Where in the hell did they come from?" DeMarco almost screamed the words.

"Texas," Jackman said. "That means they've cleaned out that state. You better hope that's not Ike McGowan's bunch. He's just as bad as Ben Raines."

DeMarco ignored Jackman as best he could and studied a map. "If they move up Highway 21 north, we can cream them. We'll have them pincered."

"They won't," Jackman said. "We're not dealing with a bunch of amateurs. That was my mistake."

DeMarco lost his temper. "Well, what the hell would you have me do, Jackman?"

"The way I see it, we have two choices: Get the hell out of here. Break up our people into small groups and start farming. That's one choice. The other is to pitch in with Raines if he'll let us."

"Have you lost your mind? Fight against Hoffman?"

Jackman shrugged his shoulders. "Hoffman isn't here. Ben Raines and the Rebels are."

"Holcomb says he's lost contact with those men on the west side of the river in sector one," the radio operator said. "He believes they walked into an ambush."

DeMarco sat down beside Jackman and waited for what he now knew were the inevitable words from the man's mouth.

He was not disappointed.

"I told you," Jackman said.

"Buddy reports inflicting heavy casualties on the enemy," Corrie said. "Fighting has died down to almost nothing. He says that by tonight, everything west of the river between 14 and 76 will be in Rebel hands."

"Ike?"

"He is in position and getting ready to shove off.

315

Striganov and West are ready to make their push and link up with us, north to south."

Ben smiled. "Okay, folks. Let's pull even with that rogue son of mine."

Striganov and West drove down hard from the north, and Ben and those Rebels in his contingent shoved off and hit hard. Mortars would cream an area and then the Rebels would come hard-charging in under cover of smoke. They would secure that sector and then wait, catching their breath, until the mortar crews had moved up, set up, and were firing for effect several thousand meters ahead of them. The scene was repeated a dozen times that day, from the north and from the south.

Ben's people pushed ten miles north that day, while the Russian and the mercenary pushed ten miles south. Now all that remained of Holcomb's forces in sector one were contained inside a pocket of land just about three miles wide and six miles long.

Ike split his command and sent two companies in from the west side of sector two and two companies in from the east side, those on the east side staying on the west side of Current River, keeping the river between themselves and sector three.

"Son of a bitch!" DeMarco cussed when he heard that. "I had Bishop all primed to set up ambushes. Just one time I'd like to see some damn Rebel commander make a mistake. Just one is all I need."

"You can count the mistakes they ever made on the fingers of one hand," Jackman said, after taking a slug of moonshine.

"And I'm getting tired of your mouth, too," DeMarco told him.

"You won't have to listen to it much longer."

"Now what the hell does that mean? Are you leaving?"

"No. But if we stay here, we'll soon be dead. That's what I mean."

DeMarco didn't say it, but he tended to agree with the man. He sighed and paced the room. If he was going to make any broad-ranging decisions, he knew he'd damn well better make them now.

As if reading his mind, Jackman said, "Forget Davis in sector two. That's Ike McGowan in there after him. McGowan is an ex-Navy SEAL and he fights with a SEAL mentality. I still got men straggling in here and can muster about six hundred. Get Bishop and Anderson on the horn and get them up here and let's get gone from this damn place."

DeMarco stopped pacing, sat down at the table, and stared at Jackman for a moment. "All right, Jackman, I'm listening. Go where?"

"Minnesota, Wisconsin . . . somewhere up there. If you want to continue fighting for Hoffman, okay, I'm in. But we are no good to him dead."

DeMarco had to admit that Jackman was finally making some sense. They weren't going to stop the Rebels here. To stay and fight was only to commit suicide. He slowly nodded his head and rose from the chair.

"Get your people together, Jackman. I'll give the orders to pull out." He shook his head. "It took us years to get this place just the way we wanted it. We pretended to be settlers and so forth, who just wanted to be left alone, and we never had a minute's problem with the locals. All for nothing!"

"Booby-trap the buildings."

"No time for that. Besides, we may come back here someday."

Jackman capped the old whiskey bottle full of moonshine and left it on the table. He stood up. "No more of that for me. I got to get back in shape, mentally and physically. I want to be ready when Field Marshal Hoffman comes across that southern border. I got me a heavy debt that I'm going to collect from one General Ben Raines."

"That's the Jackman I used to know!" DeMarco slapped him on the shoulder. "Come on, old friend. We got some packing to do and not a whole lot of time left to do it."

The Rebels picked up the signals down in Mountain Home and transmitted them at once to Ben's temporary CP and from there they went out into the field.

"DeMarco is pulling out of sector five," Corrie told him. "He's ordered his people in three and four to pack it up and get moving."

"To where?"

"We don't know. They'll keep monitoring."

"What about his men in sector two?"

"I guess this DeMarco person is leaving that bunch to be slaughtered."

"The caliber of people we're fighting continues to worsen," Ben said.

"It never was much," Cooper said.

"Every now and then he makes sense," Jersey said.

"Thank you." Cooper smiled at her.

"I said every now and then, Coop. That means not often."

Then Corrie received another message that wiped the smiles from their faces. She laid aside her headphones and said, "That was Therm. General Payon just reported a mass attack by Hoffman's people. Thousands and thousands of black-shirts hit him hard. He can't hold. He's backing up to try to save as many of his people as possible."

"Well, it won't be long now," Ben said. "There will be no pursuit of DeMarco. Advise Ike of that.

We'll finish up here and then start packing up to head back. We've got a lot of planning to do.''

Thomas entered the squad tent and Ben gave him the message. Thomas paled and swore in Spanish for a moment. "If my general is retreating, it means the situation down there is now completely and totally hopeless. General Payon is very much a man like you, General Raines. He is not a man to back up.''

"There is that line about discretion and valor. It takes a smart man to know when to apply either. All right, here it is. We don't have time for any type of delay. Corrie, order all the mortar crews we have to set up and start lobbing rounds into this section where we have them boxed. Order Ike to launch a night attack, using the same methods. We'll mop up in the morning. Rest while you can, folks. It's going to be a noisy night.''

Seven

When the shell-shocked night broke free of darkness and light spread over the countryside, the strip of land that had held the last of DeMarco's men was a smoking ruin of twisted and torn trees and craters from the impacting 81mm and 60mm mortar rounds that had been hurled into the area nonstop for hours. Those men who survived the attack came staggering out, their hands in the air. The Rebels then shifted their attentions toward sector two and began claiming the acreage by walking in mortar rounds from all directions. For forty-eight hours, the mortar barrage into sector two was relentless. With a range of nearly fifty-two hundred yards, the Rebels manning the 81mm mortars could lay back and drop in their rounds with little fear of any type of retaliation from DeMarco's troops.

On the morning of the third day of the assault, Corrie received a message of surrender.

"Cease fire," Ben ordered.

The land fell quiet and the Rebels waited in the now seemingly unnatural silence. DeMarco's men began staggering out of the smoking timber, their hands over their heads. They were rounded up, their

320

hands tied behind their backs, and tossed into trucks.

"DeMarco said we would be victorious," one of the prisoners told Buddy.

"He lied," Buddy told him, then bodily picked up the man and heaved him into the bed of a truck.

"Are you going to shoot us?" another asked Ike.

"I ought to," Ike told him. "That's what you deserve."

"Lord have mercy!"

One of Ike's special-ops people held out a Nazi flag. Ike looked at the flag, spat on it, and then looked at the prisoner. "You fly this damn thing and then call on the Lord? Get him out of here."

"What are we going to do with all these prisoners?" West asked Ben at a meeting of batt comms after sector-two had been declared secure.

"I don't know. What concerns me most is what happened to the black-shirts who pulled out of Mountain Home? I thought they linked up with this bunch of crap?"

"For about a day," Striganov said. "Prisoners I have personally interrogated say the black-shirts moved on further north. They say they don't know where they were heading. And I think they are telling the truth. I'm not at all certain the black-shirts trust this pack of rabble."

The batt comms were meeting in a large old home on the outskirts of Van Buren. Better communications had been set up, and Corrie was now able to talk directly with HQ down in Laredo.

"What's on your mind, Ben?" West asked. "I can tell something is troubling you."

"NAL paratroopers," Ben replied.

"We don't have any intel about them," Ike said. "We don't even know if Hoffman has enough of them to be effective."

"He's got everything else," Ben countered. "Why not have a division of jumpers that he's keeping out of sight? Or two or three divisions, for that matter. I'm not going to sell him short. Say he does have a full division of paratroopers. His infantry keep us occupied in south Texas and he sends jumpers in behind us. As short as we are, we'd have a hell of time shifting enough people around to be effective." Ben shook his head. "I don't like it. DeMarco is behind us now, and so are the black-shirts who were in Arkansas. And we don't have any idea how many others are north of us who support Hoffman. Five hundred or five thousand. Or more. We can't concentrate all our forces in south Texas."

Ben stared out the window for a moment. "Ike, I want you to assume command of the forces in Texas. Georgi, you, Rebet, and Dan will stay up here with me. Corrie, order all personnel from my One Battalion, and all of Three, Five, and Six Battalions, to gear up and get up here. I want armor and artillery with them. Find out from Tina and Raul how many personnel from Mexico have joined us and how the training is progressing. Also, get me the latest from General Payon." He smiled at her. "That ought to keep you busy for a few minutes."

"Ben," West said. "If Hoffman gets between us, you're going to be cut off and running."

"That's the idea. We're not going to be able to contain Hoffman at the border. But right now, his supply lines are stretched awfully thin. The further north he progresses, the thinner they'll become. When he moves into Texas, I want Payon to have teams ready to do an end-around on both flanks, and come up behind Hoffman. I want his supply lines harassed and disrupted. And I want to make that son of a bitch have to fight on three or four fronts. After reading the reports from every available source, one things stands out clear: Hoffman has never fought a guerrilla-type war. He's relied on brute force and massive troop movement to win what he's got. The Rebels have been fighting a guerrilla-type war for years. We know how; they don't. Hoffman has people who do know how, but so far they are not making the decisions.

"You all know where we have supplies cached. We have enough supplies hidden around this country to fight a guerrilla-type war for years. And it's going to come to that. Believe it. Ike, when you reach the point where you can't hold out, bug out. No last-ditch efforts. Keep in mind the guerrilla motto: He who fights and runs away, lives to fight another day."

When the laughter had died down, Ben said, "Take off, people. Good luck."

Striganov had eyed Ben suspiciously after the others had left the room. He poured a cup of coffee and sat back down with Dan and Rebet. Outside the sounds of engines filled the air as those batt comms leaving pulled out. "Now you can tell us what you really have in mind, Ben," the Russian said, a half smile on his lips.

Ben grinned, the boyish smile taking years from his face. "You don't really think I'm going to leave Jackman and DeMarco at our backs, do you?"

"I did wonder about that," Dan said.

Rebet nodded his head. "Yes. I wondered also. But I think I know the answer to General Striganov's question, now."

"Oh?" Ben asked, freshening his coffee.

"Just as soon as Ike and the others are on their way back to Texas, we take off after DeMarco and Jackman. You probably had it in your mind that you were going to do it alone. Forget it, General."

323

Ben laughed and sugared his coffee. "I did have the latter in mind, but I didn't hold out much hope of it flying."

"Perish the thought," Dan said.

"We all go," Striganov grumbled.

"What's the plan?" Rebet asked.

"We destroy Jackman and DeMarco," Ben said quietly.

DeMarco and Jackman moved out very quickly, and they weren't at all neat about their leaving. Scouts were on their butts almost from the outset. The scouts laid back and kept Ben and the others notified whenever the long columns of troops made a move.

Ben sent Striganov and Rebet and troops racing to the north, while he and Dan pulled in behind the scouts and poked along, always staying a full half day behind the turncoats. As yet, no word had gone out over the air as to exactly where Jackman and DeMarco had in mind. But Ben felt they would slip up eventually, and on the third day out, they did.

"Bingo!" Corrie said, after receiving a message from the scouts. "DeMarco and Jackman are heading for northern Wisconsin. Up in the Nicolet National Forest."

"Pull over and string an antenna," Ben ordered. "We've got to tell Georgi so he can get in place."

"Scouts report the enemy column is pulling over and seem to be calling it a day," Corrie said.

"That's even better," Ben said. "I could use a break." They were in northern Missouri, paralleling DeMarco's column over in Illinois.

The antenna strung and scramble on, before Corrie could bump Georgi, Ike roared on. "Goddammit, Ben. Where in the hell are you?"

"We found out where the escaping hens are going to roost and we will be slipping into the henhouse like foxes in a few days."

"That doesn't answer my damn question! What the hell does all that mean?"

"Relax, Ike. I'm not alone. Now get off the air so I can talk to Georgi."

"Jesus, Ben, I swear to God, I can't leave you alone for ten minutes without you getting into trouble. Will you, for Christ's sake . . ."

Ben turned down the volume and said to Corrie, "When he winds down, get Georgi on the horn, will you?"

"What if he doesn't wind down?"

"Change frequencies."

Corrie listened for a moment. "He wants to know if you want attack choppers?"

"No."

"He wants to know 'why the hell not?'"

"Give me that damn set, please. Ike, goddammit, I need the choppers to stay right where they are. Hoffman could bust through at any moment. I'll wrap this thing up here and I'll see you when I get back. Eagle out!"

Ben started laughing as soon as he broke the signal. Ike would be kicking wastebaskets and cussing and jumping up and down. The exercise might do him good. Ike always needed to lose a few pounds.

Ben was awakened in the dark hours of the morning by a runner from communications. "Hoffman's forces are approaching Mexico City, General. General Payon says there is no way he can hold. He's

325

splitting up his forces into small guerrilla-style units and retreating northward. They will be destroying bridges as they move north."

Ben acknowledged the report and looked at his watch. It was only a few minutes before he usually rose. He let his team sleep on for a little while and washed his face and hands and then shaved in cold water, only cutting himself once. As usual, Jersey was the first one of his team up. After her toilet, she joined him in the coolness of very early morning for a cup of coffee. Neither spoke until their second cup had been poured.

Jersey studied Ben's face in the dim light for a moment. "What's wrong, General?"

"Hoffman's goose-steppers are knocking on the back door of Mexico City."

Jersey said a very ugly word.

"I agree."

Corrie and Beth and Cooper joined them, each carrying a cup of coffee. Only Cooper was eating. Cooper could get out of bed and eat a raw buffalo before his feet hit the floor.

"Cooper," Jersey said. "What is that mess you're gnawing on?"

"Last night's liver."

Jersey said another extremely ugly word and moved away from Cooper.

"It's good for you," Cooper said.

Jersey shuddered and asked, "How far is Mexico City from the border, General?"

"Probably five hundred miles or so to Brownsville. Probably seven hundred and fifty to Laredo. I think we have plenty of time before Hoffman's people reach the border . . . in any large numbers, that is."

"We still have plenty of gas, General," Cooper pointed out.

"So does Hoffman." Ben spoke the words quietly. "He's agreed not to use it if we don't. That arrangement was negotiated through Payon."

"I despise that stuff," Beth said softly. "It's . . . evil."

"I agree," Ben said.

The team sat in silence for a time, enjoying the cool and calmness of early morning. Many other Rebels were up, but they moved quietly out of long habit. Ben did not have to give any orders about when they would move out. The battalions knew that they would be on the road at first light.

Dan walked up, carrying a mug of tea. "I heard about Hoffman," the Englishman said. "Three of the last great armies on the face of the earth about to engage in what could well be the greatest battle ever fought."

"I'm scared," Beth admitted. "I thought we had a lock on things. I thought the fighting was just about over. Now it's just about to begin."

"Stay scared," Ben told her. "It'll help keep you alive." He drained his mug of coffee and walked away.

"He's changed," Cooper said somberly. "I can feel it."

"The general knows that the battles ahead of us could well make the difference between liberty or slavery," Dan said. "Or it could mean the end of everything. A total collapse of any vestiges of civilization. It could possibly mean that the Rebel army, as it stands now, will cease to be and we all will be forced to break up into small groups of resistance fighters. There is a lot weighing on the general's mind."

"Hoffman had to have been planning this long before the Great War," Beth said. "Not necessarily

Hoffman, but his father or grandfather."

"Oh, yes," Dan said, sitting down with the group. "Most certainly, they were. Why didn't the United States government stop them back then, I believe is what you are leading up to? Yes. You four were children back then. You couldn't have possibly understood how the politics of the world worked. It was a sorry mess. In this country, in England, in countries all over the world. Lack of cooperation between governments seemed to be the order of the day. It just seemed that nobody could agree on anything. In one part of the world, peace seemed to be blossoming. In yet another, bloody wars were raging. As the general has told you, in all the so-called civilized, industrialized nations, governments were teetering on the edge of bankruptcy trying to be all things to all people at all times. Taxes were going up and up and up and services were going down, down, down. If you were not there, and old enough to know what was taking place, it's very difficult to explain."

"Everybody wanted something for nothing," Jersey said.

"Well . . ." Dan looked out into the graying of dawn. "Yes and no. Big governments seemed incapable of staying out of the private lives of their citizens. Governments would not allow the private citizens to protect themselves by carrying guns, but yet the courts hampered the movements of the police to such a degree the law-abiding citizen was not amply protected. In the cities, it was not safe to walk after dark. In many areas, it was not safe to walk *anytime.*"

"Because of gangs of punks?" Cooper asked.

"Yes."

"Well . . . why didn't the police go in and clean

ut those areas?"

Dan smiled. "The courts wouldn't let them."

"Colonel," Beth said. "That doesn't make any ense! All right, all right. Why didn't the citizens orm neighborhood patrols and run the punks out?"

Dan laughed. "The police wouldn't let them."

"Well, goddamn!" Jersey said. "Who was looking after the law-abiding, taxpaying citizens?"

Dan chuckled at the frustration in her voice. "Theoretically, the police. In reality, nobody. Toward the end, what happened here in America was the police developed a bunker mentality. They felt that everybody was against them. And in many cases, the nation's press certainly appeared to be. Criminals could resist arrest, but if the police used force against the criminals, they were setting themselves up for department disciplinary hearings and possible lawsuits. When you hear the general say that criminals had more rights than the victim, he's telling you the truth."

"And? . . ." Corrie asked.

"Here in America, a liberal Democrat won the presidency, the Democrats gained full control of both houses of Congress, the nation went to shit, and the Great War enveloped the globe."

"And now fifteen years later, here we are," Beth said. "Colonel, the way I read what you just said, all this was . . . well, it just couldn't have ended any other way."

"You're right. Revolution by the people was inevitable. Those in power just could not or would not see it coming."

Jersey stood up and picked up her M-16. "Seems like to me, if a person lives a decent life and pays taxes and respects the rights of other law-abiding people, they have a right to demand law and order . . . or pick up a gun and see to themselves. Colonel, cops back before the Great War, if they found a person carrying a gun in their car—a decent person, say, who was just stopped for a traffic violation—would the cops take the gun?"

"In many cases, yes. And place the person under arrest for carrying it."

"Even though the person had no criminal record and the police knew that he or she was carrying the gun only for personal protection?"

"Ah . . . well, yes. That's right."

"Then the cops didn't really know whose side they were on, did they?"

Dan blinked and looked at her for a moment. "That's . . . a very unusual way of looking at it, Jersey."

"I don't think so. I've seen all the old movies and read the books. The cops had instant access to all the information on a suspect. Seems to me like if the cops had turned their backs more often, all the criminal activity and gangs of punks crap could have and would have been taken care of by the citizens."

"Then you would have had anarchy, Jersey."

"Isn't that what we have now, Colonel?"

Eight

"Striganov is having a hell of a time crossing the Mississippi River," Corrie told Ben. "Those bridges not blown have been weakened by time and no repairs. He won't risk crossing them. He's going to have to go all the up into northern Minnesota and cut across."

Ben did some low muttering and cursing. "We have no choice, Corrie. Tell him we'll trail this bunch until he gets into position. If he gets into position in time," Ben added.

"And if he doesn't?" Jersey asked.

"We tangle with them anyway. Dan says you had some interesting comments the other morning, Jersey. What did you two talk about?"

"Conditions before the Great War."

"And your thoughts were . . . ?"

"That if the citizens had formed vigilante groups and the cops had turned their heads, maybe the Great War and the collapse of everything would never have occurred."

"It wouldn't have worked, Jersey. Law and order can never be allowed to break down to that extent. The problem was that due process was taken too far to the left and we couldn't get it turned around back to dead center. But nothing would have stopped the war. That was a political move between the colonels and the generals and the politicians of lots of countries."

"I just don't understand, I guess," she said.

"I'm not sure that anyone does," Ben told her.

"Not even you, General?" Cooper asked.

Ben smiled. "Especially me, Coop. I will never understand the mind of a true liberal. And believe me, I have tried."

Corrie held up a hand for silence and listened to her earphone. "That's ten-four," she said. "Scouts report a group of locals gathered three miles up the road. Armed and angry."

"Angry about what?"

"They didn't say."

Scouts had thrown up a human shield between the mob of men and women and Ben. He parted the scouts and faced the crowd. "I'm Ben Raines. What's the problem here?"

They had found a place to cross the river far south of their present location, now in extreme northern Illinois, and were still paralleling DeMarco's columns.

"You the head honcho of the Rebels, right, General?" a man tossed the question out.

"That's right."

"You got a Reb outpost just north of here, right?"

"Last time we checked, we did, yes. What about it?"

"We had a man hurt himself last week. Took him up there to get treatment. They refused. We're fixin' to storm that place and teach those assholes a lesson about being neighborly. And you and this bunch won't stop us either."

Approximately sixteen hundred Rebels locked and loaded. The sound was enormous in the still air. The group of about four hundred men and women paled at the sound.

"You were saying?" Ben asked softly.

The spokesman swallowed hard a couple of times. When he again spoke, his tone was quite civil. "We got a right to medical care, General."

"Who says so?"

"The Constitution of the United States."

"Go back and read it, mister. It doesn't say a damn word about medical care. Besides, the Constitution is null and void. It no longer matters. The United States of America is history. It's kaput." He chuckled at his choice of adjectives. But considering what the Rebels were facing in the not-too-distant future, learning a little German might not be such a bad idea. He cleared his head of the dark humor.

"If that's a joke, I don't get it," the local said, a sour expression on his face.

"It's a private joke. Besides, you don't look like you have much of a sense of humor. You want medical care, join the Rebel movement, form an outpost, and abide by Rebel laws. That's all there is to it."

The man shook his head. "We're not paying tribute to the likes of you, General."

Ben laughed out loud. "Tribute? Nobody pays tribute to me. We have started a limited cash money flow, but it doesn't go to me."

"I don't mean money, General. We don't like your idea of law and order."

"But you want us to provide you with medical care. It doesn't work that way."

"There is always Hoffman," the man said slyly.

Ben hit him. The punch landed solidly right on the button and the man went down and stayed down.

He moaned once, and then was still.

"Good shot, General," Cooper said.

"Thank you," Ben replied, rubbing his hand.

"What about this mob?" Dan asked.

"Disperse them. And see if you can find out what their beef is with us."

"You gonna take our guns, General?" a woman called out from the crowd.

"Should I?" Ben asked, searching the sea of faces for her.

The woman stepped out and faced him. "My name is Jean Lytton."

Ben waited. Obviously the name was supposed to mean something to him. It did not. "Fine. You know who I am."

"You have never heard of me?"

"Can't say as I have."

"I used to head an organization known as Christians for Reason, Action, and Peace."

"This seems to be the year for nutty slogans," Ben muttered. "Lady, that spells CRAP, if you didn't know."

Jersey giggled and it became infectious, spreading all around the ranks.

Jean's face turned dark with rage. Dangerous lady, Ben thought. And probably unstable. He had always felt that people who headed up those fringe groups protesting against the norm were probably about two slices shy of a whole loaf.

"Silence!" Jean shouted.

That just made matters worse. The Rebels really started laughing. Ben watched Jean's eyes. The woman was about to explode. Ben waved his people silent although he was having a difficult time keeping a smile off his face.

The citizen Ben had knocked to the ground

moaned a couple of times and tried to get to his feet. He made it on the second effort and stood in front of Ben, swaying. His jaw was swollen and blood leaked from his mouth.

"We got a right to choose what way of life is best for us," the man said to Ben.

"That you do," Ben agreed. "Any sort of peaceful existence you choose is fine with me. But Hoffman has sworn to destroy the Rebel way of life. If you align with him, then you are against me. That makes you my enemy. You understand all that?"

"And you'll do what?"

"Wipe you out to the last person," Ben said coldly.

"Attack, attack!" Jean suddenly shouted. "Destroy the infidels!"

"You have got to be kidding," a man said from out of the crowd.

"You better listen to your followers," Ben warned her. "Stand easy, people, and no one will get hurt."

"Forward into battle!" Jean shouted, then lunged at Ben. Jersey gave her the butt of her M-16 to the stomach and Jean folded. No one else in the crowd had moved.

"Watch this nut case," Ben said, looking down at Jean, gagging on the ground. "We'll stop here for the night. I want to talk to these people. We need all the allies we can get. Something is terribly out of whack here." He turned to the crowd. "In one hour I'll be set up to receive people from your group. Let's talk. Choose your spokespersons and we'll work this thing out. Good day."

It didn't take Ben long to reverse what Jean Lytton had done out of her hatred for Ben. Seems she had become incensed about some of the books Ben had written years back and had organized a movement to boycott his books. Then the Great War came and ended that. She had wandered into this area out of Chicago some years back, bringing some of her banana-fruit-pie followers with her, and had turned the community against Ben and the Rebel way of life.

"I guess we were fools, General," a woman told him. "To tell you the truth, we were afraid of you and the Rebels."

"Why?"

She shook her head. "You all, well, seemed to be so purposeful. You seemed to know exactly what you wanted and then did it without hesitation. The efficiency of the Rebels scared most of us. And you were so violent!"

"Where was your home before the Great War?"

She wouldn't meet his eyes, and Ben guessed she was from one of those suburbs of Chicago that banned guns back before the breakdown. Those types of people could never understand that when laws are passed to take guns away from law-abiding people, then only the lawless will have guns.

"I can guess," Ben told her. "But now you have guns. What changed your mind, lady?"

"Are you going to say 'I told you so,' General?"

"Oh, no. You've seen the light, so to speak. You want to become part of the Rebel movement now?"

"How could we exist without doing so?"

"With much difficulty." Ben looked at the woman. The times had beaten her down and she was mentally worn out. "Don't go into this with anything less than a one hundred percent commitment," Ben cautioned her. "What few rules we have are harsh ones, and they are enforced to the letter. We won't tolerate interference."

"I know, General. Joining your movement is

something that we've discussed, away from Jean, more than once."

"And . . . ?"

"Not everyone here will join."

"Then they're in a world of hurt, lady. They're going to be standing outside in the cold and we won't lift one finger to help any of them. I'm not saying it's right or moral, but for these times, it's the only way."

After she had left, Dan came in and took a chair. "About half of them have agreed to move north and join the outpost there. The rest of them say they'll go it alone."

"They damn sure have that right. And they'd better understand it."

"They're going to continue following the ranting and raving of this Lytton female."

"Good Lord."

"That's not all. She is demanding an audience with you."

"Send her in."

"Are you sure?"

"Might as well hear what she has to say."

She had plenty to say. "You are a heathen, Ben Raines," Jean told him. "You have no Christian attributes. You do not understand that people who turn to a life of crime are not to be blamed for that. Society pushed them to it. They . . ."

Ben waved her silent. "Lady, I don't want to hear that hogwash. I didn't believe it when governments were more or less stable, and I sure as hell don't believe it now. So get on with something else to bore me."

"You are a terrible man."

"Go on."

"God will strike you dead for what you are doing to this once-great country."

"Is that all?"

"No."

Ben sighed. "That's what I was afraid of. Get on with it."

"Armageddon is looming on the horizon like a great multiheaded beast. And the heads all have your face."

"Could I have a snapshot of that?" Jersey asked, sitting across the room. "That'd be neat."

"You shut your whore mouth!" Jean told her.

Jersey stood up and Ben waved her back. "This conversation is over, lady. Carry your butt out of here before I turn Jersey loose on you."

Jean stormed from the old house. After she had stalked away, those still following her falling in step with her, Jersey said, "That woman is about as dangerous as Sister Voleta."

"She's a disciple of Voleta," Ben spoke the words softly. "I'd bet on it. And she'll link up with Hoffman. I'd bet on that, too. We'll see her again."

"Striganov on the horn, General," Corrie called from the other room.

"Go, Bear," Ben said.

"I can't make it, Eagle. Somebody has crippled the bridges in this area. I'm having to backtrack. I'll cross over first chance I get and we'll have to tackle the groups from the south and west."

Ben thought for a moment. "Oh, hell, Georgi. We're about the same strength as DeMarco. Let's catch him and mix it up. What do you say?"

The Russian's great booming laugh came over the miles. "Hell, yes, Ben! Although I think you're up to something and the fight will be over long before I get there. All right, Ben. Yes. Let's do it."

Ben stepped to the door and waved at Dan. When he had trotted over, Ben said, "We're pulling out at first light and closing with DeMarco and his goose-steppers."

"Suits me. My people are spoiling for a fight. But what about General Striganov?"

"I just spoke with him, Dan. Hell, he's way up in Minnesota. The fight will be over by the time he even gets a good start. He knows it. And he said as much. Georgi knows I'm not to be trusted."

"I will admit that at times you do present an incorrigible streak, General," Dan said with a grin. "But if everybody wants a fight, and they do, why wait until tomorrow to move? We can be within five miles of them by ten o'clock tonight. The scouts say it does not appear that DeMarco thinks he's being followed, and security is very lax."

"Yeah. We could be all over them by dawn. All right, Dan. Get the people mounted up."

His team was already packing up what they had just unpacked. They knew Ben well.

"All right, Jersey," Ben said. "Say it."

"Kick-booty time?" she said coyly.

Cooper threw a helmet at her and she chased him out of the room and put him under a truck. He stayed there until Ben told Jersey to let him come out unharmed. It was time to go.

Nine

The scouts ranged ten miles out in front of the main column as they drove north into Iowa and then turned east, heading straight for DeMarco and Jackman's troops. By eight o'clock that evening, the column halted and the Rebels who had not followed Ben's orders to catch some sleep in the vehicles on the way over, drivers and gunners, bedded down for a few hours' rest. The Rebels had made very good time over the old country roads. The scouts had reported back that they were so close to the band of turncoats Americans they could practically spit on them.

At midnight, Ben woke his people and they were on the way, route-stepping toward the showdown, loaded down with equipment. They passed homes along the way, oftentimes the man and woman and kids on the front porch, seeing what all the marching people were about.

"Gonna lick this Hoofman feller, General?" a man called.

"We're going to kick his butt all the way back to wherever in the hell he came from," Ben told the local.

"Stick him in the butt with a bayonet for me!"

"That's a scabby bunch up the road, General," another called. "They rolled through here yesterday. Trash if I ever laid eyes on some."

"We'll take care of them," Ben assured the people. "You're all part of the Rebel outpost here, aren't you?"

"You better believe it," a woman called. "God bless you boys and girls."

"This makes it all worthwhile," Cooper said. "Makes me feel good that we're helping the law-abiding folks who just want to rebuild and be good citizens."

"I won't argue that, Coop," Jersey said. "That almost makes up for you hitting me with a helmet."

"Thanks, Jersey," Cooper said.

"I said almost."

"That means you're still in trouble, Coop," Ben told him.

"When am I not?"

"Noise discipline from here on in," Ben told Corrie. "Pass the word. The scouts are one mile from here."

Scouts had radioed back that the town was an old deserted one. They could attack without fear of harming any locals. Unless some locals collaborated with Jackman and DeMarco, and if that was the case, it didn't make any difference.

"One mile right up this road, General," a scout told Ben. "They have sentries posted around the town, but none climbed the water tower. Hawkins here just came back in from town and he says they're careless and overconfident. Smoking on guard duty, talking, and just generally not professional at all."

"Mines and booby traps?"

"None, sir," Hawkins said. "They parked their vehicles all over the town; just wherever they happened to find a spot." He smiled in the night. "Those trucks are loaded with explosives. It's going to be a really big bang."

"I certainly plan on it being that and more. Corrie, pass the word: rest for one hour. Then start moving around the town and work in to about five hundred meters. Mortar crews are setting up the 60s now. We'll mop up what the rocket attack leaves alive. Flares will go up the instant the attack begins and they will continue to light the night. By now the drivers have caught a few hours' sleep and are on their way here. They'll lay back about a mile behind us and deploy at the first pop and circle the town with Big Thumpers and machine-gun fire. Now, folks, these people are traitors. I am not particularly interested in seeing a lot of prisoners."

No Rebel had to ask Ben to elaborate on that.

"Take a rest," Ben finished it.

That nearly twenty-five hundred Rebels could completely surround the town without being detected could be broken down into two reasons: the skill of the Rebels and the laxness of DeMarco and Jackman. That laxness would cost them their lives.

Ben and his team silently worked their way into position. They were a few hundred yards from a two-story building right on the edge of town. A dozen vehicles were parked in front of and around the structure.

Ben looked at the luminous hands of his watch. Five minutes to blowdown. He lay on the cool ground and studied his darkened surroundings. Not one unnatural sound could be heard. As a matter of fact, nothing could be heard. That should have been a dead giveaway to the turncoats, Ben thought. They might be skilled woodsmen, but they weren't worth a damn when it came to urban warfare.

Corrie was listening intently to her headset. Finally she smiled and whispered, "All teams in place, General."

"Any second now," he returned the whisper.

The first 60mm mortar fell right on a truck that was loaded with explosives. The explosion completely destroyed the building the truck was parked in front of and sent a gasoline fireball several hundred feet into the night sky. Flares began popping in the skies, beginning their slow parachute drop downward.

Then two dozen 60mm rounds fell on the old town and the earth trembled under their impact. Hummers roared into position all around the outskirts of the town and the gunners began firing 40mm grenades into the confusion, the Big Thumpers spitting out death and fire.

Trucks and Jeeps were exploding inside the town, sending out death-dealing and maiming shrapnel for hundreds of yards. Those Americans trapped inside the old town soon discovered that they had no place to run. When they tried to flee the flames and explosions, the hidden Rebels lying a few hundred meters out cut them down. The fires from the burning town could be seen for miles in any direction. And they were seen. Several hundred members of the loosely knit Rebel outpost nearby stood on their front porches and in their lawns and watched and listened to the destruction of those who had turned their backs on America and who would enslave them under Hoffman's directives.

No one felt an ounce of pity for the traitors.

"Mortar crews stand down," Ben ordered.

The night ceased its rocking and trembling. The crackling of unchecked fires, the popping of burning ammunition, and the screaming of the wounded filled the firelit, leaping, dancing night.

"Move in," Ben ordered.

The Rebels worked closer. When they were within range of rocket launchers and bloop tubes, Ben halted forward motion and ordered his troops to pour it on those still left alive in the now-ruined town.

So complete was the murderous attack, so total the destruction and so massive the confusion, the forces of Jackman and DeMarco might have gotten off a hundred rounds maximum at the nearly invisible Rebels. Not one Rebel was killed or wounded by hostile fire.

"Hold your positions," Ben ordered. "Do not advance. Shoot anyone carrying a weapon. If they come out of that inferno with their hands in the air, take them prisoner."

When dawn finally lightened the eastern skies, and the fires in the town were burning down, the Rebels had taken twelve prisoners, and two of them were so shell-shocked they were reduced to near-babbling idiots.

Two of the prisoners were Jackman and DeMarco.

"I'll make a deal with you," Ben said. "Tell me everything you know about Hoffman's army—and I mean everything—and I'll let you live. If you choose not to cooperate, I'll hang you right here and now." He pointed to a huge old tree with two nooses dangling from a branch.

"Fuck you, Raines," DeMarco said. "Heil Hitler!"

"Hang him," Ben ordered.

Two minutes later DeMarco was kicking his last.

Jackman watched through horror-filled eyes. This just didn't happen in America. America gave you trials and appeals and free lawyers and free psychiatrists and lots of good press coverage from pissing and sobbing hanky-stomping reporters and all that stuff. In America you could drag out criminal trials—at the expense of overburdened taxpayers—and sentencing for years.

"The second noose is for you, Jackman," Ben told him.

"I want a lawyer!"

The Rebels gathered around laughed at that.

"Sorry, Jackman," Ben told him. "We put lawyers out of business."

"This ain't legal!"

"Who says so?" Ben challenged. He looked at his watch. "It's time for breakfast, Jackman. I'm hungry. You have one minute to make up your mind."

Jackman looked at the body of DeMarco, slowly twisting in the freshening breeze. Overhead, storm clouds were gathering. He looked at the pretty little Rebel somebody had called Jersey. "Help me!" he pleaded.

"Hell with you," she told him, and took a bite out of an apple from a nearby orchard. Cooper had gotten it for her in hopes of making up. What he didn't know was that Jersey had never been mad at him. But she wasn't going to tell him that. As long as Coop thought that she was mad at him, his behavior was exemplary.

"But you're a woman!" Jackman hollered. "Like my mama."

"If I'd been your mother," Jersey told him contemptuously, "I'd have aborted you."

Jackman looked at her, disbelief in his eyes. These Rebel women ranged from pretty to plain, but one thing for certain: they all were tough as a boot. There wasn't an ounce of pity or mercy in the eyes of any of them. His shoulders sagged in defeat as his eyes once more touched the body of DeMarco. "All right,"

Jackman said. "Whatever you want to know, I'll tell you."

Ben smiled. "I felt sure you'd see it our way."

The Rebels did not bury the dead. They just collected all the guns that were usable and then blew what was left of the town over the dead, covering them with tons of brick and stone. Then the long columns turned and headed south. Georgi had cut south after talking with Ben. That Ben had jumped the gun and tackled the turncoats without waiting for him came as no surprise. The Russian had expected that.

On the way back south, Ben sent teams out to touch base with the survivors along the way, warning them of the approach of Hoffman and his goose-steppers. Some of the people who were not part of the Rebel outpost system merely shrugged their shoulders and said they didn't give a damn. Hoffman or Raines—one was just as bad as the other.

The Rebels' usual response was, "Mister, have you got another thought coming about that."

But most of the survivors who had not yet linked up with the Rebels took this opportunity to do so. While many of them did not like what they considered to be too-harsh Rebel law, they knew that life under Hoffman would be intolerable, and that compared to the Nazis, the Rebels were angels from heaven.

Ben returned to Mountain Home and was pleased to see the town running smoothly and normally—as much as possible under the circumstances—now that the hordes of turncoats were gone.

Hoffman was steadily pushing northward, with Payon and his troops—now all split up and working in small teams—retreating toward the border, blowing bridges as they fell back.

And the ranks of the Rebels were swelling with new members, the Rebels hard-pressed to give them all the necessary training needed before Hoffman's forces struck the border.

Ben flew down to Laredo to meet with his batt comms and to meet with General Payon.

"We did the best we could, General Raines," General Payon said. "I am sorry we could not contain them on our soil."

"You did just fine," Ben assured the man. They were both about the same age. Ben had been a writer before the Great War, General Payon had been a TV news anchor in Mexico City. Neither man had wanted the job of leader of great armies. But the people had insisted they lead. So they did.

"Together we have quite a force, General," Ben told him. "I believe we can stop Hoffman. But it's going to be a long and bloody campaign."

"We will eventually stop this madman," Payon agreed. "But the cost will be heavy and God alone knows what our countries will be like when it's over."

The leaders of two of the three largest known armies on earth began planning for what both hoped would be the war to end all wars. But both knew they were old enough to have remembered that line from history class. And both now sensed that the war to end all wars would be the conflict that would end life on earth and still the pens of history forever.

Ten

The army of the Rebels and those men and women aligned with it had grown to immense proportions. Gone were the days when Ben knew, if not the name, at least the face of every man and woman who fought with him. Ben's regular Rebels alone now numbered more than twelve thousand. If the conflict that faced them dragged on, food was soon going to present a problem. The Rebels had seized the food rations from all the garrisons of Hoffman's troops they had overrun; that gave them several months more of field rations, as well as ammo. But it was not going to be enough.

"Whole blood is going to be a problem," Doctor Chase told Ben.

"Medicines?" Ben asked.

"We have enough. For several months. We can't ask those at Base Camp One to work any harder. They're working around the clock now."

Ben looked at the large room filled with people. Used to be a time, he thought, when the commanders of all Rebel forces in North America could sit around a card table and plan the next campaign. Now I don't even know some of these people. Thousands and thousands of men and women and all depending on me to lead them.

God give me the strength and wisdom to do so.

"Where is Hoffman now?"

"One week away," Thermopolis answered. "If he continues his present advance."

"He will," Ben said quietly.

They still did not have a firm plan on how best to meet Hoffman's advance, and Ben's patience was running out. It was unfair for them to sit and stare at him. He shook away that thought and turned to face the window looking outside. No, it wasn't unfair, he amended that. He'd been calling the shots for years, so why now should he expect all that to change?

He turned around and once more looked at the faces of the men and women. Well, he thought, by God, we did it. Red, yellow, black, white, and tan, there they sit. If we didn't accomplish anything else, at least thousands of people of all colors and creeds managed to come together as one, without hate, to fight the common enemy. Yeah, he thought, there they sit. All looking at me as if I was the Messiah.

"Georgi," Ben said to the Russian. "You commanded one of the greatest armies ever to march on this earth. Don't just sit there. Help me. General Payon, you've led your people for years. Dan, you were a commander in the SAS. Jump in here. West, you commanded the finest group of professional soldiers to fight anywhere; so pull your finger out of your butt and lay a plan on the table. Rebet, Danjou, Ike—come on people. Give me some help in this thing."

They sat in silence and looked at him. Ben felt a sinking sensation in his belly. Is this it? he thought. "Have we reached the end of our string?" he said aloud. "Maybe. Maybe so, people. Maybe we're all just tired of it. Weary of all the blood and pain and suffering and days and nights without sleep. The constant pounding of battle."

"Tell us what you think, General," Ned Hawkins of the New Texas Rangers said. "I'm no leader of great armies. I have five hundred people out there ready to fight and die for this country. But I'm no expert at drawin' up plans for an army this size."

Greenwalt, who commanded Eleven Battalion, said, "Common sense tells me that if we tried to meet Hoffman nose to nose, he'd chew us up and spit out blood and bone. But if we break up into small groups and try to fight him that way, we're taking an awful chance."

"But what other options do we have?" Ike asked. "Hoffman has us outmanned and outgunned. He has more helicopter gunships, more planes, more tanks, more of everything."

"So did Khamsin," Ben said. "So did nearly every other group we've ever faced. And we licked them all. All right, people. If it's going to be all up to me, here it is. We can't meet Hoffman head-on with tanks; we don't have that many. For every attack chopper we have, he has twenty. But we have SAMs. For some reason as yet unknown, he has no Big Thumpers. Those Thumpers are going to make a mess out of his light armor. So we make Hoffman break up his army. We make him fight on half a dozen fronts. We stretch his supply lines to the breaking point, and then break them. We fight the way we fight the best, as guerrillas. We are going to terrorize his troops. We are going to infiltrate his camps, cut throats while they sleep, hang his people, and in general, scare the living crap out of them. And we can do it. We have no choice in the matter. We have to do it."

"So we give up the border," Buddy said.

"Unless you've got a better plan, yes."

"So we turn Texas into a battleground?" Ned asked.

"Yes. But we won't contain them here. Before this is over, we'll be fighting all over the nation. And when that occurs, that's when we'll beat Hoffman. We'll spread him so thin he's vulnerable."

Ben eyeballed the group. "General Payon, have your people burn their uniforms and dress in civilian clothing. South Texas is your area."

Payon smiled. "I like it. We shall be poor peasants, scratching at the ground to eke out a meager existence until the enemy troops get close enough to slaughter. Then we become fighters. Yes. I like it."

"Everybody out of uniforms," Ben ordered. "We're all civilians again. How can Hoffman fight an army he can't recognize and who pops up when he least expects it, hits him hard, and then runs away? Start moving our tanks and armor away from the border. Move them north. Therm, you and your bunch are hippies again. So play your guitars, turn up the volume on that awful music, and keep your guns handy."

"Then there is no HQ Company?"

"Oh, you'll be operating. But far from here. How about a commune in Arkansas?"

"Back where I started from," Therm muttered.

"Everybody start scrounging for civvies," Ben ordered. "Get trucks loaded with supplies and start caching them all over the country. Hoffman has been warned to stay out of Louisiana. That's neutral ground. He knows if he violates our agreement, we'll use everything we've got against him. He doesn't want that any more than I want to order it done."

"Who gets Emil?" Buddy asked.

"Therm."

"Thank you so very much," Thermopolis said.

"There is one thing I think we should all do before this meeting breaks up," General Payon said.

"What is that?" Ben asked.

"Pray."